Wolf Dawson

Enjoy the read!

Charlie Russell

Wolf Dawson

A Novel

Charlsie Russell

Loblolly Writer's House
Gulfport, Mississippi

Loblolly Writer's House
P.O. Box 7438
Gulfport, MS 39506-7438
Visit our website at www.loblollywritershouse.com

First Edition: May 2007

This book is a work of fiction. Names, characters, and incidents are products of the
author's imagination. Any resemblance to actual events or persons is coincidental.
Any scenes depicting actual historical persons are fictitious.

Library of Congress Catalogue Number: 2006908659
Russell, Charlsie.
    Wolf Dawson: a novel

    ISBN 978-0-9769824-1-8
    1. Gothic – Fiction

Book design by Lucretia Gibson
Copy editor, Nancy McDowell

Printed and bound in the United States of America.

For Hip. I wish you'd stuck around to read my stuff.

Historical Note

The Mississippi to which Jeffrey Dawson returned in early
October 1874 was on the brink of internal revolution. The four-
year struggle for Southern independence had left her economy
in shambles, one-third of her male population dead or incapaci-
tated, and one-fifth of her farmable land abandoned. Honest, if
imprudent, efforts by Southerners to reestablish law and order
during the first year of Reconstruction were characterized by
the vicious and vindictive Republican-dominated Congress in
Washington as an attempt to reinstate a modified form of slav-
ery. That radical Congress used those efforts as an excuse to
sweep away the last vestiges of civil order and institute martial
law to create an electorate that would put, and keep, corrupt
Republican politicians in power across the South.

For ten hateful, post-war years, Mississippi and her sister
states watched as the despised Republican regime, ignorant of the
South's rich history and culture and contemptuous of both, deni-
grated its social and political values and made a mockery of the
very Constitution governing the nation it claimed to have saved.
Despite what the revisionist historian would have his student
believe, the actions of these despots were not for the benefit of the
downtrodden Negro, but for personal gain.

The degree of graft and malfeasance that occurred during the years of martial law and the carpetbag regime remains uncalculated. What is known is that for generations leading up to the War Between the States, the Mississippi taxpayer had demanded thrift and prudence from its legislature, and the legislators were at all times answerable to those who paid taxes. Taxes in the Old South, in times of peace, were conservative, and government was small. But between 1868 and 1875, non-taxpaying voters placed in office a string of venal legislators who not only exceeded the boundaries of good taste in their passage of legislation but also abused the privileges of office, granting themselves, among other excesses, extraordinary per diem and travel compensation.

Additionally, this post-war legislature had no qualms about extending legislative sessions, nor about the expense of doing business that came with those expanded terms. Government inefficiency and its corresponding tax increases permeated all levels of government. These abuses came at a time and place in history when Americans still took umbrage at the idea of taxation without representation, and the Mississippi taxpayer was not represented in his government.

For the proud citizens of Mississippi, who had demanded honesty and responsibility in their elected leaders, the Republican despots who usurped their state, county, and municipal offices constituted an ulcerating sore. Operating under the protection of Federal troops, the Republican regime in Mississippi created scores of unnecessary offices and positions at every level of city, county, and state government, then filled the positions with those of their own ilk, offering excessive pay and sanctioning abusive perquisites along with those offices. Between 1870 and 1874, six million acres of Mississippi's farmland were sold by the owners to pay state taxes. Thousands of dollars that could have set the state back on its feet were wasted and the human assets critical for rebuilding were forced to sell their land and move out of the state.

In 1873, the Negro electorate selected Mississippi Senator Adelbert Ames to the governorship over the secessionist-leader-turned-Republican, J.L. Alcorn. Ames, at the time of his election, was serving out a vacated seat in the U.S. Senate, into which he had appointed himself while serving as Mississippi's provisional governor, a position he'd held since 1868.

A native of Maine and ex-Brevet Major General, U.S.A., Ames admitted in later years that he should not have left the army to take up political life in Mississippi. His reason for doing so was to further the cause of the Negro, which he embraced with vigor. It is the opinion of this writer that all Mississippians would have been better served in the long run had Ames never left Maine. Unfamiliar with civil administration, Ames was also delusional in his understanding of Southern politics, and his record indicates he felt no obligation to change that.

J. L. Alcorn, the man Ames defeated, was a Mississippian. He was intimately familiar with Southern politics in general and Mississippi politics in particular. Since the arrival of Federal troops during the war, this man who had passionately supported and voted for secession had accepted reconstruction and urged white Mississippians to embrace the Negro. He warned that otherwise the Negro electorate would fall under the influence of corrupt Republicans.

As distasteful as Alcorn's postwar treachery was in the minds of white Democrats, he still would have been preferable to Ames. But with the election of Ames a "color line" was drawn across the state political scene and radical Negroes, many not even from Mississippi, demanded a Negro state, with no whites allowed to hold office.

Ames' ultimate demise stemmed from his uncompromising favoritism to the Negro. On more than one occasion, he removed capable white (northern) Republicans from important state positions, which he then filled with inept and sometimes corrupt Negroes who were often from outside the state. This appeased the radical Negro element, but alienated conservative white Republicans and more conservative native blacks. When those injured voiced a complaint, Ames responded vindictively.

Further, Ames' ignorance of black-white relations in the South in general resulted in his mishandling crises such as the one alluded to in my story, which occurred in Warren County and Vicksburg during the summer and fall of 1874.

Early in 1874, the taxpayers of Warren County, fed up with a corrupt Negro sheriff (who was the tax collector) and an inept county board of supervisors, formed a taxpayer's league, with the goal of taking the 1874 municipal election. Despite incidents of campaign violence and the looming threat of Federal troops requested by Ames, the taxpayers swept the August election.

With the distasteful municipal officials out of the way, the taxpayer's league turned its attention to county matters. Ultimately, a grand jury composed of seven white and ten black men handed down indictments against the chancery and circuit clerks for malfeasance. When evidence incriminating them disappeared from the sheriff's office, the league demanded that the sheriff resign. After refusing to do so and being run out of town, he went to Jackson and asked the governor for armed assistance to retake his office. Ames, instead of attempting to defuse the situation himself, sent a black militia against Vicksburg, setting in motion a white Southerner's worst nightmare. The most unfortunate part of this event was that Ames had a number of white militias in the Jackson area, manned by ex-federal soldiers, who were willing to support the statehouse, but Ames did not trust his white militias.

Ames was openly accused of exploiting the "color line," but his decision was as likely the result of ignorance of the South as of an intent to provoke a race war. Ensuing riots left two white and twenty-nine Negro militia members dead. Former Federal soldiers, who made their new homes in Warren County, made up the bulk of white militiamen defending the taxpayer.

On 6 January 1875, Philip Sheridan, U.S.A., who had laid waste to the Shenandoah Valley in 1864-1865, dispatched a company of Federal troops from the Department of the Gulf and reinstated the "ousted" Warren County sheriff. General Sheridan considered his tone threatening, his act effective. It would prove to be tyranny's last gasp in Mississippi.

Weighted by its own ignorance, no longer trusted by the Negro electorate it had sworn to promote and protect, and drunk on its own excesses, the Republican Party, now split into radical and conservative factions, was falling apart. In 1875, the Democratic Party took control of the U.S. House, and at home, Mississippi threw off the shackles placed on it with the defeat of the Confederacy in 1865.

The sweeping Democratic victory within the state was met with cries of fraud and corruption in the U.S. Senate, and no doubt both occurred to some extent, but what the Mississippi Democrats practiced in 1875, they had learned first-hand in 1868 and 1870. Congressional oversight during those post-war years only occurred in the case of Republican defeat. Despite the Senate's investigation, the results stuck. The entire nation was fed up with the Southern problem, and many Americans were sick of the corruption embodied by the Republican Party.

With Mississippi's decisive victory, newfound hope swept the South. The full implication of what Reconstruction had wrought had yet to raise its ugly head; but for Mississippi, 1875 truly was, as Mary Tate describes in my story, a "glorious new year."

The dismantling of Mississippi's Republican administration began with the convening of the 1876 legislature. Under threat of impeachment, Adelbert Ames resigned his governorship and left the state. The majority of prominent Republican politicians, most of whom had never acquired property in Mississippi and had not, therefore, paid taxes, followed him. Scores of state government positions created during the post-war years were abolished, salaries for other offices slashed. By the close of 1876, Mississippi's government was back under the control of her own tax base.

Wolf Dawson does not focus on the degradations of Reconstruction, but the bitter circumstances of the post-war years set the stage for this particular novel. With a hint of mystery and a bushel-load of suspense, *Wolf Dawson* is, more than anything else, a romantic escape to a historical period where the turbulent future of a beleaguered people is, for two young lovers, momentarily eclipsed by the actions of a sinister killer and the ghostly manifestation of Southern justice.

Enjoy the journey!

Chapter One

She was down there again.

Senses sharp, heartbeat quickening, Jeff Dawson tightened Deacon's reins and twisted in the saddle. By the way she ducked behind the rail fence at the bottom of the hill, her heart was racing pretty good about now, too. No doubt, she thought herself hidden, hunched between the fence and the woods beyond, but he could pick off a rabbit at dusk at sixty yards, much less take a bead on a.... He squinted. His eyes were good, but not good enough to make out her features at this distance. For that he'd need the telescopic sight on a—

With the jolting clarity of a lightning strike, the acrid smell of spent powder filled his nostrils, propelling him from the crisp, clean Mississippi morning to another place and time, to a different prey, but human nonetheless.

Silently he cursed the disturbing imagery, but not the girl for conjuring it, then drew a ragged breath. The scent of chill fall air mingled with that of—he frowned and scanned the sky—summer rain. Strange, but refreshingly so...and fleeting. Ephemeral, not unlike the girl. His gaze returned to the tree line below. From what he'd seen of her slender body, she demanded a closer look.

Juliet Seaton's heart thumped against the base of her throat. He'd turned too fast, and she guessed he'd seen her this time.

She glanced at the grand house on top of the hill, not far from

1

where he sat, tall and lean in the saddle, looking in her direction. The new owner of White Oak Glen appeared magnificent in pre-dawn light, and Juliet's loins warmed.

What did that say of her, when she could look across a dew-draped field and lust for a stranger? Sweet Jesus in heaven, please don't let him be a Northerner.

A moment later, he gave up his search, and Juliet waited for him to disappear before raising the hem of her skirt and picking her way through the wet grass to the well-worn path. The woods were pleasant now, quiet before the world waked, a canopy of oak and gum tinted with fall color. She pulled her jacket around her and crossed the path to the spring-fed creek, White Oak Glen's water source for more than a hundred years. Carefully, she stepped to the bank and breathed, testing the air for the scent of a wet dog, indicative of an angry cottonmouth. The smell of damp earth and humus filled her nostrils along with the smell of rain. She glanced at the rosy glow of the predawn sky, then squatted, cupped her hand in the frigid stream, and drank.

Nearby, leaves rustled. An eerie quiet followed. Cautious, she rose and found the path, all the while keeping her eyes fixed on the tranquil foliage shrouding the creek, her thoughts on White Oak Glen's new owner.

A sweet gum sapling shuddered suddenly, disturbing the forest near it, and Juliet jumped. The noise abated, but there was no slowing Juliet's heart, and her gaze raked the undergrowth in search of, she hoped, deer.

A whine set her pulse racing anew, but before she could sal-vage her scrambled thoughts the foliage parted, and Juliet's eyes locked on amber ones. Her mouth, moist with spring water, went dry, and except for her pounding heart, the only part of her that moved was her creeping flesh.

The thing raised its snout and sniffed the air, then, prowling low on its haunches, cleared the undergrowth. She'd never seen one of its species before. It was too big for a coyote or a dog.

A wolf, it had to be.

Silver speckled its dark-gray fur and gave it the appearance of significant age. The beast, its head still low, took a step toward her. Juliet thought her chest would explode.

The wolf stopped shy of the creek. Front legs splayed, it bowed its head and sniffed the damp leaves on the ground. Unsure of the best course for a discreet getaway, Juliet wobbled. The beast raised its head, and she froze.

Eyes fixed on her, the wolf moved to one side, circling her, coming neither closer nor moving farther away. The predator appeared oblivious of the vicious tendrils of spent blackberry and May haw scrub.

It disappeared behind a veil of bush and gray mist, and Juliet tried as best she could to keep track of its whereabouts. Within the space of a heartbeat, the beast could charge through the brush and attack her.

She continued turning, but couldn't find the thing. Then distracted by a sound behind her, she whirled and fell back, overwhelmed by the dark shape invading the corner of her eye.

A few steps beyond the shade blanketing the field, the sun's early rays glinted off the roan flank of a horse, and the roaring silence that had accompanied her terror shattered into pounding relief. Overhead, a sparrow greeted the new day with song.

Juliet blinked at her new neighbor's horse. While fear had strained her body almost beyond endurance, the benign creature stood a stone's throw away, still saddled, chomping peacefully on dew-covered grass.

While the rider...

She jerked her head back to the left.

...was here, on her side of the fence. She could almost reach out and touch him. Her mouth opened slightly. He stood near where the....

"There's a wolf!"

"Where?"

She almost pointed at him, her new neighbor, but caught herself and instead scanned the woods to his left, going so far as to bend at the waist to see between the bushes. She was immensely relieved by the man's presence and hardly concerned at all for that same man's safety. How selfish. But her body had already started to relax, and she knew the animal would not attack. The realization stemmed from more than no longer seeing or hearing the wolf. Juliet no longer sensed its presence. The thing was gone.

Inexplicably, trepidation replaced the comfort she felt with the arrival of White Oak Glen's new owner. She lifted her face and stared into the dark blue eyes of the man.

"It was there," she said, "I saw it."

Jeff gave her a half smile. She was sizing him up pretty doggone good. She returned his smile. She felt foolish, he could tell, but the pallor of her skin and the breathlessness in her voice confirmed she'd been afraid.

He stepped into the bushes. "You saw a wolf here?"

"No," she said quickly and came closer to him. "I actually saw it there." She pointed opposite where he searched. With a quick turn on her heel, she moved away from him, toward the place she indicated, and he followed.

She jumped the creek and climbed the bank to the other side. "Here"—her voice grew more excited as she spoke—"it came out from behind these bushes."

He climbed the bank and stood beside her. The ground was covered with layer upon layer of dead leaves, remnants of past falls, but he bent to survey the area anyway. There were no tracks.

When he looked up, he caught her watching him. She immediately averted her eyes. "Then, it went this way," she said, and she walked in a circular path, picking her way through briar patches until she again crossed the creek. He stayed behind her all the time, curious as to what she'd seen and equally curious about her. At the creek edge, he stopped her and looked around.

"You're sure the thing crossed here?"

"No, I don't know exactly were it crossed. I only know it kept going."

Jeff furrowed his brow.

"I heard it; I couldn't see it."

4

"Did you ever actually see the animal?"

"Yes, back where we started. I told you. I saw the entire wolf."

She probably wouldn't know a wolf from a big dog. Either way, the thing could prove a problem. Jeff stood and strode several yards in both directions along the edge of the creek, then jumped across to check the west bank. There he found what he was looking for, and he bent on one knee to study the tracks. The scent of jasmine sweetened the air, and with a rustle of fabric, the girl squatted beside him, then leaned closer to see what he had found. For certain, she was more interested in the print than in him. She looked up, her face close to his.

"Is it a wolf?"

"It is." His gaze dropped to her lips, full and, no doubt, soft, then back to her eyes. She moved away a bit and returned her attention to the marks on the ground.

"Show me how you know."

A curious request, but he'd be happy to oblige if it kept her close a little longer. He pointed to the shape and number of pads and finally the placement of the claw points in the soft earth.

"Big, too," he said, "a male for sure."

She rose and stepped away. He rose too.

"Have there been wolves around here lately?"

She shook her head. "I've never heard of any around here during my lifetime."

"Then what did your wolf do?"

Animated again, she turned and followed a path with her eyes.

"It stopped there," she said, then shot him a strange look, "about where you came into the woods."

Damn, she was pretty. Medium height, lithe, graceful. Her hair was honey-blonde, streaked with pure gold, and full of natural curl that framed her face in provocative disarray. Her slate-gray eyes stared at him now as if demanding an explanation.

An explanation for...? Ah, yes. Jeff folded his arms across his chest. "Are you suggesting I'm the wolf?"

"Are you, Mister...?

5

It occurred to him that she really didn't need his name, at all, but he extended her a hand, and she took it. "I'm Jeff Dawson, the new owner of White Oak Glen."

"Dawson?"

"Yes."

"You used to be from here?"

She tried to pull her hand away, but he didn't let go. "I will always be from here."

"You lived on the place near the river?"

"I was born and raised there."

"That boy was killed in the war."

"That boy was only wounded."

She searched his face. "Congratulations."

"For being wounded or not being killed?"

"For owning White Oak Glen."

The timbre in her voice was subtle, but he heard it and eased his hold. She removed her hand from his. Her mood had changed, and concern moved over him. In his mind's eye, he could picture a toddler with golden curls, later a little girl, but the child had held little significance for him then. Juliet had been the baby's name. Sweet Jesus, he didn't want this girl to be that baby.

"I saw you here yesterday, Miss"—he watched her eyes— "Seaton. And the day before."

She raised her chin. "I...do you think I'm spying on you, Mister Dawson?"

"Jeff. And are you?"

She shook her head. She was trying to appear nonchalant, but when she folded her arms across her bosom, her posture was more one of defiance than indifference. "I take this walk daily during good weather. I have for years. This is the first time I've met either a wolf or a strange man."

"And today near about simultaneously." He pursed his lips. "Why do you make the walk?"

She shifted a bit and faced him fully. "I enjoy the woods, and I like to check on the house."

"My house?"

"Yes, your house."

"So it's safe for me to presume your interest is in the house and not me?"

"I'm not in the habit of approaching strange men on their doorstep, sir."

"Perhaps I can change that."

Her mouth dropped open. "Oh, I don't think —"

"I meant changing your interest from the house to me."

She studied him a moment, then smiled in obvious resignation. "You correctly guessed that I'm a Seaton, Mister Dawson, so you are very much aware that White Oak Glen is my family home."

Is, not *was*, and she had indeed noted his earlier use of her surname.

"Losing it was one of several casualties my family suffered as a result of the war. I do come here every day to see the house, and I was curious about the new owner."

"Until the wolf engaged your interest?"

She laughed, and he took her hand and brought it to his lips. "Will you continue your walks, Miss Seaton?"

Again she removed her hand, and this time she moved away, down the path from where she'd apparently come. "I fear the walk might be too dangerous in the near future," she said, glancing over her shoulder. "Welcome home, Jeff Dawson."

He started after her—"Thank you, Juliet Seaton"—and accompanied her to the edge of the woods. He watched her cross the sun-soaked field, making sure she was safe from whatever four-footed beast had crossed her path this morning. Jeff rubbed his jaw. Keeping her safe from him would be an entirely different matter.

Chapter Two

Jeff kneeled and traced the outline of the track with his finger. Another wolf print. Tracks led up to and away from the ramshackle cabin, as if the thing had come to visit. Doubtless the same animal Juliet Seaton saw earlier this morning. Wolves had been scarce in these parts, even when he was a boy.

He removed his hat and stepped fully onto the front porch—there never had been a step—and the wood groaned in protest. He'd been back in the area for days. Only now had he mustered the courage to come up here.

With his push, the door squeaked open, a soft summons to a life long past. He couldn't remember a time when it was ever this still or quiet here. As if in response, a mockingbird welcomed him with a song, and a breeze stirred the leaves of the familiar pecan tree on the side of the house.

He had to dip his head to enter. He'd never had to before. The house was warm inside and smelled of cypress, but the clean scent was deceptive. The house was filthy...and empty, its furniture gone, the floors caked with dried mud and dirt. An animal had defecated in the corner, and he took a closer look. Coon. His mother would die.

His mother had died.

He peeked into the adjoining room, as empty and dirty as the one where he stood. A windowpane was out and morning sunlight highlighted what dingy glass remained. Walking on in, he played at the broken shards with the toe of his boot. So little of him was left here.

He looked around.

And yet so much.

Turning, he stepped to the back window, his footsteps echoing against an emptiness that permeated beyond the abandoned house...the deserted home...its missing family...and pierced his heart. His heart hadn't hurt in years. Now it throbbed, a painless ache in his hollow chest.

From the window, he could see his parent's graves at the edge of the woods. They'd been laid to rest beside his grandfather and Bonnie.

Sweet, pretty Bonnie. She'd been only fifteen when she was buried with the baby that never saw the light of day. Funny, she'd seemed much older to him then. And all the time she'd been a child, her whole life in front of her. A heavy price paid for the cruel amusement of others.

Jeff pulled open the back door. Again bowing his head, he walked out on the porch. Chilly air and warm sunshine hit his face. He sucked in the air and tasted its scent, once forgotten, now recalled.

The old cookhouse was to the left. Too close to the house, his father always said, but his mother had laughed—she used to laugh a lot—and said the cookhouse was right where she wanted it to be.

He stepped down into high grass that was beginning to yellow with the onset of fall. Early. Must have been a dry summer.

The grass was wet with dew, and Jeff made no sound as he moved through it. When he cleared the protection of the house, the breeze buffeted him, and he put his hat back on and adjusted its brim to protect his eyes from the sun.

Beneath the mottled shade of a huge sweet gum, he stopped and looked down at the graves, then crushed the felt hat in his fingers and dragged it back off his head. Wooden crosses marked his mama's and daddy's. They were in bad shape. Bonnie's and Granddaddy's markers were made of stone, but when they died, there'd been someone to care for their graves.

This was his first time back since before his parents died that horrible summer of 1863, the year he'd turned nineteen. He'd been with the army in Tennessee. Yellow fever, Eileen Seaton wrote. They died within two days of each other. His mother went first, but his father had been too sick with delirium to know it. "Don't come back," she wrote in the next paragraph, "there is nothing to come back to." He hadn't known whether it was a friendly suggestion or a threat. It hadn't mattered. For a long time he didn't come back, but in the end the South had called him home as it had so many young men. And, he reckoned, as it always would.

The back door banged against the wall of the house, and Jeff spun around. "Yo," an intruder shouted, "who's there?"

He narrowed his eyes on the indignant man challenging him from the porch, and a smile tugged at Jeff's lips. The old grouser had changed little over the years.

Visibly agitated at the presence of a stranger on this place, Will Howe stepped awkwardly off the porch. He'd been lame since a Yankee mini-ball caught him in the thigh. His limp was worse than Jeff remembered.

On he came, the rifle in his right hand pointed harmlessly to the sky. Jeff straightened. A short distance in front of him, Will stopped and stared.

"I'll be damned," he said, his voice low. "Jeffrey Dawson, is that you, boy?"

Jeff grinned. "It is, Will Howe, and it's good to see you, too."

Will took another ungainly step before removing a tattered slouch hat from his head. "My God," he said, his voice heavy and choked, "I thought you was dead since that day you was bush-whacked at Corinth."

"And for three days I wished I was dead, too." Jeff stepped forward, his hand extended. Will ignored the gesture and, juggling the rifle, pulled Jeff into a bear hug. Without hesitation, Jeff returned the embrace, grimacing against the crushing force of Will's burly arms. Will pushed him back and took a good, long look. "You're taller, Wolf Dawson. Your mama would be proud."

"And you're a wee bit shorter than I remember, and"—he

swiped at Will's soft belly with the back of his hand—"a mite broader around the gut."

Will placed his hand over the spot Jeff slapped and rubbed it. "Yeah, been eatin' good lately. From the looks of you, you been cared for, too." He perused Jeff head to foot. "Darned if you don't look like a damn plantation master."

Jeff threw his arm around Will's shoulders and turned with him back toward the house. "I am, of sorts."

"You bought this place back?"

"I did."

Will sat when they reached the porch. Jeff sat beside him.

"I know it's home, son, but you'll have the same trouble making a living off this patch as your daddy did. Too much low land."

Jeff looked into the nearby woods. Just beyond, the land sloped down, then rose again, forming a series of shallow hollows that ran on to the Mississippi. Only half of the one hundred and twenty acres that made up his father's farm had been farmable, the rest subject to flood.

"It's not all I've bought, Will." Without looking at the other man, Jeff glanced off toward the east, toward the morning sun, which grew warmer by the minute.

When Will said nothing, Jeff turned back around and found the older man contemplating him. "So, you are the mysterious stranger who outbid Morton Severs for White Oak Glen?"

Jeff knew nothing of other bidders. "I reckon I am."

"You have all of it?"

"All that Darnell Tackert had to sell."

Will turned away and pulled a chaw of tobacco from the pocket of his flannel shirt. He bit off a plug and offered the package to Jeff. Jeff shook his head.

"The pretty girls still don't like it?"

"I don't know why they'd like it anymore today than they did ten years ago."

"Point is you still care what they like."

"I'm still a young man, Will. Pretty girls have yet to lose their attraction for me."

11

"Well, I'm an old man, and they've yet to lose their attraction for me, either, but not so's that I'd give up my tobakky for 'em. Never did. Never will."

Will spat, arching the stream of tobacco juice away from where they sat. Jeff hid his disgust. Nasty habit. His grand-daddy had chewed tobacco, and his mother was partial to snuff. Jeff never developed a taste for either.

"I met the girl, Juliet, this morning," Jeff said softly. He looked at Will. "How many of the others are left?"

The older man sighed. "Tucker. The other boys and Jordan Seaton are gone; the war took 'em. Missus Seaton's still alive. Juliet's the youngest. Miss Eileen ain't doin' good, though. Had a bad bout with fever this past summer was a year ago. Caught pneumonia last winter. She hasn't recovered, and rumor has it she never will. Been bedridden since the spring."

"What's Tucker like?"

Will bowed his head over the side of the porch and spat again. "Worthless drunk. Only ones ever were worth anything as far as I'm concerned was the womenfolk. Eileen Seaton, she ran that place since long before the war."

"Well, it was hers, really."

"Yep, sure was, and she come from good people, too." Will rubbed his stubbled chin with the back of his hand. "Damn shame Eaton Dobbins never produced a son so Miss Eileen's husband wouldn't have ended up with it."

"She lost it to taxes?" Jeff asked. He knew what had been happening in the South since the war ended.

"Taxes are still doin' her in, doin' us all in. Hell, I've sold off a hundred and fifty acres in the last eight years. That's three fifths of my property to fill county and state coffers plundered by these thieves from up North. They keep spendin' and raisin' taxes and creatin' senseless jobs they appoint themselves to. Seatons sunk a lot into the Confederacy. The house and the women made out okay during the war. There's a tale told there, 'bout how Miss Eileen managed that."

Jeff eyed him.

"Sold her soul to a Yankee colonel as I understand it."

"Her soul?"

"Her body, then, if you must have me say it."

"Eileen Seaton?"

"Yep, Eileen Seaton. Anyways, Tackert, he was one of them Union staff officers that was in Natchez sometimes during the war. He returned in '66 with his wife. Apparently he offered Miss Eileen a good price for the house and most of the land long before them first taxes came due, and she took it. Reckon it had more to do with gettin' her the money to hold onto the original home place and three hundred acres than with anything else." Will shrugged. "For all the good it done her. Know for a fact she's down to eighty acres now, and she ain't got nobody to work that. Tucker's no good to her.

"'Bout a month ago, her sister-in-law and her two kids moved in from Alabama. Both them children are grown. The daughter, Margery, is a war widow. The son, Wex Seaton, is a Confederate veteran. He hired some coloreds and managed to get a fall crop in this year. He may prove of some value to that bunch. Too early to tell yet. Only met him once. He ain't mixin' with folks much. Least not yet, but that might be because he has too much to do gettin' that farm back in order." Will shrugged. "Whole damn family's kinda holed up of late. Ain't like in the old days."

Jeff nodded. So, there was little left of the Seatons for him to worry about, and they had been a consideration in his coming back here. His mind wandered to Juliet Seaton. He had the house and most of the land. He was home. It was over.

He set his arms on his knees and leaned forward to study Will's rifle. "And what are you doing over here this morning?"

"Darnell Tackert paid me to watch out for this place. I knew he'd sold the old Seaton property, but didn't know anyone had bought this patch. I assumed he still had it." Will picked up the British Whitworth propped against the porch and held it out to Jeff. "Yeah, it's yours. Took it from your side that day I thought you was dead."

Will expected him to take the weapon. When he didn't, the

older man drew in a breath. "Remember what you told me that day it was issued to you?"

Yeah, he remembered what he said that cold spring morning back in '64, when Captain Brand shoved the rifle into his hands and told him he was being mustered from his infantry unit to help form up a new sharpshooters battalion. The Whitworth had a range of fifteen hundred yards and was a sharpshooter's dream....

Jeff swallowed the powdered dust of dead men's bones that filled his mouth. "I told you to take it if ever I fell." He waved the rifle away. "Well, I fell. You keep it, Will. I have no need for it now and never plan to again."

Will coughed and looked away. "As good a shot as I was, I never did this weapon justice, not like you."

How good a shot he was would sicken him if he gave it much thought, and Will's unwelcome, albeit well-intentioned, praise prompted him to think. "You were as good as me, and you damn well know it."

"No, I weren't, and you know it. The son-of-a-bitch that shot you...." He turned a discerning eye on Jeff, then nodded in the direction of the Seaton place. "It was him, you know?"

Jeff's heart started to pound.

"You saw him for sure?"

"I didn't see the shot," Will said with a snort. "But I seen Tucker and Rafe after we began the retreat. Not clear, mind you, but clear enough. I'm sure it was them, like you must've been sure all these years. They'd have shot you again, if I hadn't challenged 'em."

"I've always believed it was them."

Will was quiet for a moment, then he said, "Been seein' wolf sign for days. Ain't been a wolf in these parts since the fall of '55." He nodded knowingly. "Same year your old granddaddy died." Will stared at Jeff, and his eyes glistened. "Hell, even thinkin' you was dead, I shoulda know'd you was comin' home."

Chapter Three

The front door slammed against its frame and Tucker cursed it, as if the commotion were the door's fault. Beside Juliet, Margery threw back the covers and rose, and Juliet heard her slip into the hall. Margery's hushed admonishments and Tucker's low laughter had become routine. Tonight, they added the thumping and bumping of furniture to their antics, but they made it up the stairs, the treads squeaking with each step they took. Moments later, another door slammed, this one upstairs, and a soft creak penetrated the floor joists when Margery fell, or was pushed, onto Tucker's bed. Juliet waited for the telltale rhythm signaling their lovemaking had begun.

"Come in, sweetness."

The lamp light swathed the room in a golden glow. Against the back wall, Eileen Seaton lay in bed, propped on pillows.

"Why aren't you asleep, Mama?"

"How could I be with that racket?"

Juliet closed the door behind her. Her mother whooped out a series of coughs before she raised a handkerchief to her mouth and spat up bloody spittle. Pneumonia. Juliet placed the lamp on the table and touched her mother's forehead. "You're warm."

"I'm sick. Of course I'm warm."

"Why didn't you call me?"

"And what could you have done but worry?"

Juliet drew the covers over her mother. "You've thrown up?"

"No." Eileen slapped at Juliet's hands. "Stop it and help me to the chamber pot."

15

Her mother had trouble using the bed steps, and when she stumbled, Juliet held fast to her frail hand to prevent her falling. Upstairs the rhythm began again.

"I shudder to think," her mother said, "how many women he's with before he comes home. Then Margery, good Lord."

Settling her mother on the pot, Juliet started for—

"Let them be," Eileen said, and Juliet turned and faced her.

"This is your home, Mama, not a whorehouse."

"I find Margery's lack of discretion entertaining. I do wonder, though, what Lilith and Wex have said to her regarding her conjugal visits to Tucker's room?"

"I assume they've said nothing, or the visits would stop."

"And I, my sweet, assume they are encouraging her."

The thought of a mother and brother encouraging such behavior in a woman of good breeding disgusted Juliet, but she reversed course and smoothed the linens on Eileen Seaton's four-poster bed. The sounds of human copulation overhead outlasted her mother's constitutional, and Margery cried out at the same moment Eileen lay back on the pillows.

"She's pretending to know pleasure from Tucker."

"How do you know?"

"I don't for sure." Her mother ceased her perusal of the ceiling and pulled her graying hair over her shoulder, where she began to plait it into a braid. "But I know about pretending. God knows I pretended enough with your father."

Juliet silently cursed herself for asking in the first place.

"It pleases the man, you know, to think he can satisfy a woman."

No, she didn't know, and she wished her mother would shut up. "If it is an act on Margery's part," she said instead, "she's wasting her time; I doubt Tucker will remember being with her."

"She won't care, if she can get herself with his child. Margery wants security, but she's foolish to trap Tucker."

"I hope they wed and have a son to carry on the family name."

"The family name doesn't need to carry on."

A hateful echo of a long-running diatribe. "Quit saying that."

"It's how I feel."

"And what happens to the remainder of White Oak Glen?"

"The Douglases and the Dobbinses built White Oak Glen. I would prefer the Seaton name not carry on with it."

"You won't feel that way when you hold your grandson in your arms."

"If the babe is yours."

"My child will not be a Seaton. My child will not live on any part of White Oak Glen."

"Such are the misfortunes of war and womanhood."

Juliet's eyes stung. She started to turn away, but her mother reached out and covered her hand.

"The White Oak Glen you loved is lost. Accept it."

"Eighty acres remain and so does Tucker."

"And as long as the male line survives, the Seatons and the farm will go on, eh daughter? Such a primitive thought for an enlightened young woman. Quit clinging to the past."

Juliet blinked back her angry tears, and her mother gently squeezed her captive hand. "You are the only person left who cares about the Seaton name, and there is not one thing you can do to salvage it, damn Jordan's dark soul."

But it was Juliet's soul that was suddenly on fire. "Please, stop damning my daddy in front of me, Mama. He was the father of your children, and had it not been for the war, *he'd* have never deserted you."

Eileen released her hand and folded hers across her stomach.

"Why did you do it, Mama? You had four sons and a husband fighting for the Confederacy. How could you sleep with a Yankee?" Juliet had never asked this question of her mother. Never. She had thought, even an hour ago, she'd let Eileen Seaton take the answer to her grave. Her mother's gaze moved over her face, and Juliet steeled herself against her own shameful violation of the woman's privacy. Despite having been confronted, Eileen Seaton might still take the answer to the grave. Juliet leaned closer to her mother. "When we learned they were dead, you never cried, not the first tear that I saw, but I know you grieved, Mama."

"My sons were already dead to me, Juliet. Long dead. Years before they actually died. I loved them, but I didn't like them, and I hated what they turned out to be. Their father, who I was never particularly fond of, died with them."

"But why did you feel that way?"

Her mother rolled her head away from Juliet. "I remember a boy. He wasn't wealthy. A dirt-poor farmer's son who worked hard for a living. I used to ride into the woods at the northern end of White Oak Glen and watch him work in the fields, sweating in the afternoon sun, naked to the waist. I was only fifteen. He must have been nearer twenty. Malcolm Taylor's son Job."

Eyes black as coal in the glow of the lamp, the ailing woman stared at the far wall. Nothing hung there, and Juliet surmised somewhere in the course of this digression, Eileen Dobbins was watching Job Taylor sweating in the fields.

"At night I dreamed of lying with him. I wanted it to be that way with your father, but from the start, it wasn't, and my relationship with Jordan never improved. He gave me no pleasure, but took his from me...and others."

Resigned to not getting an answer, Juliet poured water from a pitcher into a glass. "Here, Mama."

She waved the glass away. "It will make me want to visit the chamber pot again."

"I'll be here to help. You're feverish."

Eileen reached to the bedside table and retrieved a cotton handkerchief. "I wish I'd come out of those woods and given my virginity to Job Taylor, but I didn't. I saved it for your father."

"Perhaps that was the proper thing to do."

"And what purpose is propriety if one must seek pleasure in the arms of another after marriage? To have loved Job would have been better than betraying my vows, despite your father's constantly betraying those he made to me. I could have still done my duty by marrying Jordan when the time came."

And what of poor Job? Juliet touched her mother's forehead. Her fever was rising.

"But I finally knew pleasure in the arms of a Federal officer.

I enjoyed Malcolm Frank, Juliet, and I continued to enjoy him until he went back to Pennsylvania and his wife and children. It's just as well. If I'd lived with him too long, I'd probably have learned to dislike him, too."

For certain, faithfulness appeared no more one of the handsome Yankee colonel's virtues than it had been one of her father's.

"And I'm sorry, my sweet, but I'm glad Jordan didn't come home, for his sake and mine."

Perhaps her mother was right. Eileen Seaton's adultery was bad enough, but her betrayal with a man wearing Yankee blue would have been, Juliet could well imagine, unbearable for Jordan Seaton. She closed her blurring eyes and turned away. But he was her father, and she loved him.

"Juliet."

Two quick blinks and she dared look back.

"Despite the way I felt about your father, I would have never whored myself to spite him. I've too much self-respect for that. I slept with Malcolm because I cared for him. What I did, I did for myself alone." She hinted at a smile. "Men such as your father and brothers don't deserve a daughter and sister like you."

"Oh, Mama, what could they have possibly done that was so terrible?"

For a long moment, the ailing woman studied Juliet's face, and Juliet held her breath, sure this time she would receive the answer. "Something that only a wife and mother should concern herself with," Eileen Seaton said at last, "not their little princess, who needs only to remember them with love."

Juliet opened her mouth, but just as quickly, her mother raised the handkerchief to her eyes. "I often dream of my Yankee now."

Faux tears. Frustrated by her mother's lack of meaningful response and resentful of the woman's lingering affection for the man who had deserted her, Juliet moved away from the sickbed and pulled back a sheer lace curtain covering the window.

The beautiful, preternatural world, aglow with silver light, mollified her injured spirit even as its quiet solitude expanded

19

her sense of loss. A human being needed something to make life worth living, hopes and dreams and someone to share them with.

Her mother coughed, and Juliet tilted her head and listened to the violent spasm. Eileen Seaton would be gone soon, but she'd lost her will to live long ago, and Juliet couldn't understand the why of it.

A mind-splintering howl, terrifying and unfamiliar, pierced the still night, and Juliet's fingers wadded the curtains.

"Good Lord," her mother said, "that was a wolf."

A shudder moved through Juliet, stronger than that caused by the chill in the room or the despair resulting from her mother's memories. Drawn by a perverse and inexplicable foreboding, she dared to look toward the perimeter of the woods, distant but still frighteningly near the house. She saw nothing, but the thing was there, perhaps watching her silhouette against the dim light of the kerosene lamp.

Juliet backed away from the window and shrank against the wall. Her mother had sat up in bed.

"Why, I haven't heard a wolf howl in nearly twenty years. Not since Jedediah Wolfson was...." Eileen Seaton's gaze rested on Juliet. "The new owner of White Oak Glen?"

Juliet's heart skipped a beat. "What of him?"

"You've seen him?"

Yes, she'd seen him. And smelled him. And....

"Kitty says its Deke Dawson's son, Jeffrey."

Juliet took a step toward her mother. "Yes, Jeff Dawson."

"Kitty saw him. Jeffrey Wolfson Dawson. She told me when she bathed me tonight. Says he's not dead at all."

Juliet stopped at the bed. "He was only wounded."

"Killed north of Corinth months before the war ended. Tucker swears so."

"Why is it so bad, him being Jeff Dawson?"

"For Tucker it's bad, but I fear for you, too. You stay away from him, do you hear?"

Juliet gently wrapped her fingers around her mother's wrist. She didn't want to stay away from him.

"Why would Jeff Dawson want to hurt me?"

"Vengeance, my love. Vengeance."

"Why would he want vengeance against me?"

"The year you were born..."

Trepidation moved over Juliet. She knew—

"Despite what you may have heard, the Dawsons were good, hardworking people. They raised corn and cattle, and they kept themselves fed. Deke and Lilly Dawson had two children. Jeff was the younger. They also had a beautiful daughter, Bonnie."

"I know the story of Bonnie and Jarmane, Mama."

Eileen Seaton lay back on the pillow and studied her. "No, child, you *don't* know the story of Bonnie and Jarmane. If you did, we'd have had nothing to talk about tonight. Nor do you know the one of Jedediah Wolfson."

"Jed—"

Juliet grimaced at another of her mother's coughing spells. "Yes," the woman finally got out, "Jedediah. Lilly's father, Jeff and Bonnie's grandfather. I'd known him since I was a little girl. He was a very special man.

"He saw you once as a baby. I took you up there shortly after you were born. Me, you, and Kitty. I went often to check Bonnie. The pregnancy was hard for her, she was so young.

"Jedediah wanted to hold you. Kitty made such a fuss. You know what she's like. I think she expected the old man to gobble you up. But I made her give you to him. He sniffed at you as some people do with a newborn, then carried you to a rocker on the porch, Kitty right beside him, and he rocked you in his arms and talked to you as if you could understand everything he said. You never cried once. Such a good baby you were, till he handed you back to Kitty. You wailed then." Her mother laughed, a rare, but still pleasant sound. "Kitty was fit to be tied.

"Old Jedediah was fond of children," her mama continued, more to herself than Juliet, "partial to little girls. He told me despite how she got it he hoped Bonnie's babe was a girl." Eileen closed her eyes. "We never knew. Four days after that visit, they buried Bonnie with her unborn baby."

21

"And what more is there to that story?"

Eileen Seaton found Juliet's eyes and held her gaze. After a long pause, she asked, "What was he like?"

With an unsteady hand, Juliet fluffed the pillows behind her mother's head. "Jeff Dawson, you mean?"

"Yes."

Tall and lean, broad through the shoulders and dressed the part of a wealthy landowner in riding britches and black riding boots. His hair was dark brown, highlighted with auburn. His eyes were blue. He was polite, concerned, and very handsome. Juliet shrugged.

"I was too far away to tell."

"That's how you know he was only wounded at Corinth?" her mama said. "You stay away from him from now on."

She never had any intention of approaching him; he had done that. And she was glad he did.

"You marry Matt." Eileen settled into the pillows. "I know you're having doubts, but they are foolish."

"I have some concerns, Mama, is all. He's not the same as he was before we became engaged."

"His possessiveness is as much the result of your refusal to set a date as anything else. He's handsome and has land and money enough to pay the taxes."

"His father's land, Mama, and he's passably nice looking in a gawky sort of way. Even you used to call him homely."

"Your handsome hound dog." Eileen smiled. "That was years ago, he's improved."

"You've become accustomed to him is all, and his attitude toward me is more than possessiveness. He tries to control everything I do or say. He used to find me amusing, but now he's become so disapproving—"

"You are his intended now. Josephus Braxton doesn't like me. Matt's seeking his father's approval. That isn't a bad thing."

"I know, but he's almost thirty. Sometimes I fear the way Matt treats me has less to do with seeking his father's approval than with his desire to emulate the man."

22

"Sweetness, Matt is Josephus' son. The poor boy feels his father's oppression more than anyone. Give him your support. Things will change when that mean, old snake dies."

"The man isn't a day past sixty. He'll live another twenty years. Hateful, self-righteous people like him always do. I'll spend my married life wishing him dead, and that's no way to live. Everything Matt and I have and everything we do will be with the Reverend Braxton's blessings. We will live in his house, and he will tell us when to make love and when to have children, and probably insist on naming them. And Matt will let him."

"It won't be that bad and you know it. Set a date."

"First, I want us to talk about what we expect from each other in our marriage."

Eileen Seaton frowned. "I beg your pardon? Have you fallen under the influence of some Yankee female, daughter? Those expectations were tacitly agreed to when you accepted his ring. He expects you to be a proper wife, and you expect him to provide for you."

Her mother spoke tongue in cheek; nevertheless, the censure was slighting. And who decided the finer points of "proper"? Matt? "Is that what Granddaddy told you when he gave you away to Daddy?"

"Matt is not like your father."

No, he wasn't. Where Jordan Seaton could have been faulted for showing too little interest in his wife's activities and beliefs, Matt would, she feared, show too much. Juliet pulled an extra blanket out of the chest at the foot of her mother's bed and started unfolding it. Matt would try to do her thinking for her.

"You've spoken of me to Severs?"

Juliet stilled. "He came up to me Sunday at church, and asked after your health. I was polite, that's all."

"You said nothing of our financial situation?"

"Never, Mama, but all us true and faithful Southerners are in about the same fix."

"Your brother tells him our business, including my ailments." Eileen smoothed the blanket Juliet spread over her. "He stopped by this afternoon, supposedly to check my welfare, but it was you he was looking for."

Juliet lowered the wick in the lamp. "The man is nearing fifty, Mama. I hardly think he's interested in me." Juliet smirked. "Perhaps he really is concerned with how you are faring."

"With my impending death, you mean. He wants me out of the way. Then he can connive with Tucker, and it wouldn't be a great leap down for the son of a Yankee's whore to prostitute his sister."

Juliet felt suddenly stupid and naive, and she subdued her silly smile. "Tucker would never—"

"Severs wants a wife, sweetness. Tucker would marry you to that carpetbagger in an instant if he could."

"Well, he can't. It's 1874, Mama." She jammed the edge of the blanket beneath the mattress. "And why would a person of Mister Severs' esteemed stature wish to saddle himself with the daughter of a self-proclaimed 'Yankee's whore'?" She choked on the last word and turned away.

"Look at me."

Juliet did as her mother bid.

"Because you are not a whore," Eileen Seaton said. "Because your family goes back to the French Dominion. Because you belong here in a way that Severs and his ill-gotten gains never will. Mississippi is on the brink of full revolt, but he wants to stay. He's bought property and is even paying taxes. He wants social ties within this state."

"Wex says—"

Eileen Seaton's sudden twist undid Juliet's bed tuck. "Wex is showing you attention?"

Juliet's head was starting to hurt. "No, Mama, he was talking at dinner is all about the crisis up in Vicksburg."

"I'd rather you wed a carpetbagger than a Seaton. Mark my words, should Wex Seaton ever make any designs on you, it's this farm he's after. You marry Matt, the sooner the better."

Juliet blew out the wick and removed her robe. She should

send for the doctor, but Tucker was upstairs, passed out by now in Margery's arms. She'd have to wake Wex, and she hated to. He was doing too much around here, and she didn't want to be more beholden than she already was. Aunt Lilith and her two children were moved in to stay. The sooner she wed and her mother died, the happier they'd be.

Outside, the eerie call of the wolf reverberated through the night. The thing was closer now, and Juliet looked toward the window. A silvery calm lay beyond the glass. Normally, she loved magical, moon-lit nights such as this.

Tossing a loose braid over her shoulder, she placed a knee on the mattress. A rogue, she thought, listening to the fading echo of the lonesome cry. Want and need washed over her.

Again a howl, bloodcurdling...and close, rent the night.

Upstairs, a bed creaked, and Tucker cried out as if floundering in the midst of a nightmare. In the room next to her brother's, Wexford cursed.

For a terrifying moment, Juliet thought she saw a shadow on the other side of the lace curtains, but when she blinked it was gone.

Fearful the thing could see inside, Juliet lay down on the bed and pulled the covers to her chin. She sensed the beast's presence now as surely as she'd sensed it this morning. It waited just beyond her bedroom walls.

This morning she had been rescued by the handsome Jeff Dawson, another lone wolf, more dangerous than the one outside if she were to believe her mother's warning. Despite Eileen Seaton's tales of loss and unrequited love, Juliet dared not hope the dangerous Jeff Dawson would come to her rescue again tonight. Closing her eyes, she curled into a fetal ball.

Still, she could dream.

Chapter Four

att took her gloved hand. Juliet knew it was him, by his scent and by his touch. Some young women considered him handsome, and Juliet supposed that to some he was. Whether a girl saw him as tall and broad shouldered or, as Juliet did, lanky and big boned, and if, as Juliet failed to do, one overlooked his near obsessive desire to please his overbearing father, Matt Braxton was a good catch.

"Come," he said and tugged on her hand, "it's time to go."

She'd waited patiently for the funeral attendees to leave. "I want to be alone with Mama, Matt."

"People are arriving at your home by now, and your family needs to be there to greet them. Your aunt and Margery are in the carriage, waiting on you."

"Matt," his father called, "let's be on our way."

"Come on," Matt said, more firmly.

Juliet licked her chapped lips. She had to talk to her mother; she wanted to, needed to. "Send the rest of them on, Matthew. We can walk back later, you and me."

He looked over his shoulder to where, she knew, his father waited. "It's too long a walk in this weather," he said. "This is silly. Get up."

Matt would insist she obey. To make a scene at her mother's funeral would be shameful. She rose and pulled her hand from his, and disguising her frustration, she turned her back on her mother's grave. Beside her, Matt took her hand again.

"You are being unreasonable, Juliet. You've obligations to your guests and your family."

26

Which Aunt Lilith and Margery would fulfill; Aunt Lilith had told her so earlier. Her head had started to pound. Good Lord, she wished he wasn't here. He provided her no comfort. More worrisome was the realization that she sought no comfort from him.

"I know it's hard for you right now, but with your mother gone, we should wed immediately."

She stopped and stared at him. Unmoved, he stared back. "You do realize," she said finally, "that I am in mourning? Shall we go into the church right now and find Reverend Tate? I could marry in my black mourning dress."

The Reverend Braxton looked back at them and slowed.

"You are embarrassing yourself, Juliet. I only meant that you and I need to wed as soon as possible."

"I am in mourning." She ground out each word.

"No one expects you to wait out the mourning period. There is no longer a place for you in your brother's house. Your aunt and cousins wish you gone. Surely you realize that?"

Of course she realized that, but the house was Tucker's. No, it was Tucker's and hers, even if not legally hers. She had no intention of being hastened into anything—or out of anything for that matter.

"I've just buried my mother, Matthew. You and I do need to talk about—"

"All we need to talk about is a date."

"No, Matt, we need—"

"Upset or not, son, it is unseemly for your prospective bride to admonish you in public." The horrid old man had come back and joined them. He ignored Juliet.

"She is grieving, Father."

"It is hardly your fault her mother has passed on."

Juliet moved around them toward the waiting carriage, but she didn't move fast enough to miss Josephus' reference to a bauble, meaning her, a cheap pretty his son would be better off without.

Could Matt's declared affection be only that he thought her a prize? Given his efforts to reform her "child-like" behavior, she had wondered, of late, why he considered her acceptable as a wife at all.

Matthew rushed up behind her, but she held her hand out to Wexford who took it and helped her into the open carriage. She wedged herself between Aunt Lilith and Margery.

"Juliet?"

Matthew's face was more that of a riled mongrel than the hound dog she once befriended. "I wish to ride home with my grieving family alone, Matthew. We will provide comfort to one another."

Margery covered Juliet's hand with hers, and Wexford tapped Matt on the shoulder. "She's upset. Let her be for now."

Matt's glare softened, and he backed off, out of Wex's way. The latter climbed into the carriage, and Tucker flicked the reins, Briefly, she watched Matt's eyes as the carriage rolled past him, abandoned on the drive.

No doubt she would receive a stern admonishment for this rebuke. Matt was years older than she. Once she'd thought him wiser, more responsible, but his desire to marry a woman he considered, by her reckoning, "inappropriate" belied that. She hoped Matt and his parents didn't stop by the house. She couldn't bare the thought of his disappointing her anymore today.

Had she remained his friend and not become his intended, she wouldn't be dwelling on his shortcomings now, but between Matt's persistent wooing and her mother's persuasive coaxing, Juliet had allowed them to convince her that accepting the man's ring was the only sensible thing to do.

Shortly thereafter, her up-to-that-time-accommodating beau began to patronize her, deprecating her beliefs and her values and finally her behavior. Eileen Seaton had argued Matt wanted to be certain Juliet pleased his father. Juliet, however, had become less confident regarding Matt's design. No matter, Juliet did not intend to live her life at the pleasure of her father-in-law. To live her life at the pleasure of her husband seemed no more acceptable, if she and her husband did not think alike.

For almost a year now, she'd borne Matt's condescension, in part because the betrothal had served to relieve the worry plaguing her ailing mother. In turn, Juliet had used her mother's failing health as an excuse to postpone the nuptials.

She looked at the cold, leaden sky. Perhaps he wasn't everything she'd hoped for in a husband, and she wondered if, in the long run, everyone were not disappointed, to some small extent, with their mates.

Grief settled heavily on her chest, and Juliet closed her eyes tight. Her one protector was dead, and her aunt and cousins sat poised like vultures to take over what little she had left of White Oak Glen. Her hapless brother would do nothing to stand in their way.

With a good night's rest and a bright new dawn, marrying Matt might once again seem the "sensible" thing to do. Certainly is was the simplest.

Chapter Five

The auburn-haired beauty took his hat, then looked him up and down, a smile on her lips and bold appreciation in her eye. "Mister Dawson, I presume?"

Jeff was not immune to the unspoken flattery, but he suspected she earned her living making any man feel like a king. "Yes, ma'am."

She raised a brow, then artfully wet those luscious red lips with the tip of her tongue. He took her proffered hand. Soft. Manicured. "I'm Della Ross, Morton's mistress."

"Pleased to meet you, Miss Ross."

"Missus, but please call me Della."

"Della."

"Morton, Richard, and Stanley are in the"—she winked—"*drawing* room." She placed his hat on a table in the foyer and, with a smile, said, "You and I would call it a parlor."

Jeff wasn't sure he would know what to call it, but Morton Severs' town home on Pine Street in Natchez left him with the impression of a fancy New Orleans bawdy house. The woman, dressed in a low-cut, bustled, green evening gown, did nothing to dispel the illusion. Her face was painted, and she smelled deliciously feminine. Jeff guessed her to be nearing forty and, no doubt, very good at what she did.

He followed her down a dark hall decorated with gaudy red and gold print wallpaper and remembered a house he'd visited in Denver right after he'd struck it rich. He'd been younger then, with a lot to learn. Three nights and two days in that place. He loosened his tie and tried to recall if he'd learned anything new since, but he didn't think so, not when it came to debauchery.

Della led him through a pair of French doors. Morton Severs rose and stuck out his hand. "Ah, Mister Dawson, so glad you were able to accept my invitation."

"My pleasure."

"Jeff Dawson, Richard Waite and Stanley Pierce." The other two men had risen with Severs. Jeff shook their hands.

Severs glanced at the woman. "You've met Della."

She gave Jeff another wink. If Severs saw, or whether he cared, he didn't indicate.

"A drink, Mister Dawson?" Della said.

"Whiskey, thank you, and please call me Jeff." He nodded to the three men, including them in the request as he and the other three settled into their seats. Della handed him a short glass of amber liquid, and his throat warmed with the taste of it. Smooth bourbon.

Jeff could nurse three fingers of whiskey for an hour. He did not get drunk. He didn't like being out of control, and he didn't like the mornings after. Despite his dislike for chewing tobacco, however, he could be talked into an occasional cigar. He glanced at Della. He had other, more favored vices.

"We've steaks, tonight, Jeff," Morton Severs said, slapping him on the back. "Something to whet that Colorado appetite. Afterwards, we'll retire back here for a relaxing night of poker."

Severs picked up his cards, then caught Jeff's eye. "Of the portfolios I wish you to look over, two deal with gold investment, the other with shipping."

"I would be interested in reviewing the shipping, but my gold and silver investments are tied up in a company in Denver, of which"—Jeff smiled—"I own thirty percent."

Severs nodded. "I'll have the shipping portfolio delivered to you in the morning."

"Timber's good, Morton," Stanley Pierce said. At least, that's what Jeff thought he said. The men had been drinking for hours. Severs and Richard Waite could hold their liquor. Pierce didn't know his limit. Jeff sipped his third glass. The filling dinner had helped absorb his first two.

"Could be a future there. So much of this damn state's yet to be cleared." Pierce waved his hands for emphasis.

"You're showing us your hand, Stanley," Richard Waite said. He looked pointedly at Severs. "If what's happening up in Warren County is any indication, remaining opportunities are about to be lost."

"There's too much at stake for the Party," Severs said, "Grant will send troops."

"He should have done that before now."

Severs turned his attention to his cards. "He's got to give the govenor a chance to fix this mess."

"Ames..."

Jeff cocked his head to make sense of Pierce's slur.

"...made this mess."

Della sashayed over with a fresh whiskey for Severs. "You Republicans made this mess."

Severs glanced at Della, who leaned a shapely hip against his chair. He returned his attention to the other players. "Stanley's right about Ames."

As far as Jeff was concerned, Della was right. The fact that a delusional fool such as Ames sat in Mississippi's statehouse was living proof of a hate-filled, vindictive Congress that didn't give a hoot about this nation and cared even less for the Constitution that governed it. Jeff looked at Waite. "Cards, Richard?"

"Two and I think Washington's abandoned him."

"Grant won't abandon this state."

"I'm telling you, Morton, things are out of Ames' control. Grant needs to act fast and whip these Southerners back in line or kill every damn one of them."

Jeff stared at Waite, then at his cards. He couldn't concentrate hard enough to decide which ones to keep and which ones to get rid of. And, he realized, he no longer cared. "Then who would fill the state and county coffers, Richard? It's my understanding the voters don't make up a fair portion of the tax base."

Waite turned a wary eye on him, but Stanley Pierce broke the tension by raising his whiskey in a sloppy salute. "You're absolutely right, sir, absolutely right." He giggled. "Killing the goose that laid the golden egg, Richard. Foolish, foolish."

"You've had too much to drink," Waite said.

Pierce tossed in his cards. "You're absolutely right." The man reached out and stroked Della's derrière. "This is my idea of a coffer to plunder."

Unperturbed, Della took Pierce's hand and placed it on the table. "You're pathetic tonight, Stanley, dear. Stick to cards. You'll have better luck."

Waite laughed. "Excellent plan, Stanley. Excellent. Breed the South right out of these yokels."

Della lurched Richard Waite's way. "You'd have to be able to get that thing in your pants big e—"

"Della!"

Whether Severs' reproof was made to deflect Della's counterattack or to prevent the unladylike image she was about to project, Jeff didn't know, but Della clamped her mouth shut.

"Don't let 'em rile you, honey. Stanley's drunk and Richard's trying to get your goat. Go on up to bed."

She hesitated only a moment, glared at Richard Waite, then brushed Severs' forehead with a kiss.

After the door closed behind her, Severs grinned at Jeff. "Della was the wife of a Confederate officer killed at Shiloh. Now she's my mistress and a wonderful companion if I do say so myself, but I don't wish to marry her. When I consider breeding with Southern stock, I think of something a bit more refined."

"With Eileen Seaton dead," Waite said, "that worthless boy of hers just might sell you the girl."

Jeff let Waite's words sink in, but Severs chuckled. "I've considered that, but I've got to rid her of Braxton first."

"Shame to waste that honeyed ass on a piece of Rebel trash," Pierce said.

The smooth sipping whiskey that had earlier caressed Jeff's throat now burned in his chest.

Severs glanced at Pierce. "Braxton wasn't in the army."

"Were you, Mister Pierce?" Jeff asked.

All three men turned to him. Whether it was his formal
address to Stanley Pierce or something in his tone, Jeff wasn't
sure. He'd made a big mistake coming here tonight. These men
weren't honest businessmen investing in the future of the South.
They were opportunists, riding the coattails of a corrupt political machine, which had been plundering the defeated South for
almost a decade, and they had assumed him to be one of them.
He should have realized that at the moment of Morton Severs'
unexpected invitation. Shoot, the man had even asked his political proclivity, but had merely slapped him on the shoulder and
told him not to spread that fact around when Jeff told him he
was a Democrat.

"Bad leg." Pierce blinked stupidly before collapsing against
the back of his chair.

Tension oozed into the room, then flowed among the four
men. Finally, Severs spoke.

"And were you in the grievous conflict, Mister Dawson?"

"Company C, Adams County Volunteers, Sixth Mississippi
Infantry Battalion. Later the Sixteenth Mississippi Infantry Battalion Sharp Shooters." He met each pair of eyes, one by one.
"Confederate States Army. Three glorious years, twelve major
battles, and skirmishes too numerous to count. I've put the war
behind me, gentlemen, but I won't...." The words died on his
lips. His parents had drilled certain things into him growing up.
Honor, respect, plain good manners—he recalled Pierce's crude
allusion to Juliet Seaton's "honeyed ass"—how and where a man
spoke of a gently-reared woman. How a man treated a woman,
any woman.

Those things were as much a part of Jeff Dawson as the color
of his hair and the blue in his eyes. He was in Morton Severs'
home; he'd eaten his food. Regardless of how he felt about these
carrion worms, he would not shame his mother and father by
insulting Morton Severs and his friends, not while he was a guest
in the man's house.

Jeff rose from his seat and placed the card deck on the table. "I thank you for dinner, Mister Severs, but under the circumstances do not send the portfolio. I won't do business with you."

Chapter Six

A loud pop charged the cypress-scented air, and Jeff reined Deacon up to the rail fence separating his land from the Seatons'. He'd heard a commotion from a distance, but not enough to figure out what was going on. His hearing was not nearly as good as his vision, and he mused it was the strength of his eyesight that had led to the premature degeneration of his hearing. He'd snuggled a rifle up against his right ear too many times, then fired.

"You whoring bitch, let go..."

Given he was riding in the area where he'd first met Juliet Seaton, he feared it was her being beaten in the woods.

"Damn you," a woman heaved out amid a series of blows and responding grunts. "You can't git it up for me, you drunken pig, but I hear you can for her."

Definitely not Juliet Seaton. More relaxed, Jeff dismounted and stepped through a weak spot in the fence. He could see the adversaries now, and he pushed on through the foliage.

"I'm tired of you—"

Lorna Hart—her dark hair half up, half down—looked his way. Her dress was torn, her cheek bruised, but she stood tall and proud with her hands on her hips. That would leave the man on the ground to be her client. With a contemptuous smile, Lorna looked down and kicked said man in the kidney. He threw up.

"He can't keep his cock hard enough to even get in me," she said to Jeff. "How the hell is a girl supposed to make a living?"

"Get paid up-front would be my advice, Lorna," Jeff said, walking over and rolling the man onto his back.

36

Disgust swept over Jeff. Tucker Seaton was out cold with vomit at the corner of his mouth, his pants unbuttoned, and his John Willie exposed. He glanced at pretty, buxom Lorna Hart, a town whore, then back to Tucker.

"From the looks of the two of you, you got the better of him."

"I got nothin'. That's why I'm so mad." She turned and played at the torn sleeve of her dress. It was ripped at the waist, too. She looked at him, smiled, and came closer. "How about you, Wolf Dawson?" She stood in front of him and placed a hand on his shoulder. With her free hand, she reached down and stroked his thigh. "You in need of a woman?"

Jeff was only moderately surprised by her action. He took her free-playing hand and pushed her easily away. "No, Lorna, I'm not. It'll be dark soon. There's a wolf about. You need to get out of these woods."

"Oh, there's a wolf about, honey," she said and rubbed his back. "And I want him in me right now."

"What are y'all doing conducting business out here in the woods?"

"Been coming out this way to him for years. We used to go to his barn, but since his cousin Wex got here, he's in and out of the barn all the time. So now me and Tucker stay in the woods."

"Long walk for poor pay. Are you in love with him?"

"Shit, naw, honey. He's got money, always has. First it was his mama's. Now it's Morton Severs'." She looked at Tucker's battered body. "Guess he's drunk so much he don't care who he takes money from anymore."

"Could you button his pants for me?"

She snickered, but squatted beside the man and did what Jeff asked. Then she fumbled with Tucker's pockets and pulled out a worn ten-dollar note. She held it up for Jeff's perusal. "For my time, honey. He won't remember if he got anything from me or not."

Jeff couldn't care less what she took off him.

"I bet you pay in gold, don't you, Wolf Dawson?"

"I don't pay at all, Lorna...*honey.*" He stooped and, bracing himself, pulled Tucker's dead weight over his shoulder. Clumsily, Jeff straightened. As much as he'd like to, he couldn't leave him here. The nights were cold, and the son-of-a-bitch wasn't warmly dressed. Not that he would care if Tucker Seaton froze to death—along with all the other sons of Seaton. It was the daughter he was thinking of now.

"You can have me for free." As she turned to get out of his way, Lorna moved her hand over the worn bodice of her dress. "Right now."

"You've got your money. Go home."

"I need more than money. I need a real man."

Jeff led Deacon to the old house, Tucker lying across the saddle, and when he dumped the unconscious slug on the porch, he wasn't gentle about it. He'd be late getting home tonight, and he had business to take care of.

"Yo, inside, anybody home?"

There must be. Golden lamplight fell through the windows across the toes of his boots and the wooden planks of the porch.

A woman, lantern in hand, opened the door.

She wasn't Juliet.

"Who's there?" she asked.

"Jeff Dawson, your neighbor. I've brought your man home."

"Wexford!"

The cry came from a woman who'd come up behind the one holding the door. The screen flew wide, and an older version of the first woman stepped out. The younger one raised the light.

"Tucker," Jeff said.

"Oh, my." The younger woman handed the lamp to the other. "Mother, hold the light up here."

The aunt and the female cousin. He wondered where Juliet was.

"What did you do to him?" the younger woman said.

Jeff tipped the brim of his hat. He could not see her well in the dim light, but she looked to be around thirty, thin, her skin slightly pinched around the mouth.

38

"I've done nothing to him, ma'am, but bring him home."

The older woman squatted beside her daughter and Tucker. "Smell him, Margery. He's dead drunk."

"He's hurt." Margery again looked at Jeff.

"That he is, but I didn't do it." He didn't feel it would be appropriate to tell Margery that the town whore had beaten her intended. "I can help you get him in the house." Truth was he wanted to get inside and see if Juliet was home. A farfetched hope. She would have been on the porch by now.

The older woman rose. "Oh, for pity's sake, Margery, I put fresh linens on the beds this morning. I see no reason to lay his filthy carcass on one of 'em."

Seemed the best course was to let Tucker lie in filth or change his own damn sheets. The bed was his, after all.

Margery glared at her mother, then turned to Jeff. "Please, do you think you could manage the stairs with him?"

He could, and he did. Juliet Seaton wasn't inside.

"Matthew is growing impatient with you, dear."

Juliet stuck a needle into the soft, flannel fabric. The hole was no more than a separated seam, thank goodness. She owned only two dresses not boasting a patch, and this was one. "I'm still in mourning."

"Your mother would not expect you to wait." When Juliet didn't respond, her aunt sighed. "What does Matt think about your waiting?"

"He wants the wedding to take place before Christmas."

"I thought as much, and that's good."

It wasn't good, and as of right now, it wasn't going to happen. Juliet glanced at the beautiful ruby on her finger. She had wanted an emerald, but this ring had belonged to Matt's maternal grandmother.

"And what are you going to do?"

"He's given me three days to come up with a date."

"Or he'll break the engagement?"

"Or he'll—"Juliet frowned at the way her aunt was clinging

to the upholstered arm of the chair — "set the date," she answered.

Aunt Lilith let out a breath, then reached over to pat Juliet's hand. "It's good he's put his foot down."

Juliet lifted her gaze to her aunt's face, and the older woman shrugged. "To be his own man," she offered.

"He lives to please his father, you know that." She stuck the needle back into the seam and pulled the thread through. In the fireplace, a charred log fell and sent a spray of sparks up the chimney and onto the hearth. "Matt's reining in his fiancé pleases Josephus Braxton. I fear Matthew wishes to be like him."

"They are well-to-do."

"I wonder if I'll be happy with Matt."

"There are all degrees of happiness."

"And misery is not one of them."

The woman smiled. "Marriage is give and take."

"It's what Mama wanted," Tucker said.

"But I'm no longer sure it's what I want."

"Either you're going to marry him or you're not. Break the engagement or set a date," Tucker said.

Juliet bit her bottom lip, but kept focused on her aunt. "Riding over last night, I asked him what he expects from our life together. He said the purpose of marriage was clear in God's eyes and we'd work out the finer points as we moved through our married life."

"And that wasn't satisfactory?"

"It will be a little late, don't you think, if I don't fit well into 'God's plan' as Matt envisions it."

"You told him that?"

"Yes. He responded in true Matthew fashion with accusations of sacrilege. He asked his father to ride back with us 'so he would not have to make the return trip alone.' Of course, the real reason was so he wouldn't have to talk to me. Aunt Lilith, he will never talk to me, not really."

"Then who will you marry?" Tucker asked.

Why did she have to marry? But she knew what his answer to that would be. "I haven't said I'm not going to marry him."

Tucker snorted and looked away. He should be showing concern for his own future, not hers. When she had returned home last night, she found Margery cleaning superficial cuts marring his face. None were serious, but the overall condition of his bruised and battered body, coupled with his drunkenness, had been disgusting. Spiritually exhausted from her trying visit with the Braxtons, she retired without asking what happened.

Tucker downed the whiskey in his glass, and Margery rose from the chair next to his and yanked the whiskey bottle from the tabletop. "Do you want to be sick again?" In what appeared an afterthought, she snatched the glass from his hand and, glaring down her nose at him, pivoted and stomped from the room. Juliet's reciprocating snort mimicked Tucker's. He caught her eye, and she shook her head. Last night wasn't the first in recent years Tucker had been brought home in such a state. Juliet was thankful Margery dealt with him now.

The back door opened, then slammed shut. Wex said something to Margery. Juliet didn't hear the woman's response, but she didn't miss Wex's curse or the decisive tread of his booted feet moving down the hall. She glanced up when Wex entered the parlor and followed his gaze to Tucker, long legs bent awkwardly in front of him, slouching in his upholstered chair. Wex breathed in and turned to his mother.

"We lost three calves last night. One was the yearling bull."

"Good Lord, what happened to them?" Lilith said.

"Wolf."

"The wolf killed three animals in one night?" Juliet asked.

Aunt Lilith's brow furrowed. "Is it a pack?"

Wex shook his head. "To bring down something as big as—"

"It's him," Tucker said.

Lilith shifted in her chair. "That wolf we've been hearing howling in the night?"

"Jeff Dawson," Tucker answered in a flat voice, and Juliet's heartbeat quickened.

"The man who brought you home last night?" Aunt Lilith said.

"Yes."

41

Wex rolled his eyes to the ceiling, and Aunt Lilith shot him an exasperated look.

"We've got to hunt this thing down," Wex said, his eyes back on Tucker.

Tucker did not bother to turn his way, and embarrassment tore through Juliet. Wex would get no help from her brother. Even before this loss, they were going to have trouble paying the property taxes in the spring. They couldn't lose any more stock.

Securing the needle in the fabric, Juliet rolled up the soft dress, rose, and stepped over to kneel in front of her sibling.

"Tucker, you have to help Wex hunt the wolf. We've lost the yearling bull, for goodness' sake."

Margery had reentered the room and now moved behind Tucker's chair.

Bleary-eyed, Tucker blinked at Juliet. "I wouldn't hunt that thing if I could walk. It's not a wolf, it's him, I tell you, and he'll kill me."

"Then why did he bring you home last night?"

"I don't know what his motive was, but he will take the form of a wolf, and he'll rip my throat out. That's what he's after."

"Why would he, darling?" Margery cooed.

"Because..." Tucker sobbed and rubbed his forehead before returning his attention to Juliet. "He's dead! Don't you understand? The son-of-a-bitch is already dead."

"I've seen him, Tucker. I've talked—"

"I k-kill...." Brutally, he grabbed her upper arms and shook her. "I saw him killed at Corinth, dammit. I saw the yellowbelly run. He took a bullet in the back. I saw him die."

Heart racing, Juliet tore herself free. Run? She didn't want to believe that, but who was she to judge how a man behaved in battle. Rout or retreat, but she refused, at this point, to see Jeff Dawson as a coward.

"I stood over his worthless carcass and kicked him. He didn't move." Tucker's eyes, wide now and charged with hatred, stared at her. "He's a ghost, and he's after me."

Behind Tucker, Margery motioned for her to stop, and Juliet

rose and moved away. She stopped in front of Wexford. "I'll help you."

Wex Seaton was a tall, handsome man. All the Seaton men were. But Juliet knew too well there were character flaws that went with the rugged good looks. Wex gave her a patronizing smile, and she fought the urge to scream at him. It was that or sit down and cry. Her relations were taking over her farm, and why not? Without them, she and Tucker would doubtless lose this place.

Well, their helping her was one thing. Her sitting back and allowing them to rob her and her brother was another. If she did decide not to marry Matt, she could not afford to lose what was left of White Oak Glen—not to anyone. She looked again at her brother. He'd slithered back into his slouch. He'd be sleeping soon. Briefly, she glanced at Margery, who now comforted the worthless.... Goodness, she wished the woman would marry him and give him a son. For her father's line, it would be like a fresh beginning.

Juliet turned to Wex, who watched her with an amused glint in his eye. "I'm a good shot," she told him, "and we can talk to the neighbors. Surely we're not the only ones having trouble."

"It's us Seatons Dawson is after." Tucker shifted so he could address her directly. "He wants us to lose this place."

Juliet studied Tucker. That part of her brother's diatribe could be true.

"I'll dress in something more suitable," she said and moved around Wexford.

Aunt Lilith rose. "I've laundry to do this morning," she said to Wex. "Are you sure you want to take Juliet into the woods?"

Wex kissed his mother's forehead. "She's willing to help."

"But what will Matthew say?"

That question seared Juliet, but before she could say anything, Wex laughed. "You fear for her virtue?" Playfully, he perused Juliet, standing before him. "You know my little cousin is not my type, Mother. You needn't fear for her."

Chapter Seven

uliet perched on the top step and rested her eyes on the massive double door a porch-width away. Beyond that portal glittered memories of crystal chandeliers and gilded mirrors, gleaming furniture and polished floors. There had been laughter and music-filled soft summer breezes, which lulled her to sleep in the nursery next to her mother's room. She'd had a father and brothers and for a brief time, before the war, she'd been their little princess.

The last time she had crossed that threshold was the spring of 1866. She'd been eleven. She'd sworn that day she would never step inside White Oak Glen again unless the house was hers.

Juliet looked down the hill from where she'd come. It wasn't the lifestyle she missed—that had been over before she'd been old enough to appreciate it. She grieved because in her heart White Oak Glen was hers. Her young grandfather built this house in 1818, the land having come to them three generations earlier in a British land grant awarded her maternal great-great-great-grand-father for service to the Crown.

Her gaze lingered on one of four fluted Ionic columns spaced fifteen feet apart. She'd kept her juvenile vow. During the eight intervening years, she'd not so much as crossed the fence separating what was left of her family's farm from Darnell Tackert's land.

Sunlight bathed her body, warming her despite the chilly breeze that swept the veranda across the front of the house. The cold stung her eyes. She faced the door, and it was as if she'd never left.

44

She crossed the porch, and knocked on one of the ten-foot panels. Kitty Horton opened it, and Juliet's mouth fell open.

"Lordy be, sweet baby girl. What you doin' here by yo'self? You still walkin' them woods no matter my Miss Eileen told you not to, ain't you?"

Kitty hadn't been to her house since Eileen Seaton's visitation. Juliet certainly hadn't expected her to open Jeff Dawson's door, but was relieved to find a friendly, and familiar, face.

Kitty stepped onto the porch and pulled the door almost closed behind her. "How you doin' since yo' mama been gone?"

"We're doing as well as can be expected."

"Yo' aunt still there?" the Negress asked, placing her hands on her wide hips.

"Yes."

"Tucker, he still—"

"*Who's here, Kitty?*"

Kitty turned her head toward the partially opened door. "Miss Juliet Seaton, *Massa* Dawson."

Juliet couldn't see him from where she stood, but she heard him cross to the door. It swung wide. He glanced at her, then at the Springfield she held in her hands. "You've come to see me, Miss Seaton?"

"Yes."

He stepped aside. "Come in."

And she was tempted, for no other reason than to see how much she could recall.

"I'd rather not, Mister Dawson."

Perhaps he understood, or maybe he thought she was being standoffish. Whatever, he didn't press the issue. Kitty moved inside, and Jeff Dawson stepped out. He smelled of soap and leather, and for a moment she drank him in. Intoxicating. Her stomach twinged with guilt. Never had she felt the least desire to do similarly with Matt. When Jeff pulled the door shut, she backed up.

"My condolences for the loss of your mother, Miss Seaton."

"Thank you."

His eyes settled on the Springfield. "Now, you've come to shoot me for bringing your brother home? I wouldn't blame you for that."

"Did you beat him?"

"He was beat up when I found him. Passed out, too, and not from the beating."

"Where did you find him?"

Jeff stepped farther onto the porch and indicated the woods well in front of the house. "Down there, where you like to walk."

"I thank you for bringing him home."

"You're welcome."

She wanted to explain, but wasn't sure how to start. Perhaps with Jeff Dawson's having seen what her brother had become, he would consider vengeance complete and leave them alone.

"Are you hunting this morning?" he asked.

"As a matter of fact I am."

A smirk played at the corners of his mouth. "And what are you hunting?"

"Wolf."

He folded his arms across his chest. "And do you expect to find your quarry in my house?"

"Is he here, *Wolf* Dawson?"

"That depends on what you intend to do with him once you've caught him."

She felt her cheeks redden, but she refused to drop her gaze. "I intend to shoot him, sir."

"In that case, he isn't here."

She sighed. "Have you had any problems with the thing?"

"No. Have you?"

"He killed three head of cattle last night. One was a yearling bull."

The handsome Jeff Dawson frowned at her. "A yearling bull? That doesn't sound right." He made a move toward the house, but she caught his arm.

"Tucker says you're behind it," she blurted out faster than she was thinking, and she could have kicked herself. She'd come to ask if he'd had problems and if so, perhaps they could hunt the thing together. Now she'd confronted him.

"Why would I be?"

"To finish destroying us."

"And why would I want to destroy you, Miss Seaton?"

"I know things happened years ago. I know your sister died in childbirth with a baby she claimed was a Seaton—

"You were told she was willing?"

He may as well have punched her in the stomach. "What do you mean 'willing'?"

"I mean that Seaton baby she died with was the result of rape."

For a moment, Juliet feared she might throw up on his porch. "I never heard.... Mama said...."

"Yes?"

Her mother had said she didn't know the story and then refused to tell it to her. But this couldn't be true. Her family wouldn't have been part of such a thing.

"I know your sister died trying to give birth to Jarmane Seaton's child out of wedlock."

"Your mother obviously left out some pertinent facts regarding your brothers' role in my sister's rape."

So it would seem, and Juliet's ignorance was working to her disadvantage. Had she known Jeff Dawson believed his sister violated, she'd have never come here.

But she was here. Juliet straightened, and sensing the anger seething inside him, her heart pounded harder.

"But Tucker was only a boy when it happened."

"He was old enough."

Old enough for what? She didn't want the answer, not from him. She couldn't be sure he'd tell her the truth. Couldn't be sure he knew the truth. He could be blinded by his own prejudice.

But her mother's words belied that. Juliet steeled herself. "I wasn't," she said, "I played no part in it."

He was watching her hands. Without thinking, she'd balled her free palm into a fist, while with the other, she strangled the

Springfield. Conscious of his scrutiny, she eased her hold on the rifle and brought it to her side. His gaze found hers.

"What did your mother tell you?"

"She warned me to stay away from you."

His gaze fell to her lips, then moved back to her eyes. "There were other things your brothers did. Tucker included."

She felt the color drain from her face. "What?"

He moved to the door and, sure he intended to leave her, she cried out after him. "You have White Oak Glen. Isn't that enough?"

He stopped dead in his tracks and turned. Slowly he raked his eyes over her before bringing them to rest on her face. "I can think of additional payment."

Trepidation, fear, and anger swirled around her like a cyclone, and from the way he braced himself, he must have seen it. Stiff as a lightning rod, she stepped closer. "Let me tell you something, Mister Dawson, I did nothing to hurt you or your family. My people are all but gone, too. I have lost my home, and my brother is making a travesty of my father's name. If it is your plan to destroy what is left of the Seatons, be forewarned that I will not sit back idly and let it happen, and I don't care if you're the devil himself let loose from hell."

"And how would you go about countering the devil himself, Miss Seaton?" Jeff opened the front door. "Will," he called, "come on out here."

The last thing he wanted to do to this particular Seaton was destroy her, at least in the literal sense. God, she was beautiful, even dressed in worn wool, scuffed boots, and a man's tattered coat, too large for her. Possess her, yes; make her scream with want and need whenever he desired—repeatedly take Jordan Seaton's daughter until she was delirious on Jeffrey Dawson, and no part of Jordan Seaton remained.

Will walked out, pulling a suspender onto his shoulder. He looked at Juliet, nodded in greeting, then turned to Jeff.

"Will Howe," he said, "you know Juliet Seaton?"

Juliet held out her hand. "It's been awhile since you've visited our place, Mister Howe."

"It has, Miss Juliet. I'm sorry for the loss of your mama."

"Thank you."

"Seems that wolf's been giving the Seatons trouble," Jeff said.

Will placed his thumbs under his suspenders and stretched them out. "Do tell?"

"Killed three calves last night, including a yearling bull."

Will let his suspenders pop. "Did you say it brought down a year-old bull?"

"Yes." Juliet stepped closer to his side to get a better bead on Will, and purposely, Jeff breathed her jasmine scent.

He wanted to touch her, to smell her skin...to taste her, and a delicious tremble moved through him.

"Don't sound right, Jeff."

Will's direct address drew him from his erotic reverie. They'd been talking, he hadn't been listening. "I'm sorry?"

"Bull's pretty hefty prey for a lone wolf. Don't know that I've ever heard of such. And the little gal here says they was all partly eaten. We're sure there's only one wolf?"

There was a subtle smugness in Will's voice, and Jeff flexed his jaw. Will, of all people, believed there was only one wolf. "That's all the sign I've seen."

Juliet turned her attention from Will back to him. "You've seen tracks in addition to what we saw that day?"

"Yes. Closer to the river, near my folks' old cabin. You've checked with the other neighbors?"

"My cousin Wexford is doing that now. I'm supposed to meet him at home at noon."

"I won't go to your house, Miss Seaton, but I will help you hunt your wolf."

Will looked first at him, then at Juliet. "Tucker going to be part of this?"

"No." She looked down the hill. "He's feeling poorly."

Jeff caught Will's eye. The lovely Juliet didn't want them to see her face. Yeah, the bastard was feeling poorly, all right. Sick and hurting. Tucker was in no condition to help her with the farm. He probably hadn't been for a long, long time.

Will cleared his throat. "I'll tag along and cover your back anyways."

Juliet turned, her lips slightly parted. She had a question, the product no doubt of Will's comment. Whatever she would have asked, she must have thought better of it.

"Tell your cousin we'll meet him down by the creek after the noon meal," Jeff said. "I say we start with the dead animals and move outward."

"I'll tell him."

"And you don't need to come along on this hunt."

"Oh, but I must, Mister Dawson."

He furrowed his brow.

"I have to look out for my interests."

At first, he thought she was talking about looking out for her interests against him. Then he surmised her comment was on account of her cousin Wexford and his mother.

"Are you a good shot, Juliet Seaton?"

"A very good shot, Wolf Dawson."

Chapter Eight

Will squatted and studied the ground. "We're not accomplishin' a damn thing. We find tracks, then poof, they're gone, and it's as if the thing never was."

"The *thing* is a wolf," Jeff said.

"Then where do the tracks go?"

A gust of wind rustled the trees, and a roar swelled through their crowns. He and Will were well inside the woods in front of the big house. Here the vegetation grew thick and in places nearly impassable. They'd worked their way to this point from the pasture where the dead cattle lay. Most of Seaton land was cleared, except this patch on their west, but even past their property line, the land stayed wooded, full of hills and hollows and an occasional swamp for several miles to the west until it reached the river. Once, Jeff's parent's farm had abutted Seaton land. That land too was his now, the old Dawson place incorporated into the new White Oak Glen.

Jeff had found these fresh tracks a short while ago, but again the sign had stopped as though the predator had sprouted wings and flown away. The wolf had disappeared like that three weeks ago, after Juliet had seen it.

"It's Jedediah Wolfson," Will said.

"Jedediah Wolfson is dead."

"That's what we're talking about here, boy. A phantom."

"Will, dammit, you sound like a superstitious peasant." Jeff stilled and listened to thunder roll off to the north.

"Well, this ol' peasant needs to be gettin' home while the gettin's good. That weather is moving in fast. Cold'll be comin' in

51

behind it. Had too much rain last week. Creek's gonna flood." He looked Jeff in the eye. "Ain't nothin' to be done here. Not by a man anyway. A priest, maybe, but I'm not so sure that'd be the right thing to do, either. Might oughta let justice take its course."

A shudder moved through Jeff, and his chill was not the result of the blustery wind. "Have you seen Seaton and the girl?" Will was right about one thing. They needed to quit for the night.

"Passed Seaton as I was comin' this way. He was goin' home. Said he had somethin' he needed to get done before the rain started."

"And Juliet?"

"He'd gotten separated from her, but he wasn't worried. Said she knew these woods better'n any of us."

Jeff cursed. Knowing these woods was one thing. Wandering around in them with this *thing* lurking somewhere was entirely different. Unease settled over him, and he rose. "We should find her."

Will stood too. "She might have gone on home herself."

"I don't think she'd have left without telling one of us."

The wind surged and for a moment thrashed the colorful November foliage. Lightning flashed, and Jeff counted, one, two, three...the thunder rumbled, closer now and louder. Another gust swept the treetops and, with it, a sense of urgency. By his best estimate the cow path was over this way about twenty yards, and he picked up his pace.

Wex had told her an hour ago he needed to stop hunting for the day and get that hole in the chicken coop fixed before it started raining. Juliet assumed that's where he'd gone, because she couldn't find him now. She probably should get back and help with that chore under any circumstances.

Maybe it wouldn't be too awful having Aunt Lilith, Wex, and Margery here, if she could curb her resentment of them and appreciate what they had to offer.

Another gust of wind tore through the deciduous forest above her. She needed to find Jeff and Will and let them...

A tug at her skirt startled her, but a rapid heartbeat later she released her captured breath. Only a blackberry tendril.

The wind blew fitfully, then died. Dark would come early tonight. The cow path wasn't far, but given the vegetation, the going was difficult. Carrying the rifle, almost as long as she was tall, made maneuvering harder.

Lightning struck close, expanding the air with a boom that left her hair on end. Her senses absorbed the terror in the trees and in the living things inhabiting them. Inexplicably, she looked over her shoulder in search of she knew not what. The foliage was thick and gray, its shadows dark, and her spine was tingling. She faced forward, stumbled, and sank ankle deep in mud.

The wind died with her abrupt stop, and she drew in a breath. Never had she been afraid in these woods, and she needed to calm down and work her way around this low area to keep from swamping her boots.

Again she looked behind her. The rifle slipped in her hand, and her stomach tensed, but she cleared the spring-made bog. In front of her, finally, she could make out the path, and she hurried, longing for the dubious security being on it would provide. But a stone's throw away from it, she collided with a wall of stench, blocking the way.

The wind howled. Or was it...? She jerked around, half expecting to find the amber eyes of the wolf watching her, but nothing was there. She drew a breath...and with it the nauseous reminder that something dead lay out of sight. A kill, no doubt, and a clue. As much as she hated to deviate from that cow path, she needed to find the source of the smell.

She inched right. Beyond the underbrush, about twenty feet away, a swatch of bright yellow beckoned her, and she started toward the color, anxious to see what it was, then get on that cow path and out of these woods.

Breathing was now near impossible, and she gagged.

Drowning in the scent of death, Juliet parted the brush, then she fell back, away from her discovery. Bile filed her stomach and stung her throat. She covered her mouth to fight the sickness.

Then the piercing howl of the wolf obliterated what would have been her scream.

A kaleidoscope of fall colors filled her vision as she spun in search of the cow path. From somewhere, Jeff Dawson called her name. She cried his in return. Lightning struck with a boom and a cackle, shattering her precarious equilibrium and leaving her terrified and disoriented.

The wolf was here, but even before its warning howl, she'd sensed it. It had been behind her all the time, watching.

It was here now.

Juliet tripped crossing the creek, soaking her skirt before crashing to the ground with a grunt. Pain contracted her chest, and she covered her head with her arms and pressed her forehead against the damp earth.

The pain subsided, and she found her breath. With renewed determination, she pushed herself to all fours. Her knees and boots tangled in her skirt, and she rolled over and yanked at the fabric.

Then she was up and on the path and—no longer hindered by the rifle, because she'd lost it—running in the direction of Jeff Dawson's voice.

The path curved, and she followed it. Jeff was in sight, running toward her. The wind picked up, and she saw his frightened eyes widen at something closing—

Chapter Nine

The howl explained her panic, but Jeff was equally sure that the danger posed by the wolf—normally they didn't attack people—was nothing compared to that of the large oak limb plummeting toward the path. By the time he saw the bough, Juliet was under it, running blindly, and she didn't hear his shouted warning above the storm's fury.

A heartbeat after she hit the ground, he was beside her, repeating her name and praying for any sort of response, which didn't come.

Frigid raindrops pelted them. Jeff looked up the path. Will was struggling, slowed by his awkward gait, but he was coming. They were all three drenched by the time Will got to where Jeff hunkered over her. They had no choice but to move her. If the downpour continued like this, the creek would flood in minutes, and they had to get her warm.

Will pushed up one of Juliet's eyelids. "Wish we had a doctor."

Jeff snaked an arm behind her shoulders and carefully raised her upper body off the bed. "Get that coat, Will."

"She's like ice."

"I know it. I've got to get her out of these wet clothes." His own hands were so cold he was having trouble making his fingers work. He stopped a moment and looked at her. He'd patted her wild hair dry, as best he could, all the while feeling her head in search of the damage. She had a knot on top and broken skin, but there was little blood. The swelling was minimal. That worried him. Given the size of the limb and the distance it fell, there could be more swelling occurring inside her skull.

"You want me to go for the doc?" Will asked.

"I'd feel better, but you're gonna have trouble getting to Natchez.

"Nah, ain't rained enough yet. We need to let that cousin of hers know where she is, too. Be a hell of a shame to have Tucker Seaton out looking for her and maybe drown."

"From what I've seen of Tucker, I doubt he even realizes she's missing. Wexford might notice she didn't return, considering she was hunting with him, but you'll never get across that creek now. You'll have to get to them the long way, but send me a doctor first."

Jeff started unbuttoning the bodice of her dress. The fabric was worn, and the skirt had been patched in several places. He didn't recall the one she'd been wearing the day they met being so shabby. "I guess times are tough for the Seatons."

"Times are tough for most all us Confederates, 'ceptin' them that went out to Colorado and struck it rich."

"Help me here, Will. I've got to move her head again."

They got the dress off her, and he felt the corset. The pantaloons were wet, too. She was soaked to the skin. All three of them were. He'd taken his sweet time lifting her, then carrying her up the hill to his house. Her head injury scared him and justified his extra care.

He took her left hand and rubbed his thumb over a ruby ring. "Things can't be all bad."

"Matthew Braxton I reckon."

Jeff's gut tightened, and he remembered Severs' reference to Braxton several nights ago. "She's engaged?"

"Has been for over a year."

"Over a year?"

"There's hesitation on somebody's part."

Jeff looked at Juliet lying on the bed soaking wet and in her worn unmentionables. For sure, it wouldn't be the groom's. Any man looking to be wed would be a fool to hold off on her.

"That the son of that hellfire Baptist preacher up the river road?"

"That's him."

Jeff remembered Matt, a long, tall beanpole, who wouldn't relieve himself without his daddy's permission. "What the hell is he doing with someone like her?"

"Money'd be my guess. Compared to most everybody else, the Braxtons ain't had to sell off their land to meet Republican taxes." Will shrugged. "Neighbors say the boy avoided conscription by maneuvering behind Yankee lines. The Braxtons didn't risk anything in the war. Recovery for them has been easier than for the rest of us, but they ain't Republicans."

Jeff clenched his teeth and considered stripping her naked and drinking his fill, but it was none of his business if she chose to sell herself to a namby-pamby man for money.

He reached for the top hook on her corset, and Will cleared his throat. "I think the fewer of us here for this, the more she'd appreciate it. I'm gonna get in dry clothes. You got some gear?"

"Slicker in my dresser, and there's a cotton nightshirt in there, too. Get it for me, will you?"

Chapter Ten

Rain drummed on the roof and pulled her from a deeply disturbing dream, made all the more upsetting because she didn't want to leave it. Juliet rolled to her side, and the world rolled with her. Eyes closed, she waited for the horrible spinning to stop, and when it did, she peeked. A window reached for the ceiling; beneath it sat a narrow window box. A wet, gray tapestry of dreary daylight filled the opening...and, symbolically, a tiny corner of her heart.

She pushed her sorrow aside and laid a forearm over her eyes. There was something more immediate, something else she had to remember.

The mattress sank under another's weight, and she raised her arm and looked. In her dream the wolf had run her down, then subdued her with legs that became arms, razor-clawed paws that became hands. He had kissed her lips, her neck...her breasts, his tongue cold and wet, a comfort against her heated skin. Her terror had dissipated along with the evanescent beast that held her captive, and the wolf had become that very same Jeff Dawson who watched her now, his brow etched with worry.

"How do you feel?" he asked.

"I can't remember."

"You can't remember how you feel?"

"I feel horrible. I can't remember what happened."

"You were hit in the head by an oak limb a little smaller than a railroad tie."

"Oh." Well, that explained her head. "I remember this room."

"Was it yours?"

58

"Yes, but it wasn't yellow then. It was pink and white, before the war. During the war, it became grungy. Gray. The whole world turned gray."

"That was our color then, if you remember."

"I hadn't thought of it like that. Fitting, as it turned out. The room looks nice now."

"It was this way when I bought the house. Missus Tackert must have decorated it."

Juliet fought back a wave of nausea. "It's raining?"

"Yes. It stopped for a little while earlier, but it's been raining since dawn."

"Dawn?"

"You spent last night with me, and you'll be with me again tonight."

"Does anyone know where I am?"

"Will Howe. He left to get the doctor yesterday after you were hurt. He was going to try to make it to your people. Haven't seen hide nor hair of him since."

She started to sit up. "My family—"

"Lay back," he ordered, then rose and walked to the window. "Neither of us is going anywhere. You should see it down there. Your woods are a swamp. Let's hope Will's gotten word to your brother and aunt by now."

If her mother were still alive, she'd be beside herself. As it was, the others would probably be content if she disappeared. Tucker might care, if he were sober enough to realize she was missing.

Juliet drew her arms from beneath the covers and noted the long white sleeves. "We were hunting the wolf. I remember that." Slowly she lifted the blankets and looked beneath. Good lord, she was in a man's nightshirt.

She lowered the covers and found Jeff watching her.

"I undressed you."

She stared at his broad torso outlined against the hazy light from the window, and she smoothed the covers when he started back toward the bed.

59

"You were soaked to the skin and in shock, Juliet. I had to get you warm and dry. I was discreet."

"Meaning?"

Again, he sat on the edge of the bed. "Meaning I covered you with my nightshirt before disrobing you."

She wondered if he really had or was simply trying to make her feel better. There was no doubt in her mind he'd seen a naked woman before.

Her concern seemed suddenly silly, so she gave him an agreeable nod. That started her head aching, and she raised her hand to the top of it and found a tender spot. Again nausea assaulted her, and she ceased all movement. The sickness passed.

"Do you have a comb?" she asked.

He laughed. "I do, but your appearance is the last thing you need to worry with now."

"I-I..."

He reached out with long, tanned fingers and tugged a lock over her shoulder to fall across her breast. "Your hair is beautiful; it's spread all over the pillow."

Her face heated. "That's what I'm afraid of."

"A man prefers it the way it is now." He tilted his head, appraising her. "The color in your cheeks becomes you, miss."

The warmth in his voice caused her stomach to flip-flop, an unpleasant sensation given the nausea. Did he think she wanted to please him? Of course, all men would assume so, and she had asked for a comb. And if his assumption were false, why did his compliment flatter her so?

Trying to dismiss her vanity, she focused on his finely sculpted mouth set between a straight nose and a strong chin. His jaw was square, masculine; his cheekbones, high. Her gaze drifted upward, but avoided those dark blue eyes. A wisp of hair, more auburn than brown in the firelight, fell over his forehead.

She surrendered and met his eyes. He was watching her, as if trying to read her mind.

If you must know, Jeff Dawson, I think you are the most handsome man I have ever seen in my life.

"You look as though you are in agony, Miss Seaton."
Despite her misery, laughter gurgled up her throat.

*J*eff moved the chamber pot close to the bed and helped her
up. She was dizzy, unsteady on her feet, and, he could tell, hurting. He then waited patiently outside her door, listening, until he
was sure she was finished. By the time he reentered the room, she
was pulling the bedcovers over herself. He gave her laudanum for
the pain and to help her sleep and spent the rest of the day catching up on correspondence and bookkeeping.

In the afternoon, Will came back, but without the doctor, who
was treating measles on a farm south of Natchez. Keep her head
still had been the sawbones' guidance. Will proceeded to ask Jeff
if Juliet had regained consciousness and how alert she'd been,
and he'd breathed a sigh of relief with Jeff's responses. If she
regains consciousness and appears to have all her faculties, the
doctor relayed, the expected outcome was good.

Will had also gone around the worst of the flooding and
reached the Seaton farm from the east. That's why he'd taken so
long getting back. Wex and the womenfolk knew where she was
and knew she'd been hurt. "Figure you'll be seeing them as soon
as they can get over here."

That was fine. At least they knew she was alive.

Night fell once more. The rain continued, sometimes heavy.
The weather was cold, but the temperature wouldn't really plum-
met until this moisture was used up or moved elsewhere.

Periodically, he put down his novel and trekked through a
connecting room into the one where Juliet slept. Her breathing
was shallow, her skin pale and clammy. She hadn't wakened since
morning, and he was beginning to doubt his wisdom in giving her
the sleeping draught.

He finished a chapter, marked his page, and laid the English
Gothic aside, preparing to check her once again.

"Mister Dawson?"

Her voice surprised him, and he sat forward to see the doorway to the adjoining room.

On her, his nightshirt fell halfway between the ankle and the knee, and those bare feet of hers had to be freezing. He rose. Stock-still and glassy-eyed, she watched him come.

"What are you doing up?" Despite his mild censure, he was relieved she'd wakened. He stopped in front of her.

"There was more, wasn't there? Something else in addition to the limb?"

"You were frightened when I came upon you. The wolf had howled. I figured that's what scared you."

She swayed, and he caught her at the waist. In response, she put her hands on his shoulders. Her efforts appeared to steady her somewhat. "I'm having bad dreams."

Suddenly she bowed her head and tightened her grip on him. For a brief moment, she stood rigid, looking at the floor. "I'm going to be sick."

Shit! He guided her to the chamber pot at the foot of his bed, and when she squatted and stuck her nose over its edge, he smoothed her hair back to keep it clear of vomit if she did get sick. She gagged once, but after a moment raised her head and breathed in.

"Perhaps I won't, thank you."

He pulled her up when she tried to rise, then lifted her in his arms. "Are you sure you're not gonna be sick?" A beauty she may be, but he didn't want to be thrown up on.

She laid her head on his shoulder when he turned to the dark room, and it occurred to him she was only half-aware of where she was and what she was doing. "You've no business walking around," he said.

In her room, he settled her between the rumpled bed clothes and tucked the blankets around her.

"I cannot remember what happened," she said tearfully.

"That's not unusual with a head injury."

"I remember you." Her voice broke. "I remember my mother died three weeks ago."

He sat beside her and covered her hand.

"Something else happened, Jeff."

Ah, finally, his given name.

"Something awful, and I can't remember what."

He stroked her knuckles with his thumb. "Can you remember your dreams?"

"I remember one," she said, then played at her bottom lip with her teeth. Hesitant or organizing her thoughts?

"The wolf's in it. At first he's vicious, and I'm terrified, then he stands on two legs." She contemplated him intensely. "And he becomes a man."

Visions of Will's werewolf-like creature invaded Jeff's brain, and intrigued by her scrutiny, he knit his brow. "Does the man have a face?"

"Yours."

His heartbeat quickened. "And did I threaten to eat you up?"

"You did not threaten at all."

He wasn't sure he liked that. He'd hoped to threaten something. He squeezed her hand, chilled by the cold night air. She shivered, and he felt it. Her shiver was not from the cold.

And not from fear either.

"What did I do, Miss Juliet?"

A tremulous smile moved over her lovely, full lips. "You comforted me."

Unable to stifle himself, he smiled broadly, eager to know more of what was going on inside her beautiful head. "And how did I comfort you?"

"You hugged me and told me everything was all right."

And he had done just that in the wee hours of this morning when, with the howl of the wolf, she'd cried out in delirium; then he'd soothed her feverish body with a cold, wet rag. She'd been frightened and shaking, and on the threshold of consciousness.

Again, he pulled her into his arms and squeezed. "Everything is still all right, Juliet."

He eased his hold and rose. "I need to get you something to eat."

"No." She reached out for his hand. "I'm not hungry."

"You've not eaten since noon yesterday."

"I don't care. I'm not a coward, but I am frightened now. No matter what you say, everything is not all right. There's something else. It's real, and it's terrible. My mind is trying to tell me through my dreams. I'm afraid I'll remember and you won't be here."

He relented. Maybe by morning she'd be strong enough to go downstairs and eat, though what the hell he was going to feed her, he didn't know. He retrieved his book and pulled a chair close to her bed. Shortly, she dozed.

Jeff jerked forward, at the same time grabbing the upholstered arm of the chair. Something slipped from his lap and thudded upon the carpet. The world around him was scarcely brighter than the one his name, cried aloud, had torn him from, and for an instant he didn't know where he was.

Embers glowed in the fireplace before him, and the wick in the kerosene lamp beside the bed was short, good for little more than precarious assurance against dark shadows invading a child's dreams. He looked on the floor. He'd dropped his book.

Another desperate plea oriented him, and he sprang from the chair and grasped Juliet to him.

"I remember," she sobbed into his shoulder. "Oh, my...."

"Shh," he coaxed, while the pieces of his own scattered psyche fell back into place. He rocked her gently. "What was it?"

Her arms circled his chest, and she pressed herself to him as if she couldn't get close enough.

"I'm here, I'm not going anywhere."

She pushed back, and her cheeks glistened in the muted glow of lantern light. Reaching up, she touched his face.

Making sure he was really who he was supposed to be?

"A woman friend of Tucker's, Lorna Hart, she was in the woods." Juliet removed her hand from his cheek and touched her throat. "Her.... Oh God, Jeff, her head was almost severed from her body."

Chapter Eleven

"I think that we should leave her here, Matt," Wex Seaton said. "If we could cross the fields, I'd say yes, but she's in no condition to make that trip the long way around."

"We've got his wagon. She'll be fine.

Fine, hell. Jeff stepped into the room and handed Matthew Braxton Juliet's clothes, which he'd hung on the mud porch out back. That damn wagon didn't even have springs.

The man stared at the corset and pantaloons, then looked at Jeff. "Kitty Horton works for you?"

"She does, but she hasn't been here for three days."

Braxton kept his gaze fixed on him.

"I undressed her. She was freezing, and I was scared she'd go into shock. I considered her life more important than prudence." He wanted to say "...than your sensitivities," but didn't.

Braxton started out of the room. "I'll help her dress."

Jeff reluctantly watched the man climb the stairs. Ol' Matt had filled out some since Jeff last saw him, but he was still lanky. Not what anyone would call a handsome fellow with his straw-colored hair and big nose, but not really ugly either. Plain. The man was simply plain. Juliet could do worse...in regard to looks, that is. Matt reached the upstairs landing, and Jeff turned to Wex Seaton.

"I'll lend you some blankets and a pillow, too. She can't even stand up without getting sick to her stomach, and it's too damn cold for her to be in the back of that wagon."

"I could bring Margery over and let her stay with you until Juliet's ready to travel or until the creek goes down."

"That would be fine with me, but she's indicated that she's willing to go." Jeff's gut feeling was Braxton had browbeaten her into leaving, but her agreeing tied his hands. What he wanted to do was send the selfish prude packing. Juliet shouldn't get out of that bed yet, and anyone who gave a hoot about her would know that.

Jeff motioned Wex into the parlor. "Any more trouble over at your place?" He offered Wex a whiskey.

"Nothing. I checked everything at first light. All the stock is there. Then Matt showed up wanting to talk to Juliet."

Matt showed up again now, too, quietly reentering the room. *Help Juliet dress*, Jeff's ass.

"Well, speak of the devil." Wex held the shot glass up and saluted Matt. "He was bound and determined," Wex continued to Jeff, as if Matt wasn't there, "to fetch her home the minute he found out she was over here with you."

Matt glared at him, and Wex chuckled. "So, is she ready?" Wex asked the man.

"No, she said she'd dress herself."

Jeff moved toward the parlor door and listened, hoping he'd hear her fall on her face. He would send Braxton packing then.

"When she's ready, she wants to see you," Braxton said to him.

Because of Lorna, he knew. Jeff made his way back to the whiskey on the console. "You've a long ride, Braxton. Would you like a fortifier?"

"I don't imbibe spirits."

Jeff offered Wex Seaton another. Seaton, warmed from that first shot, Jeff reckoned, sipped at this one and elaborated on the damage the storm had done to his collards. Braxton paced.

"Mister Dawson?" Juliet's voice sounded strained...and her formal address grated on him.

He moved into the foyer and, spying her at the top of the stairs, cursed under his breath. "Juliet, go back to the bedroom." He hoped Braxton noted his use of her familiar name.

"I must talk to you."

"I'm coming up, now sit down."

Jeff's foot had just touched the bottom step, when Braxton passed him up, then took the stairs two at a time. On the landing, Braxton grabbed her elbow and led her back into the room.

She was seated in his reading chair by the time Jeff entered the room. Braxton hovered over her like a watchdog, his insecurity pathetically conspicuous. Ignoring the man, Jeff bent down on one knee beside her.

"You'll talk to the sheriff?" she asked.

"I'll ride as far as Natchez with y'all and talk to him today."

"I'd be very grateful."

"Why does he need to see the sheriff, Juliet?"

She glanced at her intended. "I saw something in the woods the day I was injured. Something that must be brought to the attention of the authorities."

"What?"

"A dead body."

"A...." Braxton clamped his mouth shut, then laughed nervously. "Was this before or after you were knocked in the head?"

"Before."

"Juliet, are you absolutely positive you saw something?"

Jeff didn't miss her subtle cringe. "Of course, I am."

"There's enough scandal here without your being mixed up in murder." Braxton shook his head. "Out on a wolf hunt! Of all the silly, irresponsible, childish things to do"—he threw up his hands—"and now this. What will my father say?"

He belittled and bullied her. Jeff wanted to hit him.

"I said nothing of murder, Matt. I said I saw a body."

Braxton released a put-upon sigh, then turned to Jeff.

"I do not see why you can't talk to the sheriff without involving Miss Seaton."

Jeff bristled. *Miss Seaton!* He wondered if Braxton had ever had the pleasure of spending two nights alone with *Miss Seaton.*

"I would happily do so," Jeff answered, "but I didn't see the body."

As if he were making some noble sacrifice, Matthew Braxton

straightened and thrust out his chest. "Then you must be the one to talk to the sheriff, Juliet."

"I'm certain he'll be out to talk to her, Braxton. She's in no condition to see the man today."

"Then why do you need to see him today?"

This pompous ass didn't want him to accompany them to town. Whether it was because Braxton wanted him away from Juliet immediately or because he feared what people seeing them along the way might conjecture, Jeff wasn't sure. He bit back a deprecating comment. "Because the sooner he learns of the incident, the sooner he can begin his search for the body."

Juliet turned to Jeff. "I fear the body has washed away in the creek water."

"Possibly, but it has to be somewhere."

"The river, maybe?" Wex said. He'd followed them upstairs and now stood at the bedroom door. "Who was it, little cousin?"

"Lorna Hart."

Braxton curled his lips in disdain. "If it was that trollop you saw, good riddance. No doubt the woman got exactly what God meant for her."

Jeff tensed. It was more than Braxton's sanctimonious condemnation of another human being. Juliet had seen something that frightened and sickened her. After four bloody years of war, he knew she would never totally eliminate that vision from her memory.

"Your not approving of Lorna Hart, Matthew, does not justify wishing her dead," Juliet said.

Wex leaned a shoulder against the doorjamb and stared at Braxton. "Matt is not the only upstanding Christian person who's gonna feel that way about her, Juliet. You can bet that Yankee deputy won't spend much time trying to find out what happened to her, either."

"The wages of sin are death," Braxton said to Juliet. "I did not wish her dead. I am merely saying there is no cause to become upset over her."

"There is—"

"Except that your fiancée saw it," Jeff said, rising.

Braxton glared at Jeff. "And if you had not dragged her off into the woods on something as inappropriate as a wolf hunt, she now wouldn't be burdened by what she saw."

The feel of Juliet's hand on his preempted Jeff's retort. She said, "I came to him, Matt, and please, Mister Dawson, say no more."

Jeff held Braxton's glower, but Juliet didn't want a confrontation, and Jeff didn't want trouble either. It would be best for them to go. He was sick of Matthew Braxton and more tired yet watching Juliet deal with the man. He thought of Braxton's hands on her, and his thighs weakened. Damn it all to hell! She was obviously uncomfortable around him, and given Braxton's attitude toward Lorna, he'd wager Braxton didn't know the first thing about pleasing a woman, nor would he care to. Sex to him would be a necessary evil—one he would not hesitate to participate in and sinfully enjoy—but would be appalled if his wife displayed any pleasure in the act.

Braxton dropped his stare, and Jeff stepped back and forced himself calmer.

"It's after twelve," Braxton said. "We need to get moving or night will catch us."

Wex grinned. "And with werewolves on the loose, that could prove hazardous."

Juliet looked at her cousin, then at Jeff. Jeff returned her gaze ruefully. "I'll get those blankets and a pillow."

"You needn't bother," Braxton said.

"I will bother." Jeff didn't even try to hide the contempt in his voice. "She'll not leave my house without them."

Braxton's nostrils flared.

"She'll need them, Matt," Wex said. "I can return them to Dawson when I bring back his wagon."

Juliet started to stand, and Braxton stepped over to help her. Jeff turned away. Two minutes later, arms full of blankets, he came to the top of the stairs where Wex stood watching Braxton fuss alongside Juliet.

"I could carry you."

"I would prefer to walk, thank you."

She faltered, but Braxton held her steady.

"You're going to be sick to your stomach again," Braxton said.

Worse, she was going to tumble headlong down the stairs. What was the man thinking? Jeff thrust the blankets into Wex Seaton's hands, seized Juliet by the arm, and lifted her in both of his. "Excuse me," he said to Braxton, then skirted the man and started down the stairs.

Juliet's head lolled on his shoulder. "I fear I'm going to faint."

"And it would serve you right. Why didn't you let him carry you?"

"Please slow up, Mister Dawson."

He stepped off the bottom tread and turned toward the back of the house.

"Quit calling me Mister Dawson, and if you cannot abide his touch, Juliet, how do you expect to endure the marriage bed?" He was angry and jealous and honest enough to admit it to himself, if not to anyone else.

She didn't belong with the likes of Matthew Braxton. Living with him would make a bitter, pinched old woman out of her in ten years' time. "Is the price you're being paid going to be worth it?"

She raised her head to see his face, and he glared at her.

"What do you mean?"

He was out the back door, and off the porch steps. Frigid cold pierced his body, and despite the fact she was bundled up, he knew it pierced hers, too.

"You know what I mean," he said when they reached the rear of the wagon, "your body for his money." He looked over his shoulder. "Seaton," he called out, "we need those blankets!" He turned back and met her eyes, dark gray and churning with unbridled fury, and he snarled at her, "You're no better than a prostitute."

"But the price a man pays for a wife is so much greater, isn't it, Mister Dawson?"

"And more often than not, I hear, the pleasure's not worth the payment."

Her eyes narrowed, and he was sure she hadn't experienced energy like this in days. Her anger exhilarated him, and satisfaction ran wild through his veins, filling his damn cock with blood. He so wanted to lay her in the buckboard, throw up her tattered skirt, yank down her pantaloons, and take her in front of Braxton he could hardly stand it.

"A woman could never be paid enough for what she has to put up with from a man."

"That, Miss Seaton, depends on the *endowment* offered by said man."

Those narrowed, angry eyes widened in understanding, and he grinned at her.

"But in your and Braxton's case, Miss Seaton, you'll get no better than you give."

Chapter Twelve

"*H*er mother come to me yesterday. This *Miss* Hart's been gone four days now."

Jeff made a quick count backward. That had been the same day he rescued Tucker Seaton from her merciless beating in the woods. He told Deputy Sheriff Benton Floyd so.

"You say her throat was torn out?"

"That's how Juliet Seaton described it, but you need to talk to her. She took a heavy blow to the head, and she was hysterical when she talked to me."

"Probably an animal then. I hear there's a wolf out your way."

"Yes."

"Folks tell me there hasn't been a wolf in these parts in recent memory."

"Nineteen years," Jeff clarified, "and as the story goes, he was a rare one."

He was reserving judgment on Floyd, an ex-Union soldier from Ohio. Jeff had yet to meet the sheriff, and Will told him he probably wouldn't. That man was colored—the "bone" the radicals threw to the colored voters who kept them in power. White deputies, Union men and Republicans, carried out the actual duties of the office and shared its perquisites.

"But she could have been savaged by wild animals after she was dead," Jeff said.

"You're thinkin' someone killed her?"

"I'm thinking you can't rule it out yet."

Floyd leaned back in his chair and crossed his feet on top of his desk. "She was a whore; it won't matter to most folks."

"It'll matter to her mother, and it'll matter to other people, too, if there's somebody lurking in those woods over there killing women. The next victim may not be a whore. A killer's a killer, and as far as I'm concerned, I'd prefer to live among whores than murderers."

"Well said, Mister Dawson. I'll gather us up a party, and we'll start searchin' those woods. First we need to come up with a body and make sure that juicy little Miss Seaton"—Jeff's gut tightened—"wasn't seeing things."

Chapter Thirteen

Kitty helped Juliet from the chamber pot back onto the bed. Goodness, the pillows felt nice behind her shoulders. "He sent you?" she asked Kitty.

"I come on my own." The Negress rinsed out a cotton rag, then sat at the foot of the bed. "He told me you was at his house fo' two nights. Wanted to make sho' you was okay."

"I'm not. The trip in the wagon was—"

"I ain't worried 'bout no wagon trip, child. What that Jeff Dawson act like towards you?"

A new wave of nausea swept over Juliet. She was trying to do too much and paying the price. "He nursed me."

"You was knocked out?"

"Some of the time."

"How do you know he didn't—"

An ache cramped her bloated stomach, a terrible sensation every bit as sickening as the insinuation from Kitty's lips.

"Why would he do such a thing, Kitty?"

"He whelps from vengeful stock. Lie with the devil, them. Tucker, he's tellin' you true 'bout that."

Hogwash.

"Dawson's wantin' to even things between his folk and you Seatons."

Back to Jarmane and Bonnie Dawson. Juliet could not rule out a desire on Jeff Dawson's part to avenge that perceived wrong, but he didn't need to conjure demons to do that, nor did she believe he would ever violate a comatose woman.

"To hurt you like those boys hurt his sister."

Juliet stared at the black woman. "Didn't Bonnie give herself willingly to...?"

Kitty was already shaking her head. "Your cousin raped that girl."

Juliet's quickened heart now raced. "How do you know that?"

"Ever'body know'd at the time." Kitty folded her hands in her lap. "Yo' daddy, he knowed, and yo po' mama, later.

"Miss Eileen she tell me your cousin Jarmane wanted that Dawson girl and thought it be his right to take her. He was a handsome boy, but she was a real pretty girl, too. He used to flirt with her at the church. I know cause yo' brothers teased him shamefully. Sometimes, she flirted back—oh, they really rode him on those days. And maybe he took her flirtin' for yes. Yo' mama called him a conceited ass. She said that would have been all the answer he needed, that he thought that Dawson girl would be honored to frolic with the likes of him. Maybe she should have been. Ain't for me to say, but yo' mama said she placed higher store on herself than that. When time came for him to have his fun, she said no."

"Why didn't Mama tell me?"

"'Cause she be ashamed."

Juliet closed her eyes tight to shut out the honesty in Kitty's. Jeff Dawson had told her the truth on his front porch.

"Mama warned me to keep away from Mister Dawson. Said it had to do with Jarmane and Bonnie and about the old man, the grandfather. She said I didn't know the truth." Fingers crushing the bed quilt, Juliet looked Kitty in the face. "Why didn't she tell me about the rape? Did she think me better off not knowing what drove him?"

"It weren't Dawson that mainly concerned her, child. It was the how of it, and you knowin' yo' daddy covered up the deed. She forgave him many things, but she never forgave him what happened that awful year. She didn't want you knowin', you loved his memory so. But you gots to know now, else you goin' to get yo'self in trouble with that man. Them Dawsons be dangerous people."

75

"I don't believe Daddy would have protected his nephew in such—"

Kitty held up a hand. "There be mo' to the story, baby girl. Somethin' few of the livin' know. But that man Jeff Dawson, fo' sho' he knows."

Despite the chill in her room, Juliet broke out in a sweat.

"Jeremy and Rafe, they held that girl down while Jarmane had his fun. Sullivan and Tucker, they was just fourteen and twelve, watched. According to what that po' girl told yo' mama, they all cheered Jarmane on."

Kitty's words chilled Juliet's blood and froze the sweat upon her skin.

"Them boys, they was drunk. Been sippin' stolen moonshine all mornin'. Po' girl just happened across their path. It was June. She'd been out pickin' blackberries. Her mama wanted to make a cobbler.

"Miss Eileen said it was a wonder all five of 'em didn't rape that girl. 'Bout killed Deke Dawson, Bonnie's daddy. He come with the sheriff, but your brothers and cousin said the girl was willin'. They said she only claimed she was raped after yo' brothers happened upon her and Jarmane in the woods."

Juliet sat forward and placed a hand on her forehead. Kitty handed her the wet rag. "Put this on yo' head; it'll help with the poundin'."

Pounding was right. "Could—"

"No, child. I know what you's thinkin', and it ain't that way. Lord knows yo' mama wanted it to be how her boys said, but Miss Eileen talked to old Doc Wells who tended Bonnie after. Bonnie had bruises...and she was tore bad. Jarmane hurt her. Doc Wells told the sheriff that, but sheriff sided with yo' daddy and uncle. Dawsons didn't fight it. Damage was done, weren't no fixin' it. Raisin' a ruckus would only add to the girl's shame, and there was other ways, ways outside the law, to get justice.

"Jarmane got that girl with child. Yo' mama was carryin' you, and yo' daddy told her to mind her own baby and not worry 'bout that girl up by the river.

"Miss Eileen did though. Visited that Dawson girl often. But she was too young. Went into the birthin' at eight months. Her and the baby died."

Juliet laid the empty shell of her body back on the pillows, but the physical comfort did nothing to relieve the spinning in her head or the emptiness in her soul.

"Two days after they buried Bonnie Dawson, that cousin of yours was found in the woods with his throat ripped out."

Found at the southwest corner of White Oak Glen, not far off the drive leading to the house. Juliet knew that part of the story.

"Fool sheriff said it was a wolf done it, but all us know'd it weren't the way of a wolf." Kitty's gaze met Juliet's and held. "Werewolf was what it was."

"A werewolf?"

"Yes'm."

Suspicion crept over Juliet. "Who?"

"That old man. Jeff Dawson's granddaddy, Jedediah."

"He was murdered."

"Lynched. Three days after Jarmane Seaton was killed, that boy Jeff Dawson found his granddaddy on Dawson land near the river, hangin' from a tree."

"Jeff found him?"

"He was young, too. Little. Ten or eleven."

Good God. He'd just buried his sister, then to find such a thing in a tree. "Who did it?" Juliet said. Beneath the covers, she shifted position and drew her knees closer to her body.

Kitty took the rag and rinsed it in the shallow bowl of cold water beside Juliet's bed.

"Nobody knows fo' sho'. Mean old man had lots of people hatin' him."

"You know."

"I don't know nothin'," Kitty said sharply, then placed the rag against Juliet's head. "And I ain't speculatin' neither. He was a wicked old man, in league with the devil. Most folks was glad he was gone."

"I don't believe you can kill a werewolf by hanging it."

"Who says that thing be dead? What's that howlin' we been hearin' in the middle of the night? Might be that old man's come back. Might be the ghost of that boy killed at Corinth."

"That boy wasn't killed at Corinth, Kitty. For pity's sake, you're in his house every day. And you expect me to believe you think him a ghost?"

"Hmmph. I think he's white mongrel trash don't have no mo' business livin' in yo' mama and granddaddy's house than a field nigger."

"You're obviously not afraid of him, and you shouldn't speak of him like that. He's good to you, I've seen it."

Kitty folded her arms over her ample breasts. "He pays real good. I'll take his money fo' sho', and I'm takin' good care of yo' mama's house in return. And I ain't no Seaton. Seaton blood is what he hungers for." She nodded pointedly at Juliet. "Seaton blood and Seaton shame. Don't you trust him, girl, no matter how temptin' he is."

"I've talked to my father. We will marry on the thirtieth of November."

Less than a month away. Juliet took a seat on the settee and looked at the ruby ring on her finger, then at the domineering Matt, who stood in front of the fireplace. Well, she figured she could be dominated, but it would take a special man to manage it. So special she wouldn't realize it was happening. Even more, she wouldn't care. Best of all, she'd do the same to him, and he would be as happy.

"Your mother is gone. I am your betrothed. For all intents and purposes, you are my responsibility now, and this foolishness with Dawson is a disgrace, Juliet. If people find out about your being alone with him for two nights, they'll think you whored yourself with him."

"Is that what you think?"

"Of course not, but the point is the opportunity for you two was there and given what your...." Juliet swore he bit his tongue. He thrust out his chin. "Anyway, that's what people will think."

"Only a dirty-minded, self-righteous busybody would think such a thing. I can't even remember most of my stay. In any case, I wouldn't care if people did think such."

"Well, I care."

"What should he have done, Matthew? Left me in the woods?"

"He should have brought you home."

"It was almost a mile. I had a head injury, and it was storming."

"He should have risked it."

"He didn't know if I would live or die, for Christ's sake."

Matt bent down with a swift, violent motion and caught her chin in his hand. "Do not blaspheme, Juliet!"

His hold hurt, and she twisted out of his grasp. If she wanted to blaspheme, she'd damn well blaspheme.

He straightened, nostrils flaring. "I did not like the way he acted toward you nor the liberties he took in front of me." Matt paced in front of the fireplace. "He offended me, and his actions could have disgraced you. He should have weighed the consequences before taking you to his home."

"And if my injuries had been worse, and I had died?"

"Death before dishonor."

"Soldiers' words, Matthew, easily spoken by someone whose life was not threatened."

He whipped around and stuck a bony finger in her face. "Do not use that tone with me!"

"Do you actually think I would put my life into the hands of someone who thinks as you are thinking now?"

He reared back slightly, then hid his fisted hands behind his back—but not before she saw. He would hit her. After they were married, he would hit her, thinking it his right. Missus Braxton was a shy, cowering woman. No doubt, Josephus beat her. Juliet had never seen him, but she knew now, without a doubt, that he did, or had. As terrible as Jordan Seaton may have been, he never raised a hand to her mother.

Matt put his back to her and faced the fire. "I have had all I can stand, Juliet. We shall be married on the thirtieth or—"

"We shall not be married at all."

He turned around with her words, and she held out her hand.

"What is this?" he asked, his voice tremulous.

"Take it," she said, "that is how it must be."

Paling, he opened his palm, and Juliet dropped his grandmother's ring into it.

"You are breaking our engagement?"

"I am sorry. I kept hoping for some spark between us to convince me that I would be happy with you and you with me. Time has proven the opposite, and I am glad I waited. You don't approve of me, Matthew. We would have been miserable together. Eventually, you would have probably killed me...or me you, for you could have never forced me into submission."

"I-I would have never forced—"

"You would have tried, physically and emotionally, as your father abuses your mother. Unlike her, I wouldn't have tolerated it."

His face flushed. But for the shock, she thought he might have hit her then.

"Have you talked to your aunt and brother about this?"

"And my mother before her death. She knew, they all know, I had misgivings about taking your ring."

"You can't pay the taxes on this place. I'd have done that."

Recalling Jeff Dawson's words to her, she stood. "To accept your money for my body would make me no better than a common prostitute."

Though it shouldn't have, his brutal slap caught her off guard. She whimpered and covered her cheek with the back of her hand.

Matt thrust out his chin. "To scorn the marriage bed, sanctified by God, in such a disgusting manner is disgraceful. You've no more respect for marriage than your mother did."

Hand pressed against her stinging face, she bored her gaze into his. "Leave my house. You are no longer welcome here."

He stood glaring at her, clenching and unclenching his fists, his narrow face so red she imagined his blood boiling beneath the surface of his skin.

"Your mother wanted you to wed me," he said. "She wanted me to lead you out of this den of iniquity she made and back into the fold. You've betrayed her wishes. You should be ashamed."

Ashamed? Her heart, already churning, increased its pace.

"My mother wanted me secure; she cared nothing for your so-called fold. I doubt she even believed in God's fold anymore." She braced herself, sure he was going to hit her again. She was so sick of him she didn't care, as long as he left afterward.

"For certain she betrayed her God along with her husband. Good day to you, Miss Seaton." He spat the words out, splattering her uninjured cheek with his spittle. From the chair closest to the fireplace, he snatched his hat and turned on his heel. She heard him grab his coat from the rack next to the door, then heard the coat tree fall against the wall. The door opened with a violent rattle, then slammed shut. A glass pane shattered, and pieces of it tinkled upon the floor. Upstairs, Tucker cursed.

From the corner of her eye, Juliet saw Aunt Lilith peek into the parlor. The woman's gaze met hers, then dropped to the hand covering Juliet's cheek. With a sympathetic shake of her head, Lilith crossed the room and removed the hand. Sitting on the settee, she pulled Juliet down beside her.

"I take it you wouldn't give him a date?"

Juliet felt tears well in her eyes, and she turned to the fire. She'd wronged Matt, hateful as he turned out to be. Worse, she'd wronged herself. With the tip of her tongue, she touched the corner of her mouth and tasted blood.

"I did both myself and Matt a great service, Aunt Lilith. I gave him his ring back."

Chapter Fourteen

"*O ver here!*"

The man calling couldn't be more than twenty yards in front of him, but it was hard to tell where, exactly, any of them were in the woods.

Jeff stepped forward and bogged down in the soft earth. The water had finally receded back within the creek's banks, but in some places that had taken more than two weeks. The ground remained sodden and flattened from the flood. The cold, muddy search party was well into day two of its hunt for Lorna Hart's body, and Jeff hoped like the dickens that Sikes' hail signaled an end to the effort.

"You found something?" Benton Floyd hollered from farther away.

"Yeah, I've found her, get over here."

"Where are you?"

Jeff followed Sikes' voice. In front of him now, he could see the man's red plaid shirt and tan trousers. Jeff ducked under a limb and maneuvered around a browning cedar. Sikes, a hand covering his mouth and nose, looked up as Jeff approached. Jeff gagged at the stench and immediately took a handkerchief out of his coat to hold over his own face. Sikes retreated to the cow path.

Deputy Sheriff Floyd and another deputy, this one a freedman, forced their way through the damp foliage. "My God," Floyd said, when he reached Jeff, "where is she?"

Jeff shook his head and moved forward, peering over low-growing bushes. "She's over there," Sikes forced out. "Nastiest thing I've ever seen."

82

"We need to talk," Jeff said.

Tucker Seaton looked up from the table at Hawlin's Tavern where he sat drinking with two of his cronies. The man's expression changed from surprise to fear and finally to hate in the space of a heartbeat.

"I'm not talking to you."

"Outside, or in front of your friends here, Seaton. I don't care, but we're going to talk."

Tucker looked away. It was early afternoon, and Hawlin's was relatively empty. He appeared sober, maybe only getting started for the night.

"Which will it be?"

Tucker's lips curled into a sneer. "Why, you yellow-bellied coward—"

Jeff grabbed him by the collar of his jacket and pulled him from the chair. "That's right, Seaton, I'm always the one running away."

Tucker's boots scraped on the wooden planks of the floor before Jeff twisted him around and upright, then pushed him toward the door. Tucker flailed, swinging his arms, but couldn't make contact with Jeff, who held him at arms' length. The man wasn't as sober as he appeared.

Jeff shoved, and Tucker stumbled out the door. He'd have fallen, but Jeff caught his arm. "We've got to talk to the deputy. He wants to hear your side of the story about the day Lorna Hart died."

Tucker yanked his arm from Jeff's hold. "I don't know anything about how she died. I don't remember—"

"Tell it to Floyd." Jeff stepped into the street, then looked back. Tucker didn't follow.

"You brought me home that night," Tucker said. "Did you see her?"

"I saw her, and I've made my say to Floyd. Now he wants to talk to you."

"Why did he send you?"

"I volunteered. I was part of the search party. We found her, and he wants to close out his investigation."

"What did you tell him about me?"

Jeff grinned at Tucker, still on the porch of Hawlin's tavern. "I told him the truth, Seaton, that's all."

Tucker looked around at a man, peeking outside the tavern door, then turned back to Jeff. "You know you did it. Juliet said her throat was torn up. Like a wolf would have done"—the pitch of Tucker's voice was rising with each word he spoke—"poor girl's having nightmares every night, damn you. You're trying to destroy me!"

Jeff's grin had faded. "Let's go, you worthless, putrid son-of-a-bitch." He hated the man standing before him. Hated him with a passion he couldn't believe. Him and his father and brothers. "I don't have to destroy you; you're doing it to yourself. Now get your ass down to the sheriff's office. I want to get this done, and I want to go home...to White Oak Glen." Jeff returned Tucker's glare. "That's right, you Seaton bastard. I have other ways to get even."

꧁loyd looked up from his desk and met Jeff's eye. "Seaton claims that you musta killed her, trying to frame him. Says he can't even remember leaving Hawlin's with her that afternoon."

"I didn't kill her, Floyd. I told you, she was alive when I got there, beating Seaton up pretty good. She had a few bruises of her own, but she'd have to be declared the winner of that bout."

Floyd snorted. "With him blind, stupid drunk, I'd believe it."

"Drunk or not," Jeff said, "I believe Lorna could make most men regret a fight. That woman had a mean streak in her."

"From what the coroner's tellin' me, it don't matter none. We aren't ever goin' to know how she died. Not enough left of her to tell with the swelling and bloating and plain general decay done from the time she was out there."

So nothing else would be done about this death. Lorna Hart was a whore, a dead whore, and except for her forty-four-year-old mother, no one cared that she was dead.

"Have you told Juliet Seaton about finding the body?" Jeff asked.

"Haven't seen her since that day I asked her where she'd seen it. She said she'd take me there, but I turned her down. Woods was still flooded, and she was white as a sheet."

"I'll go the long way and tell her on my way home. I think she'd like to know."

"Don't go hangin' around that place, Dawson. I know some of the history 'twixt your people and theirs, and I don't want trouble."

Chapter Fifteen

A familiar horse stood harnessed to a wagon in front of the little white-frame Methodist church just outside of town, and Jeff's heart felt a little lighter. It was Wednesday afternoon and the place appeared deserted. Damn, he wanted to see her, and he admonished himself for being a fool. He breathed the crisp fall air, cold for early November. She was here.

The minister came out the front and pulled the heavy door shut behind him. Jeff dismounted and tethered Deacon, then started up the worn path. He knew who the man was, though he didn't know him by name. A nice-looking sort, smallish, probably in his early forties.

The man extended his hand. "I'm Michael Tate, the minister here. May I help you, sir?"

Michael Tate carried a handful of books, one being the Holy Bible. Obviously, he was done doing whatever it was preachers did when it wasn't Sunday.

"I'm Jeff Dawson—"

"Ah, you're the fella who bought out Darnell Tackert." Tate shook his head. "A good man, Tackert, for being a Northerner. Had a nice wife, too. Judith was her name. She was younger than him. Died in childbirth her fourth summer here. Her and the baby. Tackert was never the same after that."

Jeff nodded politely. "I never did meet the man. Agent told me White Oak Glen's owner wanted to return to New York."

"Money problems," Tate clarified, then he smiled. "Honest, I guess. He needed to unsaddle himself from that place. Are you thinking of joining our congregation?"

"Hadn't given any thought to that, though my parents were members a long time ago."

"You're from around here?"

"My daddy had a small farm on the other side of the Seatons. It abutted the river."

"You've been gone awhile?"

"Got sidetracked by the war."

"Ah." Tate patted his lips with his index finger. "Served in the conflict, did you?"

"Sixth Mississippi Infantry Battalion, and later the Sixteenth Sharpshooters."

Tate smiled warmly and stuck out his hand again. "Chaplain, 29th Cavalry."

The smile was contagious, and Jeff took Tate's hand in new greeting. "We'd have been together at Sharpsburg."

"That we were, sir, that we were."

Jeff sobered. "Well, Reverend Tate, I—"

"Call me, Michael, please."

"Michael. I stopped, hoping to find"—he turned and pointed at the abandoned wagon—"Miss Seaton. Is she here?"

"She's visiting her mother, behind the church. She's alone. Stops by often. She's been back there awhile now. Why don't you wait on her?"

"I will."

"And think about joining us once again, Mister Dawson—"

"Jeff," he corrected, and he stepped off the path to make his way around to the back of the church.

"Jeff. We've a good group of people. Miss Seaton is a member."

Miss Seaton was engaged to the son of a Baptist preacher. Jeff doubted she'd be a member of Tate's congregation much longer.

The churchyard was roughly fifty feet behind the building, just short of deciduous forest, the fall colors of which had been subdued by the recent soaking rains.

Juliet was on her knees in front of a gravestone, her honey-blond hair glinting in the afternoon sun. She seemed sad and small, but she was, even at a distance, deliciously beautiful, and Jeff's body warmed.

A cold, north breeze accosted him where he leaned against the corner of the church and disturbed his tender thoughts. He shifted his gaze to the blue sky beyond the branches of the shedding oaks and gums, then looked back at her, his senses noting the sharp transition from brilliant blue to browns and gold. She shifted her weight and drew her coat tighter before sticking a bare hand inside its open front.

As if she sensed him, she turned and found him watching her, and he started forward. She returned her attention to the grave, but at his approach, she rose from her kneeling position.

"The rest of your family is on my land," he said, when he reached her. The scent of jasmine mingled with the sweet, crisp smells of the autumn woods, and his stomach quivered like that of a schoolboy meeting a pretty girl. "You should have asked. I would have let you bury her with them."

Juliet gave him a sad smile. "Tucker would have never asked. Besides, she wanted to be buried here. It doesn't matter. My father and brothers aren't over there. I don't know where they are. I don't even know if their bodies were placed in graves."

At one of the scores of hastily created graveyards across this country, Jeff thought, for both Blue and Gray.

"We found Lorna's body this morning."

Lightly, she touched his arm. "And how did she die?"

"The deputy doesn't know and doesn't think he'll ever know. She'd been out there almost three weeks. The body is in bad condition."

"Her throat had—"

"I know, but he argues that could have happened after she died. Wild animals."

"But, the wolf was there. You heard him."

"Yes," he said and stepped to her side and took her elbow. "But we don't know how long she'd been dead." Jeff didn't want to go into the gruesome details nor tell her Lorna had probably been dead since the night before Juliet saw her. He wondered if she knew Tucker had been with the woman that same afternoon, but he didn't say anything in case she and the fawning Margery did not. If they didn't already know, they'd find out soon enough, but he wasn't going to be the one to tell them.

She looked up at him, about to ask something else, and he spied a faint shadow on her left cheek. Curious, he turned her toward him. She met his gaze, then frowned. Cautiously, he raised his hand to her cheek, and she immediately pulled away, twisting her face from his scrutiny. She stepped back awkwardly, off balance, and he grabbed her elbow in support.

"You didn't have a bruise on your cheek when you left White Oak Glen."

She didn't try to pull her arm from his, but she did keep her face averted. "I ran into something."

"A man's fist." A statement, not a question, and he made sure his tone was cold.

"It was a slap, actually."

"A damn hard slap."

"It will never happen again."

"He promised you that? Because you're a fool if you believe him."

She turned, gray eyes churning. "He promised me nothing."

Jeff laughed in pure derision. "So, you intend to be a good little girl and do everything he says?" He yanked her so she faced him head-on. "You couldn't kowtow to a mean, opinionated, self-righteous prude like him if your life depended on it. And believe me, honey, it will!" He just might shake her silly. "Is the damn money that important to you?"

She jerked free and crossed both arms over her breasts. "You are right, Mister Dawson, I could not. Nor do I intend to bow down to any other arrogant, foul-tempered man who feels he has the right to tell me how I should live my life." She pressed her lips together. "I poorly stated the reason he would never hit me again. He will never hit me again because he'll never have the opportunity. I broke my engagement to Matthew days ago."

Jeff blew out a breath. "I'm sorry...for my behavior, I mean."

She turned and took a step toward the church, then whirled on him. "And who are you to judge why a woman marries? Why on earth do you think she marries? She marries for security if she's got a brain in her head." Tears welled in her eyes. "Do you think for love? How many men do you think marry for love?"

He looked at her and raised his eyebrows.

"Men marry so they don't have to cook their own meals or wash their own clothes," she continued.

"I don't do those things."

"And you're not married are you?" She stuck a finger under his nose. "And another reason—"

"Offspring?"

"I was coming to that. Sex."

"For sex I could visit a—"

"A whore, Mister Dawson? And probably will, even after you marry. Isn't that what you said to me the day I left White Oak Glen? Something about the pleasure being better with another than with a wife?"

"I was angry."

"About what?"

"At the thought of you marrying Braxton for his money."

"Well, have no fear for him. I have set him free."

He grinned. "Do you have another victim in mind?" He was hoping she would say him, but he knew she wouldn't. Even if such a thought had crossed her mind, she wouldn't say it.

But she ignored his question entirely. "It's a wonder men marry at all. If I were a man, I wouldn't."

"Men, like women, do want children, Juliet. Sometimes they even fall in love."

"Matt said he loved me, but I realize now he considered me an investment property in need of improvement." She rubbed her forehead. "My father married my mother for her name and for White Oak Glen."

"Those are important factors for some when looking for a mate."

90

"If you feel that way, don't ridicule me then."

"I don't feel that way, but I understand it," he said, keeping an eye on her as they walked. "For me, social status is unimportant. Must be my white-trash blood."

They had reached the back of the church, and a pale Juliet sought a porch step and took a seat.

"You haven't fully recovered, have you?"

She gave him a wan smile. "Not entirely. I need to rest for a moment. I'm dizzy."

The wind picked up, and he glanced toward the woods.

"Did my father call you that?" Juliet asked.

He looked at her. "What?"

"White trash."

"More them that depended on him. That term was standard for poorer folk, then as now. Especially when those folks are up in arms over the violation of their daughter."

"My mother told me you weren't white trash. She said your parents worked hard and fed themselves and their family."

"Yep, we always kept ourselves fed."

She was quiet a moment, then asked, "Where does the name 'Wolfson' come from?"

He sat down a step below her and turned sideways so he could see her better. "My mother was quarter-blood Creek, my maternal grandfather, half. Daddy was Scots-Irish by descent. His people came to British West Florida from North Carolina after the end of the French and Indian War. My maternal grandmother was French. She and granddaddy had five children, but only my mama lived to adulthood. She married my daddy when she was sixteen. He was eighteen, the son of a part-time farmer-Indian trader in west Alabama. Daddy was a bit of a wanderer when they met, and they ended up living with my mother's father, Jedediah Wolfson."

Jeff stopped a moment, pondering her interest, but she kept her eyes fixed on him, waiting.

"The 'Wolfson' came from his grandfather as best I understand it."

"On the Indian side?"

"Yes. The story goes way back, before the white man tainted the bloodline. Anyway, family legend has it—that means it's a Jedediah Wolfson-told tale—my great-great-grandfather killed a large wolf that had been coming out of the swamp at random and attacking villagers." Jeff shrugged. "He was only a boy; the wolf became his totem."

"Like a familiar?"

He narrowed his eyes. "A witch's familiar, you mean?"

"Yes."

"More like a spiritual guide. Guardian angel would be a closer parallel, I think, but I don't even know how accurate that is.

"Anyway, my great-granddaddy was *Wolf's son*. He married a white captive—"

"So the Indians tainted their own blood."

Jeff smiled. "It would appear so. Anyway, whoever she was, she must have worked some magic on him, because he ended up completely anglicized. Wolfson became his surname. My mama and daddy gave it to me as my middle name."

She leaned forward. "Could your grandfather turn into a wolf?"

"Those stories about my grandfather are very old, and pre-date Jarmane Seaton's death by decades.

"There are tales of shape-shifters among Indian tribes, just as there are tales of werewolves among the Europeans. Used to be, there were lots of wolves around these parts. They became rarer and rarer. Still, there were some when my family arrived.

"My grandfather was a half-breed. As such, many considered him a lesser person. People also feared him. He didn't help matters any, either. My father told me granddaddy would make up stories, and threats, to frighten our more troublesome neighbors."

"Like my family?"

"I don't think there was a problem between your folks and mine until that summer Jarmane came to stay. The point I was trying to make is that my granddaddy had been scaring the wits out of the more ignorant around here for twenty years before your cousin Jarmane was found with his jugular severed. When

Bonnie was attacked, my family had no support from its neighbors to stand up to a wealthy and influential family like yours."

He turned and looked her in the eye. "I can't tell you that my grandfather didn't kill Jarmane Seaton. I don't know. But he would have killed him as a man, not as a wolf."

"Jarmane was young and strong. Your grandfather was well into his seventies."

"And a skilled hunter." He tightened his lips. "He was more than capable of killing a so-called man who needed two others to hold down a fourteen-year-old girl while he raped her."

*A*nd they'd come full circle, right back to the incident that had begun it all.

She returned his gaze. "I'm ashamed of what my brothers and cousin did. I'm even more ashamed of my father's covering it up. Kitty Horton believes my mother started to hate him on that day, and she never stopped."

She bowed her head, no longer able to stand Jeff Dawson's scrutiny. Being here with him like this, she was even ashamed to have Jordan Seaton's blood running through her veins. To be ashamed of her father's blood was grievous to her, but God, her father had a wife and, before it ended, an infant daughter of his own. How could he have condoned his sons' vicious violation of a young girl? But maybe he hadn't. Maybe he had simply dealt with protecting his sons as best he could, if woefully inadequate by the standards of what was right.

Juliet looked up and found Jeff's eyes. He must hate Tucker and her and anyone else of his or her ilk. As her mother warned, he could well be a danger to what was left of the Seatons.

But he was so handsome sitting there, a step below her, one muscled leg stretched out before him in the grass, the other bent close to his body. Masculinity emanated from him like heat from a fire, warming her, fanning what, despite her innocence, she knew to be desire. She didn't know what he was thinking, but she was sure he could and would skillfully accommodate the need pooling in her pelvis.

Doubt swirled around her, as dizzying as her questionable equilibrium.

"Is it you, Jeff?"

"Is it me what?"

"Can you change into a wolf like your grandfather before you?"

"Like in your dream?"

Her cheeks burned. Yes, the recurring dream that had compelled her to leave her sickbed and seek him out, she'd been so frightened. Now he used her confession against her.

"Oh, I could eat you up, Juliet, but as in the case of my grandfather, I would do it as a man, not a wolf."

Her heart beat faster with the sudden fear that he had sensed her desire, but she forced herself past his innuendo.

"Tucker says you died at Corinth."

The humor left his eyes. "And why does he say that?"

"He says he saw you dead."

"He probably thought he did."

She swallowed hard and asked, "Did he?"

He rose from where he sat, and she followed him with her eyes.

"Do I look dead to you, Juliet?"

"You look...."

He reached down, took her hand, and pulled her to her feet.

"Tucker says he saw you shot in the back, running away." Her voice sounded breathless, even to her own ears.

His blue-eyed gaze penetrated her. She was unsure whether the anger she detected there was directed at her or Tucker, and she steeled herself.

"He says he stood over you, and you were dead."

"Your brother is a liar."

Her head, the blood surging through it in rhythm with her heart, pounded worse than it had in days. "In that you are not dead or that you were not running away?" she whispered.

"Both." He brought her hand to his face. "Touch me, Juliet. I am warm."

She opened her palm and gently laid it across his cheek. Beneath the surface chill wrought by the cold, she felt his warmth. He placed his hands on her shoulders.

Standing on the step above him, her face was almost even with his. A gust of wind, maybe something summoned by him she thought, tore at her hair and pushed her against him. His arms circled her shoulders. She felt helpless, but at the same time safe, anchored in his arms. His lips covered hers, and he bent her back. Her head spun, and heat, frightening yet delicious in its unfamiliarity, spread through her limbs.

Dear God, Matt had never done more than kiss her cheek.

The dizziness left her off balance, and awkwardly she clung to him. His arms tightened, him not knowing she couldn't tell right side up from upside down, and she melted into him, surrendering to his support. If he let go of her now, she would fall over, so she clung to him in case.

He cupped his hand over the back of her head, angling his lips over hers. Then his tongue was inside her mouth. A soft sound escaped her, and he abruptly pulled back.

"Is that the kiss of a dead man, Juliet?"

She closed her eyes and laid her forehead upon his shoulder. The world was spinning. She had no control, and for an instant thought she might be sick. What kind of an answer would that be for his question, and she'd have chuckled had she felt better. Instead, she pushed her arms over his shoulders, then turned her head to one side and nestled it against his neck. "I wouldn't know," she said softly, "I've never been kissed by a dead man."

"Or by a live one either I'd bet."

Had her inexperience with kissing been that obvious? She'd have pushed him away from her, but his support was essential—and he was like an oak tree, strong and solid and straight. He smelled of soap and sweat and leather. She opened her eyes and stared at the peeling wooden planks of the white building. And he stood where he was, very still, holding her.

"You're dizzy, aren't you?"

"Yes."

He chuckled and squeezed her tighter. "It would have been too much to believe you actually wanted to hold onto me the way you are."

"I am sorry."

She would have been happy to cling to him had she been sure his design was for something other than disgracing her.

"I'll take you home."

"No. Margery and Wexford are at Bolton's Dry Goods. I was to meet them after visiting Mama."

His hand caressed her shoulder. "Come on, then. I'll make sure you get there all right."

Chapter Sixteen

"Don't wake him, Margery. He worked hard today. This farm may be depleted, but it's still a lot of work for one man.

"But what if it were a scream Juliet heard?"

A howl charged the night, and the hair on Juliet's neck stood on end. She stayed in place and battled the urge to retreat from the window. It might see her if she moved.

"Good God, Mother." Margery stepped back through the hall doorway into the parlor. "The thing must be in the yard. How can he sleep through that?"

The rhythmic rocking of Aunt Lilith's chair had stopped with the howl, then a floorboard moaned and Juliet knew the woman had stood.

"Perhaps he can't," her aunt said, "but it's nearly midnight. He's not going to hunt that thing in the dark."

Steeling herself, Juliet drew back the lace curtain and stared into the silvery darkness. Why not? That *thing* was a creature of the night. Night would seem the best time to hunt it. Outside, the moon was very bright, but wouldn't be full for three more days. The beast seemed fond of moonlit nights.

Margery stepped to the window where Juliet searched for shadows, and she, too, pulled back the delicate lace. "Why does Tucker say that thing out there is an evil spirit returned from hell to destroy him? What could he have done?" There was neither challenge nor accusation in her cousin's words; she truly wanted to know. "Tucker's drinking has become so much worse since Dawson returned, Juliet. Do you know what it is?"

Did she indeed? Not long ago, she thought she did. Bonnie? Jedediah Wolfson? But surely Tucker had played no part in old Jedediah's lynching. That left whatever *it* was to have happened at Corinth.

"There's bad blood between the two families, Margery. I know my brothers played a role in the rape of Mister Dawson's sister—"

"She was willing," Aunt Lilith interjected from the other side of the room, "everyone knows that."

Juliet turned from the window and looked at her aunt, still standing in front of her rocker. "Mother and Kitty say she was not."

Aunt Lilith simply stared at her, and Juliet looked back at Margery. "The girl died in childbirth."

"What role did Tucker play in the rape?"

"He watched," Juliet said. "He was twelve. Only Jarmane actually raped her."

"And he was murdered for his sin, then," Aunt Lilith said. "That should be enough vengeance."

Juliet had not averted her attention from Margery. "Everyone said Jedediah Wolfson, Jeff's grandfather, killed Jarmane. Someone lynched Jedediah."

"And Dawson thinks it was Tucker?"

"Tucker would have been only thirteen by that time." Again, Juliet looked at Aunt Lilith. "Was it Daddy?"

"Oh my goodness, Juliet, no. No one knows who killed that old man."

"Certainly the killers know, or did." Juliet dropped her eyes. "And I fear Jeff Dawson knows."

"If it was Uncle Jordan who hanged that old man, then why would Dawson want to destroy—"

"I don't know that he does, Margery."

"Well, something does." Margery raised her voice a pitch. "With that cow and pig killed last night, we'll not be able to eat soon, much less pay the taxes."

Juliet's hand shook, and she dropped the curtain. Margery

was staring at her as if she expected her to do something. And she should, she really should.

The thing howled again, more distant now, but still too close. Lilith laid the sock she'd been darning on the sewing table next to the fireplace. "Get away from that window, girls. You're making me nervous."

Juliet stepped back and tied her robe tighter at the waist. "I heard a woman scream, I know I did."

"Yes, you said, but I heard nothing."

"I heard something strange, too." Margery dropped the curtain, stepped away from the window, then sat in the upholstered chair near her mother's rocker. "It was far away. I don't know that it was a woman. It could have been the wind. I wish Tucker would come home. I hate the thought of him out there with that thing about."

The sound she and Margery heard had been far away. If anyone were in trouble out there, they would be unable to find her. Still, it gnawed at Juliet that someone could be in danger and they were doing nothing.

The wind gusted, and she listened for a sound carried on it. If she heard another scream, she would wake Wex, no matter what her aunt said, and she would go out with him.

Aunt Lilith started for the dining room. "I'll make us some coffee. I don't think any of us will sleep until that howling stops."

Chapter Seventeen

"We've had ourselves another killin'," Will said.

Jeff glanced at the shrouded body draped over the back of the dappled gray, then motioned Benton Floyd through the door. He frowned at Will, who followed the deputy.

"I found her body at your folks' place," Will said. Jeff closed the door behind him. "She was in the house."

"When?"

"This morning at dawn. That wolf was out yelping and howling all night long. I checked up there 'cause of those tracks we'd seen that one time. Wanted to see if he'd been back."

"Had he?"

"Yes, sirree. Fresh sign all over your front yard."

Jeff stepped away from the back door and motioned the two men into the long hall that led to the front of the house. He stopped at the dining room and called for Kitty.

"Yes, *massa*?"

He hated when she called him that, and he knew she did it on purpose.

"Have you started my breakfast?"

"No, sir," she said and craned her neck through the breezeway door to see the other two men. "We gots more to feed?"

"We do, two more."

She nodded and disappeared, and Jeff led the way to the front of the house. In the parlor, he opened the drapes covering floor-to-ceiling windows. Light filled the room. "Do we know who she is?"

"Susie Watts," the deputy answered. "Little whore that fre-quented Bekin's in Under the Hill."

"How long was she missing?"

The deputy shook his head. "Don't know, but she ain't been dead that long. Last night, I'd say, but I haven't gotten back to town to talk to anyone that might've seen her. Howe came and got me a little after sunup. Thought we'd stop by and tell you first since her body was on your land."

"How did she die?"

Will caught his eye.

"Her throat was torn open like with the Hart woman," Floyd answered. He dusted his slouch hat against his pants leg. "Look, Dawson, I appreciate your invite to eat, but I'd best be gettin' back to town and start searchin' this out. I need to talk to the sheriff. I'm thinkin' we may have a real problem on our hands here."

Will pushed his plate away. "Damn good meal, Kitty."

"Watch yo' damn mouth in this house, Mister Howe, and thank ya'."

"I keep tellin' you, *Auntie*, this is a bachelor's house, and you're a servant."

Her eyes bulged, bright against her dark skin. "Servant, my ass. I run this house for thirty years. Shame Miss Eileen's not around to tell you, but I did. She run the farm, I run the house. Shoot! I spoke, them Seaton men they jumped." She laughed, and with her hands full of dirty dishes, she disappeared into the breezeway connecting the kitchen to the house.

"And so she's tryin' to make a Seaton man out of you?" Will grumbled at Jeff.

Jeff yawned and stood up. "It's not a concern of mine. She takes care of this house like it was hers, and I'd forgotten what my mama's fried chicken tasted like until I took a bite of hers."

Will followed him out back and into the frosty grass.

"What did you think," Jeff said, "when you saw the woman's body?"

Will pulled out his tobacco and cut off a plug, then offered it to Jeff, as he always did. When Jeff declined, Will shoved it into his own mouth and started to chew.

"She was turned on her side, starin' at nothin', in the room your mama and daddy used for sleepin'. Her throat"—he lifted his hand and caressed the area of his Adam's apple—"right here was gone. There was only a little blood there on the floor."

"She was dead before she got there?"

"That's my guess." Will turned and spat tobacco juice on the ground.

"Plenty of wolf tracks, you say?"

"Yep."

"How about human?"

Will pointed a knowing finger at him. "I checked before I left the first time, and I checked when I got back with that sorry excuse for a lawman. I don't think any of this is getting through to him. That gal had to be moved there by something; she didn't die in that house. Looking for human footprints never occurred to Floyd until I pointed out that he might should."

"Did y'all find anything?"

"Nope, but I think they was brushed away."

"Why?"

"Because there weren't any."

Jeff grinned. "Well, I'm sure Floyd found that argument convincing. So, he's thinking an animal did this?"

"He's thinkin' a damn monster did this."

"Not so long ago you were thinking the same thing."

"Oh, no, son," Will quickly corrected. "Not so long ago I said Jedediah Wolfson was back to help you extract vengeance from that lyin', cheatin', bushwhackin' snake, Tucker Seaton. Far as I know, that son-of-a-bitch still has his throat, and the only ones dead are the town's best whores. I don't think Jedediah would be doin' that, do you?"

"No, but I don't believe he's come back, in any form or for any reason."

"Tucker Seaton is telling his drunken cronies it's you."

Of course he was, and people would believe it, too. If there was a killer on the loose, human or other, Jeff Dawson was the new man in town. No, not new, and that made it worse, because he was intimately involved with an old horror tale.

He felt Will's hand on his shoulder. "Trouble's brewin', boy. I didn't touch poor Susie this mornin', but I looked her over good. I know there were other marks on her body. I'd be willing to bet she was raped, and then stabbed. We can hope the doctor will be able to convince Floyd of that."

"It won't matter. Even if Floyd believes she was stabbed, that still doesn't eliminate the possibility of a man-beast having done it."

Will dropped his hand. "Oh, it's a man-beast for sure, something sicker and a whole lot less human than a big wolf could ever be. And I'd bet next year's tax money he was born of woman."

Chapter Eighteen

"Gal, what you doin' over this way by yourself?"

Juliet smiled and laid the reins on the wagon seat. "I hope I'm not taking you away from anything important, Mister Howe, it having turned out to be such a beautiful Indian summer day."

"Too late for Indian summer, Miss Juliet," he said, giving her an exasperated look before helping her from the wagon, "but it is a nice day."

"I'm interrupting you from doing something, aren't I?"

"I'm mendin' harness, and I can do that the whole night long." He led her to the narrow front porch of his cabin. "You've no business out here by yourself. Thank the Good Lord you didn't cross the woods."

She took the ladder-back chair he offered. "I've been avoiding the woods of late, and I miss them, too."

"Best you stay out of them for now. There's been another killin'."

"Last night?"

"Yes, ma'am. I found the body this morning, but the woman was killed last night for sure."

She'd been right after all. Juliet parted her lips and drew a breath. "Who was she?"

"Susie Watts. Doubt you knew her. She was a lady of the evening. Found her myself over at Jeff Dawson's old place."

"I heard a woman scream last night." Self-anger eclipsed her guilt. "I knew I had, but no one believed me."

Will squinted at her. "When?"

104

"Close to midnight. We were up. That wolf was prowling and howling all around our place. No one could sleep."

"I heard it, too, but later. By the moon, I'd say around two. You say you heard the scream at midnight?"

"Yes, but surely not from the old Dawson place. I don't think even the wind could have carried the sound that far."

"We don't think she was killed there." Will sat on the porch and leaned back against a rough-hewn post.

"You think the wolf dragged her —"

He shook his head and opened his mouth —

"Did she die like Lorna Hart?"

"Her throat was tore open, that's true."

"What manner of beast are we up against, Mister Howe?"

"Now don't start soundin' like a superstitious peasant, Miss Juliet."

His words conjured Kitty's description of Jedediah Wolfson's lynching. Of course, Mister Howe was right. She sounded no better than those who had allowed that old man's death to go unpunished.

"I'm athinkin' it's a human animal," the man said, "a blood-thirsty killer who takes pleasure in killing and mutilating."

Juliet raised her hand to the collar of her dress. "But her throat..."

"It could be done with a little help from a man-made instrument. I've seen worse things done in war."

"Was she violated?"

"My guess is yes, but I don't know. Given her chosen profession, it might be hard to tell."

She understood what he meant and didn't want to encourage further elaboration about the woman and her relations with men. Will Howe was older and kind; still, he was little more than a stranger.

"You had a reason for coming up here alone, I take it?"

"I appreciate your admonishment, Mister Howe. I certainly would not have come had I known of Miss Watts' death, but since I'm already here, I'd like to discuss something with you."

"And what would that be?"

"Were you with Mister Dawson at Corinth?"

"I was with Jeff Dawson from the time he enlisted in 1861 till we lost him in November of 1864, in a skirmish outside Corinth."

"When he was wounded, you mean?"

"Yes. I thought him dead." He chuckled. "When I saw him at his mama and papa's cabin more'n a month ago, I thought for sure I was seeing a ghost."

Juliet hoped he didn't see her blanch.

"Thought there was no way he could've survived that shot to the back."

So he *was* shot in the back. She fisted her sweating palms. "You were retreating?"

Will Howe narrowed his eyes and leaned forward. "Whatcha thinkin', gal? That he bolted?"

"Tucker says—"

"Don't you believe what your brother tells you." He turned his head and spat tobacco juice into the yard. "Those of us that hadn't bolted by November of 1864 sure as hell weren't gonna bolt then. Excuse my language, please, miss."

"No offense taken, Mister Howe."

"By then we'd seen lots of action from one end of the Confederacy to the other. We was losin' the war. We wasn't such da...." He sighed. "We wasn't such fools we didn't know that. Jeff and me was part of the same company until he was pulled out in the spring of '64 to become part of the Sixteenth Sharpshooters, but we was still part of the same battalion. Anyways, Pinkston's Fourteenth Cavalry"—Juliet recognized the unit as being her father and brothers'—"joined up with our outfit three days before Jeff was shot. Only two of your family was left by then, Tucker and Rafe. Truth was, there wasn't much left of either of our outfits, and the two units was minglin' mor'n usual.

"Your brothers and Jeff avoided one another like they would someone with the plague, though. The hate showed.

"We was headed north that third day; it was right before daybreak. We know'd there was Yankees somewhere between us and Tennessee, but our scouts hadn't seen nothin'. Hadn't been any fightin' for days. Word was we were to team up with Forrest, but none of that was ever confirmed, and we never got to where it was we was headed.

"We was in some woods, climbin' yet another little knoll. Jeff was about ten yards in front and to the side of me. It was late fall. Leaves was on the ground, and there weren't no way those Yanks could have missed our comin'. They were up on the crest, all the time, watchin' us come.

"I reckon they was well hid, but Jeff saw 'em and yelled a warnin'. Even got the first shot off, if I remember correctly. Then the place was spittin' shot. I saw him throw open his arms and fall flat on his face. For sure I thought a Yankee had got him. We charged forward, screamin' and shoutin', and tryin' to figure out who was where. There was a bunch of them Billy Yanks, more'n us. We were outgunned, and worse, out-flanked. They was laid out proper to ambush us. Our retreat, if you can call it that, began shortly thereafter.

"I started slippin' and slidin' back down that hill, churnin' up mud and leaves, hopin' I'd have a chance to check Jeff, to make sure he was really dead. Tell you the truth, sorry as it is, but he'd tell ya the same thing, it was better for me if he was dead 'cause there weren't no way I'da left him there, and it was lookin' as though none of us was gonna make it out. Mini-balls were apoppin' and aflyin' every which-a-ways. Dawn was crackin', turnin' everything misty gray. I made him out halfway down the hill. Someone was standin' over him, pistol drawn. I yelled, and I was close enough to see that the man saw me. Another man pushed at the first and cried that he was dead and they should go, and they mounted quick and left. When I got to him, he was dead still, the back of his coat covered in blood. I thought he was a goner, too, and the Yanks was all over us."

Mister Howe turned his eyes from her. "I grabbed his fine rifle, and I left him there, sorry soul that I was. Left him face down in the wet fall leaves. I never touched him to make sure; there weren't enough time."

Will Howe met her gaze head-on. "We was routed that day, Miss Seaton. Not for the first time and not for the last, but Jeff Dawson weren't routed. Not that time, anyways. Sometimes tuckin' tail is the smart thing to do. But he was shot facin' the Yanks, and the ball that felled him weren't no Yankee one. He was shot in the back by a fellow Confederate."

"The men you saw, they were cavalry? You said they had horses."

"Fine horses."

"Seaton horses?" She choked on her words.

"I wasn't close enough to know for certain, but I reckon so."

That would explain everything. Tucker shot Jeff Dawson in the back. Her brother had almost let that slip a few weeks ago. That would explain his fear. Jeff knew it, too, or at least suspected. That's why it could be him killing their stock.

She closed her eyes tight. Such a cruel and petty tactic. Too petty, she thought, for that to be the case. If a man like Jeff Dawson wanted vengeance beyond possessing White Oak Glen, he would face them and take it, not play a malicious game of cat and mouse.

"Who lynched Jedediah Wolfson, Mister Howe?"

His eyes widened, but only a little. "Weren't no witnesses ever talked, Miss Juliet."

"You know."

She watched him swallow. "Tell me," she said softly, dreading the words she didn't want to hear.

"Tell you?"

"Confirm for me what I already know."

"It don't need to be confirmed for you. You was barely born at the time."

"There's more than the past at stake, Mister Howe. Was it my father?"

"Your father and your two oldest brothers, Jeremy and Rafe, rumor has it. But there were others that knew and maybe played a part. A handful of folk that was scared of Jedediah Wolfson. Nobody ever said nothin', and them that took part are dead."

"They thought Jedediah Wolfson killed Jarmane?"

"Sure they did. We all did. They thought he'd kill the rest of 'em, too, given time. So they killed him first."

"You believe he ripped my cousin's throat out?"

"And broke his neck."

Juliet shook her head slowly. "He was a poor old man, broken-hearted over the senseless waste of his granddaughter."

Will Howe gave her a sad smile. "Yep, he was that, too."

Chapter Nineteen

Juliet's tummy growled—she'd missed dinner. She hiked her skirts and climbed the steps.

Aunt Lilith, her back to Juliet, was on the porch doing laundry. Juliet heard a sob and stepped toward her, and with that footfall, her aunt jerked around. She was indeed crying.

"I'm sorry, Aunt Lilith, I didn't mean to disturb you, but you sounded—"

"I'm fine." Lilith swiped at her eyes. "Just thinking about my Tom and the decent lives we once led."

Juliet gave her a sad smile. "We're still decent. I would have helped with the wash. Why didn't you wait until tomorrow?"

Her aunt dropped the garment she was working on into the tub and dried her hands. "It's for Wex. He needed some shirts washed; they couldn't wait." She moved quickly and looped her arm through Juliet's. "Where have you been? We were getting worried." Lilith pushed her through the back door.

"I went up to see that Mister Howe. Did you know there'd been another death?"

Lilith stopped abruptly. "Who?"

"A woman named Susie Watts."

"She died like the Hart woman?"

"Yes."

Her aunt moistened her lips with the tip of her tongue. "They think the wolf—"

"Her throat was torn open like Lorna Hart's, but Will Howe seems to think a person's doing this."

"Oh, goodness," Aunt Lilith said, rubbing her own throat, "why would he say that?"

"He thinks the body was moved to where it was found."

Lilith sank into a dining room chair. "And where was that?"

"Over at the old Dawson place." Juliet sat in the chair opposite her aunt and took her hand. "I did hear a woman scream last night; I knew I did."

Lilith laid her free hand over Juliet's. "Perhaps you really did, dear, but there is nothing we can do to help that poor woman now." She looked Juliet over head to foot. "Your hair is down and your dress is atrocious, but come into the parlor. You have a visitor, and he's been waiting awhile."

Morton Severs was not the man Juliet hoped to find in the parlor. She didn't like his oily mannerisms and politic smile. Her mother had warned her to never be alone with him or do anything that would compromise her in his presence.

He stepped forward and took the hand she offered. His was soft, his nails manicured. He smelled of tobacco and whiskey and faintly of the toilet water he used to slick back his hair.

He released her hand and drew his suit coat closer around his growing paunch. "You look lovely, Miss Seaton."

Her aunt sure didn't think so. Juliet hadn't combed her hair since morning when she'd left the house, and she wore it down, pulled back with a drab ribbon.

Aunt Lilith moved quickly to take the ragged coat she'd worn up to Will Howe's. "I've made coffee. Please take a place on the settee, Juliet. Mister Severs has a question he wants to ask you."

Her mouth was dry, but she managed to dip her head in polite acknowledgement, then stepped to the settee and sat. There was no fire, the day being warm. Aunt Lilith placed the coffee service on the table in front of them and poured them all a cup. Juliet saw Wexford move up behind her. Tucker sat in his chair next to the window. She caught his gaze, and he looked away. When she turned back to her aunt, she found both her and Mister Severs watching her.

"What did you want to ask me, Mister Severs?"

He straightened and placed his coffee on the table in front of them. "It has been brought to my attention, my sweet Juliet, that you have broken your engagement to Matthew Braxton."

Her stomach tensed. "Yes."

He smiled, fishing into his coat pocket and never taking his eyes off hers. "I was overjoyed to hear it. I've spent the past several days in New Orleans looking for just the right ring"—he opened the black velvet-lined box and stuck it under her nose— "with which to present you when I ask you to be my wife."

A diamond, surrounded by diamonds. The ring was large and garish. Too large for her hand, too showy for her taste.

She did not take the ring, but glanced at her aunt who sat stone-still next to Severs. Not even the pretense of wooing. And a family audience at the proposal? Juliet tried to read her aunt's eyes, to no avail, and she returned her attention to Severs.

"The ring is beautiful, but I cannot accept it."

The man frowned, then suddenly smiled. Taking the ring from the box, he reached for her hand. She jerked it away. "I will not accept your ring. I am sorry."

Behind her, she heard Wex move. "Perhaps she needs more time to consider your proposal, Mister Severs."

"I fear my offer may not be on the table even by tomorrow, Seaton."

"That's just as well," Juliet said, "since I have no intention of changing my mind."

"Consider his offer," Aunt Lilith urged, subtle desperation in her tone, "he's a good match."

Treacherous words off Lilith Seaton's tongue. Juliet could not believe the woman had spoken them. The man was a northern carpetbagger, rapacious, dishonorable, and old enough to be her father. Juliet looked back at him. "I am sorry. No."

Severs looked around her to where her brother sat.

"Juliet, Mister Severs has offered to pay the taxes on this farm," Tucker said.

Juliet twisted around and found him. "We will pay the taxes on this farm ourselves, or we will lose it. I have no intention of selling myself into an unhappy marriage for the benefit of everyone else."

Severs reached out and grasped her hand. She tried to pull away, but he held tight. "And who is to say you will be unhappy? I can give you anything your heart desires." He smiled. "Look at how you're dressed. Someone of your beauty should be dressed in silks and satin, in high New York fashion—or Parisian, and I can take you to both cities to pick them yourself."

She yanked her hand free. "I do not love you, sir."

The words sounded foolish, even to her ears. She had not loved Matthew when she'd accepted his ring. But, she reminded herself, she had always had misgivings for taking it.

"Love has nothing to do with it."

"And love can grow," Aunt Lilith quickly amended, "as it did for Tom and me."

Uncle Tom had been young and handsome in addition to being wealthy.

Juliet moved to rise; Wex squeezed her shoulder and pushed her down. Surprised, she looked up at him.

"Get on with it," Tucker groused from his chair across the room.

Body tensing, she turned to her brother.

Severs cleared his throat. She twisted back and narrowed her eyes on him. "Get on with what?"

"I had hoped you would not force me to do this, Juliet, but under the circumstances you leave me no choice. I am confident that I am doing the right thing for your family, your brother, and for you, my dear. You will be well cared for in my hands."

She tried to swallow, but her mouth was so dry her tongue stuck to its roof.

"Weeks ago now, on that last afternoon Lorna Hart was seen alive, I saw your brother leave Hawlin's with her. You must be aware he has been seeing the woman periodically for years."

Severs squared his shoulders as if about to perform some righteous, but painful, duty. "Tucker is the last person known to have seen her alive.

"Now, I've not said anything to the sheriff. Your brother was, shall we say, quite intoxicated. It is also my understanding that another young woman was murdered last night—"

"There is no proof either of them were murdered. It might have been the—"

"The wolf?" Severs graced her with an indulgent smile. "I do not think Deputy Floyd believes that any longer. He has a killer on his hands."

Anger, frustration, and fear surged through Juliet. She rose from the settee and, with a wobbly about-face, went over to her brother. He never even had the decency to straighten from his slouch. His worthless life had become a slouch. She knelt beside him.

"Did you kill Lorna Hart?"

Tears welled in his eyes. "I don't think I would have killed Lorna."

She shook him. "You don't *think!*"

He tore himself free. "I don't remember what happened."

"Where were you last night?"

"He left Hawlin's, drunk, at ten," Wex spoke up.

"I was coming home early," Tucker said, "but that thing was out last night. I heard it, and I headed back to town."

"He doesn't know what he did after that," Wex said, "I've asked him."

He got home about an hour before dawn. Juliet knew that.

"Were you with Susie Watts?"

"I-I don't—"

"Where are your clothes? Were they bloody?"

Margery grasped the back of Tucker's chair. "His clothes weren't bloody, but his shirt was on wrong side out. He'd been with a woman, but I refuse to believe he killed her."

Juliet shot to her feet. "And if he did? Surely you don't wish yourself wed to a butcher, Margery." Margery's mouth dropped open, but Juliet turned from her. "Do you really think I'd protect a man capable of committing such heinous crimes?"

Severs took a step forward and held out a hand in entreaty.

"None of us would harbor such a man. Nor do I actually believe Tucker committed the terrible deeds. But you miss my point, sweet Juliet. Your brother was seen leaving with a poor unfortunate creature who is now dead. Of the witnesses, a number were his old comrades in arms who, like you, could not in good conscience testify otherwise. As for myself, there is something I want, and I will not hesitate to use my, shall we say, influence with the powers that be in this county to make certain your brother hangs for Lorna Hart's and Susie Watts' murders, innocent though he surely is."

Margery's gasp was faint, but telling.

The gentle shake of Severs' head impersonated an apology. "I'm sorry, Juliet, but to the victor lays the spoils."

Hateful, hateful words expressed by a lesser man, wallowing in the power granted him by a hateful people. Juliet glanced at Wex, who glared at Morton Severs with a hatred that was almost palpable, but he neither said nor did anything. Juliet dropped her gaze. Short of killing the man, she wasn't sure what he could do.

"Please," Margery cried, "the man wants you. He'll take care of you. You'll have everything your heart desires. If you don't marry him, I will have nothing. Nor will the rest of us."

I will not have a man I can love, Juliet silently countered. I will never know happiness. "No," she said, "short of a lynching, it takes time to conduct a trial, and in that time we can find the proof that Tucker is innocent. He'll have to take his chances with the authorities."

Still in his slouch, Tucker snorted. "No, I won't, Juliet. Severs has agreed, in the event you really didn't give a damn about what happens to me, to take what's left of White Oak Glen in return for his silence."

Aunt Lilith rose from her seat, and from the corner of her eye, Juliet saw Wex move. But the sounds and the sights and even the concerns of the others were insignificant.

"You would sell him what is left of our heritage — six generations, Tucker — rather than attempt to clear yourself?"

Tucker blinked in the face of her words, then tightened his

lips. "I will give him what is left of this farm if you do not marry him, Juliet. With you as his wife, he will take care of us all and assure that Seatons remain on this place. Otherwise, he'll have me tried and hanged by noon tomorrow and our father's line will be ended."

Those were her fears. She had never known them to be his, and she still didn't believe they were. But he would use her fading hopes against her now to save his worthless hide. Juliet studied Tucker a long moment, but found no remorse or misgivings, or even a second thought, in his bleary eyes. He didn't care. He would, she had no doubt, give Morton Severs the deed to their farm to spite her for defying him.

Dear God in heaven, her heart was going to burst. She turned and looked at Severs, then walked to where he waited.

"Why would you marry a woman who despises you?"

He smiled. "I wish to stay in Mississippi, to enter politics, and make a place for myself and"—he raked his eyes over her body, allowing them to linger on her belly—"my posterity. Given that I'm an outsider, I feel a Southern wife, an aristocratic one from the Old South, will prove advantageous. He lifted her left hand and slipped the ring on her third finger. "Tomorrow, at noon, at *our* Methodist Church."

"You plan for us to wed tomorrow?"

"I'll be fifty in two months. I am not getting any younger."

"I'm still in mourning for my mother."

"Fortunately you won't be for your brother."

Aunt Lilith stepped forward. "It's agreed then? Mister—"

"Morton, please, my dear Aunt Lilith." He laughed, and the older woman joined him. She'd known, Juliet realized. Her Aunt Lilith had known all along that she was going to be blackmailed into marriage. Juliet turned and met Wex's eyes, then looked beyond to Margery and Tucker, the worthless end of her father's line.

"Morton," her aunt continued, "we've waited dinnertime on Juliet. Fried chicken, won't you—"

"He is not invited to stay." Juliet turned on him. "Mister

116

Severs, I will have a lifetime of seeing you. I wish to see you no more today. Please go."

Undaunted, Severs nodded, then took her hand and brought it to his lips. She pulled away before his lips touched her. "Until tomorrow then, my dear. And I look forward to taming your stubborn heart."

Chapter Twenty

Juliet lifted her worn skirt and started to run. The sun shined on her face, warm and inviting, so at odds with the dark shadow shrouding her soul.

Lilith Seaton called after her, but Juliet ignored her, and Wex hollered for his mother to leave her be for a while. She wanted to serve dinner, Aunt Lilith had countered, and she did not want Juliet in the woods with the wolf about.

For sure her aunt meant that. She was no good to them dead.

Juliet slowed and jumped the now tame creek. Then scrambling up the shallow embankment, she reached the cow path and started running again. Her family, her horrid family, thought she was seeking solace in her beloved woods. The path curved, hiding her from the house and leading her beneath the canopy of now scantily dressed deciduous trees.

She slowed to a walk and fought back tears. She would not cry. In life there were things you had to do...but there were also things, simply put, you did for yourself.

She fisted the hand that had borne the ring and rubbed it with her other. She'd removed the thing and set it on the table by her bed. Then she'd marched through the house, retrieved Tucker's worn jacket and left through the front door. Despite Aunt Lilith's protests, she hadn't looked back.

"Tame your stubborn heart" he'd said to her. She knew what he meant. She hated him, and she hated the thought of his touching her. She closed her eyes, pondering her mother's unrequited love...or was it lust...for Job Taylor.

The big house came in view, white and impressive from this

distance, but still only a faded image of its former self. It needed paint. Darnell Tackert had paid the house little attention after his wife died, and Jeff Dawson had not done anything so far, at least to the exterior.

Juliet left the path and crossed the rail fence. Running again, she climbed the rolling hill. God, what if he weren't home. She'd wait, she thought. She'd wait for him.

There was a part of her Morton Severs would never have. That she would give to Jeff Dawson—not for Jeff, but for herself.

She was most of the way up the hill, when Kitty walked out on the broad front porch, broom in hand, and waved. "What you doin' here, baby girl?"

Her heart beat faster with Kitty's having seen her, but that wouldn't sway her course. "I'm looking for Mister Dawson."

"He be out fixin' that ol' fence at the barn."

Juliet turned away, planning now to skirt the house.

"You ain't got no business in them woods. You know what's happenin'. You make sho' he sees you home, you hear me?"

Yes, she heard her. She'd heard her most of her life. Sometimes she'd even listened. Juliet waved and started to run.

The barn was a good fifty yards behind the house, situated partway down the hill where the land leveled out before dipping into the thick woods that ended at the river.

Juliet stopped at the crest of the hill and caught her breath. Below her, the decrepit barn glowed in the afternoon sun. Once that barn had housed a score of fine horses, all gone now. Tucker had returned home from the war on foot.

Jeff came out of the barn, and her heart skipped a beat. He disappeared around the building's south corner, without seeing her. She sucked in a breath and charged forward, determined to reach him before she lost her courage.

She stopped. Sunlight beat upon the weathered walls of the barn's west side, but Jeff wasn't there. Picking up her skirt to avoid the muck, she maneuvered her way down the long side of the building and peeked around back.

His eyes were closed, his face tilted toward the sky. He had removed his shirt, and his muscular chest, glistening with sweat, tensed as he poured a bucket of water over his head. He whooped and tossed the bucket aside, swinging his head and flinging sprays of water around him like a dog that had waded from a pond. With strong hands, he smoothed the streams of water over his shoulders and underarms, then across his chest, touching the large brown nipples, prominent against his tanned skin. Juliet's eyes drifted downward to the cleft of his belly button. There she caught her first hint of hair on his torso. God was certainly making her sin easy for her. Her gaze drifted up, and she met his eyes, dark blue and intense, watching her.

Sheer determination on her part kept her legs from giving out from under her.

Lust, that was all it was. She wanted him to be her first. He lusted for her, too, she knew, from his provocative threats, his innuendo...his kiss. Was it only yesterday? After today he would have his victory and could smirk at her wantonness. She didn't care. This was for her.

Juliet wore a look Jeff understood, although it was different on her, evoking something in him that went beyond the electric charge that tore through his body. She reached out to touch his naked chest, but he caught her hand. He hadn't taken his eyes off hers, and he saw the disappointment his denial brought.

"Please," she said, "I'll never ask anything of you again."

Heart pounding, he narrowed his eyes. "Are you sure you know what you're doing?"

She stepped closer, her face turned up to his. "Kiss me, as if I weren't a Seaton, but someone new whom you could like."

At her tug, he let go of her hands. Tentatively, as though she expected him to reject her once more, she flattened her palms against his chest, and they scalded him.

"But you are a Seaton."

Her eyes dropped, and she stroked his nipples with the inside of her thumbs. Jeff sucked in air and raised his face to heaven.

Her fingers stopped their movement, and when he looked down, he found her watching him with glistening eyes. "Then have me in vengeance if that's what you want, or is there no victory if I'm the seducer?"

"What's wrong, Juliet?"

She dropped her eyes, mesmerized, it seemed, by his naked chest. Her hands moved over his ribcage in a gentle caress, stopping at the waistband of his jeans. "I want you, that's all, and I want the pleasure of your wanting me."

"Oh, I want you. I've wanted you since the moment I first saw you, but I'd like to know what game you're playing today."

"No game," she breathed out, her hand reaching for the button on his jeans. "Just mutual gratification."

It dawned on him she had known men before him, and crushing disappointment twisted his gut. Well, if that were the case, so be it; he wanted her no less. With a quick move, he yanked her to him for a punishing kiss. The soft squeak that slipped from between her lips made him pause, and he gentled, but when he pulled away, she grasped his head and forced his lips back to hers, meeting him with a hunger that devoured his senses and left him stunned and potent at the same time. He pivoted and pushed her back, pinning her between his body and the rough exterior of the barn. Instinct ruled, and he rubbed his engorged penis against her pelvis. Heat flushed his body. With a quick thrust, he dipped his head, covering her lips with his and pushing his tongue inside her mouth. She groaned and held him to her, her arms tight around his shoulders.

Jeff released her lips and kissed her cheek, her jaw. For a moment, he plundered an ear with his tongue, and she tilted her head away to give him access to her neck. He nipped her there, then licked, tasting the salt on her skin, while he traced a path down her neck to the collar of her dress. Suddenly frustrated by his own reckless response, he pushed away and glared. "Do you think to trap me, Miss Seaton?"

She stared back, shock as stark as the passion in her eyes. "Never. I told you I won't bother you after today."

121

Burning need overruled his common sense. He reached for the top button on her dress. He wanted to see her breasts. To touch them and taste them. "But what if I want to bother you? What if I want to lay with you over and over again?"

Her eyes widened, and he wondered if he had deterred her from her course. Then she shook her head and reached inside the open jacket to push his fumbling hands away. She started unbuttoning the dress herself.

"Now's the moment, Jeff Dawson. Let's make the most of it."

A thought worth contemplating. For sure, she was tempting him beyond endurance, and again he wondered what she was up to. Trying to trap him no doubt. Trap him with her body and with the possibility of a child?

The dress was open, her corset exposed beneath. His gaze clashed with hers.

She was worth the gamble.

Jeff whirled her around in his arms, and she clung to him before laying her head on his shoulder.

"Do you still get dizzy?" He entered a dim stall. "We'll use Deacon's hay, Miss Seaton, before he gets a chance to."

Not ungently, he plopped her on top of the hay, then he disappeared, and she sat up, pulling straw from her hair and wondering where he'd gone. She heard the doors groaning, and the barn darkened as they closed.

He was back, shutting the stall gate, and he came and stood in front of her. Without preamble, he unbuttoned his pants, then sat down and pulled off his boots.

More nervous now without his touch, she watched him and, in kind, removed her coat.

"Don't," he said, when she reached for the open bodice of her dress—he stood and let his pants drop to the ground—"I want to do it."

Jeff kicked his jeans away, and in the dim light, she saw him, lean and muscular, his manhood stiff and swollen. Her body tensed, but before she could think, he came to her and eased her into the straw, kissing her neck and warming her body with his. Her doubts evaporated.

"I want to make you naked, Juliet."

His voice was husky, his breath sweet. The sharp scents of the barn mixed with those of sandalwood, sweat, and musk. His mouth covered hers; desire, no longer disconcerting and twice as potent as what she'd felt with yesterday's kiss behind the church, rushed through her limbs. Juliet shuddered with the power of it and in eager surrender placed her arm around his neck and pulled him closer.

He released her lips. A soft oath escaped him, and he strained against her hold to look into her eyes. Whatever he searched for, he must have seen, because he sat up, pulling her with him, and reached for the hem of her dress. He dragged the skirt under her and up. "Raise your arms," he said, and obedient, she did. His broad, smooth chest loomed in front of her, and she reached out to touch him, but he pushed her hand away and grabbed the top hook of her corset. "I'm doing the touching now, sweetheart."

The bare tips of Jeff's nimble fingers touched her skin as he unfastened the hooks extending down the front of the garment. Furiously, he yanked it open, then growled. He forced her back and laid his body over hers, breast to breast, belly to belly, pelvis to pelvis. The intoxicating sensuality that swells with dominance and submission swept through her, and she trembled with the need to be dominated by this man. This one and no other.

He did not crush her, but supported himself with his arms, his muscled biceps flexing with the strain. "You're so beautiful," he said.

With that, Jeff rolled to his side. She still lay on her back, and he maneuvered closer until their bodies touched along their entire length. He dipped his head and took a breast in his mouth, nipping, teasing with the tip of his tongue and his teeth, until her nipple was a hard bead; and while he coaxed the sensitive nub, she arched toward him, offering him more to suckle. Warmth and wetness leaked from between her legs, and unable to help herself, she moaned.

"Hold on, honey" — he pinned her hands over her head — "I want to take my time with you."

Juliet reveled in his superior strength, unnecessary though it was; she didn't want to get away.

Holding her wrists with one hand, Jeff moved the flat surface of his tongue over her other teat in a wet swath. Surprised, she gasped, but that pleasure was quickly exceeded by the caress of his free hand inside the waistband of her pantaloons.

He watched her face while his fingers roamed over her belly to find her pubic mound. His thumb touched her genitals, and she caught her breath. She saw his smile, then felt his fist against her womanhood. Heat emanated from that spot, and she closed her eyes and writhed against his hold.

"Look at me," he said, and she did. "It's going to get better, Juliet." He kissed her temple, then inserted a finger inside her, at the same time pushing down with the heel of his hand. The sweet sensation intensified, emanating outward in waves with each press of his hand. Her thighs tensed, and she strained against the pressure, reaching for, then seeking fulfillment, something that in her inexperience she could not understand.

She cried out while she rolled her head in the hay. Lost in her orgasm, she arched her body upward, and he released her wrists to slip an arm under her back and pull her tight against him.

She was wonderful. Jeff breathed in the scent of her hair and lowered his head to kiss her neck. The faint smell of jasmine mixed with that of sweat and the tangy scent of her womanhood on his fingers. Blood pulsed through his veins. She was virgin, and she was his, or was about to be. He had never wanted anything in his life like he wanted Juliet Seaton at that moment.

He pushed her back. Pliant, she went, covering her eyes with her forearm.

"Does your head hurt?" he whispered, sitting on his knees and smoothing the waistband of her undergarment. He didn't want her to hurt, but that wouldn't prevent him from taking her now. He'd care for her head later.

"Nothing hurts." She raised her arm and peeked at his face. "I feel wonderful."

She might hurt in a minute, but he would assuage that, too. He removed her boots and stockings, telling her to lie still when she would have helped. He wanted to drink his fill of her naked breasts and beautiful face and in so doing, increase the anticipation for what lay beneath her worn-out pantaloons.

His breathing was heavy by the time he pulled the undergarment over long, slender legs, which she subsequently closed as best she could. She lifted her head to see what he was doing, then reached and covered her pubic mound. He laughed and took her hand, then kissed it. "It'll take more than that to protect you from me now, Juliet." He touched her knee. "Let me look at you." When she opened for him, he spread her wide. Again she started to reach down, but caught herself and averted her gaze from his. She was shy, and he was embarrassing her, though he didn't mean to.

Again, he eased his body over hers. "You have nothing to be ashamed of."

She placed her hands on his shoulder; he moved closer. "Jeff, I have never —"

"I know," he said and kissed her lips. "It's all right."

He ran his hand over a silken thigh and bent her knee. "Wrap your legs around me."

She did as he said, then pulled him closer.

"Hold on, baby, let me do this. I don't want to hurt you."

"It will hurt. There's nothing you can do."

"The more careful I am, the easier it will be on you."

"Thank you."

Did she expect he wouldn't care if he hurt her? Again, he stroked her clitoris, and she closed her eyes and sighed. She was wet, and he moved his engorged cock to her vaginal opening. He pushed, not quite in the right spot, and he took his penis and deftly guided himself in. She was tight, and he pushed, gently at first. She tensed, and he squirmed, trying to work his way inside her. He pushed again.

125

Juliet pulled up and hid her face against his neck. "Jeff, have you ever done this before?"

"I'm sorry?" he asked, too sharply, but he was pretty sure he'd been insulted.

She pulled back to see his face. "I meant with a virgin?"

Under the circumstances, her good humor said a lot. "No," he answered and kissed her quick on the lips. "Do you, in all your worldly wisdom, have any suggestions?"

"I think it would be best if you did it, quickly, but don't tell me when—"

He thrust, and she arched up, pinching his shoulders with her nails. Guilt and worry coursed through him, and he held her to him, one hand under her derrière, in unspoken comfort. "Is it better now?"

"That hurt."

Gently he laid her back, careful not to exit her. "I apologize, but it was your idea."

"A man of action, Mister Dawson?"

He straightened his body over hers and gazed into her eyes. "Juliet, I am laying on top of your naked body with my peter inside you. Don't you think you could use my given name?"

"I have used your given name." She smiled. "Jeff?"

"Yes?"

"Are we done?"

His mouth dropped open. "No."

"Well—"

He didn't wait for her to finish her question, but pulled himself partway out of her. Briefly, he bowed his head to again feast upon a breast, then pushed back and began the rhythmic motion that stroked and heated his engorged penis. Pulsating waves of pleasure emanated from his shaft, tensing him, exhausting him, and sating him in a physical and emotional way he had never experienced before.

He held and stroked her, kissing her eyes and her smiling lips, and finally he pulled out and tugged her close.

No, Juliet—his promise made with a tender caress, a sweet

kiss, but not with spoken words—we are not done, not by a long way. I may make love to you all night.

Chapter Twenty-one

Jeff had been up since sunup, riding around, looking for wolf tracks, and dreaming of Juliet. He hardened at the thought of her. Within half an hour of their first time, he'd made love to her again in the stall of the barn. Repeatedly he'd brought her to the brink of pleasure until she'd cried out in frustration and begged him to enter her. They'd climaxed within seconds of one other, and then and there he'd set his goal: simultaneous release with his little mistress.

His mood would have been glorious, but for a niggling little doubt shadowing the fringes of his sex-drugged mind. Her last embrace had been too tight, that last kiss too deep, as if she really thought it was to be their last. From the cover of the woods last evening, so her family could not see, he'd watched her walk all the way home. She'd turned only once, two steps outside his arms. This morning, the shimmer in her soulful eyes still filled him with unease.

He walked through the kitchen door humming the haunting notes of *Lorena*, nodded to Kitty, then hung his hat on a peg. He had convinced himself then as now that Juliet's intent had been to worry him, to compel him to a commitment he wasn't ready to make. That was a woman's way. Later today he'd go over there. They'd talk.

"Did you get yo'self some breakfast before you took off?" Kitty asked.

"No, ma'am," he said, sitting and starting to remove his boots.

"Well, it's dinner time, so you might as well forget about breakfast."

128

He pulled out his pocket watch. It was after eleven. "That's fine, Kitty, I'm not hungry."

"Hmmph."

He snapped the watch shut. "Why such a sour disposition this morning? I'm the one who missed breakfast."

She turned her stout body and glared at him. "What did you do with Miss Juliet yesterday afternoon?"

Anxiety nipped at him, then irritation. He turned back to his boot. "I don't believe my relationship with Miss Seaton is any of your concern, Kitty."

"Well, *Massa* Dawson, does that relationship you gots with her give you any say in what the hell she does?"

Kitty's voice was loud, offensive, and was meant to make a significant point. He turned his head from where he bent, fumbling to take off his boot, and stared at her.

"Well, does it?"

"Get to the point, Kitty."

"The point is that girl's marryin' that Morton Severs this mornin'."

His heart lurched into his throat. Carefully, he forced himself up on weak legs. "What are you talking about?

"I said exactly what I mean. She be marryin' that disgustin' man, and him old enough to be her daddy. Them like him come down here after the war and rob you white folks. Now Severs he's done got Miss Juliet, and I jist wondered what you know'd about it since you spent the better part of two hours with her curled up in your barn last evenin'.

"Oh, her mama would like to die, if she weren't already dead. She hate that vermin Severs. One reason she sold White Oak Glen to Mister Tackert when she did was to keep men like him from gettin' it."

"When?"

"Spring of '66, it was before them first taxes—"

"When is the wedding, dammit?" He pushed his foot back into the boot.

"Noon, I think."

"Where?" He grabbed his hat and hollered outside at Kitty's grandson Toby, who was leading Deacon to the barn after watering him.

"Methodist Church," he heard her say, then he was out the door.

"*Morton* is here." Margery came on in the small room at the back of the church and closed the door. Juliet glanced at her. *Morton.* Mister Severs was now *Morton*. It occurred to Juliet that if she played her cards right, she would be able to seduce him away from his agreement to pay the taxes on the farm. What satisfaction she'd find in rendering her aunt and cousins homeless. She looked in the primping mirror, then bowed her head. But Tucker would be cast out with them, and what was left of White Oak Glen would be lost to her forever. When she looked up this time, she narrowed her eyes, and her reflection responded in kind. Or maybe *Morton* would buy it for her.

Margery squatted at her side and gazed up with hazel eyes. "Do not worry for Tucker, Juliet. I'll take care of him."

"I want you to marry him, Margery, give him a son, someone to carry on my father's name."

Margery rose, silent, and Juliet almost laughed out loud. She sounded as if she were attending her funeral and not her wedding. She looked in the mirror. Buried, no less, in her mother's wedding gown, a beautiful dress of luxurious off-white satin, its bodice and cuffs embellished with hundreds of tiny pearls: a poignant reminder of a lost age.

She hadn't wanted to wear it, its value too precious for this travesty, but Aunt Lilith insisted. There was no time to purchase another, and it was a perfect fit.

Juliet reminded herself that her mother had not loved the man she married either. But no matter how it turned out, on her wedding day Eileen Dobbins had dreamed of one day loving Jordan Seaton. Pity was, it never happened. Only a few short days ago, when she'd broken her engagement to Matt, Juliet had been determined her life would be different.

130

Numb with the grief that comes from shattered dreams, she
glanced into the looking glass; the ghost of Juliet Seaton stared
back. Last night she found heaven in the arms of a man she would
never have, and today God would cast her into hell for that trans-
gression.

Aunt Lilith stepped up behind her and covered her carefully
curled and pinned-up hair with a net of pearls.

"You are a beautiful bride."

Her aunt dared to place her hands on Juliet's shoulders, and
Juliet fought the urge to tell the woman to go to the devil.

Lilith Seaton cocked her head to one side and contemplated
Juliet's reflection. "Morton Severs will be so pleased with you,
and you will be wealthy. You are a lucky young woman, though
you don't realize it now. Pinch your cheeks, dearest, you are so
pale."

Last night, when she'd gotten home, her cheeks had been
flushed and full of color. Jeff had put that glow there. For two
hours, he'd loved her and caressed her and lit a fire in her she was
sure no other man could ever aspire to.

He was Jeff Dawson, and he was the one she wanted.

He'd walked her to the edge of the woods at dusk after asking her to stay. He made no offer of marriage or commitment,
simply wanted her to spend the night in his big four-poster bed.
Of course, she couldn't. He'd hinted of more trysts to come. She
told him she wouldn't. She'd been honest with him from the start
she reminded herself. She'd told him she'd ask nothing more than
that one time, and she never would.

He'd chuckled at that and kissed her goodnight. "Good-bye"
she reminded him, but he refused to listen. She couldn't resist
him, he told her, and she'd let him believe that.

She had shamed herself, but for a moment she had held her
dream in her arms.

Jeff was happy with his conquest, he had made that clear,
reminding her he would be forced into nothing, sure her good-
bye was simply a ploy to coerce him into some yet unvoiced obligation.

She closed her eyes and shuddered. She was deluding herself. No matter what she tried to make herself believe, he'd be angry when he found out she'd wed another, if only for his pride.

Aunt Lilith paced nervously around the small room. Juliet looked out the hazy windows. They needed to be washed. A knock sounded at the door, and Juliet grasped the stool on which she sat. The executioner had arrived.

In the mirror, Juliet watched her aunt smile. The woman had been fretful all morning, sure Juliet would bolt, failing to do her duty to the rest of them. Lilith nodded for Margery to open the door, but before she could get to it, the door swung open. Jeff Dawson still had his hand on the knob.

Aunt Lilith stepped forward. "Mister Dawson, there is no—"

"I want to talk to Juliet alone."

Lilith frowned. "Whatever you have to say must wait until after—"

Still in the hallway, Jeff turned from the protesting Lilith. "Take one more step toward me, you son-of-a-bitch, and I'll knock you back into your pew."

Behind Jeff, Juliet saw her brother stop cold. Wex stepped forward and placed a hand on Tucker's shoulder. "Mother," Wex called, "Margery, come on. Let him have his say to her, then we'll have the wedding."

Lilith rushed out, skirting around Jeff. "Where is Morton? He will not like this if he...."

Jeff closed the door.

"What are you doing?" he asked, his voice soft. He seemed perfectly calm all of a sudden, so unlike the man who had opened that door.

Juliet sat at an angle on the stool and watched him. "I'm getting married," she said in a small voice. Lord help her, she could hardly breathe.

"You're going to marry that carpetbagging scum Severs?"

"Yes."

He pushed himself away from the door and approached her with measured steps. He was trying to control himself, she could see it in his step, in the way he flexed his hands. "Why the hell are you doing this?"

"I have to."

"Why?" he yelled, and she jumped.

She was scared for many reasons, only one of which had to do with him, and she was upset, which had almost everything to do with him. She wasn't going to be yelled at and bullied. He'd agreed to their liaison. She'd told him she'd never ask for anything again, and he had agreed—to sleep with her, at least. She rose. "I am doing what I have to do."

"Is what you did with me yesterday something you had to do?"

"What I did with you was something I wanted to do. I didn't want him to h-have...."

"Your virginity. You chose to give that to me instead of your damn filthy, thieving carpetbagger husband?"

"Yes," she spat out, "I made sure he'd never get it."

He grasped her arms and shook her. "And what about me?"

"What about you?" *You fool, what do you think about you? You're so smart, why can't you figure it out?*

He let her go with a small shove and stepped back. He was restraining himself, getting away from her, out of striking distance.

"Why did you choose me?"

She couldn't tell him the whole truth, of course. Pride and prudence precluded that. "It had to be someone willing. Someone who could have carnal knowledge of me and not care—"

"Why the hell would you presume I wouldn't care?"

She brought herself up to full height. "You said so. You implied that sleeping with me would be part of your vengeance against my family. Last night you repeatedly insinuated you believed me to be leading you into a trap. I told you I was not. Now you're angry with me because I told you the truth."

He stuck a finger in her face. "You deceived me just the same, Juliet. You used me with no regard for my heart." He started to the door.

Body shaking, she barked out a laugh. "Your heart! Not once did you indicate your heart was involved. In fact, you went to great trouble to make sure I knew precisely the opposite. What troubles you now is your blasted ego. You can't stand the fact that I was not out to trap you, and perhaps I really do not want you forever, but only for a night. That's how it was for you, wasn't it? That's how it's been for you a thousand times." She straightened, defiance and anger surging through her tense body, and her voice broke. "Well, this time you lost at your own game, Mister Dawson."

"It's the money, isn't it? You're marrying him for the money, like with Braxton. Guess poor old Matt didn't turn out to be rich enough for you."

Haughtily she held up her left hand and flashed the garish diamond at him. He stared at it a moment, then at her. "We'll see about my ego, Miss Seaton, and we'll see who really lost with your whoring last night."

He reached for the knob. "No!" She leaped forward to block his exit. "What are you going to do?"

"Have a talk with your prospective...." He clenched his teeth and strained to pull the door open against her weight. It gave, of course; there was no way she could keep him inside.

"No, please, Jeff. It's not money, it's—" his hand circled her upper arm, and he pulled, then pushed her from the door. She stumbled, but righted herself. By the time she turned, his broad-shouldered form had disappeared into the hall. She rushed after him, her trying all the while to control the train of her mother's dress. Margery, pale and wide-eyed, stood in the hall next to her mother. Jeff was past them.

"What have you done?" Aunt Lilith asked, wringing her hands. Juliet gave her only a passing glance.

At the entrance to the sanctuary, Juliet stopped. The church was full and suddenly quiet, everyone looking at her.

She squinted at the guests, then raised her hand to assuage her pounding temple. Lord help her, she could not register a single familiar face, though she had to know every person in this

134

place. She swallowed, then sought Jeff, who stood six feet beyond her. Morton Severs, dressed in a fine gabardine suit of soft gray, looked first at her, then Jeff, then took a menacing step forward. "What's going on here?" he asked.

"I need to talk to you in private," Jeff answered.

"No, Jeff, please. I'm sorry for what I said. I must—"

"I'm about to be married here, Dawson. Could our conversation wait?"

"No, Severs, it cannot. It is obvious to everyone in this room that it is your impending nuptials that I wish to discuss."

She felt the color drain from her face. "Please, don't do this."

Jeff didn't look at her.

Severs did, though. He smiled and reached for her. Mute, she started toward him.

Jeff turned to her. "Don't take another step, Juliet."

Tears welled, and she was helpless to stop them. "I'm sorry, Jeff. Just let things lie."

"It's too late."

To her left, Wex rose and Severs signaled to a man in the back of the room. Jeff turned, watching them, and pulled a gun from the rear waist of his pants. In the pews, some gasped. "I'll talk to you here then," he said.

"Jeff," Michael Tate said, hastily moving around the pulpit. "This is a house of God."

Jeff never blinked an eye, but glared at Wex. "Sit back down. I intend to tell Mister Severs something he needs to know."

Poised, Severs drew his arms behind his back. "Very well, Dawson, have your say so I can get on with my wedding. And since it obviously disturbs you"—he snickered—"my wedding night."

Juliet closed her eyes at Severs' taunting. She knew now she would be the one to pay the price for Jeff's anger.

"On the contrary, Severs, I have already had your wedding night." Jeff turned and watched her. Her lips trembled, and she waited, praying he wouldn't.... "Last night," he said, "on the floor of my barn."

She held his gaze while her world crumbled around her—not the marriage with Morton Severs, which would not happen now, not the anger her family would turn on her, not even the shame she would know among her people—but the feelings she held for Jeff Dawson.

"He forced you, Juliet!"

Aunt Lilith. The woman stood behind her, at the end of the first pew. The very sound of her voice hurt Juliet's ears.

"She came to me willingly," Jeff said, his eyes locked on Juliet. "Or do you lack the spine to deny your aunt's lie, Miss Seaton. A character trait missing in so many of your family."

She lifted her chin and glared at him. "I gave myself to him of my own free will."

A low hum swept through the gathering made up of a number of Natchez' influential citizens. Wex sat down, and the man subtly summoned by Severs stopped his approach. Jeff put his pistol out of sight beneath his jacket and turned back to the groom.

"So, Severs, do you want to risk your first-born being 'Rebel trash'? Given your feelings on that subject, it's no less than you deserve."

Severs glared at Juliet. "Last night? After we'd agreed—"

"Immediately," she said.

"We had an agreement," he shouted. Severs made to rush her, but Jeff stepped in his way.

"Don't." His tone held a cold, clear warning.

"I agreed to marry you," Juliet said. "What I did before our vows were stated is not your concern."

"The hell it isn't." Severs looked at Tucker, then back at her, the glint in his eye ominous. "You'll pay for this, Miss Seaton."

Her gaze darted to Tucker, then Severs, who had started down the aisle. "Wait."

"I have nothing more to say to you." He continued to stalk toward the door.

"Do you want your ring back?" she shouted above the din of the gathering.

She felt their eyes upon her, but didn't acknowledge them. Severs turned and marched stiffly back. Jeff moved next to her, as if he meant to protect her.

Protect her from what? He'd shamed her beyond repair.

Severs snatched the ring from her hand, then spun back to the aisle and the front door. She shunned Jeff's gaze and turned to Tucker.

"You whored yourself with him?" Tucker said loud enough for all to hear.

His reaction was the last blow. She'd been willing to sacrifice her happiness to protect him, or at least his posterity. Now the fact that Severs was about to turn him in for murder didn't appear to faze him.

"Your mother is rolling in her grave," Aunt Lilith said.

"On the contrary, I did exactly what my mother wished she had done almost forty years ago."

"How could you take such a risk?" Margery hissed. "What will happen to us now?"

Glaring at her while he did so, Tucker slid the length of the pew and stood. "You're not welcome in my house, you trollop." Without a backward glance he left the church. Margery and Aunt Lilith hurried after him. Wex pursed his lips, gave Juliet a little nod, then followed at a slower gait.

The crowd was thinning out. Juliet turned to Jeff. "How could you?"

"I was left little choice. He didn't want to talk private and you'd have married the bastard if I'd said nothing."

"That was what I was here for. To get married. To cause you no harm."

"You've caused me a great deal of harm. Reckless regard for other's feelings seems to be a Seaton trait."

"I hate you."

He thinned his lips. "I hate you, too."

Her eyes welled tears, and she looked away. The house...? She was his sister; Tucker wouldn't throw her out. But they'd make her miserable there. No one else would take her in. God, what was she to do? Become a prostitute? She should have kept Severs' hideous ring. She could have sold it.

Juliet turned her back on Jeff. People still milled near the door, so she wheeled back the other way. She'd go out the back and talk to her mother. Later, she'd decide what to do.

"Did he buy you that dress?" Jeff asked. His voice seemed to come from far away. Through a fog of tears, she looked at him.

"It was my mother's."

He took her hand. His was warm and strong.

She pulled against his hold. "Leave me alone."

But he prevailed.

"You came here to get married, Miss Seaton. I suggest we do just that."

Chapter Twenty-two

Yes, he hated her. Hated her for what she'd done, or had almost done. But he wanted her, too. He wasn't about to let her out of his sight like he'd done last night. Now he knew, dammit, there was only one way to hold her.

With another jerk, she yanked her hand free. "You must be insane. You're the last man on earth I would marry."

He glanced around them. A number of the retreating parishioners had stopped and were now looking at them. Michael Tate, who still stood beside the pulpit, threw a furtive glance to his wife Mary, sitting at the organ.

Jeff nipped the tip of his tongue and leaned closer to Juliet. "Where are you going to go? Under the Hill?"

"Why should you care?" she spat out, her pretty face twisted in anger.

So much for discretion. "If you go to Under the Hill, I'll purchase you there."

"I would not accept you as a client." The tears welling in her eyes finally overflowed. "I never asked payment from you."

No, she hadn't, though he'd been sure at the time she'd expected something.

Juliet blinked and turned away. "You made everything we did sound so...."

Ugly...dirty? "You're the one who made it sound that way with your betrayal."

"I didn't betray you." Not bothering to look at him this time, she started toward the back of the church. "And I'll take care of myself."

The hell she would. Even if she could, he wasn't going to allow it. He caught her at the door leading into the rear vestibule. "I'm offering you my name, Juliet," he said in a harsh whisper, only part of him hoping no one else would hear. "Take it."

She twisted her elbow out of his grasp. "Why would you want me? You've exposed me as a whore to everyone in this town. To every crony you have and every one you ever will have."

"Yes," he hissed. He didn't like begging and, dammit, at the moment, that was exactly what he was doing. But there was no way on earth he was letting her leave this church except as his wife. "But you're my whore, and I want you."

"Why?"

What did she want, for him to fall on his knees and express undying love? "I want the pleasure of mounting Jordan Seaton's daughter any way and any time I damn well please, and I pray he'll be watching from hell every time she screams in pleasure at my touch."

"You are disgusting." She started forward again, toward the back door, but reached it only a step ahead of him.

"I am richer than Morton Severs could ever dream of being," he said.

"You are a fool, Mister Dawson." With that, Juliet turned the doorknob and pulled.

"I have White Oak Glen."

That stopped her cold. He scooted up closer, his chest almost touching her back. His heart was racing. "I have your ancestral home. It's been passed down along the female line for generations. Why not with you? Or do you still hope your brother will amount to something?"

She pushed the door shut, and he stepped back and grasped her hand. "Marry me, Juliet. I ask you one last time."

Chapter Twenty-three

And she did.

Michael Tate had been visibly relieved to perform the ceremony. A few people, most of them elderly women, had stayed to witness whatever happened next, the anti-climax to Morton Severs and Juliet Seaton's aborted wedding. Those folks had nodded in approval when he led her back to the altar. What a way to begin a marriage. Jeff had always planned to give the deed a lot of thought, but in the end, he'd acted on a whim. A desperate, all-consuming whim.

Jeff glanced at the woman sitting stiff and silent beside him in Mike Tate's cabriolet. No, it hadn't been a whim. He'd simply been forced into the deed sooner than he'd wanted.

He and, he was sure, Mike had experienced a last panicky moment when time came for Juliet to say her vows. At the point where she was to "love, honor, and cherish," she'd hesitated. "Come now," he goaded in her ear, "you were willing to lie for Severs, why not for me?" She'd glared at him as she spat out each word.

But she had said them, then said "I do" easily enough. So had he. It was over; she was his.

For a half-hour following the ceremony, Jeff waited inside while she visited her mother's grave. He'd watched her though, from a rear window, and talked casually with a calm Mike Tate. Damn, it had been poor form to draw his gun in the man's church. Jeff was fortunate Mike even spoke to him, much less agreed to marry them.

Now, having traversed the long drive from the river road, he drove the borrowed carriage to the back door of his big house.

Kitty, hands on her hips and mouth agape, stepped from the rear hall onto the back porch.

"Well, you managed to put a stop to that marriage, I reckon, but what you thinkin' bringin' my missy here? Oh, sweet Jesus, and in her mama's weddin' dress?"

"She's my wife, Kitty." He seized Juliet around the waist and swung her out of the carriage and down to the grass. "Where would you have me take her?"

Kitty stared at them a moment, before a sad smile crossed her black face. "Lordy, baby girl"—she stepped off the porch and came to Juliet, then crushed her to her ample bosom—"he done brought you home for good."

For a moment, Jeff thought Juliet would burst into tears. Instead, she turned and narrowed her eyes on him. "Isn't he the most wonderful man."

He shot his lovely, demure bride a knowing look. "And I intend to be well-compensated for my deed." He wasn't about to feel regret or remorse over what he'd done, no matter how upset she might be. He was still angry, and with good right. He took her elbow and moved her toward the house.

"Oh," she said, "I intend to make sure you get a lifetime of everything you deserve for what you did today."

Out of Kitty's earshot, he squeezed the captured elbow and leaned close to her. "Rest assured I'll get what I deserve, Juliet, and if you're smart, you'll lay back and enjoy it."

She averted her face and tugged on her arm. Hide her tears, she might, but he wouldn't allow her to free herself, not yet.

"Will we be havin' dinner guests tonight, Mister Dawson? A party?" Kitty called after them.

He looked over his shoulder. The Negress stood where she'd stopped when she welcomed Juliet home.

"There will be no guests, Kitty. Only Mister Dawson and me," Juliet answered.

If failure to celebrate struck Kitty as odd, she didn't show it. She had to know their marriage occurred under extraordinary

142

conditions, though she had no idea how much so. He'd probably get an earful once she found out.

"How's 'bout some chicken and dumplins, baby girl?" Kitty hollered after them.

At his side, Juliet slowed, and when he looked at her, he saw new tears had welled in her eyes. "That would be nice," she said, "thank you, Kitty."

"My darlin' baby girl, she always did like her Auntie Kitty's chicken and dumplins best of all. Oh," she said, wiping at her eyes with her apron before starting toward the old cookhouse. "It be so good to have a Seaton female back at White Oak Glen."

"Her name is Dawson," Jeff said. Sweet Jesus, who was in control here?

"Yes, sir, *Massa* Dawson. She be Ol' Miss Dawson fo' sho' now. But to me, she always gonna be my darlin' girl Juliet, and she done come home."

Jeff seethed. Seaton female, indeed. He yanked the screen and grabbed the knob to the back door. With a violent shove, he managed to bang the door against the back wall. He looked down at Juliet, grasped her to him, and lifted her easily in his arms. Their noses almost touched, and she stared at him with a look of total surprise. He stepped across the threshold. "A symbolic gesture, sweetheart, representative of the male animal overpowering his mate." He set her on the floor. "Welcome home, Missus *Dawson*."

𝒮he wasn't certain that was the correct symbolism, but she didn't care to argue the point. She didn't want to talk to him. Everything he said to her had a sexual connotation. A clear implication that was what he expected from her, and little more. He moved down the long foyer, then she heard his boots on the oak steps.

More slowly, she followed his path down the great hall that split the house in two. The front door was at the far end. In the summer, her mother would open all the windows and both doors to let the breeze flow through and cool the house. Her recent stay in this house felt like a dream-visit now, and she hadn't wandered about. She pirouetted to take in the heavy moldings and carved ceilings. She recalled them. They were original to the house, built fifty-six years ago.

Near the front door, two sets of stairs, one on either side, curved up to a balcony, which looked down on the entry foyer. The balcony joined an upper-story central hall paralleling this one below it. The bedrooms, six in all, came off either the balcony or the hall and were situated on the northeast and southwest sides of the house.

A small portion of the house had been redecorated, but it was mostly drab and in want of care. That was because Missus Tackert died only four years after her husband bought White Oak Glen. Darnell Tackert's desire to refurbish died with her.

To her right was the front parlor, to the left...?

Once that room had been her father's study, and though she couldn't visualize him in it, she clearly remembered her mother there. Eileen Seaton managed plantation operations years before Jordan Seaton had left for war. Juliet wondered if Jeff would ever allow her to run this place, but she thought not.

The study was dark, and she drew back the drapes. The view from here was lovely. Her grandfather had chosen this site atop the hill so the family could sit on the porch and see the farm's original home, the simple, old farmhouse her family now occupied. Woods had grown up during the war and subsequent years, and the old house was no longer visible.

But the old place...and her brother...were still there. Juliet squeezed her eyes tight. Tucker would require help when the authorities came for him, and the family didn't have the means to provide it.

She moved from the window into the room. At its center, an oak desk graced a plush oriental carpet. Tackert or his wife must have placed the rug there; it simply did not look like something Jeff Dawson would have bought.

Her slipper sank into the carpet and her heart sank with it. Tucker would spurn her support. Not that it mattered, not after what he'd said to her in the church. Still, he was her brother. She should talk to that Deputy Floyd.

She ran her hand over the glistening surface of the magnificent desk, then she sat and opened a drawer, more to see how smooth it glided than for any other reason. Many things lay inside, but she focused on the gun. A derringer, she guessed it was. She'd heard of them, but had never seen one. Careful, she lifted it. The weapon fit nicely in her hand.

"Not much firepower unless your intent is to put it to your temple and pull the trigger."

Her heartbeat quickened, but she was confident she managed to control her visible response to Jeff's sudden appearance.

He walked into the room and sat in the chair across from her. "Do you intend to kill yourself, Missus Dawson?"

"I would shoot you before myself, Mister Dawson."

He looked at the gun she held. "Do you intend to shoot me?"

It dawned on her that he thought she might, and she placed the diminutive pistol back where she'd found it, then rubbed at the stiff collar on her dress. "I must go somewhere."

"You have no clothes."

"That's not important."

"Where do you need to go?"

She averted her eyes. She didn't want to tell him. He'd not give a tinker's damn about Tucker. "I need to go to town."

"Why?"

"Really, must I tell you everything?"

His eyes widened. "This is our wedding day, Juliet. You are still in your wedding dress. You are distraught. And now I walk into my office to find you toying with a pistol, and you expect me to let you go gallivanting into town, alone, with a killer on the loose."

"A killer killing whores to be specific, and you have declared me to be one to the entire county."

He sighed and leaned forward. "Why do you need to go to town?"

"I need to talk to the sheriff."

He wrinkled his brow.

"It's about Tucker. There are rumors he was seen with Lorna Hart the night she died."

"And?"

"And? What do you mean, *and*? Don't you see? There are those who will accuse him of having killed her."

"Have you talked to Tucker about this?"

"Certainly."

"Does he appear concerned?"

"Yes," she said. Why in the world was he asking such stupid questions having obvious answers? "I want to know what the law is going to do, what the sheriff thinks. There's no way Tucker could have killed that woman. You saw him. You found him in the woods. Oh sweet Jesus"—she rose from where she sat—"you could testify against him and, no doubt, would, but you know he couldn't even walk by himself that night."

"He could have killed her before he got to that stage, Juliet."

"But he didn't, I know it."

"I know it, too, and so does the sheriff."

She fell back into the chair. "He does?"

"Yes."

"How—"

"Juliet, your brother was not the last person known to see Lorna Hart alive. I was."

"But, I—"

"They were together. They'd been fighting. Tucker had gotten in a couple of good licks, but by the time I got there, he was nearly passed out, and she was beating the absolute stew out of him." Jeff leaned back in the chair. "I sent Lorna on her way, then I took your brother home, where I deposited him on your front porch and left him in the care of your aunt and Margery."

Juliet laid her hand over her pounding heart. "He must not know you saw Lorna."

"Of course he knows. He made a statement to Deputy Floyd the day Lorna's body was found. There's no way your brother could have killed Lorna, and he knows it."

146

***

$\mathcal{J}$eff thought for a moment that Juliet was going to faint. Then she raised a visibly shaking hand to her forehead. "Does Aunt Lilith know?"

"I don't know. What's wrong with you? I thought you'd be relieved Tucker has an alibi."

She studied his eyes, and he held her gaze. Then a primordial whine escaped her throat, and she rose from the chair.

"Did you hear what he said to me at the church?"

He opened his mouth to say that he did, but—

"Did you?" she screamed. She rounded the desk and rushed into the foyer, the train of her dress swishing along the floor. He followed her, hollering her name. She didn't respond, but lifted her skirt and started running down the hall to the back porch. When she hit the yard, he started to run, too, and snagged her arm outside the cookhouse. She whirled on him, and prudently, he let her go.

"What are you doing?" he said. "And answer me this time, because I see no reason now for you to talk to the sheriff."

The anguish moved across her face as clearly as the puckers in her chin. "I'm not going to the sheriff," she said and choked back a sob. "I'm going home. I'm going to get my things. I'm going to get my mother's things. Lilith Seaton will *never* sleep in my mother's bed."

With a swipe at her eyes, Juliet continued to the barn and left Jeff standing there, cursing himself. Morton Severs had been blackmailing her, threatening that worthless brother of hers, and Tucker had played along, him and the others. They'd sold her into marriage for Severs' money.

"Kitty," Jeff called over his shoulder, "hold off on dinner. And I'm taking that grandson of yours with me. We've got furniture to move."

Kitty's stout body filled the cookhouse door. "Don't you worry none 'bout them dumplins. They keep good. And I'm movin' into my old room back of the dinin' room, how you been wantin'. Gonna be like in the old days."

147

Jeff stopped and pivoted. "In the old days, you were a slave, Kitty. Now you get paid a nice sum each week."

She waved him on. "Slave, my ass. Shows what the likes of you know. You been listenin' to them Northerners think they know so much? I done tol' you and tol' you. Me and Miss Eileen, we run'd this place."

Chapter Twenty-four

Juliet was out of the wagon before Jeff pulled the mules to a complete halt. He tossed the reins to Toby Horton, then jumped down and hurried through the picket gate, still swinging from her push. She was well in front of him, running up the dirt path, charged up and determined to keep herself that way in the face of what she was about to do. She had been that way last evening, and realizing that, he didn't call for her to hold up, but concentrated on catching her before she plowed into the hornet's nest.

Wex Seaton opened the screen and stepped onto the porch. Behind him, the door closed with a soft pat. He partly blocked her path, but she ignored him, skirting to his left and yanking the door open. Wex moved aside; he made no attempt to stop her.

Tucker loomed in the doorway. "What the hell are you doing back here?"

"Get out of my way."

"You're not coming in this house."

His voice held a telltale slur, but he stood straight enough to offer a challenge.

"You worthless pile of horseshit, my things are in this house. I've come for them, including the things that were Mama's."

"You aren't coming in here."

Missus Seaton appeared from the darkened interior. "You are not welcome here, Juliet," she said with a thrust of her chin.

"Aunt Lilith, you go to the devil."

Through the hazy screen covering the outer door, Jeff swore he saw Lilith Seaton pale. Wex stiffened, but Jeff's hollow foot-

149

falls on the porch steps stayed whatever action, if any, Wex would have taken in his mother's defense.

Tucker teetered slightly, then supported himself against the doorjamb. "I see you brought your boyfriend," he said with a sneer. "Oh, excuse me. Your demon lover."

"Husband," Jeff said.

Tucker's eyes, already fixed on him, widened, then he shifted his body to one side and glared down on Juliet. "You married him? After everything else, you m-m-married that hellish"— Tucker pointed at Jeff—"th-that thing shouldn't be able to walk around in the light of day. Don't you realize how powerful it is?"

Jeff tensed his jaw, but Juliet appeared to ignore her brother's tirade completely and started around him and through the door. Immediately, Jeff reached for the half-open screen. At the same time, Tucker grabbed Juliet and spun clumsily around, leaving his back to Jeff. Before Jeff could move to help Juliet, the crack of a fist against bone split the air, and Jeff barely got out of the way of Tucker's falling body. The man crashed to the steps, and he lay with his head on the bottom tread, his feet on the porch proper. He rolled his head to the side and groaned.

Wex, who'd had a better view, caught Jeff's eye and grinned.

Juliet stepped forward, rubbing her knuckles. "Tucker," she said, glaring down at him from the edge of the porch, "I know you lied. You offered me to Morton Severs for drinking money. Then you had the nerve to defame me in church. You are a pathetic, drunken lout; I'm going to get my things now, and you better keep out of my way."

Tucker's head had stopped moving. He'd passed out. A pity, because she'd spoken so eloquently.

"And you'd best hope Wexford meets with enough success to pay the taxes in the spring," Juliet said to her Aunt Lilith, "because if he doesn't, I'm buying back the rest of White Oak Glen, and y'all will all be evicted."

She was sure playing fast and easy with his money.

"I don't know what you mean," the older woman said. "I truly thought it was for the best—"

"Don't you dare say it. You know how my mother despised Morton Severs, and yet you were willing to compel me to marry him against my will."

"Your brother—"

"Has an alibi and always has. Tell me you didn't know, and if it would have mattered if you did."

Margery stood in the door, her hand covering her mouth. "I didn't know," she mumbled, then dropped her hand. "I swear, Juliet. I did not know. I truly thought Tucker was in danger."

"And whose side would you have taken had you known?"

Margery's gaze flitted to Wex, then back to Juliet. She didn't answer.

Juliet stepped around her aunt and cousin and into the house.

Chapter Twenty-five

"My great-uncle Moon, he be Grandma's oldest brother, say these mules be the best lookin' ones in all Adams County."

Jeff reached up to help Juliet from the wagon. "You be sure to thank him for me, Toby."

They were fine mules. He'd bought the pair six weeks ago in anticipation of moving newly purchased furniture from Natchez to his new home at White Oak Glen. He'd need them for plowing, too, come spring.

He set Juliet on her feet, then took her hand and gently rubbed her knuckles. She flinched.

"Hurt?"

"A little." She pulled her hand away.

She'd knocked Tucker plumb out. Wex had helped Margery get him up to bed. If he'd come to before they left, Jeff didn't know it, but he and Juliet were there over two hours loading Juliet's things and the treasures that had belonged to her mother, including a cherry bedroom set.

"Put your hand in Epsom salts. I've got some in the cookhouse."

"I'm fine," she said, moving to the back of the wagon. She pulled out the sheet bundling her clothes.

"I'll get that. Toby," he said, "climb up here and start handing things to me.

"We'll unload the smaller things here, Juliet, but I'll need to hire help to move the furniture upstairs." Night encroached all around them. Short days, long nights. Jeff glanced at the sky.

152

"Looks like we're gonna get some rain. I'll put the wagon in the barn overnight."

She nodded, and a mixture of frustration and regret twisted his gut. During the trips to the Seaton place and back, and the whole time spent packing, she communicated with him in monosyllables and then only when a gesture wouldn't suffice. Dammit. This wasn't entirely his fault. If she'd trusted him with the truth instead of giving herself to him to spite Severs, he would have exposed the lie and freed her from coercion.

Even before he'd completed his argument, he recognized its fallacy. If she'd been willing to sacrifice her happiness for her brother, why in God's name would he think she'd risk putting Tucker's fate in his hands? From her point of view, he hated Tucker. Truth was, the worm was too pitiful to waste the emotion on.

No matter how Jeff tried to justify his anger, he couldn't. He'd lost it the moment he realized what had driven her to the desperate bestowal of her virginity. Juliet was a passionate and resolute woman, full of grit and spirit, if not always sound judgment. Damn, he'd been the one who'd known her last night. He shared every touch, every sigh, every sweet kiss, and rejoiced in each cry of pleasure. He and no other knew what their lovemaking meant to her. Her virtue had been a precious gift, not an instrument of spite. A part of her she wished to share with the man she...well, someone special, and she'd chosen him.

For her, it must look as if he'd thrown that gift back in her face this morning at the church. Well, he felt betrayed, too. How could she have failed to share his feelings as he'd shared hers?

Kitty came out to help carry items into the house. "Dumplins done, so's them limas and black-eyed peas. My baby girl, she always did like kitchen food best. Be a fine feast for her weddin' day.

"I know you like 'em, too," she said to Jeff, her smile fading to something akin to a sneer. "You just a po' white boy. No need to cook you fancy food."

"I'm not a poor white boy any longer, Kitty."

153

"Yeah, but yo' taste, it done be set for life."

Jeff ground his teeth. Maybe his class was too.

"Was another killin' night befo' last."

Juliet set the bowl of dumplings on the table. "I know."

"Folks in town, they startin' to talk." Kitty placed a pewter fork by Jeff's plate.

"Talk about what?"

"'Bout what's doin' it."

"And?"

"Well, mosta that spook talk comes from ignorant white trash don't know no better."

And superstitious coloreds, Juliet would wager. "What are they saying, Kitty?"

"They say it be a dark spirit. Something yo' *husband* done brought back from hell to hurt yo' family, or maybe he be the evil hisself."

Goose bumps moved over Juliet like a coming rain over an open field. She recalled her own initial reaction to the wolf, her ignorance of the beast and her fear in the face of her ignorance. Ignorance and fear. The two were linked. Juliet closed her eyes and recalled Jeff's smell, his touch. A delicious shiver eclipsed her chill....

"That is silly," she said to Kitty.

"Don't matter none, silly or not. Tales told 'bout his folks, 'specially his granddaddy, go back a long, long ways."

"I know."

"Things you know 'bout happened at the end. I be talkin' 'bout things happened long before Jarmane Seaton was even born, much less murdered." From the buffet, Kitty picked up the salt and pepper shakers and set them in the center of the table. She glanced at Juliet before doing the same with a steaming bowl of vegetables. "I remember from when I was a girl, the talk. Used to be a Perry family east of the Dawsons. Them two families never did get along—always fightin' over the water rights to that same ol' creek runs down in front of this house. Truth was though, as I heard it, Mister Perry plain didn't like living next door to an Injun. And that ol' man Wolfson, he was plenty mean in his own right. He looked like an Injun, too, but he weren't full blood. That made it worse, him bein' a half-breed."

Juliet took crystal water goblets from a beautiful breakfront and wiped them with the apron tied around her waist.

"That your best dress?"

Still holding the apron, Juliet looked down at the dark blue wool. The dress bore no patches and boasted a lovely tatted collar and cuffs, fastened with pearl buttons. She wore it for church and special occasions...such as her wedding supper.

"Except for my mourning dress, yes it is, and I refuse to wear black on the day of my marriage. Now, go on with your story, please."

"Well, ol' Mister Perry, he started gettin' real ugly. Folks say he salted the Dawsons' deep well. That's when the wolf come."

"Did it gobble Mister Perry up?" Juliet asked with a smile.

"After it killed some stock."

The smile fled her lips. "It killed Mister Perry?"

Kitty lifted her chin to expose her throat, then curled her fingers into a claw and simulated grabbing her Adam's apple. "Ripped his throat out. Missus Perry sold out to yo' daddy and moved away."

"So Jarmane's death wasn't the first attributed to Jedediah Wolfson?"

"No, darlin' baby girl. And there were others after Perry."

"No one did anything?"

"Nobody could prove nothin'. And they was mostly mean men he killed or hurt. Nobody cared for a long, long time."

"Then came Jarmane?"

"Yes'm. Ol' man crossed the line when he killed that Seaton boy. Yo' cousin was aristocracy. Ol' man Wolfson was not, neither was that girl Jarmane got with child."

Kitty stepped back and looked at the table, dressed with a white linen cloth and what little was left of Eileen Seaton's fine china. "Fit for a weddin' feast."

Juliet couldn't suppress the smile that curled the corner of her lips. "It is beautiful, Kitty, thank you."

"Why ain't you happy, girl? For better or worse, you done got what you wanted. The only thing you ever wanted."

Tears filled Juliet's eyes. "It was under the worst of circumstances. The absolute worst. I never dreamed of being married the way I was today." She swiped at a tear tickling her cheek. "It was a horrible, humiliating day. Why, he's out there right now in that dirty barn, feeding those mules in the same work clothes he wore at the ceremony. I don't think he gave any thought to anything he did this morning, up to and including marrying me."

"Oh, baby girl," Kitty said, coming around the table, "what you expect foolin' around with the likes of him?"

Juliet's heartbeat quickened as Kitty hugged her.

"The important thing is you've got yourself back home to White Oak Glen..."

Shocked silent, Juliet stared over the steaming bowls of her wedding feast.

"...just hope you gambled right, lyin' with trash and not that filthy carpetbagger."

Juliet pushed away roughly. "Don't *ever* call him that again, Kitty. I mean it. Don't you dare."

Apparently not offended, Kitty nodded. "You be right, baby girl. Him'll be the daddy of your little chilluns if he lives long enough to git you any...and if you does, too."

"I'll have to go to town in the morning and hire a few hands to get that furniture in the house." Jeff glanced up from his plate. "I want you to go with me. There's a seamstress on Pine Street. You need a new wardrobe."

She looked at him, washed and dressed in the clean shirt and jacket he'd donned when he came in and found her changed.

"I know Fran Woolsey. Mister Dawson—"

"Quit calling me that. I was Jeff this time yesterday, and I intend to stay that way for the rest of our lives." He pushed his plate away.

She *was* being silly. "Jeff," she started, "I don't want—"

"I want you to buy new clothes. You're my wife. I'm rich. I want you to look as though I care about you."

Whether you do or not. "You're concerned with what people think of me?"

"Of course, I"—he looked up and met her eyes—"You're not disgraced, Juliet. I gave you my name."

"Your name wasn't what I wanted. Your respect. Perhaps some consideration or your...."

*L*ove? She didn't say it, but she thought it; she must have. Certainly, it was the first word to cross his mind. Well, he'd been angry and hurt...and scared to death he was going to lose her. "I would have publicly raped you," he said softly, "if I'd had to."

Her mouth opened slightly. Then she shook her head and rose from the table. "I'm tired. I'll help Kitty with the dishes, then I'm going to bed."

He rose with her, his chair scraping across the wide plank floor. Her eyes met his, and defiance stared back at him. Quickly he came around the table, and she watched his every step, facing him when he reached her side.

She stiffened at his touch, and her nostrils flared. "I will not deny you conjugal rights, but you will find no pleasure in them."

To insist on making love to her tonight would be a foolish and unforgivable error. He pulled her to him anyway and kissed her unyielding lips. The chill of her response sucked the warmth out of him, leaving him with an emptiness that smacked of grief. She hated him, or so she'd said this morning. Right now, he believed her.

"I'll help Kitty. You go up to bed."

She stepped back. "Where do—"

"I'll sleep in my bed; you take your old room. Don't worry, Juliet. I'll let you know when I want something from you."

Chapter Twenty-six

"It's too elaborate, Franny." Juliet smoothed the gray wool of her dress over her bottom before again taking a seat on the dressmaker's comfortable settee. She turned the page of the latest *Harper's Bazaar*, then flipped it back, smoothing the illustrated page with the palm of her hand. Fran Woolsey sat down beside her.

The seamstress frowned. "You're being very frugal with his money. He's given you an unlimited account. Order what you want. He indicated you'd be lavish; I think he expects it."

"He said that?"

"More or less."

Yes, he would have. He'd always thought her design was to marry for money—in his case, money and White Oak Glen. She was of a mind to cancel the entire order and leave. Two blocks over, the Emporium carried ready-made clothes. They would be fashionable enough.

"I have your measurements. If you don't spend his money, I fear he will, and as generous and handsome as he is, I have my doubts about how much a young man coming from his background knows of women's fashion." She giggled. "You could end up looking quite atrocious."

"You know he would let you pick the designs, Franny."

"We would hope so, but given those conditions, why don't you?"

For the first time today, Juliet smiled. "Very well. I want this dress, but I want the neck lower, and please, less draping. I like the bustle, but could you lessen the train. I dislike long trains;

158

they are so burdensome." She cocked her head at the illustration. "On the shoulders"—she lifted her hands to touch hers—"let's use simple puffs. I don't want a lot of ornamentation."

"Color?"

"Red. Red silk, trimmed in velvet."

"Hmm, I'll check with Mister Hardy, but I fear I may have to order the velvet from New Orleans."

"That's fine. You say you'll have some of the dresses done by the end of the week?"

"I'll need to hire two more seamstresses, but I know several looking for work. He said you needed"—Franny drew her attention and smirked—"'unmentionables,' too."

What a pathetic vision she must have presented to him day before yesterday. "Black," she said.

"I beg your pardon?"

"A black corset trimmed in red silk thread."

"I'll make you a complete set of lingerie for this dress, in black."

"I'll need more. I prefer silk."

Fran reached to her left for a new pattern book. "Nightgowns?"

She did need one, but a purchase at the Emporium would be fine.

Fran opened the magazine. "Silk foulard is popular, low-necked, open to the hem. See here, I could trim the opening in lace."

"Foulard is so thin, I think—"

"You are a married woman now, Missus Dawson."

The feminine voice was unfamiliar, and Juliet looked up to find a lovely, mature woman, with auburn hair and green eyes, in the doorway. The woman smiled at her.

Of course this person smiled at her. She was, after all, *Missus Dawson.*

"Oh, Della, please come in." Franny glanced at the clock on the wall. "I didn't realize it was so late."

"I'm a few minutes early. Do continue with Missus Dawson."

"I'm sorry. I don't believe we've met."

The woman stepped forward, hand extended.

"I do apologize," Fran said, "I thought—"

"It's all right," Juliet said and took the offered hand.

"I'm Della Ross." The woman cocked her head and studied Juliet. "A friend, shall we say, of Morton Severs."

Dumbfounded, Juliet looked at the hand still in hers, and she dropped it.

A throaty laugh escaped Della Ross' painted lips. "Well, I am pleased to make your acquaintance"—she took the chair next to Juliet—"even if you do not return the compliment."

"I apologize. I-I am simply...."

"Yes?"

"Surprised."

"That he has a female friend or that he has friends at all? My dear, you must understand that anyone who has money will most assuredly have friends." She arched a lovely brow. "Wealthy men most especially have female friends."

Juliet fidgeted with her hands, before finally using them to smooth her skirt. "Of course."

"I don't believe you know much about him at all, do you?"

"I know he is a ruthless...."

"Lying, cheating carpetbagger who tried to coerce you into marriage against your will." A broad smile spread across Della Ross' face. "Oh, Juliet Seaton Dawson, you really got him good. I heard everything. Not from Morton, mind you, but from mutual friends."

Juliet glanced at Franny on her left. Coolly, the seamstress returned her gaze, and Juliet blinked. She knew without asking that Franny, too, had heard the full tale.

Juliet and Jeff Dawson must be the talk of Natchez.

"It was so rich, and Jeff Dawson's asking him if he were willing to raise 'Rebel trash,' oh, that was the best part of all."

Juliet started to get up.

Della took her hand. "Please, I do not mean to offend. I applaud what you did."

"Missus Ross," she said through trembling lips, "everyone in Natchez and beyond knows what occurred between me and Jeff Dawson. I have disgraced my family and humiliated myself."

"Oh, my dear, most of us know the fundamentals of sex. We regularly partake of it ourselves. No one knows the details of what you shared with Jeff Dawson. Only you and he know that, and I'm sure he will never tell. And as for your family...." The effect of Della's hesitation was portentous. Then she shrugged. "Well, suffice it to say that your brother alone has brought the Seaton name more disgrace than you ever could. I don't want to appear cruel, but you should be proud to bear the Dawson name."

Her brother and her mother. Della Ross had tactfully avoided Eileen Seaton's liaison with the Union colonel, but her carefully couched words indicated that she knew.

"And as for humiliation, Missus Dawson, the person hanging his head in shame over what occurred at the church yesterday is Morton Severs." Della chuckled softly. "You gave him back ten-fold for what he tried to do to you. He got exactly what he deserved."

Franny nodded in approval, and taking Juliet's other hand, she tugged her back onto the settee.

"You were his mistress?" Juliet asked Della.

"I am his mistress. For the past five years."

"You must be pleased he didn't marry me?"

The auburn-haired beauty gave her a thoughtful look, then pursed her lips. "My dear, his marrying you would have made no difference in my status. I would have continued to be his mistress. You would have been his wife, the mother of his children, and the bearer of an impressive aristocratic pedigree."

"You wouldn't have cared that he was married to another?"

"On moral or personal grounds?"

"Either...both."

"Neither."

Della patted Juliet's hand. "I am what I am, the illegitimate daughter of a prostitute. I first sold my body to a man in New

161

Orleans when I was thirteen. I married Maurice Ross when I was seventeen. I was a widow at nineteen."

"I'm sorry—"

"Don't be. In spite of his good looks, Maurice was a gambler and a scoundrel. He was not a nice person.

"Years later came the war and its armies. Needless to say, I kept busy and was well-fed for my efforts. I got in a bit of trouble in New Orleans with a northern politician several years back and felt compelled to leave the area. I'd just arrived at Under-the-Hill when Morton found me, and I haven't worried about anything since." She gave her head a gentle shake. "First time in my life I've not had to worry about anything.

"Morton likes to tell his friends I'm the widow of a Confederate officer. Makes him look as though he's raped one more part of the South in their eyes. But you see, he takes no more from me than I take from him, perhaps less so. By marrying you, he would have truly accomplished that final goal. I'm so glad you didn't allow it."

Guilt drained the blood from Juliet's cheeks. Had Jeff not shown up when he did, she would have gone through with the wedding.

"And if you're thinking I'm in love with him? No, I'll never love another man. I loved Maurice and him not for long. I care for Morton; he's generous with me." Della's lips curled into a knowing smile. "And I take good care of him in return. He's a poor lover, primarily because he has never bothered to learn what pleases a woman, and I fear he must remain so, because I am no longer compelled to teach, even if he were interested in learning."

Juliet felt returning color heat her cheeks.

"I don't mean to embarrass you, but trust me when I say you would have been glad to have me in the house downtown. He would have bothered you less."

Nausea swelled Juliet's stomach. How horribly close she'd come to a lifetime of emptiness.

But what lay in front of her now?

❦

162

The animosity was growing, feeding on fear and doubt until it sucked the life from truth and left the dry fronds of hate in its wake. Jeff had first sensed it the day they found Lorna Hart's body. Now, suspicious glances and wide berths had become more noticeable. Working white men rarely initiated hand-shakes in greeting anymore, and some were slow to take his hand when offered. So far, no one had outright refused to shake. Scared to, probably.

When Jeff walked into Hawlin's late this morning, Frank Sikes had brought himself to full height and thrust out his chest in challenge. Jeff had simply nodded in silent greeting, then ig-nored the man. He was looking for workers, not trouble, but he wouldn't run from adversity. Will had warned him of the rumors circulating among the ignorant, the prejudiced, and the just plain mean that the murders of Lorna Hart and Susie Watts were committed by some demonic man-beast, a werewolf or a shape-shifting Indian, and he, Jeff Dawson, was that blood-lusting creature. Jeff's growing up poor, then returning rich to the downtrodden South, and now his most recent coup with the aristocratic Juliet Seaton, fueled the resentment, at least among those of his birth class.

The growing isolation from his neighbors worried him. He'd lived through the same thing as a boy, when people believed his granddaddy to be the source of ill-fortune befalling unfriendly acquaintances of the Dawson-Wolfson family. Biased neighbors could prove a greater threat than the marauding wolf and a killer targeting prostitutes. He glanced at his beautiful bride beside him and flicked the wagon reins. What had he drawn her into?

Old Son increased his gait, and the cumbersome, springless wagon bumped along the rough road. Jeff bounced painfully on the seat. Juliet bounced, too. Doggone it, he was going to buy a carriage, something nice and small like Mike Tate's cabriolet.

His workday had taken longer than anticipated, and he'd left her in town shopping, in some form or fashion, most of the after-noon. Except for a jaunt to the Emporium, she had apparently spent most of her time inside Fran Woolsey's shop. He hadn't thought about her being ashamed to show her face in public, and she'd said nothing. Another thoughtless misstep on his part.

"You tired?" he asked her.

"I didn't sleep well."

"Nightmares?"

Juliet looked at him askance. "Of sorts."

"The wolf again?"

"To have dreamed, I would have to have slept." She dropped her eyes. "Mine were waking nightmares."

Fearing a rebuke, he squelched the urge to draw her head against his shoulder. Of course, she hadn't slept well. Neither had he. They needed to put their wedding day behind them.

And the dark rumors? Dear God in heaven, what was going on in Juliet's head? For sure, she was aware of the talk. That she would consider, even for a moment, his being a cold-blooded killer—and her anger and resentment would make that easier— sickened him.

With each passing hour, he wanted her more, and not just for bedding. He wanted her for a lifetime.

"The furniture is in the house?" she asked.

"Yes, the pieces were too big for the nursery." He glanced at her. "So I put them in the room next to it. The one I believe once belonged to your mother."

A pensive expression moved over her face. "The one—"

"Next to mine."

"And where do you want me, husband?"

He wanted her in bed with him, but wasn't about to give her satisfaction by saying so. "I want you in that room, Juliet. The one joining mine."

"For easier access to Jordan Seaton's daughter, whenever you want her?" she said.

He didn't want to fight. Coolly, he assessed her. "*Should* I ever want her."

Her scornful smile challenged those words and pricked his manly pride. And it hurt.

"Don't be so cocksure of yourself, honey. I've had you, remember? Don't think for one darn minute that I'm so overcome by your charms I can't resist you. You'd be wrong. As far as I'm concerned you're still a dishonest, self-centered little cheat."

A bump and they touched at the shoulders. Juliet scooted away.

"Why ever did you marry me?"

"I told you why." He urged the horse faster.

White-knuckled, she clung to the wagon seat. "Fine, then let's leave it at that."

They weren't leaving *it*, or anything else, anywhere. They were wallowing in it, this hurt that they purposefully inflicted on each other.

"*Self*-centered" rang in her head. She might not have thought out the full ramifications of her hastily devised plan two days ago, but she hardly deserved to be considered self-centered.

Juliet opened the drawer of the fine cherry dresser. Jeff was correct about this room, it had been her mother's. Eileen and Jordan Seaton had shared beds from time to time, but never a room. Pent-up grief squeezed her chest, and Juliet slammed the drawer shut. She didn't close it fast enough to prevent an unbidden sob.

Moving her mother's things to the nursery would have to wait till tomorrow; she couldn't deal with it today. Later, she would get rid of the clothing and store the little collection of sentimental treasures properly. Some she would even display.

Jeff dropped her purchases on the bed, and she jumped, then brushed away a tear. He'd caught her crying again, and she hated that. Momentarily, he cleared his throat.

"Juliet...?"

His voice was soft, a concession leading to comfort, but she would not have it. Composing herself, she turned to him.

"Do not concern yourself. Facing Mama's things is what upset me, not your frank comments."

He assessed her for what proved to be an uncomfortably long moment, then looked around the room. "I've hired painters to do the exterior of the house. You may do whatever you want to this room."

"Oh"—she swallowed—"what about the rest of the house?"

"I've hired a decorator from New Orleans. He'll be our guest the first week of December."

Jeff started to move away, but stopped when she took a step toward him.

"Do you know what improvements or changes you want to make?" she asked.

"No. I planned on reviewing the decorator's suggestions."

She nodded and backed away.

"Get your ideas together, Juliet. It's obvious you have some. We can talk about them after dinner if you want."

Chapter Twenty-seven

The wolf howled.

Juliet opened her eyes and stared at darkness. The foreboding cry came again, and she threw back the covers and rose from the bed. The door to Jeff's room was not where it should be, but she found it easily enough and opened it. Hesitant, she called his name. He did not answer, and she stepped into a black void. Blind, she shivered. "Answer me, darn you, I'm scared."

Silence roared back.

A primordial howl splintered the air, and she fell back, inadvertently forcing the door behind her shut.

From the depths of the room, she sensed movement.

She reached out and touched nothing. "Jeff?" she whispered.

"Yes," he answered.

"Did you not hear the howl? The wolf sounds as if it's in the house."

"I know," he said, his voice hoarse. His silhouette, black against black, loomed close and trapped her inside his arms. At his touch, warmth heated her skin. "Don't worry."

Her heart beat faster. Fear vied with desire.

He turned her and pushed, and she fell onto the bed. He settled over her, pinning her beneath him from the hips down. His hands grasped the neck of her nightgown and ripped it open. The beating of her heart drowned the sound of his breathing, and in an instant, chilling fear usurped desire and gave way to terror. He rose on his knees to mount her, and she reached out to ward him off. Her fingers tangled in coarse hair; her hands roamed freely over him. Thick masses of bestial hair covered his body.

She tried to break free, but he met her protest with a snarl, and when she whimpered, he held her tighter. He nuzzled the area below her ear, and

167

she arched back, away from him. His teeth nipped her exposed neck, and she cried out....

Juliet sat up with a start, the cry dead on her lips. Trembling, she drew her knees beneath her chin and hugged herself.

Outside, she heard a muffled bang, followed by a soft howl. Disconcerting yes, but familiar—the wind sighing against the north corner of the house. When she was little, she had often lain in bed and listened to it, a long-lost friend that tonight invaded her dreams and fed her nightmare. Even now, knowing what it was, she found the low moan haunting.

Beyond the window, the waxing moon, three-quarters full, hung against a glittering blanket of blue-black velvet. She kept her curtains open, despite nightfall, to savor these favored nights when the moon was brightest and the bare branches of the trees made the shadows in her room dance. It was late fall, winter waited, and the very best of such nights.

Again the distant bang distracted her, and she rose from the bed. The light from the moon highlighted her pale hands; her silken nightgown glowed a soft white. From the outside, anyone looking up would surely think her a ghost. At the window, she looked toward the woods. The trees were quaking in a wind that rose and fell in violent gusts. Above the trees, the silvery disk of moon looked down, lighting the field that fell away in front of her. Shadows played along the ground, but she could make out nothing certain. Surreal, a scene from another dream.

A frightening prospect, and she pinched herself to make sure she was awake and not about to enter yet another dimension of terror.

Outside, she heard that bang again. The barn door? For sure that was what made the racket, that darn barn door caught in the wind, and it would beat itself to splinters before daylight. She lit the coal oil lamp by her table and closed the curtains. The golden glow of the lamp replaced the silver gleam of moonlight and the room brightened. As a child, she would have crawled into bed with her mother, but she hadn't done that in a very long time.

Then again, she hadn't experienced nightmares for years.

She looked at the door separating her room from Jeff's. It didn't have a lock on it. He told her it never would. She wanted to be with another human being right now, and despite her dream, the human she wanted was Jeff. Still, she was reluctant to wake him, and she certainly didn't want to pass through the door she'd used in the dream, so she pulled on her slippers and a dressing gown and opened the door leading to the hall. Her heart beat faster when she saw his door was open. Inside, as she suspected, she found his bed empty, and the childlike fears evoked by her nightmare evaporated. Either he'd gone out to latch that barn door, or he'd left it to pound in the wind after saddling the big gelding and leaving. And where the devil would he sneak off to in the middle of the night?

She rushed down the stairs, illuminated by moonlight shining through the entry windows. Twice she called his name, but to no avail.

Clearing the last step, she turned down the wide hall leading to the rear of the house, her footsteps but a whisper against the oak floor. At the back door, she peeked out the window. The persistent banging was louder now, but there was no movement outside except for the wind shaking half-naked trees. If he'd gone to close the barn door, he'd have done it by now and come back. With a mild expletive, she went into the dining room, lit a hurricane lamp, and entered the breezeway. In the cookhouse, she pulled the tin lantern from its peg and lit it, then dropped the matchbox into the pocket of her dressing gown.

He could sense her fear, smell it and taste it like the lower animal he became when the need overtook him, an unyielding obsession to possess another, a woman. He didn't simply take her; he forced her. Choosing whores was a practical matter, not a moral one. They were easy to come by, and they were sinners. Given the nature of a whore's life, few people remained resolute in demanding justice for their brutal deaths.

And he needed them, needed them more than any other man

could. So he indulged himself, the power of life and death headier than the actual rape.

He liked to kill around the time of the full moon, his passion heated by the look on his victim's face when he raised the knife. That terrified realization of death in the whore's eyes stimulated him more than the warmth between her legs. That look was there now, on this one's pretty face. He squirmed, pushing the head of his penis against the folds of her womanhood, preparing to take her again.

The wind quieted, and he heard Juliet call her husband's name.

His stomach knotted. Jeff Dawson. *Wolf* Dawson. He looked beyond the trees and up the hill, to the columns of White Oak Glen shimmering in the moonlight. Calmly, he returned his attention to his victim and entered her again, the fourth time in the past hour. There was not a better man than him. The whore had no idea how honored she was. He kissed away the tears on the woman's cheeks, even as his fantasies turned to the unknowing Juliet and what should have been.

Juliet listened for Jeff to respond. When he didn't answer, she ran the final distance to the barn, the cold wind buffeting her in spurts, sometimes battering her to the point where she had to brace herself against it. The gale blew out the lantern, but she didn't need its feeble light. The moonbeams made objects as discernible as they'd have been at first light.

Again, the door fell back against the wall of the barn with a loud clatter, but she ignored it and rushed inside, relieved to be out of the wind, if not the frigid cold. The scents of fresh hay and manure assailed her, and her feet sank in the soft earth. She'd ruin her slippers if she weren't careful.

To her left, she heard a horse moving about and the stomps of the mules in a stall farther down. The animals were nervous with the wind and the incessant banging. The rear door of the barn was closed, making the interior of the building dark and forbidding. She pulled the matches from her pocket and relit the lantern, then walked down the stalls. The cow and Old Son, the large draft horse, were there. So were Jeff's two "handsome" mules. Why he kept them in the barn at night, she didn't know, but she presumed he feared the wolf might get to them. Why then would he go off and leave his barn door...?

A snort sent her jumping back, and with a thumping heart, she held the lantern high. Big brown eyes, bright and moist in the lantern light, watched her. Deacon neighed and brought his head over the rail of the last stall...the one where she and Jeff had made love almost a month ago.

Deacon snorted again, and she touched his soft muzzle. She was aware of his equine scent, the clash of his breath with the freezing air, and the fact that he was, simply put, there. Inescapably, the cold of the clear December night seeped into her bones, and Juliet dropped her free hand to wrap her arm around her scantily-clad body. She looked around the barn. Why she searched, she didn't know. For sure, Jeff wasn't sleeping out here.

Thighs weak and knees knocking, she again called his name. Her voice reverberated through the large structure. The door banged again, and Deacon shied with a nervous whinny. Near the front of the barn, Old Son reared and banged his hindquarters against the side of the building. Inside her skull, Juliet's head pounded in rhythm with her runaway heart.

*I*n the mottled moonlight, he contemplated his victim's face and tried to imagine Juliet beneath him, her skirt bunched at her waist, her naked thighs spread to accommodate him.

The glint of moonlight on the blade must have caught the whore's eye, because her gaze moved to the knife suspended above her head. She screamed into the night, a blood-curdling screech that sent blood surging into his penis and left it granite-hard.

There was nothing, *nothing* like this sweet ecstasy sweeping over him. He needed it as other men needed food and water and air to breathe. And he let her scream, over and over, each cry sending waves of pleasure through him like the successive thrusts of an ordinary man's cock into a woman's vagina. He laughed at her screams. She struggled, but he held her. Then he kissed her open mouth, silencing her.

He moved his head away and plunged the blade into her throat. This one made a funny little sound as air escaped the opening. For a moment, she lived, and he smiled at her, calling her a bitch and a whore. Then he rose on his knees and slammed his penis into her again and again and again until his mind exploded with the power God had graced him with. Sitting back, he ripped open the tear in her throat, covering his hands with blood. On impulse he brought his fingers to his lips and tasted the viscous substance. Tangy, metallic, powerful, and he licked his fingers clean. This trick he'd not tried before, and he liked it.

Exhaustion swept over him and with a throbbing head he fell on all fours, his half-naked body looming over the dead woman. No, not exhausted, sated.

Through the brambles, he stared at the vision of White Oak Glen, his insignificant victim forgotten, his thoughts on Juliet Seaton...Dawson. He stuck the knife in his boot and rose.

The scream of terror soared on the wind, and Juliet spun to face the secured double door at the rear of the barn. The horrific sound emanated on the other side of that door, from the not-too-distant woods. That scream expanded onto another and another until Juliet wrapped her arms over her head and pressed them against her ears to shut the cries out. The lantern swung from her fingertips and hit against her head.

The screams stopped abruptly, and the cold discomfort of the night seeped beneath her skin and into her blood. Another victim was dead; she knew it without having to see a body. She dropped her arms and watched Deacon fidget in his stall.

A howl cleaved the night and touched her with its immediacy. Deacon reared, then screamed. Juliet's heart was trying to fight its way out of her chest. She struggled to the gaping barn door, her movements slowed by the soft earth covering the dirt floor.

Again, the door banged against the exterior wall. She crossed the threshold and reached for....

Air lodged in her gullet, and her outstretched arm fell to her side. From her other hand, the lantern slid over numb fingers to land with a soft clink in the muck. Behind her, the animals stomped in fear, but Juliet could offer no comfort. Her entire being was riveted on the large lupine, its dark eyes fixed on her. The beast stood within arm's reach, and it blocked her escape.

The hair along the animal's back rose on end, and the wolf lowered its head to sniff her feet. Juliet closed her eyes tight and held her breath, and when the nightdress kissed her calves, every part of her stiffened, but for the uncontrolled chatter of her teeth. The beast maneuvered all the way around her, brushing the nightgown against her shins, her calves, and her knees. The cold caress ceased when the beast arrived back where it started. Its ribs brushed the hand at her side. Had the thing been a dog, she would have petted it.

When she opened her eyes, the wolf was still there, watching her, waiting, it seemed, for her to respond. In surrender, she inhaled, and the essence of summer rain overwhelmed the stench of urine-soaked hay and manure, and for a moment, her fear. Through trembling lips she said, "Please, go away."

Jeff called her name, desperation in his voice and in the pounding of his feet. She jerked her head one direction, then the other. He rounded the corner of the barn and almost collided with her.

His body was shaking so hard Jeff couldn't have steadied the rifle and fired it if he'd needed to. Never once had he been like this in wartime. But in battle, all he'd had to lose was his life—he lowered the rifle—not this beautiful woman, who stood before him in the moonlight. Eyes wide, she stared at him. He thought she was in shock.

"What happened?"

Her eyes glistened. She said nothing, and he knew it was because she couldn't.

173

He stood the rifle against the barn wall and gently shook her. "Why did you scream?"

With a shake of her head, she stepped to him and curled her arms around his waist.

Her warmth scorched him. She was without the stiff corsets and stays, or whatever the hell women called them, and too scantily clad to be out on a night like this. Not that he was much better. He'd dressed hastily, too, grabbing whatever was at hand.

"The wolf," she said against his chest. "Did you see it?"

Ah, she was coherent. Terrified, but coherent.

He laid his head on hers, holding her, trying to give back to her the heat she passed to him. "No," he said, "where was it?"

She pushed away and searched the nearby ground. He followed her gaze, then picked up the lantern, which sat on the ground beside her. A chill moved through him that had nothing to do with the cold night. He dropped to one knee and, guiding her out of the way, held the light higher. The thing had walked completely around her.

"It came this close to you." It wasn't a question, the tracks had already provided him the answer, but Juliet nodded anyway. He rose, drawing her to him. This time she was not as pliant.

"What are you doing out here in the dark? You heard the thing howling. You had to know it was about."

"I heard only the wind."

"The wind? I hear the wind moaning around the house constantly, Juliet. These were blood-curdling howls, less than an hour ago. They brought me out of bed in a full sweat."

She stared at him. "I was sleeping. Oh, goodness, I did hear them, but I believed them to be part of my dream."

He stared back at her, then placed an arm around her shoulders, and he bent, intending to pick her up.

"No," she said, "I'll walk. I'm all right now with you here, and you need to carry the rifle. We have to shut this door, too. The animals are frightened."

The animals were, in fact, calm. The wolf was gone.

No tracks led away from where she had stood.

174

—⋆—

"𝒟rink this," he said, pouring her a shot of whiskey. Juliet waved the glass away.

He pulled out the chair next to her at the table. "Drink it. You're cold and frightened. I'm scared you're going to go into shock."

She downed the stuff quickly, knowing it would burn, then waited for the resulting wave of nausea to pass.

"If I haven't gone into shock by now, I doubt I will."

Kitty tromped in from the breezeway, a porcelain pot of hot coffee in her hand. "You ain't got the sense God gave a Bessie bug, girl. What you mean goin' out there in the dark?"

"The barn door was banging, Kitty, didn't you hear it?"

"Yes, I heard it, and I left it go. I'd done heard that wolf, too. Lordy, child, I weren't goin' out there."

"I didn't hear the wolf after I woke. All I heard was the racket down by the barn."

"So you goin' to go alone and shut that barn door? Wake that man"—Kitty glared at Jeff—"him's the one needin' to do that."

"I didn't know..." Goodness, she wasn't going to admit that.

"Kitty," Jeff said, "that's enough fussin' at her. We've got a good two hours before dawn. You need to get back to bed."

Once Kitty's door closed, Juliet reached for the liquor bottle and poured another shot. Throwing back her head, she downed it, then covered her mouth, more symbolic than effective in holding back the vomit. No matter, she didn't throw up.

Jeff closed the bottle and set it on the polished breakfront. Probably afraid she'd end up like Tucker.

"Why did you go out there?" He sat down in front of her.

"I woke up. I had another dream."

"One with the wolf walking on two legs and talking to you?"

"Yes." His summary was sufficient, and she wasn't about to delve into the details of the nightmare. "The wind was howling, and I could hear the barn door banging. When I realized you weren't in your room, I thought you'd gone outside to latch it. But it didn't stop." She looked up and glared at him. "I decided

175

that you must have left the barn door open after saddling up and leaving."

"You thought I'd gone to town?"

"I considered that possibility."

"And you went out to check?"

"I went out to close that noisy door. I couldn't sleep for it."

He looked amused. Well, for sure, he didn't believe that was the real reason she'd gone out, and in truth, it wasn't.

"I was in a hurry. Guess I didn't secure the latch good after I checked the animals." He laughed shortly. "That barn needs some work."

"Jeff?"

"What?"

"The scream you heard?" That topic appeared to sober him somewhat. "I heard it, too. Right before the howl."

"It wasn't you who screamed?"

"No."

"Are you sure? You were so scared—"

"That was before the wolf howled, remember? I never made a sound. I was too terrified." She reached over and touched his hand.

He twined his fingers with hers and squeezed, providing her the support she needed. He always did. Instead of using him that day four weeks ago, she should have confided her predicament. He wouldn't have betrayed her, she knew that now, not even to hurt Tucker.

"That means there's another woman out there," he said. "And she is, no doubt, already dead."

Chapter Twenty-eight

"Oh hell, Floyd, this weren't done by no wolf." Will Howe's voice grew louder with each word. "It's a man."

"Or no ordinary wolf." Against the glare of morning sun, Benton Floyd squinted at Jeff.

Jeff returned the deputy's silent accusation with a cold stare, and Floyd looked away.

"Or no ordinary man," Will countered. "Some person that's less than human, for sure, but it ain't no werewolf."

"Even you believed those stories about Jedediah Wolfson, Howe, and you damn well know it."

"Jedediah Wolfson never did anything like this."

"That's not what I hear tell about the death of that Jarmane Seaton all them years ago," Hank Fletcher said.

Will spit on the ground at Fletcher's feet. "It's the likes of that Jarmane Seaton who'd be doing something like this."

Floyd waved at the blanket-covered body of Ann Davenport, a twenty-two-year-old prostitute who worked the streets and taverns along the river. "I don't know for sure these women are being raped."

"Well, you've figured out they're being murdered, haven't ya?" Will said. "Or are you havin' doubts about that, too? Think maybe they're takin' their own—"

"Will," Jeff said. He caught Will's eye and shook his head. Lord, the man was being confrontational this morning, and Jeff knew his old friend was trying to defend him.

"You know, Howe," Frank Sikes said, "they coulda earned their pay, then that thing kills them."

177

"So, now you're thinkin' they're leavin' town with a wolf?"

"Maybe he becomes a wolf after he leaves with them," Sikes tossed out.

Will straightened awkwardly. His leg had been bothering him lately, and Jeff suspected the cold weather had a lot to do with that.

"I know what you're wantin' people to think, you ignorant ass," Will said to Sikes. "You're one of Severs' cronies, stirrin' up trouble."

"I've had my suspicions about some things from the start."

"And what are they, Sikes?" Jeff's voice dropped the frigid air a couple of degrees.

Frank Sikes met his eyes and glared. "None of this happened till you got here."

"I was born and raised here. You're the newcomer, not me."

"I hear tell it happened more than once before you left for war."

"It happened only once during my lifetime," Jeff said, "to a raping bastard who deserved to have his throat ripped out, but I didn't do it, and there's nothing but a lynch mob's leavings to say my grandfather did. The people who murdered Jedediah Wolfson didn't even have the courage to identify themselves. And I can tell you something else. If me or my grandfather were the ones doing this, we wouldn't be raping and murdering young prostitutes—we'd be finishing off what was left of the Seaton males."

Jeff stepped to one side and kneeled beside the shrouded body on the ground. Despite the damage done to the body, little blood stained the grass and dry leaves. She'd been moved here. "Whoever is doing this becomes a monster after he picks up his victim, Floyd, but he doesn't change form to do so." Jeff pulled the blanket back. "Look at the bruises here on her wrists, and here on her thighs. This woman was forced, and it's the work of a human male."

Floyd shook his head. "It's always on or near your land."

"This is Seaton land—"

"Just a few yards from Dawson's, Howe," Sikes said. "Same with Lorna. And Susie Watts was found in his family's cabin."

Jeff's heart was pounding. He was out last night. Out after the wolf. What was Juliet thinking in the light of day?

"Enough, Sikes," Benton Floyd ordered. "How 'bout gettin' this poor gal out of here. I need to go on over and talk to Wex and Tucker Seaton. Let 'em know another corpse has shown up on their land."

"Then where was he when he weren't here last night?" Kitty started kicking the yards of velvet curtains into a manageable pile while Juliet, looking down on the black woman from the vantage point of a stool, balled her hands into fists.

"He was out hunting the wolf. He said he heard it. You did, too."

"Don't know what you thinkin' taken these heavy curtains down this time of year. Supposed to do this come spring." She looked up, hands on her hips, the pile of curtains wadded at her feet, and a challenge in her eyes. "Might be he's the wolf."

Juliet climbed off the stool and moved it to the center window on the parlor's front wall. Morning light had flooded the room with the removal of the heavy drape, and the sunshine had briefly lightened Juliet's mood, as well. "How can you say that, Kitty? I saw the wolf, and I saw Jeff."

"At the same time?"

"Not exactly —"

"No," Kitty said, pointing a finger at her, "I heard your story last night. First there was the wolf. Then there he was after that wolf done up and disappeared. How you know they not one and the same, and he killed that girl befo' —"

"No more!" Juliet's nails dug into her palms. "I've known and loved you all my life, Kitty Horton. You are as much a part of the Seaton family as this house, but I will not listen to you speak against him. You work in his house now. Not mine and not my mother's. His."

"You know the stories told 'bout his granddaddy —"

179

"Yes, I do. But I never heard anything about him murdering women. Have you?"

"No, but this ain't him, this is his grandson."

"Jeff does not turn into a wolf."

"Maybe he be doin' it as a man," Kitty said softly.

"You see and talk to him every day. You knew him when he was a little boy. Why would you say such a thing?"

"Lot's happened since them days. Rapes and murders and years of war. That do something to a man sometimes. Makes him snap." She snapped her fingers in unison with her words.

"That could be said of most of the male population around here. Anyone could be doing this."

"Not everyone has werewolves in the family."

"There was no werewolf. His grandfather was reputed to be a shape-shifter."

"It all be the same. Some calls it one thing, some another. But it all be the same evil thing in league with the devil."

Sweet Jesus in heaven. How many other people were thinking like Kitty? The woman wasn't isolated here at White Oak Glen. She had friends and extended family. They were all gossiping, spreading falsehoods, and feeding a growing frenzy.

"It's a lie, Kitty. I don't know what's happening out there, but I do know Jeff Dawson is not doing it. I want your loyalty and support. If you're not willing to give that to him, then I insist you give it to me or I want you to leave White Oak Glen today."

Kitty stared at her, and Juliet glared back. It would kill Kitty to leave White Oak Glen again. She had been so certain everything was going to be like "old times." Well, the old times were gone, and unlike Jordan Seaton, Jeff Dawson took a great deal of interest in this farm. Juliet would feel fortunate if she were ever able to wrest full control of even the house from him.

"Why you protectin' him, baby girl? He hurts you, like your daddy hurt my Miss Eileen. I know you two don't share a bed."

Guilt swept Juliet with the realization that Kitty's animosity toward Jeff might stem, at least in part, from the black woman's loyalty to her.

180

"Oh Kitty, he doesn't hurt me like Daddy hurt Mama. I care deeply for him, but we have some problems with trust"—Kitty's eyes widened—"that have nothing to do with the absurd notion that he's a werewolf. I know you are aware of the conditions under which we wed. We hurt each other, and now we have to work through the healing."

"Hmmph," Kitty snorted, more like her old self. "Healin', my ass. Not sleepin' with that man ain't doin' one damn thing, but sendin' him to bed with another."

Which, no doubt, she suspected he was already doing by raping and murdering prostitutes. Kitty bent and started gathering the discarded drapes.

"You needs to get that mess fixed in the bedroom upstairs, missy." Kitty looked over the reams of dusty drapes she was holding. "Know for sure where yo' man is at night instead of stumblin' around in the dark lookin' for him." She ambled toward the door. "And I ain't goin' nowheres. This be my home, and I ain't leavin' you, not knowin' what I do 'bout his people. But I'll support you like you ask. Least till it be proven he's a killer."

"You support him when you're with others," Juliet stated firmly, stepping after Kitty's retreating back.

The large black woman looked over her shoulder. "I can do that, my sweet baby girl, but many already got their own opinion. Folks scared now."

Yes, scared out of their ignorant minds and looking for someone to blame.

Chapter Twenty-nine

"Floyd ain't got no business bein' deputy nor sheriff, neither one, in this county. He don't know nothin about this state or the South, and he don't give a hoot about us taxpayers those bastards in Jackson are robbing."

Jeff couldn't stifle a grin. "Are we still talking a murder investigation here?"

From the chair on his porch, Will spat tobacco juice into the grass. "Puttin' their thievin' asses in the most important jobs in the state and wastin' our money is what I'm talkin' about. They couldn't run a murder investigation if they wanted to. Ain't one of 'em qualified."

"There's many a man who came to office under similar circumstances, who don't do anything but sit on their rear ends and line their pockets."

"Yeah, and we're under the thumbs of 'em right now. Hell, there's those born and raised here would hide a killer just to spite the so-called Congress of the United States and their puppets."

"Maybe a killer killing one of those thievin' puppets," Jeff said, "but I hope not one killing our own women. And never fear, Southerners will regain control. The Republicans are losing their grip. The rest of the nation is fed up with 'em, too."

"Well, I don't know how much time you got. If Floyd don't get a handle on things, you're gonna be facin' a mob."

"An experienced lawman would be lost with a case like this. At least he's trying."

Will sat back and grunted. "Yeah, well, we'll see what you're sayin' when there's a noose 'round your neck."

"That sounds like Southern justice."

"Oh no, boy, they'll truss you up all nice and tight and hang you all legal-like in the light of day. If they can make it look legal, then it is legal."

Jeff feared that possibility less than swinging in the dark of a new moon, the victim of frightened, faceless men, his neighbors, more than one Confederates like him.

"I talked to Miss Juliet this morning about her run-in with that thing," Will said. "Wolves don't act like that."

"I know."

"Do you think she's telling her story right?"

"I saw the tracks. The thing circled her."

"It was getting to know her. Know her scent."

Jeff felt the hair stand along the back of his neck. "Are you thinking it's planning to make her a victim?"

"I'm...." Will furrowed his brow. "I thought you didn't believe in the thing?"

Jeff pulled a blade of grass from the ground and chewed on it a moment. "I don't know what to believe. But I don't like the thing sniffing around Juliet. She said its shoulders fell even with her waist. Do you realize how big it is?"

"Prints already told us that."

"And where did it come from? There hasn't been a confirmed report on a wolf in these parts in over twenty years."

"'Cept for what killed Jarmane Seaton."

"There was no sign."

"Seaton's jugular was missing."

Severed, not missing. "There's sign this time, Will. At least one of the things out there is a wolf."

"Sign that stops in mid-step. I'm not convinced there's a wolf, period."

Jeff shifted his weight; his rump was going to sleep sitting on the floor of Will's porch.

"You know," Will said, "I saw them tracks of the thing killed Josh Perry all them years ago. Big, like this one now."

"You're making a point?"

"Hell, boy. Perry was on a rise that overlooked a path your granddaddy was know'd to walk every mornin' before sunup. Perry's Kentucky rifle was still in his hand when we found him. He was waitin' to bushwhack Jedediah."

A slow smile curled Jeff's lips, and he drew up a knee and laid his arm across it. "Granddaddy loved to tell and retell that one, Will. But you know what? He never once admitted being the one who killed the man."

Will leaned back. "Course he wouldn't."

Jeff laughed. "He let folks believe he'd done it. He used that story to enhance the rumors. Josh Perry's untimely slaying by a vicious wolf played right into Granddaddy's hands."

Will leaned forward, arms on knees. "And Jarmane Seaton?" Jeff said nothing, and Will nodded sagely. "Tell me, son, how many times have you heard of a lone wolf attacking a man, tearing his throat out, and breaking his neck?"

Fifteen years had separated those two deaths that were, for all intents, identical. Behind him and Will, the sun was setting, and the shadow of Will's cabin shaded the ragged yard. Jeff looked toward the darkening woods. The day had been cold, the night would prove worse, but they were prepared. With moonrise, he and Will would venture back toward White Oak Glen and wait...for what he wasn't sure. He only knew that since early fall, when the wolf arrived, weeks would go by with no sign of the animal and no death. The moon would be full in two days, but as best he could recollect, there'd been no killings on the actual full moon, but always a few nights before, and so far, there'd only been one killing per month. December's killing happened last night with Ann Davenport. Finding something tonight was a long shot, but Jeff was uneasy with the rumors and more so with the beast's interest in Juliet. As best he knew, she was the only living person to have seen the thing, and she'd seen it twice.

Jeff closed the bedroom door with a soft click and removed his heavy woolen coat. Moonset occurred three-quarters of an hour ago, the wolf not having made its presence known. Neither

Jeff nor Will heard any screams in the darkness, and Jeff assumed their culprit had not murdered another woman this night.

He stretched his aching limbs. The failure of the wolf to manifest itself was a significant disappointment. A distant howl would have been enough to assure Will that he was not the wolf. Jeff knew Will didn't believe him to be a woman killer, but Will did believe Jedediah Wolfson could change from man to beast at will. He suspected Will considered it a possibility he could do the same.

"Where have you been?"

He whipped around from the high-backed chair over which he'd draped his coat. Instantly, his testes tightened. Juliet was so damn beautiful, slightly unkempt, with wisps of hair escaping from the golden braid over her shoulder. Faint shadows lay beneath her eyes. She hadn't slept.

He raised the wide-brimmed felt hat from his head in mock salute and tossed it on the chair, then proceeded to remove his britches. He'd be a sight for her in his red underwear. Watching her, he pushed at the waistband and smirked.

Her nostrils flared. "The sun will be up soon, Jeff. Where have you been all night?"

His gut clenched at the tremor in her voice and the anger in her stance. "You think I've been out murdering women, Juliet, is that what you think?"

"Your murdering women is not what I fear, you horse's ass." She stepped forward, and the scent of jasmine engulfed him. For a brief instant that smell was the only thing registering in his head. Then she grabbed his shirt, pulled him roughly to her, and sniffed at him.

He laughed. "Something you learned from your friend the wolf, sweetheart?"

"Something I learned the first time we made love."

"The only time we made...." He narrowed his eyes. "You think I've been with another woman?"

She swallowed—her pride as well as her spit it seemed. "Have you?"

185

Jealous. The woman was jealous, and suddenly every fiber of his being tingled with desire.

"Should I have been?"

"What kind of a question is that? You're married to me."

"In name only. You've not shared my bed since we wed."

Her eyes glinted, and his penis surged to life. "That was your doing," she said, "not mine."

"The hell you say."

"Yes, I do say. You put me out of your room."

"What did you expect? You told me you hated me. Did you think I'd drag you to my bed and force myself on you?"

"Who said anything about force? We had a deal. I become mistress of White Oak Glen, and you take"—she tightened her lips—"you lie with Jordan Seaton's daughter whenever you wish."

"And you would have been accommodating?"

"Certainly. I live up to the bargains I make."

"You didn't with Morton Severs."

Her eyes widened. "He is the one who abrogated the agreement, not I."

Jeff coughed out a laugh. "After you gave yourself to me."

"I didn't promise him a virgin," she said loudly. "I agreed to marry him to protect my brother. He deserved what he got."

"And so do I," he said, his voice cool.

And he did deserve what he got. Thank sweet heaven she was what he wanted.

"Look between my legs, Juliet."

She hesitated, then looked at the crotch of his woolen underwear. Defiantly, she raised her eyes and met his.

"I want you now. Are you ready to live up to your end of the bargain?"

"Have you been with another?"

"Qualifying the agreement, sweetheart?"

"Yes," she hissed, "have you?"

Damn, she was jealous. Whether it was a matter of how she felt about him or simple pride, he didn't know. "Did I smell like I'd been with another?"

"No."

Jeff grinned at her, but said nothing more. After a moment, she tightened her lips and snatched for the buttons at the neck of her nightgown.

He watched her, amused by her rough movements. When she was done, the nightgown gaped open to reveal the gentle swell of her breasts. Anticipation sobered him, and his breath came harder.

"Undo your braid."

Her gaze flicked to his in surprise, but she reached up and removed the ribbon holding her hair. He helped her pull out the plaits, then ran his fingers through the silken strands, caressing her scalp with his fingertips.

He stepped back. Her hair hung in dark golden waves over her shoulders, and his erection strained against his underwear.

"Remove your gown." To his own ears, his voice sounded hoarse and distant, and he didn't fail to notice Juliet's subtle stiffening with his words.

"I've asked nothing of you so far," he said, cutting her off when she started to speak.

Glaring at him, she curled her fingers into the nightgown.

His body trembled with self-imposed restraint, and he wished like hell he had something cold to drink. But he held himself in check and watched the hem rise.

"You'll turn around, please?"

He almost fell forward. He did allow his parched mouth to fall open, but that lapse was momentary. Recovered, Jeff found her eyes, then cocked his head in disbelief. "I will not. That would defeat the purpose."

Juliet dropped her gaze, and the nightgown continued to rise, exposing her calves, thighs...his breath caught in his throat when the dark triangle of her pubic mound came into view, then her flat belly, and finally her luscious breasts with their large, dark nipples. She pulled the gown over her head and tossed it aside, wrong side out. She caught his eye, but only for a moment. He wasn't interested in her face right then, but focused his attention

187

on her naked body. When he again sought her face, she was blushing and had turned her head to the side. Such a lovely profile. She moved her hands....

He stepped forward to stop her from covering herself and, smoothing his hands down the length of her arms, he pinned her wrists behind her in a gentle hold. "I have embarrassed you, again," he breathed in her ear, "and I apologize. I didn't mean to, but you are so beautiful to look at."

She turned her face to his in invitation, and he caught her lips, tickling them with the tip of his tongue. Instantly, she opened her mouth, and he entered. She maneuvered closer to him. Pulling back, he dipped his head and took a breast in his mouth. She groaned, and his tongue swirled over her nipple until it was a hard nub. He freed her wrists and embraced her before flattening a hand over her slender bottom. She was tight against him, and he held her there, assuaging his stiff penis against her pelvis. She whimpered. Sheer masculine need surged through him, and holding her by the neck, he plunged his tongue inside the recesses of her mouth before he lifted her in his arms, and hers circled his neck. He found her lips again and, hugging her naked body, turned to the bed and laid her on the chintz spread, then pushed her into the pillows.

His eyes raked the length of her, and she bent one knee, drawing it up to cover her womanhood. In the soft light of the oil lamp, her hair and pale skin glowed against the dark green silk. He grasped his shirt and pulled it over his head.

"It's cold in here. Why didn't you say anything, my nude beauty?"

"Because this is what you want. Isn't that my role, to please?"

So that was how she was going to be. If he hadn't been so hard with want, he might have mustered the strength right then to plop her back in her own damn bed, but he wasn't going to punish himself because of her stubborn pride, and he hadn't forgotten the groan of pleasure she'd been unable to suppress when he'd suckled her breast.

He yanked at the bedspread and kissed her brutally before

tucking her beneath four layers of quilts and blankets. "That's right, Juliet. My whore, my money, my pleasure."

Or so she thought. He would make her scream in satisfaction tonight if it killed him.

Still in his woolen drawers, he rose and made a fire in the grate.

"It seems a lot of trouble to go to," she said, "for a few minutes pleasure."

"Did I spend only a few minutes with you the first time we made love?"

"It didn't take you long, as I recall."

"We were together for more than two hours and a goodly portion of my pleasure, and my stimulation, derived from fulfilling your desires."

She shook her head. "Things are different now."

"How so?"

"Because I know you want me to scream out in pleasure to mock my father, who you hope is watching us from above."

Ah yes, the cruel, goading words he'd spoken on their wedding day, because he was too angry and prideful to tell her the truth. The old anger surged through him anew—twice as strong this time because moments ago he'd thought they were so close. Methodically he pushed his drawers over his hips and stepped out of them.

"From hell, Juliet, not from above. And yes," he said, "I hope the bastard is watching me arouse his daughter, and she *will* scream out in pleasure, I'll see to it."

She sat up, eyes hard. "You are as disgusting as ever, Jeff Dawson. I can't tell you how much the thought of our copulating while my father's ghost watches excites me."

The thought didn't excite him much either, and he snatched the covers from her naked body. Five feet away the fire hissed and crackled and bathed them in amber warmth. Her jaw locked, but she lay back stiffly on the pillows. "You can't rape me, I won't let you. I won't resist. I told you I'd live up to my part of our agreement, and I will."

189

"Yes, because you worry what your neighbors will say if you can't keep me home."

"And why should I care what the neighbors think after what you've told them." She smiled sweetly. "Truly, sir, I simply wish to be what you want me to be."

The hell she did. She was still bitter and angry. She'd come to him before she was ready—done it because she felt she had to, and now her resentment was besting her. Well, he had his pride, too, and he wasn't going to leave her any. Not this time.

"You plan to give yourself to me, and think I'll be happy with what you offer, but you plan to give nothing, emotionally, of yourself in return?"

"Why should you care?"

He grinned, hoping the expression appeared as unpleasant as he felt. "And what victory would I find in that, Juliet?"

"And that's what I am, isn't it? A victory over the Seatons."

Right now the Seatons, in the form of the youngest female, were winning hands down, and that angered him. With one quick move, he fell over her, pinning her to the mattress and covering her mouth with his. She responded immediately, wrapping her arms around his shoulders and pulling him to her. Her tongue twined with his. He felt one foot move over his rump. Then he felt the other. She had positioned herself for his entry. Just get it over with, that's what she wanted. She was still tight and dry, not ready for him at all. Well, she wasn't going to get her way, and he was going to shock the hell out of her at the same time.

With the heel of her foot, Juliet coaxed Jeff forward. He responded by nuzzling her behind the ear. She tried to pull away, but trapped beneath him, she could go nowhere. He was angry, but he wasn't responding in an angry way. He was going to try to force her to enjoy him. Well, she wasn't going to let that happen.

He kissed her again, and she responded in kind, hoping to light an irresistible fire in him before he managed to light one in her—the memory of his touch was too strong, and now the feel of his hands and his tongue ignited the smoldering embers.

Cupping her jaw in his hands, Jeff tilted her head back, and with his tongue, he traced a path under her chin and down her throat, stopping between her breasts. His path deviated at that point, licking a wide swath beneath a breast, then circling the nipple with that same insidious tongue before taking it in his mouth and suckling. She arched against him, half resistance, half surrender. He knew it, too, damn him. Holding her down at the shoulder, he covered the other breast with a large, callused palm and began to knead, intermittently pinching the nipple until it was erect. He shifted his body in response to her moan and suckled that breast, and she despised herself for her body's betrayal. She pushed him away at the shoulders.

"Take me, damn you. I want you to now."

He caught her hands and thrust them above her head. Below a lock of auburn hair that fell across his forehead, his blue eyes bored into hers. He was so handsome.

"In good time, sweetheart."

Veiled anger oozed from him. She closed her eyes. Why had she provoked him? Pride, anger, resentment at what she felt was her duty—incited by Kitty's words.

Then he'd failed to come home tonight.

"Look at me."

She opened her eyes to find him on all fours, his arms and legs straddling her body. She was no longer pinned beneath him.

"Look at my chest," he said, bending his head to kiss her behind the ear.

She did and her heartbeat increased.

"Look farther down, Juliet."

Instead she looked in his eyes.

"You say you want me. Look down at me."

She tightened her lips, but obeyed.

His penis was large and stiff, jutting out from a dark nest of pubic hair, ready to enter her. She met his eyes and smiled, again stroking his legs and rump with her foot.

He smiled back. "Just one more thing to do, sweetheart, and that's get you ready."

He moved away from her, but she sat up after him. "I am ready."

He laughed at that and pushed her back. "Who do you think you're talking to? You're the novice here, not me." He returned to her breasts, licking, kneading, and suckling, then left them tingling and ran that wayward tongue down her torso to swish at her belly button. He moved lower, and she started to sit up. "Lie down," he said and skipped to her knee. Relieved he passed over her womanhood, she did.

Sitting on the back of his legs, he raised her calf high, caressing it between the ankle and knee with the tip of his tongue. At the back of the knee he stopped, then bent the leg and kissed her inner thigh. She sucked in a breath of air. All she could see of him now was the top of his head, but she felt his tongue moving relentlessly up her thigh. His thumb touched her womanhood, and she gasped. He chuckled and slid his tongue upward.

She startled and sat up, and he immediately rose to face her. "I said lie down."

She tensed. "You're not going to do this to me."

"What?"

"Sodomize me."

"Yes, I am."

"No."

She pushed at him, but he caught her wrists and, crushing her to the mattress, pinned them above her head. Bringing his face close to hers, he said, "Do you see the suspenders over there on the chair?"

Dread crept over her, and she looked, but didn't allow him the satisfaction of response.

"There is so much more to lovemaking than sticking one's cock inside a woman and ravishing her, Juliet. There's any number of delicious perversions. Sodomy is one; bondage another. If you don't lie still and leave your hands right where I have them, I'll tie you up with those suspenders, and I'll still have my way with you."

"What you are proposing is deviant."

192

"Then you have a lifetime of deviance before you."

She opened her mouth to speak, but he kissed her quick, then licked her ear. Liquid heat warmed the apex of her legs. He moved over her again, caressing her body with his tongue, and she steeled herself against his onslaught.

So be it, she told herself. This perversion, by its very nature, would revolt her and spare her the humiliation of expressing the pleasure he was so sure he'd earn.

She closed her eyes to shut out his sorcery, but the magic was in his fingers and his tongue and closing her eyes made her body more sensitive still. So she opened them and watched his head and squirmed when his breath caressed her genitals, but he held her tight at the hips.

"Shh, baby, it's gonna be all right."

He licked her, and she jumped, the shock deliciously painful. Damn him, damn him, damn him.

She pushed away with her foot, a tactical error, for it opened her legs more to him, and he flattened his palms on her thighs, spreading her and leaving her open and exposed. Totally vulnerable.

"I'm going to feast on you, Juliet. I'm going to gobble you up, and you're going to love it."

No longer resisting his machinations, she arched back. The tip of his tongue, soft and moist, touched her womanhood, and without conscious thought this time, she closed her eyes and whispered his name. His tongue was moving over her with ferocious force, and she pushed against it. Sensation pooled between her legs, then expanded to an all-consuming pressure....

Jeff raised his head and moved his body, then filled her with his manhood before beginning the cyclic thrusts she remembered from their first time. He grasped her to him, and the pressure surged over her body in waves of uncompromising pleasure. She cried out, clinging to and pushing against him as she drew out the last tiny spark of pleasure, coincident with his final grunt.

He was still inside her, her head on his shoulder, and her arms and legs, so weak they might have been atrophied, tangled around him like a muscadine vine. With a pleasant shudder, Juliet pulled back. Jeff sat straighter and watched her. At that moment, she swore his eyes reflected the same shock she felt.

Juliet was looking at him as if she had no idea who or where she was. Never in his life had he experienced anything like their simultaneous orgasm. She hadn't, for sure, and from the sound of her release, he knew she had enjoyed immense pleasure.

Only then did it dawn on him he'd won.

She looked around, then started to disentangle herself from him. He wasn't going to have that. The victory was his. With lupine agility, he rose and swept her into his arms. Spinning around, he headed for her bedroom where he plopped her naked body atop her bed. Wide-eyed, she stared at him.

"The next time you need me, ask. I can be accommodating, and that's the only way you'll have me." He turned and left.

Chapter Thirty

He wished she'd slammed the door after him when he returned to his own room that night, or rather morning, but she hadn't. She'd closed it without making a sound. Her anger would have justified his preemptive strike. Now, he figured either she didn't care or she was hurt. Given those options, he hoped for the latter.

She'd risen an hour or so after their tryst, and he doubted she'd gotten any sleep at all. After accepting that she wasn't going to come crawling back to him, he'd fallen into a deep, physically-sated slumber where he'd remained for most of five straight hours. When he woke, he heard her calling to the painters outside.

That had been yesterday.

Juliet hadn't exactly been hiding in her room, but even after a day and a half, she was still having difficulty meeting his gaze. He hoped it wasn't because she was ashamed of crying out during their lovemaking and told himself her reticence stemmed more from damaged pride than anything else. He had possessed and dominated her, even though she'd sworn he wouldn't. Thank goodness she lacked the experience to realize she had done the same to him.

"Water him for me, Toby, then rub him down," he said, handing the gelding's reins to the young Negro. "Mister Howe's here?"

"Yes, sir. Got here 'bout an hour after you left."

Jeff had been to Will's place this morning, wanting him to come and help check the woods in daylight. He wasn't convinced Benton Floyd was looking for anything that would shed useful light on the killings. Like the night before it, there'd been no

195

howling last night. Tonight was a full moon, then it would begin to wane. Jeff didn't expect another killing for a month. Again and again the monster would kill until they caught it...*him.*

He pushed open the cookhouse door, and Juliet's laughter died on her lips. His eyes found hers.

She sat at the small table in the back of the room, near the stove. Will sat across from her. "Thank goodness you're back," Will said. "Might be I can win a game now."

Jeff dropped Juliet's gaze and took in the checkerboard between his wife and his friend. Juliet rose.

"Now that your regular opponent is back, Mister Howe, I'll see to the builders."

Jeff watched her slender back disappear into the breezeway. She had the architects working on a design to make the kitchen part of the house proper, and a contractor was adding indoor plumbing to the old nursery, which Juliet was converting to a real bathroom. He wondered if she'd chosen that room to convert because she didn't plan on bearing him children.

Will motioned him to Juliet's seat and set up the board.

"She beat you?" Jeff asked.

"Two out of six games."

Well, damn, he'd best limit his game with Juliet to sex. He rarely beat Will at checkers. It had gotten to the point he didn't like playing with him.

"You've never played her?"

Jeff removed his hat and eyed the board. "Don't play checkers unless you're here, Will." He looked up. Will's blue eyes pierced him from beneath bushy eyebrows.

"Things still not right betwixt you two, are they?"

It was none of Will's concern.

"She's yet to forgive you for your wedding day?"

Jeff placed an index finger on a checker and moved it. "I'm beginning to doubt whether she ever will."

"Hmmph. You two are a fine couple. Handsome the both of you. You'll make beautiful children together."

Jeff glanced at him. "Don't you have to have sex for that?"

196

Will frowned, then laughed. "Don't believe you ain't beddin' that girl, Wolf Dawson. You're a damn disgrace to manhood if you're not."

Yeah, he bedded her, but not nearly as often as he'd like.

"Went up to your place early," Jeff said. "Wondered where you were. Wanted to check the woods the back way."

"Did you?"

"I checked, but didn't find anything. The killer moved those women from wherever it was he murdered them, Will. I'm sure of it. He puts them out where they'll be easy to find. The place, or places, where the killings happen could yield evidence as to who he is. Assuming this bastard's reasonably intelligent, that could be another reason he moves the bodies. I've talked to Floyd about getting hunting dogs in here."

Will jumped him, looked up, and winked. "You ain't too sharp this mornin', boy. What did he say?"

"He's not convinced the bodies are being moved; he can't understand a killer wanting the bodies to be found."

Will's eyes bulged when Jeff double-jumped him. "Well, I know a fella named Jim Ferguson lives about two miles north of me. He's got good hunting dogs. We need to talk to him."

"We can talk, but I doubt it will do much good. "

"Why not?"

"I've got two problems. First the search will include Seaton land. Tucker won't cooperate, and, second, as in days of old, the common folk are rallying 'round the Seatons. People from these parts are becoming less and less willing to work for me."

With his chin, Will pointed to the door through which Juliet had disappeared. "That why she's dealing with the workmen?"

"That's one reason." He smirked at Will. "The main reason is she's plain good at running the house, and she knows what she wants."

Will chuckled at that. "Guess we knew that, didn't we? She knows what she wants and goes after it." He gave Jeff a knowing nod. "Like the day before you wed. They might have forced her to marry Severs, but she damn sure got who she wanted before they did." Will leaned over the board. "Girl loves you, son, whether you or her realizes it. Get her into bed and make some babies."

"Mary?" Juliet rose so quickly, she had to grasp the arm of the settee to keep from falling back onto it.

"Hello, Missus Dawson." Mary Tate, pulling mittens from her hands, stepped into the parlor. Michael Tate followed. "Kitty said we'd find you in here. We gave up on getting a formal invitation, so we just took it upon ourselves to come on our own."

"I'm sorry, Mary, we've had no visitors."

A light laugh bubbled from Mary's throat, and she handed Juliet her coat. "Michael and I thought so. Lying low, considering the wedding?"

Heat washed over Juliet. She didn't want to think about her wedding day, much less discuss it with the minister's wife. How sad, she thought, hanging Mary's coat on the hall tree, that she would always remember her wedding day with a cringe.

"I told Michael," Mary said, taking a seat when Juliet reentered the parlor, "that we must get you and Jeff out of this self-imposed purgatory and back into the fold with your friends and neighbors."

Juliet had neighbors, but she didn't consider many around here friends. Her mother had become a recluse following the war, and Tucker's drinking had exacerbated the family's isolation. Juliet was a member of the Methodist Church, her family had attended it since her grandfather's days, but beyond Sunday service she played little role in the congregation.

With characteristic efficiency, Kitty appeared with the coffee service, and Juliet asked after Jeff's whereabouts. At the barn, Kitty told her and said she would fetch him.

Mary giggled. "I don't think you know this, but Missus Iverson stayed and watched your wedding. Ida was with her. They were sitting on the bride's side. Did you see them?"

Except for her family, Juliet could not recall one face from the pews. She shook her head. The Iversons had been members of the Methodist church for as long as the Seatons and the Dobbins before them. Missus Iverson was nearing eighty. Her daughter Ida, a war widow since '63, lived with her. Juliet certainly hadn't made out a guest list, and Aunt Lilith had scarcely been in the area long enough to know who to invite to the ceremony. More than likely, half the congregation had crashed the aborted Seaton-Severs ceremony.

"Anyway," Mary continued, "Ida told me her mother leaned over to her after the vows and said, 'That was the most romantic thing I have ever seen in my life.' Ida asked her what she was talking about, and old Missus Iverson told her daughter she was a nitwit. She was talking about 'how that handsome young man rushed into the church and told everyone he fornicated with Juliet Seaton in his barn, just to keep her from marrying that awful old Yankee, then married her himself.' I do believe, Juliet, Missus Iverson thinks Jeff made the whole story up."

Juliet mouthed a silent "O." For certain, Mary was trying to make her feel better. Missus Iverson was senile, for Pete's sake.

"The point my lovely wife is trying to make," Michael said, taking Juliet's hand, "is that many people are happy for you and pleased Morton Severs received his just deserts. No one worth worrying about is judging you."

Della Ross had intimated the same thing, but Juliet thought she'd understood that woman's motive.

"Christmas is in three days," Mary said quickly. "Michael is planning a wonderful service, and we'll have a potluck after in the vestry. Slim Bowers is finding us a tree this year."

Michael Tate rose when Jeff entered the room, and Jeff took the man's hand in a friendly shake.

"Mike and Mary have come about Christmas," Juliet said from where she sat next to Mary. "It's in three days."

Poor Juliet sounded bewildered, and he wondered if she had indeed lost track of the date. "I know, sweetheart."

She smiled at the endearment, and that gave him heart.

"We've come to invite you to the Christmas Day service and

potluck," Mike said to him. "We've not seen you since the wedding."

"We fear you've been suffering from embarrassment," Mary added. Quickly, she glanced at her husband, and he nodded at her. Thus encouraged, Mary grabbed Juliet's hand and beamed first at her, then Jeff. "History is being made in Warren County right now. The entire South is about to rise up and throw off these petty tyrants who have made a mockery of honesty and decency, not to mention the Constitution." Again, she turned her enthusiasm on Juliet. "We're gonna run these filthy Republicans out of Dixie altogether. Oh, you two, 1875 is going to be a glorious year. We want the Dawsons to come and make themselves part of our little community's future."

Jeff couldn't help but smile. He glanced at a patently dumbfounded Juliet. She wanted to say something to him, he could tell, but suspected she found it awkward to speak in front of the excited Mary. Throwing off the venomous Yankee horde was one thing, having Christmas with her neighbors was another; and the latter, Jeff was sure, explained Juliet's reticence.

"You don't have to make a decision now," Mike said, watching them. "We wanted you to know you were welcome." He stepped away from the women and motioned for Jeff to follow. Discreetly, Jeff caught Juliet's eye. She bit her lip, and he winked, hoping to reassure her. Social interaction at present made his bride uncomfortable. As for him, he wanted to make a place for himself. That's why he had come home. He looked beyond the dingy parlor to the open foyer and listened to the hammers and saws singing in the soon-to-be bathroom upstairs. Within two years, White Oak Glen would once again be a showplace, fit for entertaining.

He followed Mike into the foyer, while a spirited Mary chattered on. Once she got going, it seemed, Mary was one of those talkers who didn't require much in the way of response.

"I hope Grant doesn't send in troops; Mary will be devastated," Mike said when they were out of earshot.

"Whether he sends them in or not, Mike, it's over. The very

fact that Ames has been asking for Federal troops since four months into his administration tells the tale. I don't think the rest of the nation will tolerate reinstating martial law in the South. Except for the parasites still feeding off the carnage, Northerners want to put the war behind them."

Mike sighed. "You need to shove some things behind you, too. You really need to come Christmas. There are dark rumors circulating all over this part of the county."

"About the murders?"

"And the wolf." Mike shook his head. "There's little I can do to sway the talk going around in the dens where those unfortunate young women came from, but the people in my church are your neighbors. They need to get to know you."

Jeff shot him a wry grin. "A lot of them do know me. There are still some left who knew my grandfather. That's where the legend comes from, Mike. Until now, shape-shifting has never been attributed to me."

"I don't believe in such tales, my friend. As far as I'm concerned, werewolves died out in the Middle Ages. Most reasonable people believe the same way I do."

"The mutilated bodies of those women are more than just scary stories. They're real."

"And a real man with a twisted passion is producing them."

Out of the corner of his eye, Jeff saw the women step into the foyer. Mike had his back to them.

"You've a passion for one woman, Jeff. I've seen that, but I don't believe it's twisted, and I see she remains very much alive."

Jeff's eyes met Juliet's. Mary cleared her throat, and Mike jerked around. Color flushed Juliet's cheeks, and Mike smiled in obvious embarrassment. Then he looked at his wife. "I think it's time we left, my darling defender of the Cause."

When Jeff turned from showing the Tates out the front door, he found Juliet, arms folded beneath her breasts, watching him. "If the Reverend Tate only knew," she said with a smirk, "that I am the one with the passion." She dropped her hands to her sides. "And you a beleaguered Puritan."

With a haughty toss of her head, she turned her back on him. He snagged her wrist and yanked her back to him. When he turned her in his arms, she lost her balance and fell against his chest. Not giving her a chance to recover, he found her mouth and plundered its interior in a passionate kiss. To his surprise, she responded in kind, circling his neck with one arm and greeting his tongue with hers. His body was trembling by the time he pulled back to see her face.

"Does this make me a slut, Jeff Dawson?"

"Yes, and I like it."

She smiled sweetly. "And do you intend to do anything about it, darling?"

He narrowed his eyes and caressed her left breast, and she sighed.

"I could take you on this floor right now," he said, "and you would not resist me."

Her lips curled. "Yes you could, you bastard, and we both know I'd love it. But you won't, because I have to *ask* first." She raised her brows, mocking him. "And that, sir, is something I have no intention of doing." Holding his biceps, she steadied herself on her feet. "Now, if you are done with me, I will check on the painters."

Chapter Thirty-one

"Where's your husband?"

From where she stood on the shaded front portico, Juliet shifted her gaze from Wex to her brother. "He's not here."

Tucker pulled the rifle he toted from his shoulder. "Sleeping? Been out all night again?"

She whipped her head back to face Wex, who stood at the bottom of the porch steps. "There's been another murder?"

Wex shook his head, but before he could speak, Tucker said, "He's killed another cow. Mutilates our stock on a routine basis."

Tucker wasn't drunk, but he'd been drinking. She figured he wouldn't have the courage to be here otherwise.

"Juliet...," Wex began. Tucker stepped forward, his mouth set in an angry line, but Wex held up a hand. "Let me handle this."

Chest heaving, Juliet focused on her cousin, his green eyes watching her from beneath the brim of his hat.

"Was the cow eaten?" she asked.

"Partly."

"So you are implying that Jeff snuck out last night, killed a cow, then sat in a cold, dark field and ate it raw?"

"A wolf—"

"I'd believe it," Tucker said. "The man isn't human, I'm telling you. He's dead, and what you sleep with at night is a demon."

He's not dead," she said, "your bullet missed—"

"No, it didn't. I..."

Tucker reddened, and Juliet drew herself up stiffly.

"A vital organ," she finished. Good lord, she hoped her look conveyed the contempt she felt. "You sicken me, Tucker. You shot a fellow soldier in the back."

Instantly, Tucker composed himself. "You think that's unusual? It was the perfect way to get rid of someone you didn't want around. I wasn't the first soldier to use that tactic, and I won't be the last."

Adrenaline surged through her, overpowering what had become mild but persistent nausea. "Rafe was part of it, wasn't he?" Of all her brothers, black-eyed, black-haired Rafe had been her favorite.

Tucker's ensuing smile was downright ugly. "It was his idea. We knew the minute we joined up with the Sixth Mississippi we needed to get rid of him." He leaned toward her. "Too much had happened in the past. Him or us. You think he wouldn't have done the same, given an opportunity?"

She wanted to cry, but instead, she bridled. "No, I don't. The difference between you and Rafe and Jeff Dawson is that you and Rafe behaved like cowards. You were afraid of him because of what you'd done to his sister, afraid and ashamed. You lacked the courage to admit your guilt or face him like men. Get off my land, Tucker."

"Your land?" He howled with laughter. "Got it back, didn't you, little sister. Whored your way back into White Oak Glen, like our m-mother w-whored herself...."

Bile burned her chest. Behind her, on scaffolds, the painters worked, but she knew they were listening to the exchange.

She felt dirty.

Head bowed, Tucker swiped at his eyes, and Wexford pushed his shoulder. "Go home, Tucker. I still need to talk to Juliet about the wolf. That's why we came here, remember?"

Tucker looked up quickly, the rims of his eyes red. He stepped back and looked at the house. "The man is dead," he shouted, making sure the painters heard. "He's a demon, and now he's a butcher."

Her body shaking with cold fury, Juliet charged down the steps. Wexford forestalled her attack with a quick arm hook around her waist. Tucker was already making his way down the long slope toward the woods and home. He turned back once to taunt her. Juliet pushed on Wexford's constraining arm, and he let her go.

"We've suffered no attacks," she said, anticipating his question. "Perhaps that's because we have only two horses, a milk cow, and two mules, and they're locked safely in the barn at night."

"I can't lock up twenty head of cattle every night. I've got to kill this monster."

Juliet brushed a wayward strand of hair off her forehead. "And you want Jeff to help you hunt it?" She folded her arms under her breasts. "Well, I will not have him with you, Wex, not with Tucker. He'd go out and never come back."

Wexford glanced at the painters. "Let's walk," he said and touched her arm. He guided her away from the house, not speaking until they neared the woods she loved.

"Something else is at work here, Juliet," he said.

"What do you mean?"

"This creature is not a normal wolf."

"I think everyone would agree with you on that. It's large and smart, and—"

"What of the women?"

"Jeff doesn't believe the wolf is killing the women."

"The arrival of the wolf and the murders coincide."

He helped her climb the rail fence, then jumped the barrier to stand next to her on the Seaton side. The cow path was a few feet away, and beyond that the cold creek gurgled its way to the river. She stepped forward and breathed in the frigid air, then drew her shawl over the sleeves of her wool dress. It was damp and even colder in the shade. She hadn't been here since the day she'd crossed from the old house to White Oak Glen and given herself to Jeff.

Why was she here now?

Wex moved up behind her and attempted to direct her toward the path, but she stood her ground. She didn't want to go farther into the woods. The white columns of her home stood well behind her, but still were in sight. She and Wex had come far enough.

"What are you trying to say, Wex?"

He snorted. "Don't you see what's happening?"

Pretentiously, she widened her eyes. "You mean you understand it?"

"Maybe we should listen to Tucker."

"For what possible reason?"

"He could be right about some things."

"He is no more than a back-shooting coward, twisted by fear and guilt into—"

"A wolf is eating our stock, Juliet. A man isn't doing that. The women are raped, a wolf isn't doing that."

"That proves there are two different killers."

"What if it's a combination of the two?"

"A man-wolf?" she asked, not trying to hide her irritation.

"Don't discount the possibility."

"And my husband is supposed to be it?"

"There's the family legend."

"Not of rape."

Wexford placed his hands on her shoulders and gently shook her. There was no threat in his touch, but there was arrogance in his eyes, and Juliet reflected once again on how good-looking Seaton men were and what a pity the majority had few other positive traits.

Still, it was unfair to attribute her father's, brothers', and Jarmane Seaton's shortcomings to Wex. He had come here four months ago and worked her farm like a dog, shunning friendship, even help, unless he were desperate. Yes, his efforts were in his own self-interest, but the benefit went to all, while her brother drank his life away and squandered what little the family had left.

She shook off his hands, and he stepped back.

"What are you up to?" she asked. "I know you well enough to know you've not fallen prey to Tucker's nonsense."

She turned to go, but he seized her arm. "I have to consider the possibility you're in danger where you are."

His domineering angered her almost as much as his promoting himself to family patriarch. Maybe his game was too clear. Well, she was a married woman. She had never been his responsibility and never intended to be. She lifted her arm to free herself, but he tightened his grasp.

Bushes rustled behind them. Wex pivoted, his gaze skimming the thick foliage. Her heart quickened its pace, and a breeze stirred the dead leaves still clinging to branches far above their heads. "It's the wind," she whispered, managing now to detach her arm from Wex's hold.

He jerked back around at the sound of her voice. Uneasy, she stepped toward the fence and the clear field. "No," he said and quickly glanced at the big house, "it's because Dawson is..."

A feral grin marred his face, and he reached down to pull a knife from his boot. A low growl vibrated through the quiet spot where they stood. Between clenched teeth, Wex drew a breath. "You need to get home," he said, "and hurry."

"I can't leave you here. Come back with me. We'll find—"

"Go!" he said, his eyes fierce. "Do what I'm telling you, right now; I'll watch and make sure you're okay."

The howl pierced the serenity of the cold, clear day and shattered it. The painters were off the scaffolds before Juliet got inside the house.

At the entry to the dining room, she collided with Kitty and bounced off the larger woman. She almost fell. "Is Jeff back?" she forced out.

"Rode past the house not ten minutes ago, headed for the barn." Kitty was drying her hands, nonstop, on her apron. "Oh my lordy, lordy. What that thing doing howling in broad daylight?"

A shot rang out. Juliet, shaken by the report of the rifle, flung the back door open and charged toward the barn. She arrived winded to find Toby trying to settle a spooked Deacon. "Where is Mister Jeff?" she managed between breaths that pierced her aching side.

207

"Went looking for you, Miss Juliet." Deacon shied, and Toby tightened his grip on the harness. "Said he seen you in the woods."

"He heard the wolf?" she got out.

"No, ma'am."

Juliet stared at him.

"Yes, ma'am," he amended, "I guess he did, but he done gone and left me with the horse befo' that wolf howled."

Breathless, hurting, she plunged through the structure's rear exit. She stopped when she reached the fence and ran parallel to it, searching the woods that loomed beyond. Jeff hollered back when she cried his name, and the scattered bits of her sanity settled back into a semblance of self-control.

"Where are you?" he shouted.

"At the fence. Wexford is in there somewhere, hunting the wolf. He has nothing but a knife."

She stopped moving, trying to see him. "Jeff?"

He didn't respond. Maybe he thought he shouldn't...or he couldn't. Juliet dropped her shawl and cleared the fence.

"Answer me! Are you all right?"

"Don't you come in these woods," he shouted back.

Too late for that. Careless, she tripped and almost fell on her face. More scared than angry, she struck out at the dead summer brambles, which had snared her. "Where are you?"

"Be quiet!"

She all but swallowed her heart. She and her big mouth were forcing him to give his location away. Juliet yanked on the offending blackberry tendril and fell, off balance, through less vicious foliage into a clearing.

"If I find you in these woods—"

"Now you shut up!" she screeched, and flattening her palms against the leaf-covered ground, she pushed up. If someone were trying to shoot him...

The presence of the huge, gray beast lying two body lengths away banished the sudden, overwhelming scent of summer rain from her senses. Juliet eased back to her knees. The animal made no move to rise. It seemed neither curious nor threatened, but watched her with its amber eyes. Heart pounding against the base of her throat, she mustered the courage to take her eyes off the wolf and search for a sign of Jeff. She desperately wanted to call for him now—she returned her focus to the beast—she wanted him to actually see the thing, but she feared, in addition to her other concerns, calling out would upset the animal. "Strange" was the term Jeff and Will used to describe its behavior that night at the barn. She figured its behavior now would be considered likewise.

Steeling her trembling body, she maneuvered low on her forearms and brought herself closer to its eye level.

"Who are you? Jeff?" She waited. "Jedediah Wolfson?"

The animal rose to its impressive height. In her haste to rise with it, she got tangled up in her skirt, lost her balance, and tipped to one side. In the span of one racing heartbeat, she took her eyes off the beast and looked up to see Jeff glaring at her from behind a stout bush.

"Why the devil are you in these woods?" His voice bristled with the edginess created by worry dissolved into anger, and he started to force his way through—

"Wait!"

Quickly she searched the clearing, then returned her gaze to his, not as angry now.

"You saw it again, didn't you?"

She rose and stepped to where it had rested. "It was here, right here." Turning on her heel, she scanned the nearby woods, but knew she'd find nothing. After a half-hearted effort, she gave up and turned to where Jeff kneeled, studying the spot she'd pointed out. He blew out a breath and rose.

"There's no sign, Juliet, not even a track."

"There must be sign of some sort." She fell to all fours and began brushing dead leaves aside, searching for what he might have missed. "It was lying right here. I talked to it."

"Juliet?"

In exasperation, she jerked her head up and looked at him. "Did it talk back to you?"

209

Chapter Thirty-two

Jeff closed the front door a bit too hard. "What were you doing down there with Wex Seaton?"

Juliet was shaking, events only now catching up with her. Kitty rushed into the foyer from the dining room, but Jeff grabbed Juliet's elbow and pulled her into the parlor. "She's fine, Kitty," he called over his shoulder. He closed that door, too, but more softly. Juliet glanced at the portal. Her architectural plans called for its removal, along with most of the wall, to make a grander entry into this room.

"Well?"

She frowned at him and tried to remember what he'd asked, and he must have realized her confusion, because he said, "Wex Seaton—what were you doing with him?"

"Oh, that's right." Warm all of a sudden, Juliet dropped her shawl. "He and Tucker came by."

"Tucker came here?"

"Yes, he did." She sank onto the settee and rubbed her forehead. "Jeff?"

"What?" Anger clad the word.

"I'm going to be sick."

He cursed. "Put your head between your legs and hold it."

Hold it, he said. Out of the corner of her eye, she saw him move away. Easy enough to give orders when you're not the one assailed with nausea, but she did as he said and closed her eyes at the same time.

He stuck their only spittoon under her chin and held it, all the while smoothing wisps of hair from her face while violent retching tore her insides apart. Done, she wiped her mouth with the back of her hand, then vomited again.

"It's the fear," he said softly. "Sometimes it takes awhile to take hold of you."

"And how do you know so much about fear?"

"Years of war and death, sweetheart. Fear and I are old, acquaintances."

She looked up and found his eyes. "Did you lose your meals, too?"

He handed her a handkerchief. "In the beginning. Stopped later, though. Don't know whether I got used to being afraid or just ran out of food."

Her gaze dropped to his lips. Such a handsome mouth. She wished they had the kind of affection for each other that allowed her to lean over and kiss him. She grimaced. Even under those circumstances, she doubted whether he would want her sour kiss right now.

"Are you better?"

She nodded, and he rose and set the receptacle aside.

"Tucker and Wexford?" he prompted.

"You fired the shot?" she blurted out.

"What?"

"The shot in the woods?"

"No," he answered slowly, "I shoot only if I know what I'm shooting at. I've yet to see your wolf."

Juliet swallowed. "It must have been Tucker then. Wexford didn't have a gun." She turned her face to Jeff's. "Did he shoot at you?"

Calm, Jeff sat beside her. "I don't know who fired that shot or whether it was fired at me."

But he did. He had some idea how close a bullet had come to him. His voice sounded anxious when he'd called to her from the woods. She touched the arm Wexford had seized so roughly. How long had he planned on keeping her in the woods? Long enough for Jeff to return home and come looking for her so Tucker could shoot him?

211

"Why did they come here?"

Juliet blinked at his voice. "The wolf killed another one of their cows last night."

"And they think I did it?"

She frowned. "We have to go to the Christmas service."

"Why—"

"They think you're the beast, Jeff. Tucker thinks you're a ghost. Wexford thinks you're a werewolf, or so he says." Juliet meshed her shaking fingers together in her lap. Anger and fear were chipping away at her temper. "Anyway, that's what they claim."

"They're not the only ones."

"And that's why we must go to the service. I can't believe Wexford gives any credence to this foolishness. Tucker's brain is pickled, so there's no judging what he thinks any longer." Cold now, she drew her legs beneath her. "But in both their cases, they will feed the frenzy and use people's fear against you. We really must go."

"They'll be there?"

"I don't know, and I don't care. They can leave if they don't like our company. Mike and Mary invited us personally." Lord, if only she could lie down and close her eyes....

"Mike and Mary Tate do not make up the entire congregation."

"I am confident they discussed the invitation with the other members. They've extended a hand. I think we need to take it."

"I'm willing to go."

"Good." Strained by events, Juliet thought of her bed and started to rise.

He pulled her back. "Why were you in the woods with Wex Seaton?"

"We were talking...about family things." She looked at Jeff. "I thought he wanted to get away from the painters."

"You could have invited him into the parlor for tea."

She didn't miss the subtle sarcasm in his voice. "Tucker was with him at first. I don't want my brother under this roof."

212

He didn't ask her why. Tired, she closed her eyes. He thought he knew the reason, and perhaps he did. For her, delving into who had pulled that treacherous trigger at Corinth many years ago was something she didn't want to discuss with Jeff. She no longer cared what happened to Tucker, but she did care if Jeff Dawson hanged for killing him.

"Why did you go into the woods?"

She opened her eyes and found him watching her. "He led me down there. As it turned out, he wanted to warn me about you, but we only crossed the fence." She peered at him. "Are you sure you were not fired at?"

"You think they planned to ambush me?"

"I don't know, but that shot worries me. Tucker had a rifle. Wexford wanted us to walk along the path, I think, but I'm no longer comfortable in those woods, not since I saw Lorna Hart's body. We stopped at the fence and talked there, but right before we heard the wolf, he became persistent, and I can't help but wonder—"

"You shouldn't have gone with him."

"I realize that...." She caught accusation in his eyes, and her heart started to race agian "You think me part of the—"

"I wouldn't be living in this house with you if I had even an inkling of such suspicion. Wexford seems an okay sort, but he's still a Seaton. If nothing else, he could compromise you, by insinuation if not by deed."

Well, for pity's sake. Juliet tilted her head, not even trying to suppress the slow grin shaping her lips.

"Go ask your painters," she said. "We remained within their view the entire time, and I'm sure they were watching, given the words already exchanged between Tucker and myself. We provided their afternoon entertainment."

"Sure, that's what I'll do. Go out and ask them if they saw my wife and her gentleman friend down by the creek. And what do you expect they would construe from that?"

She felt better than she had in days. "Why, that you are jealous, darling. That's certainly what I'm thinking."

"Don't flatter yourself. Like you, I'm concerned with appearances, and for you, such behavior is absolutely forbidden."

His cold, analytical appraisal dampened her. "And why is that?"

"Because you're a woman and you bear the children."

"I see—an amendment to our agreement. I thought my only obligation to you was sex."

His jaw tightened, almost imperceptibly, but she saw. "That's what I expect from you, yes, but accidents happen, and should one befall you, I want to make sure it's mine."

She felt the blood drain from her face, but she looked him squarely in the eye, praying he wouldn't see how his words had wounded her. "Rest assured, husband, any 'accidents' that occur will most definitely be yours."

He'd hurt her, damn it. What she was supposed to feel was insult, not injury. If she would draw back and punch him as she had Tucker, he'd feel a whole lot better.

He hadn't meant what he said, but her smug satisfaction at his perceived jealousy irritated him. The truth was he'd been scared for her. He didn't know the intended target of that bullet. His best guess was Tucker thought he saw something in the woods and took a potshot at it. It could have been him. He looked at his wife. It could have been something else. Drunks made dangerous hunters. But who or what was he really aiming for?

By dragging her off to those woods, Wex Seaton had placed Juliet in danger. Calculated, inadvertent, or just plain reckless, Jeff didn't like it. He hadn't gotten to know the man well, and he wasn't sure he trusted him. Sure, he was an agreeable enough fella when you were in his company, but by all accounts, Wex wasn't a sociable sort. He had found an opportunity at Eileen Seaton's farm, and he'd moved in and taken over. He'd failed to take Juliet, however, and Jeff wondered if Wex had ever considered doing that or if he were considering it now.

Chapter Thirty-three

Juliet had set the table with what was left of her mother's fine china and the crystal Darnell Tackert left as part of the settlement on the house. There were no silver place settings. Eileen Seaton had hidden her silver in 1863 in anticipation of Federal troops, then sold it years later in a desperate attempt to raise money.

While she and Kitty prepared Christmas Eve dinner, Juliet made notes of what she needed to complete the Dawson dinner service; she'd been remiss in not setting the household up better. Jeff made it clear she was to spare no expense in provisioning their home, but surviving the postwar years with her mother and brother had made Juliet frugal. Spending money on luxuries was particularly difficult for her.

She stepped into the dining room, smoothing the front of the green silk tulle evening dress she'd picked up at Fran Woolsey's yesterday. Jeff stood at the buffet, pouring them both a glass of wine. He glanced at her, his eyes resting, for a moment, on the square neckline of the dress.

He was in black dinner dress replete with jacket, ruffled shirt, and a western tie. The stark color added to his height and strength.

"I like green," he said, handing her a glass of wine. "I'm glad you picked that color for tonight. You are beautiful."

"Thank you." At a faint queasiness, she rubbed her tummy and hoped he didn't notice. She didn't want anything to spoil the evening she had planned. "And you are very handsome."

He pulled out her chair. "You and Kitty have outdone yourselves for only the two of us."

She took her seat; food would help her stomach.

In the center of the linen-covered table, a roast of beef surrounded by carrots and potatoes glistened in candlelight from the chandelier.

"Kitty is gone?" she asked.

"No, she wanted to wait and clean up. Toby is waiting for her." Jeff glanced at her. "They've not far to go. They'll be fine."

They would be. Neither Toby nor Kitty would appeal to the killer, and Juliet no longer believed that the wolf was a threat to humans.

"They'll be back the day after Christmas." He placed a piece of meat on her plate, then scooped up a spoonful of vegetables.

"Did your father serve the meals at your house?"

He laughed. "My mother waited on my father hand and foot. If he'd tried to serve a meal, he'd have dribbled it over the table, and she'd have hit him with a serving spoon.

"No, I saw this once in a Denver mansion, the father of five serving Christmas Eve dinner to his family and guests. Of course, his sweet wife had worked all day preparing it—he had the honor of serving it."

"I'm sure he provided the food for the meal."

Jeff nodded, taking his seat. "And a good provider he was, too. Gold, silver, and finally a railroad magnate. That's where I should have sat out the war, in Colorado."

"Why did you come home?" she asked softly, placing a small piece of roast in her mouth. The meat was delicious.

"I never intended to, didn't have the heart to come home to nothing. While I was in prison, I became good friends with a fella by the name of Nate Calvin. He nursed me before and after a Federal doctor dug the bullet out of my back.

"He was a good twenty years older than me, and all he talked about while we sat in that Yankee hole was the war ending and California." Jeff shrugged. "I decided to tag along. We never made it any farther than Lone Pine, Colorado, on the western slope of the Rockies. Some fella there had just struck silver. We sold our two sorry horses and laid a claim. Three weeks later, we found silver. Six months after that, we had a working silver mine and hit a vein of gold.

"Seven years we worked that mine and two others. They all tapped out, but by then we'd invested our take to form a consortium. Nate had a head for business. He died of pneumonia last April, and I sold seventy percent of my holdings to a big banker out of New York. I kept thirty as a steady income."

Down the length of the table, he held her gaze. "What does bring a Southern boy home, Juliet? I can't explain it, but whatever called to me is as strong and passionate as that big muddy river to our west and soft and sweet as a magnolia blossom." He looked down at his plate. "Maybe if I'd met someone in Colorado I wanted to spend my life with, I'd have stayed. As it turned out, there wasn't anything there to take the place of Dixie in my heart."

Her stomach quaked, and she fought down a greater touch of nausea, all the while wondering if she would ever be that most important thing in his life. "Tell me more about your grandfather."

"My mother's father, Jedediah?"

"Yes. You told me he was the son of a shape-shifting Creek Indian who had a wolf as his familiar—"

"Totem."

She looked up from her potatoes. "'Totem,' I'm sorry, and his mother was an English captive?"

Jeff wiped his mouth with a napkin. "Great-grandma wasn't just any English captive. Apparently she was the beautiful red-headed daughter of a wealthy planter from south Georgia.

"Now, according to the story granddaddy told me out behind the barn, it was in the guise of the wolf that my great-granddaddy sodomized his beautiful prisoner."

Juliet's stomach flip-flopped. "How did he—"

Jeff leaned forward. "By sodomize, I do not mean the perverse pleasure I inflicted upon you the other night. I learned that in a Denver bawdy house. I doubt that my grandfather would have imagined such an act, and I'm sure he wouldn't have discussed it with me, if he had.

"No, I mean he reportedly had sexual intercourse with her in the form of an animal."

And that wasn't perverse?

"Nine months later my grandfather was born."

"And did the wolf marry the Englishwoman?"

"Yes, but as a man. According to my granddaddy, his daddy could take on the form of a wolf at will, but must have derived particular pleasure from animal sex."

Juliet stared at him. He stuck a piece of meat in his mouth and chewed, not dropping his gaze.

"Capturing that young English beauty was probably the best thing that ever happened to my great-granddaddy, because whatever he was doing to her, in any form, she liked it. When she was finally rescued, she wouldn't give him up."

"What a strangely romantic tale," Juliet said softly.

Jeff gave her a long perusal, then smiled. "I find 'erotic' a better word for it—or dirty perhaps. Mama would have died if she'd known Granddaddy told it to me."

He returned to his meat. "Great-grandma's daddy wasn't only rich, he was powerful, and my great-grandfather ended up an influential mediator between the British and the Creeks and ultimately received a land grant in Georgia from the British government. According to Granddaddy, my great-grandfather was a staunch Tory. He lost his holdings during the Revolution and came west to Spanish Natchez." Jeff looked up and shot her a grin. "Whether there really were any holdings, I don't know.

"Now the way old Jedediah told the tale, the ability to change into wolf form passed down through the generations."

"Did you ever ask your grandmother?"

"My maternal grandmother died in childbirth a few years after my mother was born. Granddaddy never remarried.

"And you, Jeff?"

Suspending his fork halfway to his mouth, he looked at her. "And me what?"

"Did you inherit the ability?"

"My father was a white American male."

"Your mother—"

"That's it, Juliet! My father had sexual intercourse with a female wolf." His lips curled into an incredulous grin. "That explains the affection he always displayed for my mother."

She would have been devastated by his mocking words had it not been for the amused look on his face. Goodness knows what images must have passed before his eyes. For sure, it was silly—the implication he had made, anyway. "I didn't mean that your mother and father performed...."

"My mother and father had sex, Juliet. That's the one thing I'm sure of and the only one."

She turned back to her own plate. The meal was good, her nausea was passing. "You like the story, don't you?"

"Which one? The one about my great-grandparents or the one you just created about my parents?"

She reddened, and he chuckled. "I love the story, Juliet, and I enjoy telling it. Granddaddy did, too. It and the ones he embellished in front of the fireplace after the sun went down." He winked at her. "The ones not so off-color he couldn't share them with me and Bonnie in front of my mother."

Juliet tensed at his mention of Bonnie, but he didn't appear preoccupied with his sister's memory.

"They got better every year."

Disappointment gnawed at her. "You don't believe he could change into a wolf, do you?"

Quiet blanketed the room. Carefully, Jeff cut a potato in half. Juliet waited, holding her breath, and her palms started to sweat.

"I did, up until I was eleven." He looked up. "Then one night, not long after Bonnie died, he didn't come home. Daddy and me went looking for him next morning. It was me who found him, hanging from a white oak tree close to the river." Jeff glanced away and with a softer voice said, "I couldn't get up that damn tree to get him down. Tore my hands up trying. My hands and my face were covered with blood and snot and tears from me crying and wiping and trying to get up to that limb. I knew then he wasn't a spirit."

She could hear the grief in his voice and in his words, and her bottom lip quivered with an empathetic tremble.

He speared a piece of the potato and shoved it in his mouth. "Nah," he said, pushing the food to one side, "in spite of the fact he allowed someone to kill him, I think he was one of the greatest men who ever walked this earth." Pointedly, he looked her in the eye. "But he was only a man, sweetheart."

Juliet caught her unsteady bottom lip between her teeth, while Jeff washed his food down with wine.

"Jedediah Wolfson knew the call of every bird, the name of every plant and tree, and the track and sign of every animal roaming those woods you love so much. He taught me to recognize a lot of them, but not nearly all. I'm a pretty good tracker. That's why I'm so frustrated by your friend the wolf."

"My friend the wolf?"

"You're the only person I know of who's seen the thing."

"But you and Will Howe...darn it, everyone says the thing behaves strangely."

"Very."

"Well, I'm simply trying to figure out what it is."

"It's a wolf." He folded his napkin by his plate and rose.

"But he must be more—"

"He is not Jedediah Wolfson. Him I saw buried." He reached out, took her hand, and pulled her to her feet. "And I'm sorry I'm unable to fulfill your fantasies, but I'm not him, either."

Implying she had some dark desire to have intercourse with a wolf? Perhaps it *was* time for dinner to end.

"Kitty," she called down the breezeway, "We're done."

Kitty appeared as Juliet was picking up the coffee service. "Since you are determined to stay until we finish our meal," Juliet said, "will you cut the pie and bring it to us in the parlor?"

"Thank you," Juliet said and took her serving of pie.

Kitty handed him his. "Soon as I wash these plates, me and Toby be leavin'. Be back day after tomorrow. Only reason I'm goin' is the *massa* here insists I take off Christmas."

220

"In the old days, the master gave you Christmas off. I doubt there were complaints then."

Kitty's gaze didn't waver, and Jeff flexed his jaw. The woman didn't think he was good enough for Juliet. Now he sensed Kitty didn't want to leave Juliet alone with him. He found those doubts particularly disturbing. The point of going to church tomorrow was to get to know people. Well, Kitty lived in his house. If her trust was in jeopardy, what good would socializing do?

"We'll be fine, Kitty," Juliet said. "I know how to clean up."

Kitty snorted. "They's a second pecan pie on the breakfront, sweet baby girl, for tomorrow."

"Thank you, Kitty. Merry Christmas."

Jeff watched the Negress lumber out of the room, then he stoked the fire. This December had proven a cold one, and he was thankful the furnace was working efficiently. The fireplace he tended now served more for atmosphere than anything else.

Juliet had draped pine garland along the mantle. He glanced around the room, but spotted no mistletoe. She'd probably been unable to find any. He wiped his free palm on his pants leg, then placed the poker in the stand and, hot as hell, stepped away from the fire.

Juliet sat on the settee rubbing her fingers together. He was as nervous as a raw recruit on the eve of his first battle. She looked up with a little smile, and Jeff reached into his coat pocket and brushed his fingers over the small velvet box he'd secreted there. He cleared his throat.

"I have something for you," he said and wrapped his hand around the box. Damn, if he weren't careful, he'd crush the thing.

Juliet straightened, a look of surprise on her face, and he glanced at the small hand now splayed across her belly. His heartbeat quickened with the memory of Severs' flashy diamond on that hand. His was so different, and he prayed she didn't throw it at him.

He pulled the box from his pocket, but he didn't hand it to her. Instead, he sat next to her, and he opened it and removed the ring he'd ordered from a Natchez jeweler four weeks ago.

221

Still as stone, she waited beside him. He leaned over, took the hand covering her belly, and slipped the diamond- and emerald-set gold band on her third finger. Damn, the thing fit.

"I didn't have a ring for you when we wed"—he met her eyes—"everything happened so suddenly. I hope you'll accept this one."

Then he held his breath.

Head bowed, she removed her hand from his and flexed her fingers. After a moment, she balled the hand into a fist and covered it with her right hand. "How did you know?" she said, her voice edged with emotion.

He still couldn't see her face. "How did I know what?"

She jerked her head up and gazed at him with bright, tear-filled eyes. "I love emeralds."

"I didn't know. I told you I like green. Your biggest failing is your eyes are gray."

"My biggest?"

"Physically, I meant." He sat still, listening to his heartbeat in his ears, and waited for her validating response.

"Well, I like green, too," she said. "Pity your eyes are blue." She leaned over and surprised him with a peck on the lips. "Thank you, Jeff. It is beautiful." Then she swiped at a tear, gave a little laugh, and rose. "I have something for you, too."

Composure seemingly regained, she walked to a small secretary sitting against the wall separating two of the room's floor-to-ceiling windows and returned with a bundle wrapped in brown paper and tied with a green silk ribbon. She handed it to him with a shy smile.

"I didn't know what to get you"—she retook her place next to him—"but from what I've seen between you and Will Howe, I think you may enjoy this."

He looked at her.

"I spent your money on it, if that's what you're wondering."

"I was wondering what it is."

"Open it."

She was like a child, more excited than he was. He dropped her gaze and tugged on the ribbon.

It was a chess set of white marble and black onyx, stored in a hinged wooden box lined in blue velvet. "Exquisite" defined it perfectly. He'd come across the term in one of his recent English Gothics and was proud to put the word to use.

"Do you play?"

He never had and started to—

"I can teach you," she said quickly and picked up the wrapping and smoothed it flat.

Again he opened his mouth to speak.

"There's a game table in your study. You never use it. We could move it in here by the fire."

She was bubbling at the prospect of teaching him the game. The chess set was as much for her as him, but instinctively he knew she was drawing him to her, sharing with him a special part of her past.

"Come," he said, rising and lending her a hand, "help me with the table."

They spent hours in front of the fire with intermittent breaks to feed the flames and get coffee and a second piece of pecan pie. She'd hoped for a nice evening teaching Jeff to play chess. His perfect gift had transformed the night from pleasant to wonderful.

Chess was a favorite of her mother, who'd been taught the game by Juliet's grandfather, the one who'd inherited White Oak Glen as a young man and built the big house here in 1818. Juliet learned the game as a child and considered herself adept at it.

But Jeff Dawson was a quick learner. The first two games had proven easy wins for her, while Jeff learned the moves of the different pieces. He seemed to forget nothing that she said, he never asked her to repeat anything, and when his pieces fell to her, he didn't argue, understanding immediately what he'd done wrong. The third game had lasted over two hours before she managed to get him in checkmate. The present game was now in its third hour and the wee beginning of Christmas Day, and she was beginning to worry he might actually beat her.

"You've played this game before?"

He broke his concentration on the board and looked up. A lock of hair fell rakishly over his brow. "I have not. You are simply an excellent teacher."

Darn him. He was an astute and intelligent man, and she was falling asleep over the board. She watched him tap an index finger against his handsome mouth. Then he narrowed his eyes and raised a hand, moving his queen. "Check," he said.

She clapped her hands, tossed him a satisfied smile, and took his queen with her bishop. "Check," she echoed.

He never even blinked, but moved a castle, taking her bishop. "Checkmate."

Her eyes dropped from his face to the board, and she scanned the pieces and calculated her options. She had none. He'd led her into a trap and, in her smug conceit, she'd followed.

"You're falling asleep, Juliet."

Now he was being kind, trying to make her feel better.

"We could play one more."

"Can't stand to lose, can you? You won three games, and I've won one."

"You were learning on the other three."

He laughed. "And now I know the game, I will be a more worthy opponent for you in the future."

"We could make a wager."

He sat back with a smile on his lips and glitter in his eyes. "You have nothing to wager, my sweet, except your body. Let me see...my money against your body. I could win you, but you'd win either way."

Her stomach dropped with his words, and her spirit drooped with it. This is not where she'd wanted this conversation to lead. He was so sure of himself and so critical of her unbridled passion. She gave him a smile she didn't feel. "I wanted a surer bet. If you win, you get me, and if I win I get you, but since such a wager does not interest one with your fortitude, I'll retire." She rose, shrouded by his discerning gaze. "Thank you for what was, until now, a most enjoyable evening."

She looked at the beautiful ring on her finger, then leaned

224

over, her breasts pushing upward against the square décolletage of her bodice. She hoped he looked and suffered, but her doubt was as strong as her hope. He appeared to do neither, and when she kissed the corner of his mouth, he made no attempt to take her lips. "Thank you for the honor of your ring."

And your name. Lord knows where your child would have been raised without it.

He watched her go, the gathered fabric, soft and smooth over her derrière, suggestive of what lay beneath. And he wanted what was beneath. Erotic thoughts of his great-grandfather and the man's English bride flitted through his head, and he imagined Juliet stripped and on all fours, her rump caressing his pelvis.

It had been a most enjoyable evening, and it should have ended in only one way, the two of them tangled together in his bed. He'd hurt her feelings at the end, and she'd countered by tempting him. He'd proved resolute.

But he was the loser for not allowing her the victory.

Chapter Thirty-four

"Does he know?"

Another wave of nausea washed over her, and Juliet closed her eyes. This time she held back from retching. "No, I haven't told him."

Kitty handed her a wet cloth. "You ain't gonna keep it secret much longer, baby girl, you bein' sick like you is. Yo' mama, she always got real sick like this. Do you know when—"

"Six weeks. It would have to have been the first time we...."

"You done missed your monthly time?"

"There was some blood three weeks ago, when it should have been. There's been more spots, yesterday the most recent, but I know that I'm pregnant, Kitty. There have been changes in my breasts and in my appetite."

Juliet sat on the floor next to the chamber pot, and Kitty took a seat on Juliet's bed.

"Is he here?" Juliet asked.

"He left right after breakfast. Said he needed to get to the bank in Natchez, and then he was goin' on over to that Mister Mathington's place."

"Yes, he told me last night. He wants to look at horses."

Jeff wanted to raise quarter horses. He wanted to raise cattle, too, and cotton. Other than his allusion to "accidents" the day Wex lured her to the woods, he hadn't said anything about wanting to raise kids. Well, she had to tell him they were about to; she just wished he liked her more. Kitty took her left hand and helped her to her feet. "Sho' is a pretty ring, girl. He puttin' his scent on you in all kinds of ways."

Juliet sat down in the high-backed, upholstered chair next to the bed and held her head, pounding now from the vomiting. How fitting Kitty should use such a base analogy.

"Them folks nice to y'all on Christmas Day?"

Ah, Kitty's words hadn't been mere coincidence. She had been thinking of the wolf.

"They were all friendly enough. I wasn't comfortable with the women." She laughed softly. "And even less so with the men."

"You can't hide forever for what you done. That's what yo' mama tried to do. Shamed she was she laid down with that Yankee."

Juliet didn't think so. Eileen Seaton was a natural recluse, and the loss of the world of which she'd been a prominent part had left her nowhere to go. Nowhere she'd wanted to go.

"How they treat him?"

More and more Jeff was becoming "he" and "him," no longer Mister Dawson or the "massa" with which Kitty teased him.

"Friendly, too."

But she knew there were a few old-timers left, those who remembered Jeff's origins and the tales of Jedediah Wolfson.

"The church had a tree; it was a cedar. I thought it was pretty, but Jeff said it was the ugliest Christmas tree he'd ever seen. He says in Colorado they use spruces." Juliet gave Kitty a little smile. "Margery was there."

"Hmmph."

"She's pregnant."

"Oh, good lawd! Tucker's?"

"Certainly."

"And I bet she walked around with her head high, didn't she? Plannin' that the whole while. And you hidin' in shame, and you never plannin' on trappin' a man."

"It's not common knowledge, Kitty, so don't tell it. She and Tucker are to wed Tuesday week, the fifth. I hope it's a boy, a boy to carry on the Seaton name."

"Don't tell me she done invited you and yo' husband."

"No. Jeff and I are the last people Tucker would want there."

"Cousins. Young'uns will be first cousins."

Juliet jerked her head up. "Don't say anything to Jeff about our baby. I want to tell him myself. I just need to find the right moment."

And that had to be soon. She wanted him to forgive her and want her for herself, not want her because of the baby. Right now, she wasn't sure how he would react to the news. Some days it seemed they still had so much to work through.

$\mathcal{I}$t was dusk; the workers were gone. Juliet told Kitty they would eat later tonight since Jeff was getting home late and it was New Year's Eve.

He had called her name from downstairs moments ago. He always did that, to assure himself she was in the house and safe, she believed. That thought warmed her. She pinched her cheeks and stood, smoothing the red silk over her hips. She'd been sick most of the day, but was feeling fine now. In the morning when they woke, she'd tell him about the baby. But tonight, she wanted him to hold her in his arms with no strings attached. She wanted to know he cared for her even if he didn't say "I love you." She wasn't asking for love yet. His liking her enough to be pleased about the baby would do.

Heart pitter-pattering, she started down the steps. Jeff had his hand on the rail and his booted foot on the first step before he looked up and saw her. For a moment he stared, and she liked what she saw in his eyes. His mouth opened, and he started to speak.

"It's New Year's Eve," she said, preempting him.

"Where did you get that dress?"

She swallowed. "You bought it for me."

He took several steps up, bringing them face-to-face. "Did I pay a lot of money for it?"

"Yes."

He reached up and, with his index finger, traced an erotic path down her throat and over the raised mounds of her breasts, barely touching the velvet framework of the décolletage.

"And what am I going to get out of it?"

"What do you want *out* of it?" she said softly.

He splayed his hand over her throat, caressing her with his fingertips. Her nipples tingled and for a moment she lost herself in anticipation of his body.

"You're trying to seduce me, Juliet."

"Am I succeeding?"

He took one more step, putting him one tread below her, and she had to look up at him. He still smelled of the cold outside and faintly of sandalwood. A delicious shiver passed through her, then panic when she realized he could step around her and continue up the stairs alone. She thought that was what he was going to do. She started to speak, and when she did, he covered her mouth with his. He was rough, but she didn't care. There was an urgency about him and perhaps there was anger, she wasn't sure.

"The workers are gone?" he asked.

"Yes."

"No one here but us?" He bent his head and kissed her neck.

She closed her eyes and lifted her chin, giving him easy access to her throat. "And Kitty. She's in —"

"The cookhouse. I saw her when I came in."

She moaned, and he moved his hands to the bodice of the dress and ripped.

$\mathcal{E}$yes wide open, she snatched the bodice of the dress and pulled it together. His erection pressed against his breeches, and he shifted his weight, moving closer.

Her lips parted in apparent disbelief, and Juliet strained back. Her game had turned. He was back in control, of sorts. He'd ached for her since the wee hours of Christmas morning when, letting his pride get in the way of his common sense, he allowed her to go to bed alone. This evening she'd again challenged that pride and, damn her, she'd won once more. He wanted her, and he would have her, and that's exactly what she wanted. But he didn't have to be happy about it. He seized her by the shoulders and pulled roughly at the fabric. She tensed at the same moment a subtle whimper escaped her lips. Immediately, he looked into her glistening eyes. Her chin puckered. Dear God, he'd frightened her. That he had not intended to do.

He eased his hold and dipped his head, gently kissing her neck, then earlobe. "Indulge me, Juliet. It's a fantasy I've had to rip a beautiful dress off a beautiful woman." He kissed her along the jaw line and felt some of the tension leave her.

"It was a very expensive dress."

"I'll buy you another." He found her lips and silenced whatever protest she might have made.

With the palms of his hands, he briefly covered her breasts, then continued to force the fabric, but more slowly, careful not to frighten her again. He perceived the exact moment need replaced the tension in her body.

The dress was gone. Juliet stood before him dressed in black corset and pantaloons, both trimmed in red thread and ribbons. Provocative body armor, and aroused as he was, he hated the thought of doing battle with undergarments. He wasn't even going to try to figure out how to undo the corset, and he didn't want her help. He wanted to strip her naked himself.

From the back of his boot, he pulled a knife and held it up for her perusal.

"Oh," she said simply, but the slight astonishment in her voice told him she'd tensed again.

"Do not fear. This is for the clothes, not for you."

"Jeff, please, this underwear was extremely—"

"You can have me," he growled, "but on my terms."

She let him turn her so that her back was to him, and he slid the knife between her shoulder blades and under the satin laces of the corset. The tip of the knife touched her pale skin, and she flinched, but he didn't cut her. Moments later the strapless contraption fell away, and Juliet caught it in her hands.

Turning her around, he took the corset from where she held it against her and dropped it over the side of the stairs.

She started to cover herself with her hands, but he pulled them to her side and said no. Her breasts were full, their large nipples begging to be suckled. He took one step down, and with a dip of his head, he took one in his mouth. She gasped and arched against him. A shudder moved through her and passed to him, and with an unbidden groan he let go of her hands. Immediately, she grasped his shoulders, steadying herself while he lowered his body, his hands caressing her ribs, her belly, then her hips before untying the silk ribbon that kept her pantaloons gathered around her waist. He pushed the soft garment slowly to her ankles. The hard oak stair tread hurt his knees when he kneeled in front of her, but he found his reward in gently spreading her thighs and licking her womanhood. Her fingers squeezed his shoulders and he heard her gentle sigh.

Wet and warm, she smelled of musk, and tasted of woman, and his penis swelled in response. Urgent now, Jeff moved his lips and tongue back up her body, between her breasts, taking a moment to lick a nipple. Straightening, he picked her up in his arms. The pantaloons fell from her foot to join the remains of her ruined dress on the treads. She looped her arms around his neck, and he kissed her deeply, then he climbed the remaining stairs with quick, decisive steps. "My room," she whispered.

Her bed was turned down; a fire roared in the fireplace. Yes, she had planned this, but she hadn't planned everything that was to come. His hands and arms and thighs shivered with tension and sweet agony.

He laid her on the bed and, not bothering to undress, roughly rolled her onto her stomach, grabbed her thighs, and pulled her to her knees.

"What are you doing?" she asked.

"Showing you how a wolf makes love."

"Do wolves make love?"

"How they mate then, if you prefer."

She liked "makes love" and recalled the tale he had told her Christmas Eve about his great-grandfather and his captive bride. She tried to look behind her, but could see little more than him unbuttoning his breeches. Then one of his hands was roaming

231

over the cheeks of her derrière, and she felt the soft head of his penis stroking the cleft that secreted her vaginal opening. His other hand fumbled with her hair, pulling it partially down, then tangled in it, gently tugging her head back, holding her to his will with the threat of pain. But there was no pain, and he did not act on the threat.

She twinged when he entered her. He filled her more deeply, and when he moved against her, he created a sweet subtle pain that she ignored, concentrating on pleasure and the erotic vision of what they must look like coupled as they were. Jeff let go of her hair and wrapped his hands around her thighs, pulling her to him, pushing her away. His penis hit her deep inside, and a small pain accompanied each thrust, indicative of the depth to which he penetrated her. He sucked in a breath and pulled her bottom to him, squeezing her thighs and gyrating his pelvis against her, each brief thrust of his hard body matching a corresponding wave of pleasure she knew rushed through him. He cried out and again tangled his hand in her hair, gently pulling her head and back against his chest. He kissed her ear and, at the same time, covered a breast with the palm of his hand.

"It was no good for you?" he asked after a moment.

"I-I did not—"

"I can fix that."

And he could, she knew. The position, their intercourse, and his orgasm already had her at fever pitch. Freeing her hair, he squeezed his legs against her thighs and stroked her genitals. Adeptly, he worked the tender folds of her womanhood before his fingers stiffened. He nuzzled her beneath the ear and she turned her face to the side, offering him her lips, and he took them in a heated kiss. The pressure grew and exploded in waves of ecstasy, followed by a dull cramping pain across her back. She blocked out everything but the feel of his shirt and his warmth against her, and the subtle cramp that would not go away. He smiled at her when she twisted to find him.

"Better?" he asked.

"Yes."

But she really wasn't sure. Goodness knows the climax had been wonderful, but that faint, nagging pain plagued her. For a moment, she pulled her gaze from his, turning enough to see the whole of him. But for his open breeches, he remained completely dressed. She opened her mouth to ask him to undress, to lie down with her, to cuddle her...to stay the night. He pecked her quick on the lips, and with one deft move, stood on the floor and began buttoning his pants.

She sat on the bed and drew her legs together. "You're leaving me?"

"We're done here, sweetheart."

She should have known it couldn't be this simple, but given..., she caught her trembling bottom lip between her teeth. The cramp remained, and warmth spilled from between her legs. His juices, leaving her as he was leaving her.

"Do you need something else?" he asked.

Love and forgiveness and to forgive in return. "Other than money and sex, do you have anything to offer?" She raised her head in haughty defiance. "Go ahead and leave me. I don't care."

He stood motionless.

Again the warm wetness. Swept with dread, she raised her rump, then covered her mouth to silence the wail surging up her throat; and the disappointment of Jeff's rejection drowned in the blood pooling beneath her bottom.

He hadn't missed the disappointment in her voice, and his slowing heartbeat had kicked up a notch with the hope that she might surrender her pride and ask him to stay. Instead, she looked down. He followed her gaze, and his gut squeezed with her first frantic, "No!" A string of "no's" echoed that first one.

He stepped forward, but she wouldn't look at him. Drawing her knees to her breasts, she wrapped her arms around bent legs and drew her body into a tight knot, as if in some way the act could stem the flow of blood. The pool increased, and he knew this was no monthly flux.

"God, Juliet, what's happening?"

She'd closed her eyes and rested her cheek on her knees, the answer to his query a senseless drone.

"What's wrong?" he hollered, at the same time touching her shoulder. He wanted to shake an answer out of her, but feared hurting her more.

Sucking back a sob, she opened her eyes and lifted her head. A sheen of tears covered her cheeks. "Get Kitty."

He opened his mouth to ask his question once again, but she screamed at him. "Get Kitty, Jeff, I'm losing our baby!"

Chapter Thirty-five

ex Seaton scraped his boots off at the back door, then stepped inside the semi-warm enclosed back porch that led to the dining room. There, he removed his jacket and hat, and with a dejected shake of his head, he walked into the parlor.

His mother sat in front of the fireplace making alterations to Margery's original wedding dress, the one she had worn eleven years ago when she'd wed James Dooland, her dashing Confederate captain. As best Wex could piece together—he hadn't made it to the wedding—Margery lived with the man only two weeks before his furlough was up and he had returned to war. James Dooland didn't come home; he was buried near Atlanta, Georgia.

"What's wrong?" his mother asked, halting the nimble movement of her fingers.

Wex moved a chair closer to the fire and sat. "We lost the bull last night."

"The wolf?"

"Well, I didn't do it."

"I never thought you'd done it," she said, her voice caustic. "But I cannot believe a lone wolf brought down a full-grown bull. Our neighbor in the big house must have been involved."

Wex leaned forward, elbows on knees, and rubbed his hands over his face. This could do them in. They needed that bull, and they couldn't afford to buy another. Even if they made taxes this year, they wouldn't make them the next.

"He's not killing these animals. A beast is doing it, a savage one."

He dropped his hands and turned to his mother. "Did you hear anything from the cattle, any cries or bellows during the night?"

She narrowed her eyes, as if unsure what he was asking.

"Anything to make you think something was disturbing them?"

"No."

He sighed. "Neither did I, and I'm a light sleeper."

"Wexford, a single wolf doesn't attack things as large as — "

"I know the thing is a wolf, Mama. I can tell by the wounds, but you're right, it wouldn't naturally choose something as big as a bull. And I don't understand how it can come upon the animals without alarming them."

"You're giving me the jitters, son. Pretty soon you'll be supporting Tucker with his ghost stories."

Wex looked over to the chair Tucker occupied when in this room. Supporting Tucker's ghost stories might prove a good idea.

"He's still asleep," his mother said. "Wasn't quite as drunk last night, was he?"

Wex glanced at her, then turned his gaze to the flames.

"You were with him?" she pressed.

She knew he'd been with Tucker, at least part of the time. She had asked him to stick close, for Margery's sake, to keep Tucker out of trouble. His babysitting tended to keep him out of trouble, too, or so she thought. "He wasn't with another woman," he said. "Truth is, he gets so drunk, he's no longer able to perform for the girls."

Lilith's ensuing snort was a fitting response for a most unladylike topic. "They don't care if he can perform or not as you so delicately put it. All they care about is the money he lavishes on them, and we've too little to spare."

Wex stood up and put another log on the fire. "He has his own source of income."

"Morton is still propping him up?"

"Yep, he was there last night at Hawlin's, celebrating the New Year buying drinks for Tucker, Sikes, and a few others." He stoked the fire. Darn, it was turning into a hard winter in more

236

ways than one. "Trouble's brewin' there. Severs is bitter over Juliet's betrayal. He wants revenge on Dawson."

"She humiliated the poor man is what she did."

His mother's sympathy for the carpetbagger irritated him. He gave her a long perusal and wondered why she hadn't set her cap for the man. She was still pretty, and the two were about the same age. But then, age was key. Lilith Seaton was past safe childbearing age.

"You tried to force her into a marriage against her will. You should have known she wouldn't take it lying down," he said.

"You didn't try to discourage the ruse."

"I thought she'd refuse the marriage outright. I had no idea she would actually sell herself to protect her worthless brother, though I think her agreeing had more to do with Tucker's threat to deed Severs the farm if she didn't." Wex grinned ruefully. "Ol' Tucker is sometimes smarter than we give him credit for."

"Well, we'd probably be better off at this point if she hadn't given in. Whatever Morton is goading Tucker to do could backfire on us. We don't need to anger Dawson more."

"What's he going to do, kill our dead bull?"

She punched the needle into the white satin and rose to face him. "He could kill Tucker."

"Would that really be so terrible?"

His mother stared at him a moment, then closed her eyes. "In the long run, maybe not, but it would be nice if he lived long enough to marry your sister. For that matter, Dawson could kill every one of us." She retook her seat and picked up her sewing.

"Maybe Tucker will kill him."

"Do you really think he could stay sober long enough?"

"With his cronies' help he could manage. You can bet Severs will happily provide him support, then let Tucker take the blame."

"And leave your sister's child without a father?"

"That baby will never have a father worth speaking of. It'll be better off with its uncle."

"Stop it, Wexford. I don't want you involved with this, and I want you to make sure Tucker does nothing foolish."

"I have no intention of getting involved, Mother, under any circumstances, and that includes throttling Tucker."

His mother was quiet so long he looked at her and found her studying him. "Dawson's being dead appeals to you, doesn't it, son?"

Her words, both the ones spoken and those not, seeped in. "Obviously you've considered the possibilities."

She opened her mouth, then shut it. After a moment, he grinned. "That would leave the beautiful Juliet with his money, eh, Mama?"

She dropped her eyes and sewed another stitch. "As long as you are not involved in murder, the situation could work out nicely."

"Advantageously, you mean."

"I'm thinking you've considered the 'advantages' yourself."

"There's a lot about me and my feelings for Juliet you misconstrue."

"Do I? I apologize. You are attracted to her?"

"Very."

"Why didn't you act before now?

"Before now, I had no reason to. Besides, she was engaged to Braxton when we got here, and Aunt Eileen would have never blessed Juliet's marriage to a Seaton. You know how she felt."

"But after she broke her engagement?"

"A good point to recall, Mother. It wasn't me she ran to when Severs tried to blackmail her. And"—he laughed—"what good would she have been to you then. That was before she became heiress to Jeff Dawson's money."

Chapter Thirty-six

There was nothing Kitty could do except clean up the mess and provide comfort. Even with only limited knowledge of a woman in the family way, Jeff knew Juliet had lost too much blood. Desolate, he picked up the pieces of the beautiful dress and delicate undergarments from the stairs and floor, while Kitty fussed with the distraught Juliet behind the closed door above him. Juliet didn't want him in the room. She didn't want to see him.

Kitty spent most of New Year's Day boiling and bleaching sheets and rags. So much blood from one woman carrying a tiny thing that never developed into a real child. How quickly the passion had degenerated into misgiving and loss. He'd been too rough. His touch would have been so different had he known she carried his child.

But would that have prevented the loss?

No, Kitty told him later in the day. "Her body weren't ready for this pregnancy. I think the first time some wombs refuse to let this happen to it. That baby be something strange, and it wants to be rid of it."

"But that's what a woman's body was designed for," he had argued.

"I know," she said, her voice full of unexpected compassion, "but that don't mean a body's never been pregnant befo' has to like it. Shoot! A body don't ever have to like it. My body gave birth to four fine boys, and it never liked none of 'em bein' there." She set a cup of coffee in front of him. "And other folk think maybe somethin' be wrong with the baby and nature doin' what's

239

needed by gettin' rid of it. You drink your coffee now, and I'll get you somethin' to eat. Don't you worry. My sweet baby girl will have other children."

He wasn't concerned about children, not yet. But he was weary with worry over Juliet, over her grief, her sense of loss. He couldn't shed the belief he was in some way responsible for the miscarriage and wondered if Juliet thought so, too.

*J*uliet watched the darkening sky through her windows. Kitty opened the curtains hours ago after coaxing her to eat a little chicken soup and cornbread. Clouds had gathered during the course of the afternoon, and now the wind picked up and blew in gusts, creating that familiar, lonely howl, which today seeped into her soul, as grief gripped her heart. The horrible bleeding had lessened, but remained heavy. She told herself the remains of her baby had long washed out of her, but Kitty said the bleeding would continue for several days, like her monthly flux, but heavier.

She closed her eyes tight against the angry sky, but she could not shut out the howls of the wind. She had wanted the baby. Wanted to see Jeff's eyes warm in care and tenderness when she told him. Now she'd never know how he would have reacted. He could not share her loss, he'd not known of the child until it was gone.

A soft knock sounded on the door joining their rooms, and her heart began to pound. She didn't want to face him, and he must have realized that because he didn't wait for her response. With the opening of the door, she remained on her side, facing away from him, her cheek on the pillow.

The feather mattress gave beneath his weight, and she huddled farther beneath the covers.

"It's cold in here," he said quietly. "I need to check the vent."

The vent was closed, and Kitty had not started a fire in the fireplace; Juliet hadn't wanted her to.

"Juliet? Talk to me."

"What can I say to you?"

Silence, and her heartbeat quickened with fear he might leave

240

her. Despite her earlier reluctance to face him, he was here, and need for him, greater than anything she'd ever known, devoured her. If he left her now, she would go insane.

"Did I do this?"

Guilt and remorse drove the emotion in his voice. She moved her arm and pushed the covers from her head. He was sitting on the edge of the bed in a clean, white shirt and leaning toward her. One hand he'd placed flat on the mattress beside her covered hip, the other he held fisted across his breeches-clad thigh.

He was so handsome...and so sad, and she needed him so much. Juliet blinked back tears at the realization he needed her, too.

"You helped me make the baby."

"I mean the miscarriage."

She felt her chin puckering, and her eyes stung. "Of course not, why would you think that?"

"I was rough. I-I—"

The tears welled up. "It wasn't you. I'd been spotting. Kitty says sometimes...." Convulsed with grief, she could not continue.

"You'd been bleeding?"

"Yes." Juliet turned from him and tried to fight back the tears. One rolled down her cheek anyway, and she swiped at it with the back of her hand.

"Then why—"

"I had to t-tell you." She stopped a moment to fight off a sob. "I was sick every day and so afraid you'd realize I was pregnant before I told you."

"Why didn't you just tell me?"

"I wanted you to forgive me first, to want me." She closed her eyes tight. "To sleep in bed with me every night like I was your wife and the mother of your child and not some whore you bought for an hour's pleasure."

"You think I thought of you like that?"

She blinked. "You had a right to think of me like that after what I did. I know it's my fault. I know I agreed to be what you said you wanted. I knew that probably meant you enjoyed having a physical relationship with me. But I wanted us to be more."

241

Disbelief haunted his eyes, and he shook his head. Without hesitation he stretched his hand across her blanketed body. "We are more, Juliet. We've always been more. I gave you my name. Who knows why people fall in love, but I have loved you since the moment you looked at me down by the creek and said, 'There's a wolf'. "

"But at the wedding...." She pulled a hand from beneath the covers and tentatively placed it in the one he offered.

His fingers closed around hers, and he rubbed her knuckles with his thumb. "It was a lie to protect my ego, and my heart. I'd have killed another man before I let him touch you. You were mine. You gave yourself to me. I wasn't about to let you go, and I refused to believe you wanted me to."

"And I didn't. My feelings for you were what finally compelled me to break my engagement to Matt, and no sooner had I done so, then it seemed my dreams were stolen from me."

"By Severs?"

"By my family, by duty. Oh, Jeff, I'm sorry for using you that night. I didn't think you wanted me, not to marry, not then. We hardly knew each other, and there was so much wrong between...." She breathed in. "I certainly didn't think you'd help me protect Tucker. But I wanted you. For a moment in time, I wanted to be yours and you to be mine."

His fingers tightened around hers, and she sat up.

"Tell me why?"

"Because I loved you, but there was no time for love to grow."

He tugged on her hand and pulled her to him. Heat and hardness and the scents of soap and sandalwood seeped through her cotton nightgown and her senses and embraced her wounded psyche. Her arms circled his neck, and in final, sweet surrender, she started to cry. "I don't want to fight anymore." She hid her face against his throat. "I'm so sorry I lost our baby."

"I'm sorry we lost our baby, too, sweetheart."

She hugged him tighter, losing herself in his warmth and his strength, providing him hers in return. She felt the subtle tremors racing through his body and knew he, too, had surrendered to the emotion passing between them. Her loss was his and always would be.

"God, Jeff, I love you so much."

He kissed her cheeks and lips and wiped her tears. She responded by kissing his wet cheeks. Then he stood and lifted her in his arms. "Now, I'm taking you with me, where you belong."

Jeff had already turned back his bed and propped the pillows for her head. Gently, he laid her on the side closest to the fire that roared in the fireplace and tucked her in. He had planned on moving her to his room this evening, and that realization almost moved her to tears once more.

He sat on the bed and leaned forward to kiss her long and slow. Breaking the kiss, he said, "Kitty made dinner, cabbage and black-eyed peas, money and luck for Mary's grand new year that's coming. I've eaten. I'll bring you yours." He looked around. "The dresser is empty, and there's plenty of space in the wardrobe. You move your things in as soon as you feel better." He stilled, and his eyes held hers. "And when you're ready, we'll make another baby."

Chapter Thirty-seven

Jeff woke, alert.

Juliet lay cuddled next to him, sleeping soundly. He'd feared she wouldn't be able to. They'd lain awake talking for hours, her sometimes crying for the child they'd lost or for her mother. He wasn't always sure which. She was depressed, but he no longer doubted her need for him. She wanted him, and God knew he wanted her. They'd make other children and raise them here at White Oak Glen.

The north wind sighed softly around the side of the house. In the distance, a horse neighed.

He rolled his head on the pillow and listened.

A flickering light played on the far wall. The room was cold, and it struck him that the fire in the fireplace had long gone out. Away from the house, Old Son cried out, and Jeff's heart beat a little faster. Careful not to wake Juliet, he sat up and looked over her, out the back window. Instantly, his heart crashed against his ribs, then he was out of bed, scrambling for his boots.

In the dining room he almost collided with Kitty, who hollered at him what he already knew: the barn was on fire; his animals were trapped inside.

"Go get Toby," he cried, not breaking his stride when he got to the breezeway leading to the cookhouse.

"Lordy, Massa Jeff, ain't no way we gonna save that barn."

"I'll get the animals out. You get Toby!" he yelled over his shoulder.

The frigid air braced him as he raced to the barn. From a distance, he could see that the fire was along the back wall of the

244

building. The hay had caught, and soon it would reach the loft. Strangely, the double doors, one beating with the wind against the structure's front wall, stood wide open, and Jeff wondered if Toby was already there.

He stopped at the entrance. Above him, smoke billowed, and amid the din of roaring, crackling flames, the inside of the barn was horribly bright. The stalls were open, the animals gone. He tensed, but a sixth sense warned him he was too late, and when he spun around, a shovel's spade filled his vision. Then pain and light eclipsed the brilliant rage of the fire.

Juliet heard Kitty cry out, then the slamming of a door. She reached for Jeff and found the spot where he should have been still warm.

The room glowed orange. Disoriented, she sat up. She was in Jeff's room, *their* room.

Outside something banged, and her heartbeat quickened. It was that barn door, again.

She threw back the covers and moved her legs over the side of the bed. Throat dry, she looked out the window and saw the flames from the glowing building.

Lord God in heaven, the animals! Jeff would be trying to get them out, and from the looks of things it was too late. She didn't bother with her robe. She couldn't live without Jeff Dawson.

"Where is he?" she screamed at Kitty, who headed down the foyer toward her.

"He's gone, he's done gone to that barn." Kitty wrung her hands. "I started after Toby like he told me, but I done seen 'em down there, baby girl. They dressed like Ku Klux with their heads covered in sheets so no one knows who they are."

Juliet's head whirled, and her chest ached from a heart now racing out of control.

"Where's Toby?" she cried.

"I didn't get him. He can't go out there with..."—Juliet started around Kitty—"No!" Kitty grabbed her. "You ain't goin' out there neither."

Juliet turned on the black woman in a fury and tore her arm free. "Don't touch me! Don't you dare try to stop me, Kitty." She rushed toward the back door. "Either help me or stay out of my way."

There'd be no help. Toby wouldn't dare confront anyone who looked like a Klansman, but she knew these barn burners weren't Klan. Adams County was not and never had been a Ku Klux stronghold. Worse, Juliet doubted how much Kitty would be willing to sacrifice for a man she believed might be a monster.

She burst through the back door, ignoring the cold, hard ground on her bare feet. Picking up speed, she sprinted around the cookhouse, then tripped on the hem of her nightgown and fell to the ground with a painful grunt. Before her the fiery barn illuminated the night. Silhouettes milled in front of it while the gusting wind fanned its flames into the treetops. She choked on the air in her lungs and forced herself to her feet. Jeff was inside that inferno—she knew it.

She had no weapon and no help, and the terror of losing Jeff touched her sanity. Jedediah Wolfson's name tore from her lips, invoking a spirit whose ghostly existence hovered at the fringes of her conscious thought. Her anguished cry, shielded by the roar of the flames, went unheard by the attackers, and was, in essence, a silent plea disseminated by the wind.

Faith renewed her strength, and she arrived at the barn un-noticed by the raiders. Inside the burning building, a man stirred.

It was Jeff, and he was alive!

He tried to rise to escape the insidious flames. A hooded man, his back to her, raised a rifle and took aim inside.

"Wing him," one shouted, "let him burn."

A shovel lay on the ground behind the shooter, and Juliet picked it up. Wielding it with rage and strength she didn't know she possessed, she brought it down on the man's back. He arched up, his arms spread wide, and the shot went wild.

The shooter fell, then rolled away from her. His three cohorts, their faces also hooded, turned. Two of them rushed her, but Juliet managed to grasp the fallen rifle before a body blow slammed her to the ground and knocked the wind out of her. Debilitating pain left her aware of only the muffled shouts to grab her. Then someone cried out Dawson was on his feet, and behind her, Kitty screeched for the white-trash coward to let her baby girl go. Juliet heard a thud. Kitty screamed again, her cry followed by a muffled, masculine curse. Juliet closed her eyes and fought back the pain. She heard a slap simultaneous with a shout to "get the nigra bitch."

Juliet's pain ebbed, and she filled her lungs with air before kicking out at the man holding her. Her world was spinning out of control. Then the screams, the thuds, and even the roar of the fire muted, and the air convulsed with the mind-splintering howl of a wolf that seemed to emanate from nowhere, yet was everywhere, echoing around them.

"Oh God, oh God...."

Toby's voice.

The man pinning her let her go. Juliet didn't see what the others were doing, and she didn't care. Holding the rifle, she scrambled up and faced the searing heat. In front of her, Jeff stumbled toward the front of the barn. The cloaked assailant standing closest to the entry turned and let out a warning shout just as Jeff struck out with his fist. It was a flailing blow, but surprise worked to Jeff's advantage, and the man fell backward, away from the burning structure.

Juliet started toward Jeff, hurt and in need of her help, but steel-like fingers dug into her shoulder. With a desperate cry, Juliet turned on the hooded man holding her back. Behind him, Kitty raised the commandeered shovel and brought it down on his head.

Free at last, Juliet focused on Jeff, but now two men pulled him back and held him. The one he had punched rose and moved in to counterattack his helpless opponent. To her side, Juliet heard another thud and Kitty's angry curse, telling the good-for-nothing trash to keep down. Juliet presumed she'd again clobbered her victim with the shovel.

Jeff doubled over from a punch, and all else around Juliet

ceased to register. Raising the rifle, she moved forward, screaming for the men to stop. The hitter pulled his fist back again, ignoring her, and she fired—not into the group—she feared hitting Jeff. Her aim didn't matter, the proximity and sharp sound of the blast served its purpose, and the beating stopped.

"Let him go, you filthy cowards!" Beyond them, a deafening racket obliterated her words as the rear of the barn collapsed in a hail of sparks and billowing smoke. She wanted Jeff away from these men, away from the precarious structure.

The hitter moved closer to her. "What are you going to do? You can't kill another human being."

Hot anger scorched her veins, followed by an icy calm.

Juliet pointed the rifle at the speaker. "You care to risk that?" she shouted over the roar of the flames, licking through the front roof of the barn.

"Yes."

She took two desperate steps forward, keeping the rifle on the talker. He laughed at her, and as the wood hissed behind his back, he turned and looked toward the raging flames. "Throw him back—"

Juliet screamed and raised the rifle as a second otherworldly howl rose above the manmade horror. One of the two men holding Jeff abruptly let him go. "If this son-of-a-bitch is the wolf," the man yelled, pointing at Jeff, "then what the hell is that?" The man whirled and ran for the woods.

Jeff turned on his remaining captor and knocked him to the ground. The man scrambled to get away, but Jeff kicked him before he could get back to his feet. The downed man tore at his hood, an obvious hindrance now to his defense; and the most odious of the group, no doubt the leader, that same man who had cried out to let Jeff burn and who had dared speak to Juliet, started toward the struggle. Juliet, rifle at the ready, pushed in front of him, and he stopped.

It was hot where they stood and bright, the entire front of the barn now crackling in flames. "Still think I won't shoot you?" she cried over the din. How she hated him, this person who stood

248

before her. He said nothing, but she could see his eyes beneath
the holes cut in the cotton cloth. She had his full attention. Her
heart pounded anew, no longer in fear, but in anger. "Take off
your hood, you coward. I want to see your face one more time
before I kill you."

"You won't kill me."

"Take it off, Tucker!"

He whipped the hood off his head and threw it at her, catching the rifle barrel, for which he immediately lunged, but Juliet
was already squeezing the trigger. Tucker flew backward, the
crack of the rifle drowning his cry. Bile burned her throat, and
she stepped forward and glared into his shocked gaze. Blood was
creeping over his britches and oozing between his fingers, which
clutched his outstretched thigh.

"I most certainly will kill you," she said, her voice cold. She
took another step closer to him and settled the rifle, then cocked
it. Tucker's eyes widened, and she relished the satisfaction. "In
fact, that's exactly what I intend to do."

$\mathcal{A}$ shot had exploded simultaneous with the punch that left
Jeff's opponent unconscious and Jeff crashing to his knees. He
jerked his pounding head around and, with renewed vigor, wiped
the blood dripping from his nose to his mouth on his shirtsleeve
and the metallic taste from his senses. This fight wasn't over.

Steadying himself with one arm, he twisted his shaking body
toward Juliet, ten paces away. Tucker Seaton, propped up on an
elbow, lay on the ground in front of her. She was talking to her
brother, but Jeff couldn't hear her words. He didn't need to. He
knew the stance, the aggression in her movements—the fear in
Tucker's eyes.

Jeff rose, and the ground swayed briefly beneath his feet. To
his left, Toby Horton stood holding an ax handle. Whether he'd
used it, Jeff didn't know. The point was he was here. Not far
from Toby stood Kitty, shovel in hand, ready to pound the
hooded prisoner sprawled at her feet.

Jeff motioned Toby to the man he'd beaten senseless, then

moved toward Juliet. Kitty was saying something to her, trying to sway her intent, but Juliet appeared undeterred. Steady as a rock, cold as death, she'd kill her brother if he didn't stop her.

She couldn't see him yet, and Jeff stopped short, fearing he'd frighten her. "Juliet?" he said, speaking as softly as he could and still be heard above the flames.

"Are you all right?" She wept out the words, and he sensed warmth and emotion flow back into her. Still, she didn't lower the rifle or turn from Tucker.

"I'm all right. Put down the gun, sweetheart."

"No!" She shook her head, but some of her resolve left her; he could almost feel it.

Kitty started to speak, but he waved her down, and she shut her mouth.

"You don't want to kill him, honey."

"He needs to die, Jeff. We'll have no peace as long as he lives. He's a back-shooting coward." She started to cry. "They put you in that barn. My God, you'd have burned to death if he'd had his way."

"I know," he said, stepping closer. He touched her arm, but she held steady. "Look at me, Juliet."

She sucked back a sob, then started to shake.

"Look at me."

She looked the other way. "Let me kill him. Why would you care if he died?"

"I don't give a damn about him, but I care the world for you." He pushed at her arm, trying to force it down. For a moment she resisted, then gave him a wall-eyed glance, her cheek glistening with tears.

"It's not easy to kill a man, Juliet, but sometimes it's easier to kill than to live with it afterwards. I know about killing. I never want you to. His being your brother would make it ten times worse. Give me the rifle and come to me."

She loosened her grip, and he took the weapon. Holding the barrel up, he folded her into his arms, and she clung to him and sobbed against his chest.

At their feet, Tucker fell back, the tension dissipating from his strained body almost as quickly as his blood flowed onto the cold ground. Jeff shook his head. They needed to get that bleeding stopped or the bastard was going to bleed to death, and Juliet would have killed her brother as surely as if she'd fired that second bullet through his heart.

Chapter Thirty-eight

"Somethin' ain't right here, and it happened since you come back."

Jeff squinted at Kitty. Even that small movement hurt. "You mean the wolf, or the killings, or my good neighbors trying to kill me last night?"

"There be those who say the cause is one and the same." She set a bowl of grits in front of him. "And that ain't no wolf out there, neither. Not that was howlin' last night. Oh, it might look like a wolf..."

He focused on her concessionary statement — no one had seen the thing except Juliet.

"...but it ain't one. That thing be a spirit of some sort, a demon maybe, and it come to help you last night."

Despite his throbbing head, he couldn't resist a smile. Notwithstanding the truly important concerns arising from last night, Kitty was concocting ghost stories. But finally she was confronting him face to face instead of whispering to others behind his back.

He filled his spoon with hot grits and blew on them.

And she'd been out there, she and Toby, fighting for him...or maybe they'd been fighting for Juliet. Whichever, Kitty was no longer hiding her doubts.

"I don't know what's out there, Kitty, but I imagine it's only a lone wolf."

"You heard it howl." She leaned toward him. "You heard it, you know you did. Ain't no wolf ever had a cry like that. None I ever heard."

He wondered how many wolves she had heard over the course of her life. Still, he agreed with what she implied. He'd heard plenty of wolves in the Rockies during winters so bitter the beasts couldn't find enough to eat and a man had to fear for his life when crossing paths with a pack of them. Never had he heard a howl as otherworldly as he'd heard last night. He shuddered, but told himself it was from the cold.

The door to the cookhouse slammed, and Jeff listened to Will's awkward gait moving up the breezeway. His old friend entered the dining room and frowned at Jeff. "Well, boy, it's colder'n a witch's tit out there, and you need a new barn."

Jeff pointed to the chair opposite, and Will sat.

"You wantin' some grits, Mister Will?" Kitty said.

"And coffee, too, thank ye, Auntie." He studied Jeff. "That knot on your forehead's big as a chicken egg. Wonder the blow didn't kill ya."

"Got a hard head. Swelling's on the outside. Might be uglier, but it's a hell of a lot safer."

"Nose broke?"

"Nope."

Kitty set a mug of steaming coffee in front of Will. He'd been here since sunup. Toby had fetched him on his way back from Natchez after summoning the sheriff. Deputy Floyd was who showed up. He arrested three men shortly before dawn, Tucker Seaton and two little known neighbors, Lewis Greenwood and Barnabus Clayton. Tucker had sneered when Floyd asked him the name of the man who got away.

"Total loss," Will said, "all your winter feed."

"Well, I only have two horses, a pair of mules, and a damn fine milk cow, so the feed lost wasn't that much. I'm thankful they got the animals out."

"Hell, yeah"—Will snorted—"they'll burn a man to death, but they'll save the animals. Lost your equipment, your wagon."

"Lost my saddle. I bought that saddle in Denver." Jeff smiled wryly. "Still have all my teeth, though."

Truth was, given all he could have lost last night, he really didn't care. He had his life — he looked toward the ceiling and the bedroom upstairs — and he had the woman he loved. The material losses he would absorb.

"She finally sleepin'?"

"Yep."

Juliet hadn't left his side while they waited for Floyd. Kitty brought them coats and helped stand guard while he tied up the prisoners. Kitty had also been the one to work on Tucker's leg. Juliet wouldn't go near her brother.

Not knowing who the fourth man was, Jeff had spent an anxious two hours sitting in the glowing embers of the fallen barn, wondering if that person would return and take a potshot at him from the safety of the woods. He'd little choice in that, though. Tucker couldn't walk and the man Kitty cold-cocked still hadn't regained consciousness by the time the deputy arrived. As for Jeff, he was dizzy from the initial blow dealt to his head, and Juliet was weak from her own ordeal. Kitty might have been willing to drag one man the fifty some-odd yards to the safety of the house, but he didn't think she'd have stood for three.

"Yo, inside, Jeff Dawson?"

The call came from the front of the house. Jeff rose, and Will followed. Wexford Seaton, on foot, waited at the bottom of the front porch stairs. He held the reins of his quarter-horse mare. A body lay draped over her back. Jeff met Wex's eyes.

"One of Floyd's deputies stopped by this morning and told us that Tucker, Greenwood, and Clayton are under arrest for burning down your barn. Said one man escaped."

Jeff nodded and didn't bring up the attempted murder charge.

"Well, Dawson, I think I may have your fourth man." He indicated the body lying across the saddle. "It's Frank Sikes. His jugular's severed."

"Where'd you find him?" Jeff asked, coming off the porch.

"Our northwest quadrant, edge of the woods, right where he would have been if he'd been high-tailin' it away from your place."

Jeff lifted the blanket covering the body. Maybe it was nothing more than the result of his own beating during the night, but to Jeff's eyes, Sikes' face looked pale blue, and specks of purplish blood dotted the cheek turned to him. Queasy, Jeff dropped the blanket. He didn't look closely at the neck wound.

"You're taking him to town, I suppose?"

"I am."

"I'll tag along with you, if you don't mind."

Wex shrugged. "Fine with me."

"I thought for sure you were the fourth man, Seaton."

"Yeah"—Wex shifted his weight—"I figured you probably did, but I do my midnight prowling with easy women, not trying to kill ghosts."

Jeff smiled at the irony before turning to Will. "You'll stay with Juliet until I get back?"

"I'll be stayin' for longer'n that, boy. Little gal asked me to this mornin' before you got her to go on up to bed."

Jeff grasped Will's beefy shoulder. "Thanks, friend."

Chapter Thirty-nine

"According to the coroner, an animal killed Sikes. Under the circumstances, the likeliest beast is a wolf."

Jeff had arrived home, dead on his feet, not a quarter of an hour ago to find Will and Juliet in front of the parlor fireplace, Kitty with a big pot of chicken gumbo in the cookhouse, and everyone waiting supper on him.

"How—"

"Sikes was killed in the same way an animal kills its prey," Jeff said, anticipating Will's question. "It went for his jugular. The way old Doc Maynard explained it, the women's wounds started here"—he pointed to the area of his Adam's apple. "The killer inserted a knife right under the chin, cut, and then literally ripped their throats out. They died of asphyxiation."

"Sikes bled to death?" Juliet said.

"Well..." Jeff glanced at Will, who grinned at him.

"Neck broke, too, weren't it?"

"Yes."

Will slapped his knee. "Knew it. I darn sure knew it."

Jeff swallowed and took Juliet's hand. She was a pale but still stunning beauty in green taffeta, so dark it was almost black. In deference to her grief for their lost child, he reckoned.

"There's something else that you need to know, sweetheart." Damn, he didn't want to tell her this. "Tucker and the other two are out of jail."

She stared at him. "Why?"

"The bail hearing went before Judge Whitley at ten this morning. The charge was arson."

"Arson?" she hissed. "What about attempted murder?"

"Tucker says it didn't happen. Says burning down our barn was revenge for killing his stock, and he regrets his poor judgment."

Her eyes opened wider. "Barn burning is abhorrent enough to merit their being hanged as far as I'm concerned. Did anyone listen to you?"

"I wasn't there. I didn't know they'd see the judge today. The prosecutor has dropped charges of attempted murder."

"How could he? What did Floyd say?"

"They're all in the same pocket, Juliet."

"Morton Severs'."

It was a statement on her part. She knew—better than him— how justice worked since the end of the war. "I think they probably all share a common pocket, but you're right, it was Severs who paid their bail.

"Tucker's laid up pretty good with that leg." He squeezed her hand. "It'll be all right."

"How can you say that? He's laid up only until he heals. They tried to *kill* you." She blinked rapidly and looked away. She was tired of crying, she'd told him so before going up to bed this morning.

He stood and placed a hand on her shoulder. His beautiful wife was angry and scared and frustrated, all on top of grieving. He wished she could rest.

"What did Wex say about the wolf?"

Jeff shrugged. "Not much, honey. He's always known he had a wolf killing his stock."

"He didn't say anything about you being a werewolf?"

"Not in front of me."

"We have no one to turn to."

"There are good people here," he said, kneeling on one knee beside her. "There are the Tates and Wallaces, the Barbers"—he nodded at Will—"and Will is going to stay with us awhile."

"But when will it ever be over? Is Benton Floyd doing anything to find the murderer?"

"Murderers," he said. "There are two if you count the wolf."

"You mean Sikes' killer?"

"Yes."

"Oh, Jeff, that wasn't murder. That was justice, and though I never told him to kill Sikes, I did call for the beast last night."

Chapter Forty

January was halfway gone already. The moon waxed, and Jeff worried. He fought to focus on a human killer, but the shadow of that wolf clouded his mind. No matter how often these past two weeks Juliet defended the thing, he wasn't resting comfortably, knowing it was out there. She honestly believed it came to their aid the night of the barn burning because she called it, and he hoped like hell no one else got wind of the fact she thought she could conjure it at will. Their neighbors had proven they could be dangerous, but that wolf was dangerous, too. Undoubtedly, it killed Sikes. Eliminating it from the scene would solve a lot of problems—not all, perhaps, but some. He needed to hunt it down and destroy it.

"We'll build a brick pillar here, hollow in the middle."

Jeff reoriented and listened to what Bill Tillman, the contractor for the new bath, was explaining to him.

"In addition to supporting the water tank on the roof, it will serve a secondary purpose by hiding the pipes. We'll put the water heater here." The man moved around the mess in what was once the Seaton nursery. "The tub will go here. Every time you get ready for a hot bath, all you'll have to do is open the faucet and climb in."

"The toilet?" Jeff had acquiesced to this contraption under duress. Flushing nasty things through pipes in the walls of one's home was anathema to him. His daddy would not have liked this, not one damn bit.

"Here," Tillman said, "close to the tub. Your wife did a nice job of working this out. She knows exactly what she wants."

Jeff warmed with his recollection of Juliet sitting between him and John Rich, the decorator from New Orleans, and describing her proposed changes for the house. Fortunately, Rich worked with an architect, and that's what, it turned out, Juliet's "decorative" changes required. Except for commenting on a few details regarding his study, Jeff had said nothing and tried to concentrate on her enthusiasm. Distracted by her jasmine scent and her proximity, his only intelligent thought had been how glad he was she was making the effort on the house, meaning he didn't have to. That had been just last month, before they made up.

"Yeah"—he averted his eyes and smiled—"she makes a habit of getting what she wants even before she knows she wants it."

"Good way to do it," Tillman said, "as long as she knows she's got what she wants once she's got it."

And she does, Jeff thought minutes later as he crossed her old bedroom into theirs. And thank goodness it was him.

Juliet was rising, none too early.

"You should have waked me," she admonished.

"You're tired. I want those dark circles gone from under your eyes."

She started to throw back the covers, but he moved fast and stayed her.

"What now, husband?"

"I may not be able to make love to you, but I sure can kiss you," he said and proceeded to do so. After a moment, he pulled back. "I just talked to Tillman. The bathroom is, as best I can tell, coming along nicely."

"The barn?"

"Ted Clements will be here this afternoon."

"I thought you were going to do it yourself?"

He shook his head and kissed her again. "Changed my mind. Decided that since I have to rebuild the thing, I may as well make it bigger."

"How much bigger?"

"Double its size."

She gave him an appraising look. "For your horses?"

He grinned. "Yep, and I'm putting in a full loft."

Leaning forward, he touched his forehead to hers. She circled his neck with her arms and drew his lips to her lips. Liquid heat rushed through him.

She kissed him passionately, and he groaned. Immediately, she let him go. "I'm sorry, Jeff, I forget sometimes it's not as easy for you—"

"It's all right," he said, his voice husky.

"It's not."

He took her lips again. "Juliet," he whispered after the kiss, "how much do you know about sodomy?"

Her smile was downright sinful. "Only the perverse act you performed on me. Why?"

"Are you interested in getting even?"

"Oh, yes, my darling, I certainly am."

*J*uliet brushed her fingertips over the textured surface of the wallpaper. This set of samples held more promise than the two previous ones she'd looked at. She lifted the page and looked at the sample beneath it. Pretty, and she smiled to herself. Despite her late start, she'd accomplished much today, dispensing retribution on her husband included. Jeff had left their bedroom this morning a happy man.

"It's that Faye Greenwood."

Juliet jumped and wiped the sinful smile from her face. Kitty had snuck up on her and now stood in the parlor doorway watching her with concern in her eyes.

"She be out front with her two little 'uns. Says she wants to talk to you."

Concern, Juliet realized, that had nothing to do with her and Jeff's mid-morning tryst. She set her wallpaper samples atop the existing stack on the floor—there was no room left on the piled settee—and rose. Faye Greenwood was the wife of Lewis Greenwood, one of the men who participated in the barn burning two weeks ago. She knew the woman, but not well. They'd met at Josephus Braxton's church while Juliet had still been engaged to Matt, and she had no idea at all what would bring this person to her home.

The porch was cold and windy, but Juliet felt no compunction to ask the woman into the house. The children, a small tow-headed boy of about five and a darker-haired toddler girl sitting on her mother's hip, almost caused her to change her mind. Steeling herself, Juliet pulled the front door closed behind her. Faye Greenwood was a tall, willowy woman with dull hair and pale, green eyes, which now bore into Juliet. Obviously, she hadn't come to apologize for her husband.

"Missus Greenwood?"

The woman situated the baby on her hip, nodded stiffly, then rolled her strained lips together before licking them. "Something killed our cow last night."

So, it had finally happened to someone other than the Seatons. Juliet folded her arms over her breasts.

"Your man did it," the woman said.

"My husband was in bed with me the whole night."

"I don't think so."

"I would advise you to take my word for it and be more concerned with how your own husband spends his nights." Juliet turned to go back in the house.

"We needed that cow. We saved for months and months before my little one here was born. My babies need that milk."

Juliet glanced at the little girl, who watched her with wide blue eyes and a small thumb stuck between pink lips. She could give the woman money for a new milk cow, though for the life of her she couldn't think why she should. She knew for a fact the Greenwoods had a large family base and also the support of the Baptist Church.

"My husband did not kill your cow, Missus Greenwood."

"Then he knows who or what did."

"The wolf killed the cow, you said so yourself."

"I said 'something' killed the cow."

"For your children's sake, I am sorry." Juliet reached for the door.

"I want compensation."

Juliet dropped her hand and spun around. "Do you intend to compensate me for my barn?"

"I had nothing to do with that. And my man said it was to get even for Tucker Seaton's stock that Dawson's been killin' off."

"First, my husband hasn't killed any Seaton stock. Second, Tucker wouldn't know what stock he's lost and what he hasn't. He hasn't counted, fed, or even looked at a cow in over a year. What Tucker does want is Jeff Dawson dead." Juliet narrowed her eyes. "Does your husband know you're here?"

"No, but I had a hankerin' to give you a piece of my mind."

"There's no piece of your mind I wish to have, Missus Greenwood. It is decidedly lacking in intelligence and sound judgment."

Faye Greenwood's mouth dropped open.

"And let me tell you something else. New Year's night, I hit your husband in the back of his head as he raised his rifle to shoot my unarmed husband. Barn burning is bad enough, but your husband was part of a cold-blooded plot to commit murder."

"That's not what the judge thinks."

"I was at that barn, Missus Greenwood, and the judge is in Morton Severs' pocket. You are married to a dog, who accepted blood money from a thieving carpetbagger to harm a tried and true Confederate veteran."

Faye Greenwood's eyes opened wide. "He was trying to help your brother. He didn't know—"

"Oh, Missus Greenwood, he's no better than a turncoat scalawag. Your husband trespassed on our land and tried to kill the man I love with no more justification than pure meanness and his own ignorance. He's nothing but a lowly coward who wore a sheet over his head to hide his face. He deserves to lose more than a cow."

"Now, you see—"

"No, I will not. You came here today looking to bully me into covering a loss that neither my husband nor I caused you. I pity your children more for the man who will raise them than for their temporary loss of milk. Get Morton Severs to replace your cow.

For Jeff Dawson to do so would be a false acknowledgment of guilt. And as long as you have that man to take care of you, don't ask me or mine for another thing, and you and yours stay off Dawson land."

Her entire body was shaking when she slammed the door behind her. Kitty waited inside the entry.

"Your Master Dawson probably would not approve of the way I handled that."

Kitty shook her head. "Oh, no, baby child, you done right. There's some things best handled by a woman, and another woman's one of 'em. You is feelin' guilty 'bout them little 'uns, but you oughtn't. Reason she brought them over was so you'd feel bad. They'll be okay. That gal's daddy hid his coin from the Yankees back in '63. Ain't none of his kids missed a meal or a tax payment. That old man, he don't like that Lewis Greenwood neither as I hear tell it, but he won't let his grandbabies do without."

Chapter Forty-one

Roxanne...perfect...he'd paid for her before. She knew and trusted him. Her place was on the outskirts of town, up the road a little from the Methodist Church. Everything out that way would be deserted. It would be easy to get her into the woods, to take her over and over while she struggled beneath him on the cold ground, their fornicating watched by a waxing moon.

He loved this time of month. People lately talked of nothing but werewolves, but the fools didn't understand what they were talking about. For centuries the common folk had misinterpreted what the beast really was. He knew because he was one, as surely as he knew that other thing out there was something different.

He smiled at the pretty, young woman who approached him. She traced her index finger from his collarbone to his left nipple in silent greeting. Unseen in the dark, he tugged on her hand, pulling her with him. The changes in the moon altered his mind and his body. He was better, stronger—more virile and more potent.

Tonight he would howl.

"Your whiskey, darling."

Morton Severs scowled at the glass of amber liquid, then looked at Della. "You're going up?"

She gave him a provocative smile. "I am. I hoped you'd come with me."

His mood immediately mellowed. Della was a lovely woman, more refined as a mistress than the streetwalker he'd picked up on Silver Street years ago. "Let me drink this. It'll help lighten my mood."

She moved behind him to rub his shoulders. "I can get you in a better mood."

He closed his eyes and started to relax, her adept fingers working the tension out of his muscles.

"You went to visit Tucker Seaton today?"

"Yes, he's starting to get around some. Damn, I still cannot believe those worthless fools let Dawson get away, and Seaton allowed his sister to shoot him to boot. Under different circumstances, I'd consider the entire event comical.

"Seaton has drunk so much liquor in the past four months he can't think properly anymore. He actually believes Dawson is dead, a ghost and an evil spirit to boot, which transforms into a wolf to wreak vengeance on his enemies. So I planted the seed he should kill the thing." Severs looked over his shoulder at Della. "Tell me what kind of imbecile would try to kill something he believes already dead?"

A perplexed look moved over her face. "How would you get rid of such a thing, Morton?"

He sat forward in frustration. "Are all you Southerners lunatics, Della?"

She dropped her hands and sighed. "Must have been losing the war that did it to us."

"Losing the war, hell. The war was a symptom of your problem, not the cause. You were lunatics before the thing began."

"You're digressing, darling," she said. "Does Dawson know you were part of the plot to kill him?"

"If he's got more of a brain than the rest of you, he does. I was the one who bailed the bungling idiots out of jail."

She came around and sat in his lap. Her hands around his neck, she kissed him deeply, and his blood heated. Of all the things he'd taken from the South, Della Ross was his favorite.

"You need to put Juliet Dawson behind you, Morton, before you pay too high a price for your obsession."

He untied her dressing gown and reached for a breast. "I'm

266

not obsessed with her, Della. I'm obsessed with the fact that she and that son-of-a-bitch she married made me the laughing stock of Natchez."

He caressed a nipple. Della arched back and moaned.

"Am I really such an awful man, honey?"

Della chuckled and straightened in his arms. "When you're not plotting murder or slander, no." She kissed him before he could respond. "But remember, darling, I'm thirty-eight years old and have no illusions left. Juliet is nineteen and deeply in love with Jeff Dawson. What you would have forced on her was tantamount to rape, rape that would last a lifetime."

He snorted and slapped her playfully on the hip. "If she loves him, good. I regret the fact his death will leave her a wealthy widow. Knowing she will grieve at his loss gives me some satisfaction."

"Leave them be, Morton."

Leaving Juliet and Jeff Dawson to live happily ever after galled him. "I need to be rid of him under any circumstance. A few days after those imbeciles botched the barn burning, I found out that Dawson had bought Timothy Morrison's share of Delta Shipping."

"I didn't know you were interested in purchasing another—"

"I'm not. Delta Shipping is a competitor. I wanted it to fold, and it was about to. It won't now, at least not anytime soon, with the money Dawson's got to put in it."

"You are solvent, established. You're taking a risk—"

"Despite Phil Sheridan's blustering over fixing the problem up in Vicksburg, it's only a matter of time now before the South will be back in Southern hands. Southern boys who never bore arms against the United States will grow up and vote. A Seaton for a wife would have put me in good stead—some of those sons of the South would have been mine. That won't happen now."

She pursed her lips. "So, find a more willing daughter of the Old South."

"Perhaps, but Juliet was by far the most appealing for both her bloodlines and her beauty." He shook his head. "Damn, I hate Jeff Dawson." He tightened his lips and glared at her. "I'm going to get even with him, Della, him and his bride."

She caught his jaw in her hand, and smoothed his mustache with her thumb. "I'm in the mood for a rough ride tonight," she said, rising from his lap. "Finish your drink and come upstairs." She smiled wickedly. "You can pretend I'm Juliet Dawson."

The thought of a little tender abuse sent blood rushing to his penis, and it stiffened, straining against his trousers. "I'll be right up."

Breath heavier, he watched the gentle sway of Della's hips as she sashayed to the study door. She looked back once over her shoulder, flagrant promise in her eyes.

Severs leaned back in his chair. He, the circuit court judges, and the prosecutor shared the political and monetary perquisites protected by the Republican party's justifiable gorging on its victory over these traitors. Jeff Dawson, of course, was financially capable of countering their "influence" beyond their circle, but even if he were to stoop to such a tactic, Dawson was still a disenfranchised Democrat and an ex-Confederate to boot.

He took a sip of whiskey. The fine bourbon burned his gullet and warmed his stomach. If these murders kept up, he wouldn't even have to worry about Dawson facing trial. The locals would lynch him out of sheer terror. Fools. Didn't they know the bogey man did not exist?

On the porch outside, he heard a noise. He turned to the window an arm's length away, but saw nothing beyond the lace curtains, golden in the soft glow of lamplight. Severs closed his eyes. He'd give Della a little more time to get ready. Given his mood, if a rough night was what she wanted, he certainly was ready to accommodate her.

After a moment, he flexed his shoulders and rose. Again, the sound. Frowning, he stepped toward the window. Inexplicably, the hair rose on the back of his neck. He hesitated, then cautiously extended his hand and drew one curtain aside.

His hand twisted in the delicate lace, and his entire body convulsed in a sudden, but short-lived fit that left him clawing at his throat. On the other side of the glittering window pane, red eyes glowered at him.

Without warning, a twisted, bestial face smashed against the glass. Severs jumped, then gurgled a soundless scream, and the hideous countenance snarled, exposing sharp canines gleaming with the slobber drooling from its jowls before it pulled back.

Shards of glass and splintered wood spit at him, and Severs raised his arms to protect his face. His stiff fingers, still tangled in the lace, ripped the curtains from their rod; the racket muffled his cry. The thing's impact sent him plunging back into the chair. Pressure squeezed his throat, and he curled the fingers of his free hand into coarse hair, ripe with the sickening-sweet scent of days-old death. A violent twist of his neck eclipsed the stench and his need for air. The chair toppled to the floor, and he and the horrible thing that throttled him toppled with it.

Juliet opened her eyes. The weight of Jeff's arm was warm and heavy across her waist. Turning to him, she reached up and touched his shoulder.

"Jeff?"

"What?" He sounded as if he'd been awake a long time.

"Something woke you?"

"Yes," he grumbled, "you."

She shuddered and snuggled closer to him. "Something woke me, too."

She felt him tense and knew he was wide-awake now, alert, probably listening for sounds of another attack on his home.

"What was it?"

"In my dream, it was a scream."

A howl tore through the darkness, and Juliet sat up. At her back, Jeff cursed and pushed himself into a sitting position, then pulled her into the safety of his arms.

"Someone else has died," she said.

"The wolf—"

"No. The man did it. The wolf warns when someone is dead."

"He'd do better to warn us beforehand, sweetheart."

269

It was dark in the room. She could not see. Gently she clasped the arms that held her. "You think me foolish?"

"I think you're beautiful. But I think you're trying hard to believe in something that doesn't exist."

"How do you explain the things it does? Why does it attack your enemies?"

"I don't know, but I don't want you trying to make friends with it, do you understand?"

"It's a protector, not a friend. It's not really an animal, you know." She reached over her shoulder and touched his mouth. "You're laughing at me."

He kissed the palm of her hand, and she felt him move to her side from where he pushed her back onto the pillows. "I'm smiling at your faith."

Again the wolf's cry tore through the night, eerie, more banshee than wolf.

"He's so sad," Juliet said softly.

"Sad, my ass."

"He grieves, Jeff."

Down the hall, Will called to Jeff.

"I'm coming," he called back. His accompanying curse whispered across the darkness, and she felt him lean over her. "Well, my darling, I planned to take your mind off wolves and death and coax you back to sleep, but it seems I will be up the rest of the night."

She circled her arms around his neck. "I thank you for your consideration, sir, but I doubt what you planned would put me to sleep."

He laughed at that and threw back the covers.

Grabbing her robe, she climbed out of bed after him. "I'll get the coffee started, if Kitty hasn't already."

Chapter Forty-two

Jeff took a seat on the bench in front of Benton Floyd's desk. He and Will had found the woman not long before dawn. Jeff had not known who she was, but Will had. "Roxanne Champion," he had told him with a heavy voice. "A young prostitute with a heart of gold."

Like the other three women, her throat had been torn out. Again, Jeff suspected she'd been raped, but the concept seemed incongruous to Floyd, who maintained it made no sense to rape a whore.

"What did Doctor Maynard say about Severs?"

Floyd tossed his hat on top of his desk and pulled out a chair. "Same thing as he did about Sikes. Whatever killed Severs went for the jugular. Della Ross heard it crash through the window. It was gone, and Severs was dead, before she got downstairs."

"And Roxanne Champion died like the other three women?"

"That's what the doc says." Floyd blew out a tired breath. "So what we've got is a depraved human male killing women." He scrutinized Jeff. "But what about the men, Mister Dawson?

"According to your coroner, it's a wolf."

"A wolf conveniently killing your personal enemies. Funny thing, that, don't you think?"

Jeff started to the door. He really didn't know what to make of it, but he wasn't in the mood to be bullied. "They made themselves that, not me."

"You suggestin' Tucker Seaton, Lewis Greenwood, or Barney Clayton should be sleeping with one eye open?"

"If they sleep at all."

271

"Is that a threat?"

His hand on the doorknob, Jeff sighed. "All I'm saying, Deputy Sheriff Floyd, is you should have kept their asses in jail."

He lifted his face to the clear sky and blinked away tears wrought by sun and frigid wind. The scents of blood and fear stung his nostrils. Memory only, for neither clung to him in the light of day. They'd found Roxanne's body...but before that they'd found Severs with his severed artery and broken neck.

There was room for only one wolf here, him. But it had been Jeff Dawson who had captured their neighbors' attention, Jeff Dawson who twisted the minds of the ignorant toward the concept of a werewolf, Jeff Dawson who took credit for *his* handiwork. It had been Jeff Dawson who turned the head of the impetuous Juliet Seaton. Resolved, he grimaced at the noon sun. Jeff Dawson would pay a heavy price for treading on his territory.

The time had come to bring *Wolf* Dawson to his knees.

Juliet sat in the parlor, looking over a treatise on gas lighting. She wanted it, but Jeff was afraid of it, just as he detested the thought of a toilet and feared a kitchen in the house proper. She smiled to herself. It was hard to imagine him afraid of anything, but he balked at certain advancements, particularly those that violated tenets as old as time. Still, she found she could manipulate him on certain things, and once the lighting was in the house, she knew he'd love it.

"Juliet?"

Margery stood in the entryway, Kitty close behind her.

"For pity's sake, Margery, did you walk here?"

"Yes."

Through the woods where this morning another body had been found, not to mention the weather was miserably cold. Her cousin looked awful.

"Kitty, would you bring us coffee?" Juliet said, rising.

Kitty relaxed her stance and disappeared.

Juliet cleared a place on the piled settee. "You've been ill?"

"Only the morning sickness."

"Please, sit."

Margery wrung her hands but didn't sit. "Juliet, I've come to ask you to intervene."

"With Tucker?"

"No, good Lord, with your husband."

"Whatever do you mean?"

"With the killings! For the love of God, Juliet, burning the barn was tit for tat; it's not worth murdering your brother."

Juliet's heart beat faster remembering the hatred that had almost consumed her New Year's night. "My brother tried to kill Jeff, Margery."

Margery didn't challenge the words, but smoothed her skirt under her and finally sat in a chair across from Juliet. "Tucker has not been himself lately."

"Tucker hasn't been himself for years, he just got worse when Jeff came home." Juliet watched Margery's jaw tense, and she bridled. "Do you know why? Do you know why Tucker spouts that nonsense about Jeff being a ghost?"

Margery shook her head.

She didn't know, and she didn't want to know. But it was time she learned the truth.

"Ten years ago, during a skirmish outside Corinth, Tucker and Rafe shot Jeff in the back and left him for dead."

Margery leaned forward. "He was afraid, Juliet. It goes back to Jarmane's death and the death of that old Indian Jedediah Wolfson. Don't you see? He thought he had to get rid of Jeff Dawson or die himself."

So she did know about Corinth. Tucker had told her. Doubtless he'd been in a drunken stupor when he made that confession. Juliet couldn't see him telling it otherwise.

"What do you want from me, Margery?"

"Make him stop." Her words faded into sobs, and she hid her face in her hands.

"He isn't doing—"

273

"He'll kill them all, you know that! He'll kill every man there that night. Do you want your brother dead?"

Juliet rose. "Jeff wouldn't kill anyone except in self-defense." At least, she didn't think he would.

Margery barked out a harsh laugh. "Is that what you call what happened last night?"

"You think Jeff killed that woman?"

"What woman? I'm talking about Morton Severs."

Juliet stared at her.

"Oh, for the love of Christ, Juliet, didn't you know? Mister Severs was murdered in downtown Natchez last night, in the house of his mistress. Something came through a window and ripped his throat open."

Juliet rushed into Jeff's arms and clasped him to her. She'd been walking the floor since Margery left, escorted by Toby to ensure she got home safely. Jeff knew Severs was dead, his apprehensive hold told her that, and when he started to speak, she told him that she too knew of Severs' death.

"Do you understand what is happening here?" she asked.

"No, and please don't tell me you do, but I am moving Toby from that shack to the house for a while."

"We're under siege?"

He stepped around her so she couldn't see his face. "There've been no direct threats against us."

She stepped close and touched his arm. "The authorities are trying to blame Severs' death on you, aren't they?"

"Will, Michael Tate, Wex Seaton, and I intend to stay in the woods tonight."

An indirect answer, but one that told the tale loud and clear. Juliet's heart began to pound. "What are you hunting," she said softly, "man or wolf?"

He pivoted slightly and looked her in the eye. "We don't figure the woman killer will strike again for another month."

She held her chin high, but tears blurred her vision of him.

He turned full on her and stuck a finger under her nose—

"Don't you dare cry, dammit, Juliet"— and he yanked her to him when she began to do just that. "That thing went into town last night and killed Morton Severs. I've got to do something to prove it isn't me!"

She pushed back so she could see his face. "You won't be able to kill the beast, even should you attempt such an awful thing. And it would not be in your best interest to do so."

"If you believe that, then why are you crying?"

She wiped her wet cheeks on his shirt, then laid her head against his chest. "Because I'm scared for you. I don't want you out there. I don't want Tucker—"

"Tucker won't be with us."

Again she pushed away and found his eyes. "If Wex is out there with you tonight, Tucker will know it."

"Wex wants the wolf as much as I do."

"I don't care. Even if he's not in cahoots with Tucker, you can't rule out Tucker's acting alone."

"Next month maybe." He dared to smirk at her. "He's still not getting around well, I hear."

"You *hear*?" She resisted the urge to smack him. "Darn it, you are focused on the wrong enemy. The ones who would kill you are all around us. Oh, Jeff, the only way I can bear the thought of you going out there tonight is knowing Morton Severs' killer will be out there, too, protecting you"—she furrowed her brow— "and you want to *kill* him."

Chapter Forty-three

"You're going to help them hunt that so-called wolf?" Tucker asked.

Wex Seaton took a long look at his cousin, sitting in his favorite chair, his injured leg propped on a stool. He was getting around a little better now, but two weeks ago, he hadn't even been able to go to the church for his wedding. Michael Tate had come here to do the honors. Mike, his wife Mary, and a handful of guests. "I am," he answered.

"You need to shoot Dawson."

Wex loaded his Springfield. "Wouldn't do any good. You've already tried that, twice, and I can't afford silver bullets."

Tucker closed his eyes. "Hand me the whiskey."

Wex was surprised Margery hadn't poured it out, but reckoned he was the reason. Tucker wasn't the only man in the house who enjoyed a stiff drink. He stooped in front of the cabinet. "Margery will knock me upside the head if she finds out I've given you whiskey." He took a shot glass and poured Tucker a drink. Picking up another glass, he poured himself three fingers, then refilled Tucker's empty glass. With a dashed look, Tucker watched him put the whiskey away. He didn't ask for the bottle.

"Where are the women at?" Wex threw back his head and downed the burning liquid.

"Your mother is doing the wash. Margery went over to see Juliet."

"Juliet? Why?"

"To beg for her intervention so Dawson doesn't kill me, I imagine."

Wex gave a short laugh, at the same time pulling on his coat and slipping a box of cartridges into his pocket. "Dawson's not going to kill you, Tucker, not if you leave him be."

"It's not Dawson, I realize that now. It's something else. Something he's called out of hell. He sent it after Severs last night, and I've got to kill him before he sends it after me."

Wex stopped and studied his brother-in-law. "I'm glad you are no longer trying to kill something you say is already dead." He reached for the door.

"You're going now? It's still daylight."

"There's planning to do."

"Wex?"

He turned, curious at the desperation in Tucker's voice.

"Tell me the plan. I'll help you kill him."

"The wolf?"

"Dawson."

"I gave you that opportunity not too long ago, in broad daylight, remember?" Wex looked at Tucker's injured leg, stretched out straight and elevated on a stool. "One thing's for sure, you wouldn't be able to run away this time."

"That thing was in the woods that day, watching me...protecting him."

Wex gave him a deprecating smile, and Tucker grasped the arms of the chair and pulled himself forward.

"Nothing's changed, Wex. You think I'm so stupid I didn't know your plans that day you led her into the woods. I saw you with her, how you were acting." Tucker settled back and sneered at him. "You want her for yourself. Juliet will be wealthy when Dawson is dead. You can marry her and work your own place."

Wex fought back the hatred surging through his body. This useless piece of fodder actually thought that he was working this place for Tucker's benefit. "I'd be working White Oak Glen to be specific, Tucker. But I find the thought of wedding a woman for money emasculating. The thought of working for a man who can't relieve himself without a drink to help his aim is scarcely more satisfying." Quelling the urge to strike Tucker, Wex leaned close, wishing he could at least force the contempt he felt for the man into a stream of vomit and throw up in his face. "You want Jeff Dawson dead, you kill him yourself. I fight my own battles, for my own reasons. Right now I'm hunting a wolf that is killing your stock." Wex straightened and took a step back from where Tucker sat.

"That's no wolf. That's a demon doing Dawson's killing. Kill Dawson, and it will go back to hell where it came from."

"And what are you going to do if Dawson himself returns from hell and"—Wex jumped at Tucker with both feet—*"gets you!"* He laughed and turned his back on Tucker.

"Obviously you think me a fool, Wexford, but you're equally foolish if you think you can destroy the thing without my help."

"Actually, I would consider your help a liability, and yes, I do intend to destroy the thing."

"You can't destroy a spirit any better than I can."

"Oh yes, I can."

"How?"

"There's only one way, Tucker boy, and that's by destroying its Godforsaken soul."

Chapter Forty-four

uliet and Kitty fed the men a good hot meal, and Will protested that if Juliet didn't stop forcing food into him, he was going to fall asleep in the woods and his snoring alone would dissuade the appearance of the beast.

But Juliet could keep Jeff safe inside the house only so long. She trusted Will Howe and Mike Tate, but despite Wex's personable mood, she did not want him in the woods with Jeff. Wexford didn't like Tucker, she'd always been aware of that, but the two did have a common cause, and the killing of Seaton stock was a problem that most certainly bothered Wexford more than it bothered Tucker. And despite the disparaging words Wex used in reference to her brother when she'd asked after Margery's health earlier this evening, Juliet wasn't comfortable Wex and Tucker didn't have a plan to do Jeff harm.

At the back door, Jeff bent his head to kiss her good-bye, and the day's worth of trepidation grew into an almost debilitating fear. Throwing her arms around his neck, she pulled him to her. "I love you more than life itself, Jeff Dawson. Please take care tonight. If I should lose you, I will surely die."

"If anything happens to me tonight, spend the rest of your long life enjoying my money. That's what I want."

Tears filled her eyes. How could he ask such a thing of her? "Without you, I'll have no life." She almost begged him not to go, but bit her tongue instead. Her protests would serve no purpose but to fill him with misgivings, and in the end he'd go anyway.

The men and their lanterns disappeared over the rise, beyond which lay the remains of the barn. In the yard, where she fol-

279

lowed, Juliet watched stars twinkling in the black sky. It was a clear, cold January night, and quiet. The full moon was tomorrow night. Her gaze rested on the deserted rise. They would be moving in four different directions by now, and with moonrise, they would extinguish the lanterns. Even in the forest, the trees stripped bare by winter, there would be plenty of light for them to see by.

Kitty turned her toward the house. "Come on, baby girl, be awhile befo' that ol' moon come up."

From the window in the master bedroom, Juliet watched the soft yellow lights from the hunters' lanterns maneuver through the desolate woods, disappearing over hollows and behind trees, then reappearing again. After a quarter hour, she no longer saw them at all.

"I brought you coffee," Kitty said from the hallway. Juliet drank the cup alone in the dark. Shortly before moonrise, she gave up trying to find the men altogether and joined Kitty and Toby in the warm, well-lit dining room downstairs. She laid out paper and pens, and for a space of time she searched the house for a straight edge with which to work on house plans. Concentration eluded her, but finally she settled at the table. The night could prove long.

The moon rose in the east. Juliet couldn't see its ascent from the dining room. That was as well. Sometime before midnight, Kitty shook Toby awake for the third time. "Git, boy. You go lie down in my bed back yonder." She waved toward her bedroom door, closed off from the dining room. "I can't take no more of yo' snorin'. I swear you is just like yo' granddaddy."

Juliet looked up from her most recent sketches of the proposed kitchen and listened to Kitty harangue the young man. Compliant, Toby did as his grandmother said, and Kitty closed the door behind him.

"Lordy, I hate that racket." She lumbered back toward Juliet. "I'm goin' to make us some cornbread and buttermilk, girl, what you think?"

"My appetite is poor, Kitty, but I'd like some more coffee."

"Why don't you go on to bed? They won't be back till dawn."

"I'd not sleep a wink. Just the coffee, please."

Kitty yawned. The older woman should try to sleep, but Kitty wouldn't go to bed and leave her up alone.

The ticks from the clock sitting on the sideboard resonated through the quiet room. Perhaps she should pretend to rest, that way Kitty could do likewise. She glanced back to her drawings and....

Juliet started with a rifle's report a good distance from the house. A heavy footfall punctuated the final echo of the gun, and Juliet looked up to find Kitty watching her from the breezeway.

"Was prob'ly nothin', baby girl. One of 'em saw somethin' in the dark is all."

Not one of those men would have fired at nothing. The incessant ticking of the clock continued, monotonous, even nerve-racking now.

Kitty moved. "I'm gonna make that coffee. You sit tight."

Will Howe jerked with the blast, then twisted around to where he figured the shot came from, the southwest quadrant of Seaton land, the section closest to the big house. He rose from his hiding place. There'd been no shouts, and there should have been. They'd agreed to give warning if anyone saw something. If the shooter had not cried out, it might have been because he'd been unable to. Wex Seaton was the one posted in that area.

Will shouted for Jeff.

Lilith Seaton looked up from her reading. Margery, alert, was leaning forward on the settee. "That was a rifle shot," Lilith said.

"Yes, I fear it was."

Worry, aggravated now by the tremor in Margery's voice, gnawed at Lilith's gut. She hadn't seen Wexford before he left. Night hunting was a sport she'd never been comfortable with her son taking part in. She shuddered. Even less so of late.

"I wonder what happened?"

Lilith looked at her daughter's bruised cheek and the swollen right eye, partially shut. "I don't know, darling, but I'm sure it is too much to ask that—"

"Don't say it, Mother."

"You argued with him about going out there, didn't you?"

"His leg pains him greatly, and it's d-dangerous for him."

"When will you ever learn?"

"He was drinking. He would have never hit me otherwise."

Lilith marked her place with a ribbon and closed the Bible with a snap. "Margery, he will be drinking the rest of his life."

"Perhaps if Dawson really were gone...."

Lilith frowned at her daughter. "Listen to yourself. Who did he blame before Dawson came back? And he hasn't the guts to try and kill Dawson alone. That means he must be planning to involve Wex." Worse, the drunken ass could shoot the wrong man out there in the dark. Despite what she'd said to Wexford New Year's Day, they'd all, Margery and her baby most particularly, be better off if Dawson did kill Tucker.

"Perhaps Wex will get Dawson then," Margery said.

Lilith didn't believe for an instant Wexford would work with Tucker to perform murder. Tucker was too unreliable. Alone perhaps...

What had they come to? Slowly, she traced the gold inlay of the Bible with a fingertip. But killing Jeff Dawson wouldn't really be considered a sin in God's eyes if the man were trying to destroy the Seatons. This was a matter of survival. Wex's wooing Juliet would be a different matter. He'd have so many dark secrets to keep from her. But Lilith was confident Wex would be good to her. She would, after all, be his wife.

She returned her gaze to her daughter. "Did Tucker indicate Wex was going to help him kill Dawson tonight?"

Margery shook her head and resumed knitting. "I'm not sure what Wex has planned, Mama. Tucker was in a horrible mood. Wex taunted him this afternoon."

"In what way?" Wex was a loner. He avoided trouble, and he avoided drawing attention to himself. Then again, knowing how contemptuous he was of Tucker, he might have done something, hoping to provoke his cousin into going out tonight and getting his stupid self killed.

"He implied Tucker was a coward and stupid for thinking killing Dawson will end the evil spirit. Tucker no longer believes Dawson's dead, Mama, but he thinks if he can kill Dawson's corporeal body, he'll put an end to the evil spirit Dawson controls."

"Good Lord," she said and rolled her eyes. "I imagine he got that idea from Severs. And how could Wex possibly fault that?"

"Don't laugh at him."

"I'm cringing, not laughing. Well, what did Wex say?"

"Wex spouted some nonsense apparently about destroying the thing's soul."

Lilith heard the words, but it took her a moment longer to comprehend them. When she did, her heart plummeted to her stomach. She stared at her daughter's pale, battered face, more grotesque now than it had appeared moments ago. "He said that he was going to destroy Jeff Dawson's *soul*?"

"Something to that effect."

Lilith could feel the blood draining from her face. Margery's eyes widened.

"Oh God, Mama, what's wrong?"

Silently, he closed the cookhouse door. The Negress, Kitty, had entered the larder. If he were lucky, he wouldn't have to kill her. He didn't want to kill her. That would use up some of his strength, and he needed all of it to thwart the unholy spectre of Jeff Dawson this night. From the worktable, he picked up a cast-iron skillet and moved toward the door the woman had entered. Inside the dark room, her shuffling stopped.

"Who's there?" she said. He rounded the table, placing himself outside the larder door, and when she came in view, he slammed the skillet against the side of her head. The force of the blow sent her crashing into the wall, and she fell in a heap to the floor.

Calm, he stopped and listened. Silence. Juliet hadn't heard

the disturbance. Grasping Kitty under her arms, he dragged the large woman into the larder and closed the door with an almost silent click.

*P*ulse racing, Juliet grabbed for the front door.

"Juli..." The cry died on Wex's lips, and he dropped his fist. She swung the door wide. "Jeff's been shot," he said between heaving breaths.

"O dear God, please no!" Juliet raced back from where she'd come and snatched her coat off the peg by the back door. Her heart was bursting. She knew this was going to happen. Knew it! Stifling a sob, she leaned into the dining room and yelled for Kitty. What in sweet Jesus' name was the woman doing? Body straining, Juliet cursed and stepped forward. She needed her to get things prepared. "Kitty!" she screamed.

Toby stuck his head out of the back room.

She grasped the doorframe to keep from collapsing. "Toby, find your grandmother. She's in the cookhouse. Jeff's been shot. Then fetch Doctor Maynard."

"Where is he?" she cried, bursting through the front door. She yanked the door shut behind her. Wex was already on the ground, heading toward the woods. The closing of the door shrouded what little she could see of him in darkness.

"Beyond the creek." He tossed the words over his shoulder, then stopped to take her hand. Gently, he squeezed her fingers, and she resisted the urge to snatch her hand away and hit him with it, to hurry him on, faster. She didn't want comfort. She wasn't a widow yet. She wanted her husband.

"Where was he shot?"

"Chest," Wex said, picking up speed and pulling her along. "It's not good, Juliet, I won't lie to you."

She twisted her face. "Who did it?"

"I don't know. We were separated. I heard the shot and then a cry. When I called for him, he didn't answer."

And how much of what he was telling her was true? Did Wexford's urgency reflect true concern or was it merely a ploy to deflect suspicion from his participation in a premeditated plot to kill her husband? Juliet's knees weakened, and that would mean Wex's taking her to him was nothing more than a ruse to cover up his involvement.

They crossed the rail fence onto Seaton land, the nearly full moon lighting the way. With her free hand, Juliet touched Wex's arm. "Did he speak to you when you found him?"

In front of her, Wex did not answer, lending credence to her worst fears, and she quaked at the realization that the man she loved might already be dead.

Jeff entered the back foyer. "Juliet?" he called and stepped into the dining room. Juliet's drawings lay spread across the table. "Yo, has Wex been back here?" Where the devil was—

"Back here, Mister Jeff," Toby yelled from the cookhouse. Desperation edged the young man's voice, and Jeff's concern for Wex Seaton dissolved into a dread of something unknown. He passed through the breezeway, Will on his heels.

To his right, Lilith Seaton burst through the outside door of the kitchen and, seeing Jeff, rushed to him. "Where's Juliet?"

Jeff's breath caught. "I don't—"

"Over here, Mister Jeff." Toby had appeared at the larder door, and Jeff turned his back on Lilith and hurried to the young man. But Kitty lay on the larder floor, not Juliet. Anxious, he bent on one knee, taking in the trickle of blood that inched its way, barely discernable against her black skin, from Kitty's temple to her jaw. Jeff reached for a wrist. She was out cold, but her pulse was strong.

He twisted around to Toby. "What happened?"

"Don't know. Miss Juliet, she yelled at me to find Grandma, 'cause"—the young man narrowed his eyes and scanned Jeff's body—"you'd been shot. You don't look shot to me."

"Where is Miss Juliet?"

"She done left with somebody, running down to the front of the house before I found Grandma like this."

Lilith Seaton was in front of him again, shoving him at the

shoulders. "Wex has her. He'll kill her, like the others. I've sent Margery for the sheriff. For the love of God, find them."

Her words settled like lead in Jeff's stomach. He rose, breaking contact with Lilith. "Where did he take her?"

Lilith shook her head. "To the woods, where he took the others. I don't know."

"Don't move your grandma," he called to Toby as he rounded the worktable and reached for the cookhouse door. Each victim had been found in a different spot. Where they'd actually been murdered was still unknown. Hands unsteady, he fumbled a moment with the knob. Behind him, he heard Will ask Toby how long it had been since Juliet left the house.

The frigid night air slammed into him. To his left, someone approached at a lope. Hope, then apprehension, tangled his gut. Michael Tate, only now emerging from the woods.

The unearthly cry of the wolf reverberated through the night. Jeff's throat went dry, and he felt the hair on the back of his neck stand on end. A breeze kicked up, cooling his tortured mind. *A warning* Juliet had said last night when Roxanne Champion died. If so, would that thing protect Juliet as she had earlier intimated it would protect him tonight?

Jeff threw back his head and cried Juliet's name.

The howl of the wolf shattered what little cohesiveness remained of her senses. A warning cry, or one of mourning like that of a banshee.

Wex stopped with the howl and pivoted, as though trying to determine what lurked in the dark woods surrounding them. Fear charged the air, and she heard him threaten the beast before again taking her hand and pulling her over a fallen tree trunk. "Don't be afraid of it," he told her. "You're with me."

"I want Jeff," she said.

Abruptly he stilled, then gave her hand a painful squeeze. Around them intense shadows fluttered in the glow of the moon. They were well away from the creek and the cow path now. "The clearing where we're headed is up here," he said in response.

From somewhere, the night called her name, and her heart skipped a beat. She could have sworn....

"He's here," Wex said.

His words obliterated all other thought from her mind and she bounded around Wex. In the silvery light, she could see his form on the ground, and with a sob, she lunged toward the prone body. She groped and touched, trying to roll him over, feeling for warmth, any sign of life. There was none. Chest tight, stomach clenched, she breathed, then screamed, "He's dead!"

All but dead herself, she hugged his body to her. Reverently, Wex squatted by a cold lantern and lit it, bathing her and Jeff in golden light. He rose. "I am sorry, Juliet."

She turned her face up to his. "You know what really happened," she snarled. "Tell me!"

"I killed him."

She curled her fingers into claws, but before she could mount an attack, Wex took the toe of his boot and rolled the body of Juliet's beloved in her arms, and she steeled herself to look at his handsome visage once again. Familiar eyes, but glassy now and vacant. A sob caught in her throat. Grief mixed with relief, guilt with joy. She was holding Tucker. For the span of a heartbeat, nothing registered but the fact that Jeff was not dead.

But Tucker was. She jerked her head up. Yellow lantern light exposed Wex's ghostly face, all glittering eyes and contrasting shadow. Evil. This was a man she did not know.

"Why?" she asked. Her teeth started to chatter.

"His presence would have spoiled my plans for you tonight."

Frigid cold seeped through her skin, but her shudder had nothing to do with the night air. "Where's Jeff?" she whispered.

"Hunting a wolf—and a killer, 'bout now—I would imagine." He smiled, a feral upturn of his lips that exposed his teeth. "He's alive, Juliet, but he'll wish he was dead when he finds you, sees you after the true wolf is done with you."

Juliet's body started to quake. "You killed those women?"

"Yes."

"Did you have a reason?"

"I needed them." He looked to the dark sky, and she followed his gaze beyond the naked treetops, stark and spindly against the midnight-blue backdrop of the night. His eyes rested on the rising moon. "I come into these woods with my mates and breed them, over and over again."

Slowly she removed her arms from around her brother and pushed away. The movement made a noise, and Wex instantly turned his demented stare on her. He set the lantern down, gently, then knelt on one knee and reached for her. Still on the ground, she scrambled back. He made no move in pursuit.

"The fear in their eyes. Mere sex couldn't satisfy me, and they knew after the third copulation I was no ordinary man." He pushed himself to his feet and with one deft move, bent and pulled a knife from his boot. Momentarily, he stared at it, turning it in the lantern's glow, then he glared at the false light. "We don't need this," he said, reaching for the lantern.

With his distraction, Juliet tried to find her feet, but he whirled, and in two quick strides, straddled her.

"You're not going anywhere, Juliet."

Her head throbbed in rhythm with her pounding heart. In the distance, she heard shouts. But before she could scream, he bent low and held the knife to her throat. "Shut up."

She didn't make a sound, and he smiled. "That's a good girl. Now lie flat and pull up your skirts."

"You go to the devil."

He pressed the point of the knife to her throat, near the center of her larynx. "I am the devil, Juliet. Everyone thinks it's him, but I'm the dominant male here, and you are about to know why."

Supported on her elbows, Juliet coughed in reaction to the knife's point against her throat. She tilted her head back and breathed in...

...*summer rain.*

Wex stiffened and glanced toward Tucker's body. "My God," he said, moving the knife-wielding fist to cover his nose and mouth, "he's begun to stink already."

Confused, but only for an instant, Juliet stared at Wex.

He coughed, apparently to rid his senses of the vile odor he smelled, then leaned his face close to hers. Over his shoulder, Juliet saw a shadow. Invigorated, she again breathed in the reassuring air.

"You're not the wolf, Wex," she said, focusing on his maniacal face. "You heard it minutes ago."

"I'm not that beast, no, but it can't stop me, not in human or animal form. It never has. I know now that it's afraid of me."

"You're wrong." She watched it at Wex's back. Tall on its haunches, the beast paced at the edge of the lantern's light, its coarse black-gray fur on end along the full length of its spine. The fiend emanated a silver phosphorescence, and it watched them with glowing red eyes. So ominous was the supernatural presence Juliet had to steel herself in the face of it, and suddenly her lips trembled with the full impact of the truth. "It *is* a spirit. Jeff's guardian spirit. Its purpose and its strength is for protecting Jeff." She sought Wex's eyes. "That's why it couldn't stop you from murdering the others."

She felt Wexford tense, then he laughed. "Trying to trick me, Juliet? I know there's nothing there."

"It's behind you."

His lips curled into a hideous smile. "But you're not Dawson. It can't save you any more than it could save the others."

Wex reached down with his free hand and yanked on her skirt. "I'm going to show you what a virile male animal really is."

"You are nothing more than a deviant man, a rapist and a murderer."

He sneered. "Do you think you can make me feel remorse? I have no moral values where taking and killing a slut is concerned."

"What gives you the right to judge me or any other woman?"

"I don't judge." He snorted in contempt. "People don't care if I kill a whore; so, they're the ones who judge. But the reason I chose you tonight is because you belong to Dawson. By destroying his beautiful mate, I will destroy him. Possessing your body before I take your life is more satisfying still. In my mind, and in his, that will prove I am the superior being. The very existence of Jeff Dawson and his family legend causes me extreme pain. "

The man was totally insane.

Again he yanked at her skirt. Grinding her teeth, she reached to stop him, but gasped when cold steel again touched her throat. He pushed, and she choked.

"Raise your hips."

Briefly, she closed her eyes and did as he said. With one hand, he pushed the skirt up and pulled her pantaloons down. Chilled air caressed her calves and thighs. Wex maneuvered awkwardly over her, keeping the knife at her throat, and wadded the pantaloons around her ankles. The ground was as cold as the air. Her shivers were out of her control. Her very soul was frigid.

He raked his eyes over her naked legs, then met her gaze, the knife still pressed against her throat. She had not yet recovered from the miscarriage, but even without that, the thought of Wex Seaton's entering her was devastating.

"Lay back." His voice was husky. When she didn't immediately respond, he prodded her with the point of the knife, and she laid her head on the ground. Still astride her, he scooted forward and rose on his knees. "Unbutton my pants."

With trembling hands, she did as he said.

"Touch me. See how hard I am."

When she did nothing, his mouth screwed up in anger, and his handsome face became monstrous. Tightening his hand over the hilt of the knife, he pulled back and struck her, forcing her head to one side with a violent smack. "Do as I say, damn you."

Her face stung with the senseless blow, but the knife was no longer at her throat. She would touch him all right.

A soft sound, a whine, or perhaps it was a growl, stayed her. Juliet watched Wex turn and bring himself face to face with the beast, its snout inches from his nose.

Wex screeched like a girl and propelled backward off her. She sat up, free, then yanked at her pantaloons. Wex kept moving away. A choked gurgle issued from his throat, and he pushed back farther on his heels. He had not let go of the knife. The wolf stood at her side; it made no threatening move toward either of them, but held Wex mesmerized.

Juliet scrambled to her feet. Wex reached to the back of his britches and brought his arm around in one motion. He pointed a pistol at the wolf. Juliet screamed and reached down for the lantern, three feet away. The pistol shot ripped through the night at the same moment she swung the lantern at arm's length and tossed it into the brittle woods. Flame exploded amid the trees, lighting the clearing like day. She tripped and fell in the effort, but struggled back up, keeping her eye on Wex, who was turning every which way, searching, she presumed, for the wolf.

Eyes glowing with the reflected flames eating the forest, Wex settled his gaze on her. She'd tarried too long, and before she could hike her skirt and get moving again, he rushed her toward the fire, catching her when she reversed direction. She screamed Jeff's name, then ducked her head beneath Wex's precarious grasp in an effort to spin around him. She would have escaped, but he caught the back collar of her coat and, with a twist, slammed her to the ground.

Air rushed from her lungs, and Juliet closed her eyes to better deal with the pain and dizziness. The crackle of the flames filled her ears, the scent of wood smoke her nostrils. He rolled her over, and she coughed. Harried, he started to tear at her skirts, and she kicked out, a foot glancing off his thigh. He grunted at the blow and looked down. She followed his gaze to the unbuttoned pants exposing his genitals. He'd lost his erection. His face contorted in anger. "You bitch!" He pulled her head up by her hair, and she flailed at his hand, desperately trying to free herself from his hold. Tears of anger, frustration, and pain ran down her cheeks. Out of the corner of her eye, she saw him raise his free right hand above her. Resistance evaporated. She felt the heat from the flames on one side, the stinging agony in her head, and loss in her heart. *O God, Jeff!* She looked up. Wex held the knife above her.

"It's over, Juliet. I can take you once you're dead. I've done it many times."

"They'll be here soon." But her voice was weak with surrender, the threat empty.

"And Dawson will find you dead."

Chapter Forty-five

From a knoll, Jeff looked down at the well-lit clearing and felt again the familiar kick of the Whitworth against his shoulder. The rifle's accompanying blast exploded into the night. Two hundred yards away, the bullet threw Wex Seaton off Juliet as if someone had hit him with a club. Fortunately, Jeff's target had been silhouetted against the burning woods, as had his wife. Choking back a sob of relief, Jeff wiped the sweat from his forehead. It was the first time he had killed a man that nausea hadn't assailed him. But in this case he hadn't killed a soldier fighting for his country. He'd killed a monster.

Will's fingers clamped his shoulder. "I can't believe you made that shot in the dark at this range, and shootin' at a shadow to boot. Ain't never gonna be another shot like you, boy. You was born with an eagle's eye."

A swamp hawk's actually. Anyway, that's what his granddaddy Jedediah, who first put a rifle in his hand, had always told him.

Taking his Springfield from Will, he handed him back the Whitworth and took off at a lope.

Juliet cried out for him once, and he answered, telling her to stay put, he was coming. When she finally espied him emerging from the darkness beyond the clearing, she let out a strange, soft whine and ran into his arms. She clung to him, then ran her hands over his body as though to confirm he was real. He clasped her to him, stilling her. "It's okay, sweetheart, everything is okay."

"He told me you were shot." She pushed him back to arms' length. "When we got here, I thought you were dead."

293

She turned and nodded at the ground, where another body lay. "But it wasn't you," she said and melted to him again, "it's Tucker. Wex killed those women. He said he was the real wolf. I think he was jealous of people believing you were the killer."

"He shot Tucker?" he asked, maneuvering Juliet against his side and holding her around the waist. He stepped toward the body.

"Yes, he said that Tucker would have ruined his plans for tonight."

"I would imagine so. No matter how Tucker felt about you, I don't think he would have sat back and let Wex rape and murder you." His gut tensed at the word rape, and he turned her to face him. "Sweetheart, I love you more than anything in the world, and I want you to know that no matter what happened before I fired that shot I—"

She placed two fingers against his lips. "He didn't rape me, Jeff. The wolf stopped him."

He narrowed his eyes. He'd heard the thing howl, but only once. "The wolf?"

"He's still here. Can you smell him?"

"I smell rain," he said, glancing around him before looking up at the sky where he saw absolutely nothing but smoke.

She laughed through her tears. "That's him. Even with the wood smoke, we can smell him."

His heart skipped a beat. "Where is he?"

She turned, scanning the woods beyond the dying flames. "He's been here with me, waiting on you." She pointed. "There, do you see?"

My God, he did see it, in the shadows, watching them. The thing was ominous. Instinctively, Jeff's fingers tightened around the Springfield. How many human throats had it torn out? Two he knew of for sure.

Juliet laid her hand on the rifle. "Don't," she said, and took a step closer to the fading ribbon of flame that separated them from the hellish-looking beast.

Jeff reached for her and pulled her back.

But she tugged at him, and they stepped closer. "It would do no good to shoot him. Wex tried that. If he wished to kill us, we'd be dead. Think of the number of times he could have killed me."

Jeff stared at the animal, huge for a wolf, hoary and coarse. It stood stock-still, its glowing eyes watching him from twenty paces. And it *was* him it watched, he was sure of that.

"That thing likes you, you know," he whispered in her ear. "Maybe it considers me another threat?"

"Yes," she said softly, still looking at the wolf, "he was partial to little girls." Juliet turned around to him suddenly and smiled, so bright and sincere it surprised him after what she'd been through tonight. "I was the one who saw him, but he was always with you. From that very first day, he was in the woods because you were there, that night at the barn, the day Tucker tried to ambush you. You were the reason he was about. He's your guardian angel." She blinked back tears. "He loves you."

"What are you talking about?"

"Jeffrey Wolfson Dawson," she said, exasperation evident despite her tearful tone, "don't you know yet who he is?"

He shook his head. "It is not a he, Juliet. It's a wild animal."

"*He* is your grandfather," she stated firmly and turned back.

Even though he knew she was going to say that, his vision blurred. He couldn't quite blink back the tears fast enough. Not because be believed what she said, despite how much he wanted to, but because he knew she did. She really, truly believed that wild animal was his granddaddy.

"Jedediah Wolfson," she called, "it's over. You can rest."

In awe, Jeff watched the animal raise its snout and let loose an unearthly cry, summing up the events of this violent night. But this time, for the first time, that howl did not chill Jeff's blood. Whatever the cursed thing was, it did appear to be on his side.

Behind him, Will swore, and Jeff looked around. Will and Michael Tate had stopped at the edge of the clearing, and Jeff suspected they no longer wanted to enter.

"Where is it?" Will asked.

"Over..."

But when he turned to point, there was nothing to point at. Jeff moved in front of Juliet and searched the place where the wolf had stood.

"He's gone," she told him matter-of-factly.

"Will he be back?"

Slowly she shook her head, then looked at him with shimmering eyes. "I don't know. Maybe, if you need him. What do I know of Indian spirits, Wolf Dawson?"

"Regarding that particular spirit, sweetheart? My guess is more than the Indians."

"Got him through the temple."

Jeff turned at Will's voice. His old friend had rolled Wex's body over and now studied the single shot that killed him.

"I was aiming for his heart," Jeff said.

"The hell you were. You were looking at him from the side." Will looked up with an emphatic nod. "Damn good shot, boy. No doubt in my mind you got the bastard where you wanted."

Chapter Forty-six

"Will Aunt Lilith be charged?"

"I doubt it." Jeff pulled his undershirt over his head. It was evening and the end of a very long day. He had spent most of the afternoon in town.

"She knew about him all along?" Juliet asked.

He'd returned home to find her resting upstairs, and now he crawled into bed next to her and drew the covers over them. Last night he'd almost lost her. Today, during the long hours in the sheriff's office and later in the courthouse with the coroner and the judge, all he'd dreamed of was getting home to her.

Floyd had taken Juliet's written statement early this morning at the house. Now she wanted to know what else had happened. Despite Jeff's being sick of talking about the gruesome events of the night before, he pulled her close. Her warmth revived him.

"She had suspected him for at least the past nine months," he told her. "That's the real reason they left Alabama as quick as they did. Apparently he killed two women there. Your Aunt Lilith found his bloody clothes following the second murder. She put two and two together and confronted him. He told her he'd killed an animal, and he always had something with him, apparently, even after they came here. Rabbit, coon, but there was too much blood on his clothes to have come from those small animals.

"She wanted to believe him, so instead of pressing the issue, she packed them up and moved west. Their prospects in Alabama had about tapped out anyway. After they lost the plantation to taxes four years ago, Wex couldn't find steady work. Last year, he went up to Knoxville. After eight months, he came home."

She raised her head off the pillow. "Do you think he killed anyone there?"

"I sure wouldn't rule it out. Floyd'll talk to the law up there and find out if they had any murders similar to ours."

Juliet put her head down and snuggled close to him. "I can't believe it was Wexford. For weeks my mother slept under the same roof with him."

For weeks so did you, he thought.

"What of Sikes and Severs?"

"The coroner says a wolf killed them. That sits fine with the prosecutor."

"I wonder what our neighbors think," Juliet said softly.

"I figure they'll keep what they think to themselves and stay on our good side. How is Margery?"

"She's upset, but she'll be all right." Juliet placed her hand on his naked chest, and heat emanated from that spot. "Tucker hit her, you know?"

He hadn't known, but he had no trouble believing it.

"Jeff, we'll need to—"

He took the offending hand and brought it to his lips. "We'll take care of her, sweetheart."

Immediately she shifted her body and stroked his nipple with her free hand.

"It's still too soon," he said, his voice filled with warning.

In the light created by the full moon, he saw her smile. "I'll touch you," she said, "and you touch me."

He was instantly alert. "What did you have in mind?"

Her arms circled his neck, and she drew him over her. "There is so much more to lovemaking than sticking one's cock inside a woman and ravishing her, Wolf Dawson. There's any number—"

He silenced her parroting with a passionate kiss.

"We made love of sorts the other day," she said, shortly after. "I made you happy. You made me happy. Let's do it again."

"Let's do," he whispered in her ear. "And since this is your idea, I'll even let you go first."

298

If you enjoyed this escape, indulge yourself further with Charlsie
Russell's first novel

The Devil's Bastard

Natchez on the river, 1793. The Spanish Fleet controls the
Mississippi, and the Dons rule their rowdy British and American
subjects with a patient hand. The location is strategic, the land
fertile, and within two decades, cotton will be king. Into this web
of international intrigue, the rich and powerful Elizabeth Boswell
welcomes her orphaned grandniece Angelique Veilleux and intro-
duces the impoverished beauty to a world of privilege. But
power has its enemies and wealth demands a price. Rumor has
it Elizabeth's success stems from dalliance with a lustful demon
that still prowls her family farm of De Leau outside Natchez.

At the center of this ominous legend is Elizabeth's grand-
son, the handsome and dangerous Mathias Douglas who saves
Angelique from degradation and death near the end of her
journey to Natchez. Mathias is the son of the doomed Julianna,
Elizabeth's only daughter. Mathias' father, locals whisper, is
Elizabeth's demon.

Despite the dark rumors, Angelique cannot quell her feelings
for Mathias, for whom she would make any sacrifice. An outcast,
Mathias is cruelly tested by the temptation of Angelique's affection. Determined not to dishonor her, he callously puts her aside.
But Elizabeth has other plans and offers him the family farm at

De Leau to marry the girl. Soon Angelique finds herself desperately in love with the man who has conquered her body and possessed her soul.

But something in the swamps surrounding De Leau stalks her, and nightmares invade her dreams. What she perceives as Mathias' indifference to the threat leaves Angelique isolated and afraid. She begins to doubt her grandaunt's motives for sending her to De Leau, as well as Mathias' role in Elizabeth's plan. Resolving her doubts means uncovering the secret of Mathias' sire.

From Mathias and Angelique's first meeting to Elizabeth Boswell's revelation at story's end, *The Devil's Bastard* is a splendid read. First and foremost a sensual romance, it is also a well-researched historical with a haunting mystery.

And coming in April 2008 is Charlsie Russell's

Epico Bayou

Lionel Augustus, rogue and unscrupulous opportunist, died a wealthy man; and, as is all too often the case, deceitful and greedy relatives celebrate his passing. But his older sister and younger brother were not, in the end, fawning enough to secure the good graces of their not-so-loved brother. Lionel Augustus could have written the book on greed, graft, and ruthless business behavior, and he did read his siblings like that proverbial tome. In death, he continues to thwart the hungry carrion that would exploit his countless years of soul-sacrificing spoils. Instead of distributing his ill-gotten gains to his brother and sister, he left the bulk of his significant estate to his estranged bastard son, Clay Boudreaux, and his beloved grandniece, Olivia Lee. Together these latter personify the honor and gentility of the aristocratic Old South Lionel revered, but of which he, as a land-grabbing, tax-paying, Johnny-come-lately "bastard who had worn blue," was not part.

There was but one stipulation to Lionel's will: honor and gentility must wed.

For reasons of their own, the two young people agree to marry, sight unseen. But only days after her marriage by proxy to Deputy Sheriff Clay Boudreaux of Galveston, Texas, Olivia learns her husband has died in a house fire and her extended family is contesting her granduncle's will. Exacerbating her situation, a mysterious stranger claiming to be Troy Boudreaux, Clay's older half brother, invades Olivia's opulent home and accuses her of hiring him to kill Clay…and after that dirty deed is done…hiring yet another cutthroat to kill him. The last murder failed, and Troy's here now to assume his bother's identity and lay claim not only to Clay's inheritance but also to his treacherous bride.

It would appear honor is dead and gentility is a mere smoke screen.

The interloper, be he Clay or Troy, has reasons for keeping his identity in doubt, and Olivia has sound reasons for confusing her role in Clay's alleged murder. For both, their reasons have to do with murder, attempted murder, duplicity, and trust. Neither is sure of the role the other plays in the Machiavellian plan of Lionel's ruthless siblings, nor is it totally clear Lionel's brother and sister are the only masterminds behind the plot, or plots, to sabotage the terms of Lionel's will.

Set on the Mississippi Gulf Coast at the turn of the last century, Charlsie Russell's third novel is a compelling charade, pitting the wit and will of one wary lover against the honor and sheer determination of the other, while the sinister machinations of dangerous foes force them into a grudging alliance. Though the tangled mystery sets this novel apart from her prior edgy Gothics, *The Devil's Bastard* and *Wolf Dawson*, Ms. Russell's *Epico Bayou* still features those tried and true elements of suspense, sensual romance, and historical setting that characterize her work. Pure escape. Don't miss this journey!

About the Author

Charlsie Russell is a retired United States Navy Commander turned author. She loves reading, she loves history, and she loves the South. She focuses her writing on historical romance set in her home state of Mississippi.

After seven years of rejection, she woke up one morning and decided she did not have enough years left on this planet to sit back and hope a New York publisher would one day take a risk on her novels. Thus resolved, she expanded her horizons into the publishing realm with the creation of Loblolly Writer's House.

In addition to writing and publishing, Ms. Russell is the mother and homemaker to five children and their father.

To learn more about Charlsie Russell and Loblolly Writer's House, visit www.loblollywritershouse.com.

Loblolly Writer's House

Order Blank

Tear this sheet out and

Mail order to:

Loblolly Writer's House
P.O. Box 7438
Gulfport, MS 39506-7438

Item	Price*	Qty	Total
The Devil's Bastard	$16.00	_____	_____
Wolf Dawson	$16.00	_____	_____
		Shipping free:	0.00
		Total payment:	_____

Would you like a signed copy?
Tell me how:_____
_____

Send to:

_____
_____
_____

*Price includes 7% Mississippi sales tax
For Bookseller rates visit: www.loblollywritershouse.com

Loblolly Writer's House

Order Blank
Tear this sheet out and

Mail order to:

Loblolly Writer's House
P.O. Box 7438
Gulfport, MS 39506-7438

Item	Price*	Qty	Total
The Devil's Bastard	$16.00	_____	_____
Wolf Dawson	$16.00	_____	_____
	Shipping free:		0.00
	Total payment:		_____

Would you like a signed copy?
Tell me how:_____
_____

Send to:
_____
_____
_____

*Price includes 7% Mississippi sales tax
  For Bookseller rates visit: www.loblollywritershouse.com